SHADOWS IN THE NIGHT

Lila's Disappearance

A Garth Myers Mystery

by

Frank Doyle

On the M.A.R.C. Publishers

(www.onthemarcpub.com)

Copyright Page

Dedication

For all the teachers and mentors in my life. It takes a village!

Epigraph

Beneath every reaction lies a catalyst no one sees.

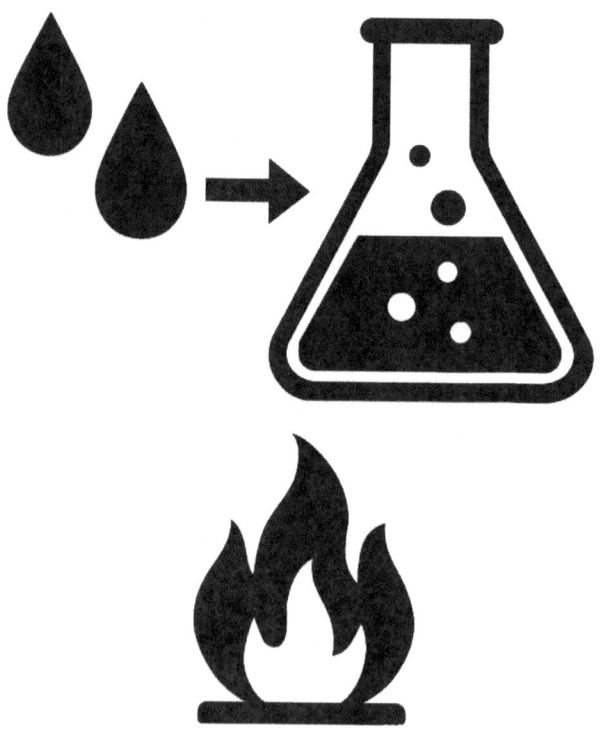

In the Sub-basements of the House of Usher

What in the name of cryptozoological fuckery does (this) mean?
A character in Shadows in the Night.
Full fathom five thy father lies
Of his bones are coral made;
Those are pearls that were his eyes:
Nothing of him that doth fade,
But doth suffer a sea-change
Into something rich and strange.
Sea-nymphs hourly ring this knell
Ding-dong.
Hark! now I hear them, ding-dong, bell.
            Shakespeare, Ariel's song from The Tempest

1. Poe

What you hold in your hand is something rich and strange. This preface may assist in your encounter with this vast and startling work. Therefore, regard these paragraphs as one reader's personal introduction to the Garth Myers mystery *Shadows in the Night*. There are as many interpretations of a literary work as there are readers. So this writing does not pretend to be authoritative. Certainly, I don't purport to reflect the opinions of the enigmatic and pseudonymous Frank Doyle, the author of this novel. No doubt, he or she would be aghast at the opinions ventured here.

Despite its length, this novel's story is simple enough to be written by water on water. A young woman has gone missing at a large public university in Wisconsin. A private investigator, Garth Myers, investigates her disappearance. This part of the novel is rendered in vigorous hard-boiled prose a bit like Raymond Chandler or James Elroy. This style is congruent with the genre, detective fiction. Suspicions lead the hero along with several sidekicks into a maze of partially flooded tunnels and chambers under a lake. This watery maze was constructed, at least in part, to conceal sinister experiments conducted by shadowy government agencies. The depths of this labyrinth are physiognomic, an intricate, pulsing network of valves, sphincters, and subterranean chambers in the form of membranous sacs and tubes. This part of the book, comprising most of the text, is written in ecstatic ejaculatory phrases. The novel is about what happens to the doughty protagonist and his comrades inside this vast cadaver with a lake draped over it like a sheet covering a corpse. The maze is infested with creatures that may be monsters or gods; it is in perpetual state of dissolution. The transformations enforced within the labyrinth are grotesque, calling into existence a remarkable prose style that is similarly grotesque. In equal parts, the book is about mutability and prophecy although, as imagined in the novel, prophecy is revelation of a repressed or forgotten past, not a vision of things to come that is prophecy as memory or the return of the repressed.

The deep structure of the book inherits aspects of Edgar Alan Poe's The Fall of the House of Usher. Like the labyrinth in *Shadows in the Night*, the gloomy House of Usher represents the body and spirit-form of Roderick Usher. Poe translates Usher's dissolution into the decomposition of the house, perched on the very vertiginous brink of a lake, a dark tarn. Spaces and furnishings represent aspects of the soul. At the center of the festering House of Usher, incestuous siblings act out a gothic drama that involves derangement of senses (synesthesia) and premature burial. *Shadows in the Night* is about siblings who are marked and, therefore, bound to one another. The action in *Shadows* takes place in a crepuscular series of crypts and passages that seem to be constantly collapsing and flooding with water that bears bioluminescent traces of sentience. The House of Usher is alive, more alive than its moribund inhabitants. Similarly, the tomb-like cells and pits under the lake in *Shadows* are spaces in which the book's inhabitants are buried alive. The cracks slashed like scars across the facade of the House of Usher ultimately are activated so that the whole edifice plunges into the dark waters of the tarn. For several hundred pages, the nightmarish labyrinth under the Wisconsin lake is contorted with spasms of its imminent collapse. Even the thematic material is similar: Garth, the protagonist of *Shadows*, is forced to confront terrible memories that the waters of the lake have washed away, blurred and erased; similarly, the neurasthenic Roderick Usher, acting as a kind of sleepwalker, has put his sister in the tomb while she is yet alive a somnambulant act that he does not remember until the walking specter of his sibling appears before him, hectic with the marks of her interment alive in the grave.

This kind of content comes from somewhere deep in the soul, a place that is either drowned at the bottom of a lake or buried alive. The structure can't support the violence of this repression and it collapses under the strain.

2. A Distributed Intelligence

Almost fifty years ago, I was a student at the University of Minnesota. I commuted to campus working there from 8:00 to 4:00 on my studies. More or less by accident, I took up occupancy in the main reading room at Walter Library, a majestic structure on the east bank of the Mississippi on the hillside overlooking the river. A thousand yards upstream, the steep gorge compressed the river into a sluice that poured over falls that had been rationalized and tamed by the Army Corps of Engineers, tilted slabs of concrete replacing the rocky and savage cascade split by islands that had once been at that place. The walls of the gorge on the east wall of the river were full of grottos and cisterns and spillways, artifacts of 19th century milling activities once powered by the current. Some ancient brick mills still stood like Etruscan ruins on the hilltop. With my friends, I spent many hours, drunk or stoned, touring these devastated industrial places. But that is another story outside the scope of this essay.

2

I discovered another eerie refuge in the stacks at the Walter Library. And, it is here, that I encountered a form of diffuse, distributed intelligence similar to what the protagonists of Frank Doyle's novel meet in the crumbling industrial labyrinth under the shoreline of Lake Monona. One day, after working in the reading room at the library, I got up to stretch my legs. I found a nondescript entry into an unfamiliar part of the building behind a big wooden desk that never seemed to be staffed. The threshold opened into the library's stacks, a great gloomy repository of books and periodicals in which no one had any interest.

The stacks occupied a huge vault, a sarcophagus-shaped chamber organized into levels at eight-foot vertical intervals. Floors and ceilings were made of metal grates like caging. The shelves were similarly gun-metal grey stretching for about a two-hundred feet with aisles ending in walkways at the cubes perimeter. A row of study-cubicles lined the rear wall of the space, cold hollow shells pressed up against the concrete boundaries of the stacks. (Sometimes, you came upon students sleeping, slumped over the cold metal desks on more than one occasion I napped in this place myself.) No one was around and the stacks were dark. You had to flip a switch to bring a flicker of light onto the dusty and disheveled volumes on the shelves. Metal grate stairways at the corners of the square space led up and down to other levels. A central shaft dropped into the basement and the library's many sub-basement, an imponderable void in which lower levels were simply swallowed up by the gloom.

About six levels were open and readily accessible and you could ascend (or descend) the corner steps they clanked like the rattling of sepulchral chains under foot. But below the sixth level, the cage closed off the passage with a grated, barred wall. It was like being penned in some sort of cage, possibly inhabited by wild things. Somehow, I figured out a way to slip around the barriers. Perhaps, I dangled over the center void, dropped my feet down to the guardrail on the level below and, then, entered the forbidden zone. (If this is how I entered the closed stacks, I shudder to think of the danger and wonder how I ever was able to climb up and out of lower levels but youth is reckless.) The forbidden stacks were, in fact, no different in form or substance than the levels above that were readily accessible, but the sheer fact that I wasn't supposed to be among these books gave them an aura slightly phosphorescent with danger and prohibition. The lower levels and the cage of metal plunged down and down into the darkness and I don't know that I ever sounded its bottom. Because both abandoned and neglected the volumes imprisoned in those depths seemed faintly abject and discredited. There were bound volumes of journals about phrenology, mesmerism, spiritualism, racial eugenics, colonialist anthropology. The books were all grim and dark and, although they didn't seem to have ever been opened, let alone read, they had a dog-eared aspect it seemed as if someone or something had been incessantly reading the books, carefully returning them to their stations where they stood sentinel over questionable branches of knowledge. I particularly recall a German book, a heavy as a brick, with cover dripping with dust: *Geschlechtsitten der Naturvoelker* (*Sexual Customs of the Indigenous People*) the book was copiously illustrated with black and white pictures which you could look at for hours without understanding exactly what the pictures were supposed to be showing. The volume was surrounded by a half-acre of books about homosexuals, transvestities, and other paraphilias. On the level above, there were digests of municipal law, codes of ordinances for cities and townships, dogbite and zoning statutes. Below, there were illustrated accounts of train wrecks, airship explosions, deadly fires, all sorts of catastrophes that left rows of mutilated corpses sprawled in rows on the charred ground.

The forbidden stacks were fascinating but frightening as well. The vast array of books was a distributed intelligence, a system of cross-referenced knowledge, paranoid and conspiratorial. Sometimes, voices whispered in the darkness and the clatter of feet on the metal steps high above resonated in the lower levels of the great concrete vault, echoing and quivering in the air as if invisible readers were walking nearby, urgently moving among the dark books on their dark shelves, researching obsolete and discredited knowledge. When the sense that I was being watched became too urgent, I fled upward to the light and, then, for half a day couldn't shake the feeling that I was under surveillance.

Perhaps, dear reader, you have had a similar experience. If so, you are eminently qualified to venture into the purulent labyrinth that is *Shadows in the Night.*

3. Correlations

The hectic action in *Shadows in the Night* embodies principles of perpetual metamorphosis and prophecy. These foundational principles, in turn, suggest other literary works correlating to the themes in the novel. I don't suggest that *Shadows* alludes to these works or is motivated by them. I am not proposing anything so crass as influence. Rather, invoking the concept of distributed intelligence, a sentience that is scattered across space and time, but, nonetheless, accessible, I invoke these parallel writings as evidence that others have thought closely on similar themes and that the comparison of the texts might be mutually illuminating.

Edmund Spenser published his allegorical epic *The Faerie Queen* in its most complete form in 1596. The titular Queen is Elizabeth I and the first three books of the huge poem were presented to her in 1589. Spenser says that the book is cloudily enwrapped in allegorical devices, a complex mock-heroic narrative that encompasses commentary on political, chivalrous, and theological subjects. Elizabeth was a virgin queen and her death was accompanied by fears of civil war; she left no successor to the crown, thereby plunging the State into uncertainty. Spenser feared that this uncertainty might lead to political chaos and violence. In this context, he wrote his famous Mutability cantos, first printed posthumously in1609 as an appendix to *The Faerie Queen;* most texts publish the cantos as the last book, Book VII, of the epic. These philosophical stanzas address the question of whether change necessarily results in chaos or whether the center, as it were, can hold notwithstanding the violent transformation of political and social norms. The issue is debated by the gods who have been called to a colloquium on a hill rising over Spenser's Irish manor house. The proponents for order in the universe are guided by Jove, the paternal

4

god of law; Jove contends with the titaness, Mutability, a giant figure that embodies the entropic aspects of existence. The text resembles *Shadows* in its commitment to embodying abstract principles in concrete forms the Titaness Mutability appears in her moist and tidal form as Lake Monona in the novel; the Host giant, Garrett, is a conservative figure and emblem of protective order: he is like Jove in Spenser's poem. Both works stand for a paradoxical proposition that there is order in the universe but that this invariant order is one of metamorphosis the world is an order that is comprised of constant transformation: things emerge from the flux, exist and pass away; everything is transient: human beings can evolve (or devolve) into strange, luminous personages, shadowy giants lurking at the bottom of things. Ultimately, for Spenser and, also, for Doyle, the alleged author of *Shadows in the Night*, Nature and Human Being in Nature are constant but the constancy is defined by continuous mutation. An analogy is the Second Law of Thermodynamics: heat flows downhill, dispersing into cold, and entropy (decay and chaos) characterize all living systems nonetheless, this principle is expressed as a law, that is an invariant formula applicable to all systems.

Sometime between 1804 and 1820, the British poet William Blake wrote: There is a void, outside of existence, which if entered into /Englobes itself and becomes a womb. These lines are from Blake's *Jerusalem, the Emanation of the Giant Albion*, one of 12 prophetic books written by the poet between 1789 and 1820. In these books, Blake establishes an elaborate private mythology consisting of various heroes and titans and their emanations. The poet uses this *mythopoeia* to reveal fluxions in his own psyche, most importantly the clash between the cold, armored entity Urizen (Your Reason) and various female figures that represent sexual liberation and love. As with Spenser and Doyle's book, the conflict is between a terrifying freedom characterized by ceaselessly evolving forms and stultifying logic and the law. Personages split off from one another and personality traits (or complexes) are embodied in emanations, some of them giants, either merciful and benign or wrathful. Garrett in the Heart Basin at the center of the Monona maze seems to be an emanation from Garth the similarity of the names implies something close to identity, although, it seems, that Garrett, the drowned brother, represents an aspect of Garth that the scientist has suppressed, albeit unsuccessfully. Blake's prophetic books are apocalyptic, revelations of things seen in a strange space that is either void or womb. Similarly, Garth, the protagonist in *Shadows*, records in the first person the things that he sees and hears in the chaos of the labyrinth where various personages, extruded as it were from the self, seem to embody various externalized psychological processes. I don't suggest that the novel derives from Blake. My hypothesis, however, is that the book's structure and its immense elaboration of what seem to be psychic processes of self-realization, addiction, and alienation runs parallel to Blake's mighty project.

Of course, there are obvious parallels as well to *Solaris*, both in its novel and film versions. Like the seas on the ocean planet Solaris, the waters of Lake Monona are sentient and capable of interacting with human fears and desires. Solaris is bliss-bestowing but destructive; the intelligent waters grant wishes but, also, harbor our fears, that can be materialized in

5

wrathful personages. Probably, the most immediate parallel to the metamorphic transmutations in *Shadows* is the Stanislaus Lem novel *Solaris* and the two films derived from it, directed by Andrei Tarkovsky and Stephen Soderbergh respectively.

4. Sobriety

Doyle, under another name, writes books about recovery from addiction. Garth Myers, the protagonist in *Shadows*, is a recovering alcoholic and some of the most pungent, and vivid, scenes in the book detail AA meetings. The descent into the turbulent chaos of Lake Mononas grottos and flooded tunnels can be imagined as an allegory for relapse and recovery. Alcoholism creates chaos and relapse triggers emotions of self-loathing and terror. It might be argued that Garth became an alcoholic as a result of his trauma suffered as a child when he almost drowned in the lake that both beckons and threatens throughout the novel. Indeed, Garth's drinking may have been a self-defensive mechanism to erase his drowned brother, and, apparently, alter-ego, Garrett. Either Garth drank to forget Garrett or the booze itself erased the lost brother from the hero's memory. It's not clear what happened in the icy depths of the lake when Garth almost drowned with his future sister-wife Regina. Regina escaped due to the intervention of someone named Druitt. Garth was pulled down with his brother Garrett although there is reason to believe that Garrett is really just another manifestation of Garth the similarity in the names argues for this proposition as does certain language in the book creating ambiguity as to whether the text refers to Garry (Garth) or Garrett. Indeed, I think it's probable that the trauma of near-drowning caused Garth to split into two emanations (to use Blake's prophetic scheme) , that is, Garth, the rational, scientific professor and private eye as opposed to the gentle, somewhat passive, alcoholic Garrett.

The tidal surges of Lake Monona and its fluxions may represent, on one level, the seduction of relapse. Battling against relapse, Garth takes comfort in his relationship with sponsor and mentor, Bob Thomas. In several of the visionary scenes under the lake, Bob Thomas acts as guide, his inscription B.T. marks the path downward into the chaos. Indeed, Thomas as a retired maintenance worker literally knows the pathway through the maze of watery (boozy) chambers, fissures, and tunnels he embodies the memory of relapses and, also, the memory of recovery from them. Thomas plays the role of Virgil to Garth's Dante as the hero navigates the infinite perils of the drowned passages under the lake. In one key passage, Garth finds Thomas' sobriety medallion in the muck in a tunnel. Thomas' serene admonitions are one of the talismans that Garth uses to navigate the sentient tides of relapse. After the protagonists have been retrieved from the flooded tunnels, Thomas, thought to be dead, resurfaces and remarks to Garth that now, at last, you've reached bottom, a jesting reference to the AA doctrine that drunks don't seek help until they have hit bottom. Finally, the form of the book recognizes that mutual assistance is necessary for a successful life: no one makes it on their own, another concept fundamental to recovery through Alcoholics Anonymous.

5. Rhetoric

Probably some learned German, in a Teutonic rhetoric manual, provides a name to an obsessively recurring pattern in *Shadows in the Night*. My study does not disclose that term and, so, I will simply describe this rhetorical tic. A sense impression or emotion is briefly named; then, the text says not X, not Y referring back to the predicate impression or emotion. So: A, not B, not C. There are variations on the pattern. Sometimes, the logic is Not B, Not C, A. Sometimes, the not clauses are expanded into four or, even, five examples of what the predicate is not. It's a peculiar minuet of affirmation and negation. And this particular rhetorical blossom is everywhere in the novel, sprouting up all over the place. Here's an example from the novel's Epilogue: A small warm thrum. / Not pain. / Not fear. / Recognition. By my count, this prose pattern appears 15 times in various similar iterations in the book's last 100 pages. In lieu of a technical term for this figure, I'll call it: *Knock! Knock! Who's there?* (I think the expression may be a form of *litotes*, affirming something by stating its opposite, although, strictly speaking this seems inaccurate since the not clauses are not necessarily the opposite of the sense impression or emotion stated.)

A critic (Sartre, I think) once argued that a novelist's prose style is a reflection of his metaphysics. This stylistic reflex suggests the scientific sensibility of the narrator, Garth the hero's mind works on the basis of careful taxonomic discernment, that is, distinguishing one thing from other things that may be closely related. *Knock! Knock! Who's there?* insists that related sensations or observations may be adjacent but are not the same. This rhetorical device has additional functions, central to the books themes: it emphasizes the final understanding serving as a kind of exclamation point in the text and also induces suspense there is a delay before final recognition at least in the most frequent iterations of the figure (that is, not A, not B, but C). This molecular, as it were, formula pervasive in the writing reflects the overall structure of the book which consists of revelations emphatically and suspensefully made. Most importantly, *Knock! Knock! Who's there?* is an application of a form of dialectic to the prose: it's like a doctor's differential diagnosis in the vortex of the flooded caverns and tunnels, the scientifically inclined protagonist rules out other possibilities before reaching a final conclusion as to what the lake desires.

Fundamentally *Shadows in the Night* is pointillist in its technique. The narrative is painstakingly built from fragmentary bursts of sensory data or emotional responses to that data. It is a vehemently present tense. In prose, a pointillist narrative does not accommodate itself well to flashbacks or exposition. Hence, the device of signaling, as if the novel is a film-script, when a flashback occurs. (Notice that the flashbacks are also rendered as mosaics of sense impression and emotion.) The pointillist style atomizes the narrative into clouds of impressions; hence, exposition and backstory are also suppressed; one has the distinct feeling that the book begins *in media res* and, further, ends in the middle of things as well.

Make no mistake about it: this novel will exhaust you. There's too much of it and the telegraphic pulses of the prose are sometimes awkward: more gasps and ejaculations than narrative. Perhaps, this is not the book at first blush that you would like it to be; it's too long and repetitious. But length and repetition are techniques as well and forms of rhetoric. The experience of reading this novel with its propulsive forward energy is one of total immersion. It's not merely the characters who feel like they are drowning. The reader is drowning as well in a nightmare of chutes and ladders, an inescapable maze made by some sinister software, endless dark and rotting passages that are perpetually in a state of collapse: it's like a maddening first-person shooter in which there is nothing to shoot.

By length and repetition, this book transcends itself: it's a barbaric yawp, primitive in some respects, sometimes dull but, nonetheless, mesmerizing. The book sucks you into its vortex. *It is visionary in every sense of the word.*

John S. Beckmann   December 7, 2025

John Beckmann is a lawyer practicing in a small town in southern Minnesota. His writings may be seen at https://prairieuprisinghome.blogspot.com

Dramatis Personae

Garth Myers — Engineering professor, recovering alcoholic, reluctant PI.

Regina Evert — Biochemistry professor; Garth's closest intellectual equal and first wife.

Sheila Lammers — Department administrator; instinctive ally and quiet backbone.

Detective Martinson — Madison PD; stubborn, intuitive, and often one step behind.

Evan Patel — Graduate student collapsing under secrets too heavy to carry.

Lila Wilcox — Missing undergraduate researcher.

Bob Thomas — Garth's AA sponsor and spiritual compass.

PROLOGUE

Activation Energy

Every spark begins in stillness.

They say every reaction needs a little push. Chemists call it activation energy—that tiny shove the universe gives a molecule before it changes shape forever.

People aren't that different.

We like to pretend we're stable, predictable, content to drift in our beakers as the world warms and cools around us. But one small shock—a bad phone call, a strange footprint on your porch, a former wife asking for help—and suddenly you're somebody else. A reactant on the way to becoming a product.

My shock came on a Monday morning in October of 1996. The lake outside my window was still and black, pretending it wasn't capable of killing a man in seconds. But I knew better. Lakes lie. I learned that when I was seven, maybe eight, lungs full of Lake Monona in Madison, until a stranger's hands hauled me back into the world.

Ever since, water and I maintain an uneasy truce. It stays outside. I stay alive. Most days, that's enough.

I wasn't planning to solve any mysteries that morning. I had a Thermodynamics I lecture at ten, office hours after, and a racquetball match I was destined to lose later that afternoon. A life well-ordered in its mediocrity.

And then Regina—my first wife, my best friend, the only person who has ever seen me without all my disguises—left a message on my machine.

"Garth... call me back. It's important."

Regina never says *important* unless someone's life is about to shift.

Turns out mine was the one that shifted.

That's the problem with activation energy: once you cross the threshold, reactions tend to run their course. Even if they take you places you wish you'd never gone. Even if they drag you back toward the water.

ACT I

Lila's Disappearance

When the truth knocks, it doesn't matter whether you're ready. It only matters who opens the door.

CHAPTER 1

The Reaction Begins

Every shadow forms the moment light decides to move.

The lake looked dead that morning.

Lake Monona can pull that trick sometimes—lie still enough to make you wonder if it stopped breathing overnight. Wisconsin lakes do that in October. They turn into cold slabs of pewter, flat as an autopsy table and twice as unfriendly. Some people find it peaceful. I find it ominous.

I stood at my kitchen window with a mug of over-extracted coffee, watching dawn soak slowly into the horizon like an ink spill reluctant to clean itself up. My reflection hovered on the glass—unkempt hair, hollow eyes, the general aura of a man who'd argued with his own thermostat and lost.

A loon cried somewhere across the water, its call echoing through the early fog. That sound always hit me in the ribs. Something about its loneliness. Something about mine.

I took a sip of coffee. It tasted like regret and burnt toast—my preferred flavor profile.

Monday. October. 1996. Though honestly, it could've been any year from the last decade. Routine can blur time if you let it.

But even before the real trouble started, I knew something was wrong. There was a tension in the air, a subtle shift in equilibrium. Sometimes an engineer—chemical at that—can feel that moment before a reaction goes from quiet to explosive. In thermodynamics, we call it metastability. In life, we call it dread.

My house on the lake creaked as it warmed. The furnace hummed inconsistently, like it was clearing its throat before delivering bad news. I rubbed the back of my neck and checked the time. Too early for office hours. Too late to pretend I might go back to sleep.

Across the kitchen, the answering machine blinked—one steady red pulse.

A lighthouse warning of rocks ahead.

I walked over, hit Play, and listened as the tape clicked itself awake.

"Garth... call me back. It's important."

Regina's voice.

Even distorted by cheap plastic and static fizz, it carried weight.

I exhaled slowly. *Important* from Regina Evert covered only three possibilities: a research disaster, a personal crisis, or something that would ruin my day, my week, or my sanity. She never used the word lightly.

I played the message again. Then again. Still important.

I set down the mug, grabbed my coat from the peg by the door, and stepped outside into the chill. The air tasted metallic, like someone had scraped iron filings across the sky.

The '89 four-speed automatic F150 sat in the driveway looking as tired as I felt. Rust creeping around the wheel wells. Passenger door that didn't open from the inside. A heating system that worked on an honor system. Madison winters are hard on trucks—and on men.

The engine started on the second try, coughing out a cloud of exhaust that drifted across the yard and evaporated into the lake fog. NPR murmured politics and grain prices through the speakers, too soft to be helpful and too persistent to ignore.

Driving along John Nolen Drive, I glanced again at Lake Monona stretched like a bruise against the city. The water was perfectly flat. Perfectly quiet.

Too quiet.

My chest tightened.

A memory surfaced, uninvited and sharp: Lake Monona Madison. Age eight. The world turning upside down. Water closing over my head. Cold hands pulling me down instead of up. The taste of panic—metallic, raw. The certainty: *I'm going to die.*

I blinked hard and forced the present back into focus. Traffic. Dawn. Madison. Not 1970. Not drowning.

My palms were slick against the steering wheel.

I rolled the window down and let the cold air slap me awake before the memory swallowed me. Water and I maintained an uneasy truce—we had for decades—but some mornings the old fear rose without warning, like a submerged log drifting up from the depths.

I pulled into the Engineering Hall lot with two minutes left before campus security started ticketing anyone bold or stupid enough to park illegally. On a good day, I was both.

The hallway smelled like chalk dust, industrial cleaner, and graduate-student despair. Familiar. Comforting, in a bleak kind of way.

My thermodynamics students filed into lecture like refugees fleeing from calculus. They stared at me with the kind of hope only people very unprepared for an exam can muster.

"Morning," I said.

A few mumbled greetings. One girl winced as if sunlight hurt her.

I launched into entropy, boundary work, and why the second law of thermodynamics ruins everyone's day sooner or later. Usually my jokes land—small, nerdy explosions of humor that keep the class awake. But today my timing was off. My mind kept drifting to Regina's voice.

Garth... call me back. It's important.

After class, I lingered longer than necessary. Erased the board, rewrote an equation just to erase it again. My office was three floors up, but my feet started carrying me across campus instead.

Toward Biochemistry.

Toward Regina.

The sky had darkened into an ugly, sullen gray. A wind picked up, dragging leaves across the sidewalk like reluctant dancers.

The Biochemistry Building smelled like ethanol, agar, ambition, and fear—memories of my early career mixed with too many late nights spent with pipettes and regret. Students hurried past me in lab coats, muttering about assays and deadlines. Science is the only field where people panic quietly.

Regina's office door was open a crack. Light spilled out onto the linoleum.

I knocked once.

"Come in."

Her voice was taut. Not good.

The office looked exactly as I remembered—organized chaos. Books stacked like geological formations, glassware on the windowsill, framed photos of conferences we'd attended together. A few pictures were newer: her with a woman smiling warmly, then another, then none. Regina's romantic life had seasons—warmth, storm, thaw.

She stood behind the desk, arms crossed, hair pulled back so sharply I wondered if it hurt. Her glasses sat on a stack of enzyme-kinetics papers, abandoned.

"Thanks for coming," she said.

"You sounded worried."

"That's because I am."

I took the chair across from her. It squeaked—protesting my weight or the conversation it was about to witness.

Regina hesitated. Regina never hesitates. That alone put me on alert.

"It's Lila," she said finally.

"Your undergrad researcher?"

"She's missing."

A knot formed in my stomach.

"How long?"

"Three days."

"Has she contacted anyone?"

"No. Phone off. No email. She didn't show up for the lab, for class, for her tutoring shift. Her roommate says she didn't take clothes or her backpack."

"And campus police?"

"Filed a missing-person report and did nothing. They say she's twenty-one and 'probably blowing off steam somewhere.' But that's not Lila. She's responsible. She's... steady."

"Steady people disappear too," I said quietly.

Regina's jaw tightened. She hated when I said things that were true but unhelpful.

"There's more." She reached into a folder and handed me a printed email.

Lila's message. Sent the night she vanished.

Dr. Evert,

Something's wrong in the basement lab. I can explain, but not over email.

Please—can we meet after hours?

—Lila

"Which basement lab?" I asked.

"That's the problem," Regina said. "As far as I know... there isn't one."

She paced behind the desk, restless energy radiating off her like heat from a Bunsen burner.

"She knew things, Garth. She was sharp. Curious. Maybe too curious."

"Curiosity didn't kill the cat," I said. "But it probably made the police report more interesting."

Regina shot me a look that could curdle milk.

I lifted my hands in surrender.

"Look," she said, voice softening. "I know you have that PI license. And... you've helped before. I wouldn't ask if I didn't think something was wrong."

I should've said no. I had lectures to prepare, papers to review, a life to keep small and predictable.

But Lila's email burned in my mind.

Something's wrong in the basement lab.

My heartbeat quickened.

"This doesn't sound like a normal missing-person case," I said.

Regina leaned forward. "That's why I'm coming to you."

A flashback surfaced—me and Regina, twenty-five years younger, exhausted at a Michigan lab bench, her leaning over my shoulder correcting my pipetting angle, telling me, *You overthink everything, Garth. Just act.*

Here she was again, telling me without saying it.

I nodded. "I'll look into it."

Relief washed over her face, followed by fear.

"I'm... worried, Garth."

"About Lila?"

"Yes. But also... about what she found."

Rain began tapping lightly against her office window. Small, uncertain drops.

"You think something illegal is happening," I said.

"I think something dangerous is happening."

The room felt colder.

"You'll start with the lab?" she asked.

"Of course."

"And be careful."

"I'm always careful."

Regina raised an eyebrow.

We both knew that wasn't true.

I walked out of her office, the hallway feeling darker than when I'd entered. Students rushed by, oblivious to the crack forming in the calm surface of their world.

Outside, the rain had become steady—thin needles pricking my skin. The sky brooded. The lake beyond the buildings loomed like a secret waiting to be found.

I made it halfway to my truck before another flashback hit: the lake sucking me under, weeds tightening around my ankles, sunlight warping above, unreachable, my lungs burning, my mother screaming from the shore. Darkness—then air filling me again.

Someone had dragged me out. Someone whose name I never learned.

I stumbled, bracing myself against a lamppost.

Madison blurred. The rain, the pavement, the rush of cars—smearing into one long gray streak.

But Lila's words cut through the haze:

Something's wrong in the basement lab.

I straightened, inhaled slowly, and pushed the memory down where it belonged. Not gone. Never gone. Just buried deep enough that I could move.

I climbed into the F150 and started the engine. The radio crackled between stations, finally settling on a jazz piece that sounded like a trumpet player losing an argument with his own sadness.

I pulled out of the lot and drove toward the Biochemistry annex—the part of the building nobody talks about unless something breaks or someone disappears.

Rain streaked across the windshield in diagonal slashes. The city lights blurred. Lake Monona loomed to my right, an unblinking eye watching me.

And I realized something that made my pulse quicken: my life had felt static for years. Predictable. Safe.

But now?

Something was stirring beneath the surface—a reaction beginning. A shift that couldn't be undone.

And I was already in too deep to pretend otherwise.

CHAPTER 2

Regina's Fear

Terror grows fastest in the spaces we try to face alone.

The rain was still coming down when I walked back into the Biochemistry Building, only now it had shifted from a steady drizzle to something more committed. Not a storm yet—just an insistent tapping, like the sky trying to get someone's attention. Maybe mine.

Hallway lights flickered overhead, humming like they'd missed their morning coffee. It was late morning by then, but the building still felt half-asleep, the way academic labs often do on Mondays before the caffeine pipeline kicks in. Graduate students slouched past with clipboards and bloodshot eyes, as if competing in some unspoken contest of exhaustion.

Regina waited for me outside her office. Arms folded. Jaw tight. She looked less like a biochemistry professor and more like a prosecutor about to deliver a closing argument.

"Come on," she said softly. "We need to talk somewhere private."

We walked down the corridor to a small conference room—one of those narrow rectangular ones with mismatched chairs and a whiteboard permanently stained with blue marker. Regina closed the blinds, shut the door, and sat across from me. Her posture was too rigid, too careful.

"I didn't want to say everything in the hallway," she said.

"Understood."

Regina rubbed her eyes, smearing whatever minimal makeup she'd bothered with that morning. "I keep trying to convince myself this is nothing. That Lila just… disappeared on her own terms. But I know her, Garth. Something's wrong."

"Tell me everything," I said.

She picked at the corner of the table before speaking. "Lila isn't the type to vanish. She's quiet, yes, but responsible. Focused. She's been working on a protein engineering project that—well, it's ambitious. She's been pushing herself. But disappearing? No. Not Lila."

"And the email?" I asked. "'Something's wrong in the basement lab.'"

Regina swallowed. "That's what scares me. Because as far as I know, there's no basement lab."

"You've been here twenty-plus years."

"Exactly." She pushed her hair back behind her ears. "I would know."

I leaned back in the chair. "Tell me about the project she was working on."

Regina sighed. "Directed evolution of enzyme variants. A routine concept, but Lila's approach was unusual. She was experimenting with multi-site mutagenesis using a new technique she'd borrowed from... from someone outside the department."

"Who?"

Regina hesitated. "She wouldn't say."

That wasn't good.

"Has anyone else in the lab mentioned seeing her act differently?" I asked.

"There's a postdoc... Evan. But he's been skittish. Nervous."

Evan Patel. I'd seen that kid hovering earlier like a bird afraid of its own shadow.

Regina looked away. "There's something else."

I waited.

"She came to my office last week. Said she found something strange while running an SDS-PAGE." Regina paused, then clarified, "Protein gel. Pretty basic procedure. But she said the bands didn't make sense."

"In what way?"

"She said she saw a band where no band should be. A size that didn't match anything in her constructs."

"Contamination?"

"She didn't think so. She repeated the experiment twice. Same result both times."

"What did you tell her?"

"I told her to rerun it a third time and show me the results. But she never did. And then she sent that email."

I nodded slowly. "So she sees an anomalous protein, panics, and then finds something 'wrong' in a basement lab that shouldn't exist."

Regina's eyes stayed locked on mine. "You think this is connected."

"Yes."

A beat passed. The room felt smaller.

Regina lowered her voice. "This... whatever this is... it might not just be a missing student. It could be something else."

"Something like what?"

She shook her head. "I don't know. But I'm terrified it's something illegal. Or dangerous."

I let that sit for a moment.

When Regina is frightened, I pay attention. She's too rational, too meticulous, too controlled to be shaken by shadows.

But today she looked genuinely scared.

"Let me see her bench space," I said.

She nodded and stood quickly, like motion alone could keep panic from catching up.

We stepped into the hallway. A pair of grad students trudged by, not even glancing at us. I wondered if they knew their classmate was missing. Probably not. Academia trains people to mind their own business—sometimes to the point of cruelty.

We headed for the lab, passing a row of clean rooms and tissue culture bays. The air smelled like ethanol and stale ambition.

Regina swiped her badge. The door clicked open.

The lab was a long, rectangular space lined with stainless steel benches, plastic pipette boxes, and stacks of glassware drying above sinks. Machines hummed—a centrifuge, a shaker, an ancient-looking PCR machine that had probably been purchased before the Reagan administration.

Regina led me to the back. "This is where Lila worked."

The bench was neat, which for an undergraduate was unusual enough to qualify as a red flag.

"She never leaves this clean," Regina muttered. "Something's wrong."

I scanned the space.

Her lab notebook was missing.

Her pipettes were lined up perfectly.

A half-finished column purification stood in the rack—ligands still bound, resin drying.

The timer on a small centrifuge blinked 04:57, as if someone had stopped it mid-run and forgotten about it.

"Students don't leave mid-purification," Regina said, voice trembling. "They don't."

She wasn't wrong. Labs run on routines. On discipline. On gradients and gradients alone.

I crouched down and checked the floor around the bench. Nothing unusual. No spilled buffers, no broken glass, no notes.

"She left fast," I said.

"Too fast," Regina whispered.

There was something else—some faint, chemical smell I couldn't place. Not ethanol. Not acetone. Something metallic, almost sweet. It lingered in the corners like a secret someone had tried to mop away.

"You smell that?" I asked.

Regina sniffed the air. "Yes. I noticed it yesterday. I thought maybe it was a contaminated reagent."

"No," I said. "This is something else."

I walked toward the side of the room where a locked cabinet sat. Heavy padlock. Thick steel. Most biochemists kept sensitive enzymes behind these, but something about this one bothered me.

"Who has access to this?" I asked.

"Only faculty," Regina said. "It's where we store restricted materials."

"Lila?"

"No. Not students."

"How about Evan?"

She hesitated. "Officially, no."

Unofficially, with grad-student resourcefulness and a screwdriver—anything was possible.

"What's inside?" I asked.

"DNA libraries. Enzyme variants. Some old radioactive kits that would give any federal inspector a panic attack."

"And any dangerous proteins?"

"Nothing that should be accessible without supervision." She paused. "But I haven't checked recently."

I put a hand on the steel. Cold. Too cold. Almost refrigerated. That meant either the AC was broken or something inside was running too hard.

I tapped it once. "May I?"

Regina unlocked it.

Inside were trays of neatly labeled vials.

And one empty slot.

"What goes here?" I asked.

Regina frowned. "There should be a plasmid library there. A small one, but proprietary."

"Who last checked it out?"

"Nobody. Not since spring."

She looked at me, horror softening her features.

"Garth... are you thinking what I'm thinking?"

"I hope not," I said. "But I might be."

I closed the cabinet and locked it again.

"Did Lila ever talk about anyone following her? Anyone threatening her? Anyone she didn't trust?"

Regina swallowed. "She mentioned someone once. Said a man kept showing up at the lab late at night. Not a student. Not faculty. Someone she didn't recognize."

My blood chilled. "Security?"

"No. She asked. They had no record of anyone from Facilities scheduled to be there."

"Did she describe him?"

"Tall. Thin. Wore a baseball cap. That's all she said."

"That's not much."

"No," Regina whispered. "But it's enough."

I walked the perimeter of the lab, examining shelves, equipment, and notes. Nothing obvious jumped out—but the lack of anything was its own kind of clue. If something happened to Lila, her disappearance was too clean. Too intentional.

"Let's check something else," I said.

Regina followed me into the hallway. We reached the stairwell.

"What are you doing?" she asked.

"'Something's wrong in the basement lab.'"

"There is no—"

But I was already descending.

The stairwell grew dimmer as we went down. A flickering bulb buzzed overhead, casting shadows that jerked in and out like startled ghosts. The lower levels of science buildings always feel a bit haunted. Too few people. Too many secrets.

At the bottom landing, a service door waited—unlabeled metal, scratched, neglected. The kind of door that pretends to be boring but isn't.

I tried the handle.

Locked.

I leaned down. The metal was slightly warm.

"Regina," I said quietly, "why would a room that doesn't exist be warm?"

Her hand flew to her mouth. "Garth—"

I touched the frame. There was a faint vibration. Something was running behind that door. Something big. Something mechanical.

"Do you know what's behind here?" I asked.

"No. That used to be a storage area, but... I haven't seen anyone use it in years."

"Does anyone have access?"

"Maybe facilities... maybe administration..."

I stepped back. A number stenciled near the floor caught my eye: B3-11.

A room number. Which meant it wasn't storage. Storage doesn't get numbers.

"Where's B3-12?" I asked.

Regina paled. "There isn't one."

I made a mental note.

We walked back upstairs. The hallway felt colder on the return. Students moved around us, oblivious to the crackling tension building beneath their feet.

Regina stopped suddenly. "Garth, you'll be careful, right?"

"I'm always careful."

She raised that same skeptical eyebrow she'd been using on me since graduate school. "That's a lie."

"Fair."

Her voice softened. "I'm serious. I don't want anyone else getting hurt."

Something in her tone told me she wasn't just afraid for Lila.

"I'll keep you updated," I said. "And Regina... thank you for calling me."

She nodded and turned away so I wouldn't see her face crumple.

Class was letting out in a nearby hallway—students pushing through doors, laughing, arguing, checking their pagers. A faculty member with a lopsided tie rushed by, muttering about a grant deadline. Life went on around us as if nothing unnatural was unfolding.

But something was unfolding.

I felt it.

A tremor in my gut—the instinct that years of problem-solving had sharpened. A reaction had started. And once it started, there was no undoing it.

I made my way toward the exit, pulling out my car keys.

That's when I saw it.

The door to an equipment room—one that was always locked—stood slightly ajar. A thin line of light spilled onto the floor. I reached for it and gently nudged it open.

Inside, a piece of equipment hummed faintly.

A centrifuge. Running.

No one was around.

The display read:

11:13 PM — Run Complete

Lila disappeared the night before.

And someone had used this centrifuge after hours.

I scanned the room quickly. A faint shoeprint—wet, smeared—marked the floor near the drain. A lake-water smell lingered subtly.

My heart thudded.

I stepped back, letting the door fall halfway shut behind me.

Someone else had been here.

After Lila vanished.

Someone with access.

Someone who didn't want to be seen.

And something about that lake–water smell twisted my stomach.

Rain pounded the windows harder now.

I exhaled slowly.

"Great," I muttered. "Just great."

Because the first physical clue had surfaced, and it was worse than I'd feared.

Not a sign of Lila.

A sign of whoever didn't want her found.

CHAPTER 3

First Clues, First Lies

The truth rarely breaks—it unravels, one thread at a time.

The centrifuge kept humming in the back of my mind long after I left the equipment room. Machines shouldn't run alone at night. Students don't sneak in to spin samples at 11 p.m. And missing undergraduates don't disappear without leaving a trace.

I stood in the empty hallway, listening to the rain pelt the windows in steady sheets. The building had gone quiet—the kind of quiet that feels purposeful, like someone hit Mute on the world. I didn't like it.

I exhaled slowly and started walking back toward the main corridor. Halfway there, I heard footsteps—soft, hesitant, the kind made by someone who isn't sure they want to be heard.

I turned.

Evan Patel stood near the corner, eyes wide behind thin rectangular glasses, his lab coat hanging crookedly like he'd thrown it on during a fire drill. His hair stuck out in uneven tufts, and his hands were clasped together so tightly his knuckles glowed like bone china under fluorescent lighting.

"You... you're Dr. Myers, right?" he said.

His voice trembled not from cold but something closer to fear. Fear or guilt. Or both.

"Yes," I said. "And you're Evan."

He swallowed. "Regina said you might be... asking questions."

"I am."

His eyes darted down the hallway as if expecting someone else to appear.

When no one did, he stepped closer.

"I—I didn't do anything," he said quickly.

"Most people don't begin conversations that way unless they did."

"I just mean... I didn't. Whatever happened. I wasn't involved."

He wasn't just shaking. He was unraveling.

"What makes you think something happened?" I asked.

He swallowed hard. "Because Lila is missing."

"And?"

"And because she was scared."

There it was.

The truth, in rusted pieces.

I kept my voice soft. "Scared of what?"

He hesitated so long I thought he wasn't going to answer. Rain drummed against the building, a steady percussion.

Finally, he whispered, "The basement."

Good. That made two of us.

"What do you know about the basement?" I asked.

Evan glanced around again. "Not here," he said sharply. "Please. Not here."

I studied him. His eyes darted to the equipment room behind me. When they saw the slightly open door, he flinched—just for a moment—as if seeing it triggered something he wasn't ready to face.

"Fine," I said. "Let's go somewhere else."

He exhaled, relieved.

We walked toward the stairwell. Evan's shoes squeaked with each step, and every sound seemed louder than it should be. The hallway lights buzzed overhead—flickering occasionally, like they were trying to tell us something.

Outside, the rain had intensified into a gray curtain. Students hurried under umbrellas while the unlucky ones sprinted bareheaded through puddles. Evan and I sheltered under the awning for a moment. The scent of wet pavement and dead leaves filled the air.

"I know a place," I said.

We headed down the street to a small coffee shop wedged between a poster-print store and a futon outlet—a relic from a decade earlier, with mismatched tables and a counter staffed by students who looked like they'd aged ten years too fast. The chalkboard menu listed items like "Existential Mocha" and "Breakup Latte."

We grabbed a corner table. Evan wrapped his hands around a cup of peppermint tea like it was a life preserver.

"Tell me about Lila," I said.

He took a shaky breath. "She was brilliant. More brilliant than she knew. Most undergrads struggle with basic transform protocols. Lila... she breezed past all that. She had this way of seeing patterns nobody else noticed."

"Patterns," I repeated. "Like what?"

"She kept asking questions about... things we weren't supposed to question."

"Such as?"

"When certain equipment was used. Who had access to some of the restricted areas. Why didn't the inventory numbers line up?"

Inventory.

My mind jumped back to the missing plasmid library.

"Did Lila say anything was stolen?" I asked.

"No. Not stolen. But... moved." Evan's eyes dropped. "She said something was being kept in a place it wasn't supposed to be."

A pulse of adrenaline flickered in my chest.

"And she found out where?" I asked.

Evan's hands trembled around the tea. "She thought so. She said she saw... people down there."

"In the basement."

He nodded once.

"People who weren't faculty?"

Another nod.

"People who weren't students?"

A third nod.

"Did she describe them?"

He hesitated. "She said one was tall. Pale. Wore a baseball cap."

Regina had said the same.

"And the other?"

"She didn't get a clear look. But she said they had a badge."

"Security?"

"No," Evan whispered. "Different. Not campus security. Something else."

The kind of "something else" you never want in an academic building.

He took a shaky sip of tea. "She told me she was going to confront someone. She said she'd found proof."

"Proof of what?"

His eyes filled with tears he tried to blink away. "I don't know. I swear. She didn't tell me. She said it was safer if I didn't know."

"And then she disappeared."

He nodded.

I leaned back. "Why didn't you tell Regina?"

"Because I.." His throat tightened. "I was scared. And I didn't want anyone to think I was involved."

Guilt radiated off him in waves.

"Evan," I said quietly, "you need to tell me if someone threatened you."

He lowered his head. "I—I found something taped to my locker door last week."

"What was it?"

He reached into his coat pocket and pulled out a folded piece of paper. He slid it across the table.

I opened it.

Block letters. Sharp strokes. Ink pressed so hard it almost tore the page:

STOP DIGGING.

My stomach clenched.

"When did you get this?" I asked.

"Two days before she went missing."

"And you didn't think to tell anyone?"

"I was scared," Evan whispered again. "I still am."

I folded the paper and placed it back on the table between us.

Fear hung between us like static, humming, waiting.

I softened my tone. "Evan... what do you think happened to Lila?"

He shook his head, tears threatening again. "I think she found something she shouldn't have."

"And?"

"And I think someone made her disappear."

The words landed heavy.

Evan wiped his eyes, trying to regain composure. "I should go. I need to get back before my shift starts."

He stood abruptly, nearly knocking the chair over.

"Evan—"

He shook his head. "I've already said too much."

Then he hurried out into the rain.

I stayed behind for a moment, processing his words. Outside, Evan disappeared into the gray, swallowed by the downpour and the campus like he had never existed.

Stop digging.

A threat. A warning. A promise.

Someone didn't want that basement disturbed.

I stood, paid for the tea, and stepped back out into the rain. My coat was soaked within seconds. I made my way to the F150 and sat inside, water dripping from my hair onto the steering wheel.

The sense of unease thickened.

I turned the key. The engine coughed twice before starting.

I needed to see the security logs.

Back in the truck, I turned the heater up and tried to shake off the feeling that something cold had settled under my skin. Rain hammered the windshield with growing intensity. The sky had darkened into a roiling bruise.

I needed one more stop before going home.

The Biochemistry Building looked even worse in the rain—a hulking gray monolith streaked with water. I swiped into the building and headed straight for Lila's apartment address—Regina had given it to me earlier.

It was a modest two-bedroom on the second floor of a converted house. The hallway smelled like stale pizza and wet carpeting.

I knocked.

No answer.

I knocked again.

A timid voice called out, "Who is it?"

"Garth Myers," I said. "I'm looking into Lila's disappearance."

The door cracked open. A young woman with red-rimmed eyes and a blanket draped around her shoulders peered out.

"I'm her roommate," she said softly. "Mara."

"I'm not with the police," I said, "but I'm trying to help."

She opened the door wider.

"Come in," she whispered.

The apartment was small, cluttered with textbooks, empty mugs, a dying plant, and the faint smell of incense trying and failing to cover something sour—fear, grief, or just old laundry.

"Have you heard from her at all?" I asked gently.

Mara shook her head violently. "She wouldn't just disappear. Lila wasn't like that."

"Did she seem scared recently?"

"She seemed... off. She said someone was watching her."

"Who?"

"I don't know. But she stopped going out at night. She kept checking the windows. And she slept with the lights on the last two nights."

Not good.

"Do you know if she had enemies?" I asked.

Mara scoffed weakly. "Lila? She was too nice for enemies."

"That's not always how it works."

Mara hugged the blanket tighter. "The night she disappeared, she told me she was going to meet someone in the lab."

My chest tightened. "At what time?"

"Around ten-thirty."

"Did she say who?"

"No. She just said she needed to show them something."

"What?"

Mara's voice cracked. "Proof. She said she had proof."

My pulse quickened.

"What kind of proof?"

Mara shook her head, eyes filling with tears. "She didn't tell me. She said... the less I knew, the safer I'd be."

The same thing she'd told Evan.

A pattern was emerging.

I made a note of a photo on Lila's desk—herself with Regina during a lab outing. She looked happy. Confident. Alive.

Now she was missing.

I left the apartment with a heaviness that settled into my bones.

Night had fallen by the time I drove back toward campus. The rain had thinned to a mist that clung to the windshield in ghostly fingers.

There was one more thing I needed to do.

I turned onto a side road and parked near the loading dock behind the Biochemistry Building. The area was dimly lit, with only one flickering lamp casting a sickly yellow cone onto the slick pavement.

I stepped out.

The air smelled of ozone and wet concrete.

I approached the service entrance—the one nearest the basement stairwell.

Rainwater pooled around my shoes.

Then I saw it.

A faint smear on the concrete, near the doorframe. Dark. Muddy. Distinct.

A partial footprint.

Not large. Not small. But unmistakably wet.

And smelling faintly of lake water.

Lake Monona.

My breath caught.

Someone had been here. Recently. Someone who had been in that water.

A chill slid down my spine.

Then the door—

a heavy steel door that had been shut tight when I walked up—

shifted.

Just slightly.

A soft metallic creak.

Like someone... or something... pulling back from the other side.

I froze.

The rain quieted.

The whole world seemed to hold its breath.

"Hello?" I said softly.

No reply.

I stepped closer.

Inside, a light flickered—just once.

Then darkness swallowed the room again.

I reached for the handle.

It was warm.

Warm like the basement door earlier.

Something ran behind it. Something with heat.

And maybe—

someone.

My hand shook.

I pulled back.

Not tonight. Not alone. Not until I knew what lived behind that door.

I took a slow step backward, then another, rain soaking through my collar.

I turned and walked away, each step echoing louder in my ears.

As I reached the truck, the door behind me let out a soft, hollow thud.

Like a heartbeat.

Like something waiting.

Watching.

Plotting.

CHAPTER 4

Sheila Joins the Investigation

Every new voice shifts the frequency of the truth.

Morning came reluctantly to Madison, sliding into the world like someone nursing a hangover. A thin mist hovered over Lake Monona, not quite fog, not quite rain—just enough to blur the line between water and sky. I watched it through my windshield as I sat in the UW parking lot, drinking lukewarm coffee and trying not to think about the footprint I'd found near the basement door the night before.

Not a good way to begin a day, but then again I've never been great at beginnings.

My Nokia 9000 Communicator buzzed.

Sheila.

I sighed and answered. "Morning."

Her voice was clipped, practical. "Where are you? You're not in your office."

"How do you know that?"

"Because I checked. Twice."

"That's unnerving."

"Garth, it's eight-thirty. Your office hours start at nine. You vanish before nine, I assume two possibilities: you're dead or you forgot."

"I didn't forget."

"So you're dead."

"I'm fine."

"That's debatable."

I stared at the windshield. "I'm in the lot. Drinking coffee badly made by a machine that hates me."

"Well, good. Come inside. You look suspicious sitting alone in a truck staring at the window."

"Who told you I was doing that?"

"I have eyes everywhere."

I hung up before she could say more.

Sheila has been my administrative assistant for almost ten years. She knows every student's GPA, every professor's vice, and every secret the department tries to bury. If the university had a nervous system, Sheila Lammers would be its amygdala—sensing danger, assigning meaning, making snap judgments that are correct nine times out of ten.

I stepped out of the truck and walked through the quad. Students drifted past wearing oversized sweaters and headphones, immune to the grayness of the day. Campus always had a pulse in autumn—slow but steady, like the city breathing before winter smothered it.

Inside the Engineering Building, the hallway lights buzzed their usual morning complaint. I walked past the bulletin board of undergraduate announcements, past the trophy case with dusty plaques, and toward my office.

Sheila waited by my door, arms crossed, hair pulled back tight, expression set to *I know everything and I disapprove.*

She looked me up and down. "You didn't sleep."

"I slept."

"You didn't."

"I might've."

"Your shirt is buttoned wrong."

I glanced down. "No it's—"

It was.

She stepped forward and fixed it with the kind of brisk efficiency only a former schoolteacher or army sergeant could manage.

"There," she said. "Now tell me what's going on."

"I don't know what you—"

"Garth, spare me. Regina emailed me last night."

Of course she did.

Sheila walked into my office and shut the door behind her. "She's worried. And if Regina is worried, I'm worried. Now talk."

I dropped into my chair. The room smelled like old paper and burnt dust—comforting, in a nostalgic kind of way. My desk was its usual chaos of journal articles, unfinished problem sets, and half-written notes. Sheila took the only clean chair.

"Lila Wilcox is missing," I said.

Sheila blinked once. "Oh God. The girl from Regina's lab?"

"Yes."

"When?"

"Three days ago."

"Have you talked to the police?"

"Yes. They're useless."

"That tracks."

Sheila leaned forward. "What's your role in this?"

I sighed. "She asked me to look into it."

Sheila didn't blink. "Of course she did."

"I found some things," I said.

"Like?"

"Her lab notebook is missing. A centrifuge was used at 11:13 p.m. the night she disappeared. Security logs don't line up. And someone left a footprint outside a restricted door in the basement."

Sheila stared at me. "Footprint. Basement. Garth, what exactly are you involving yourself in?"

"I don't know yet."

"And that's what scares me."

Sheila stood and moved to the window, watching students cross the courtyard below.

"I liked that girl," she said quietly. "Always polite when she came by to drop off forms. Bright eyes. Big plans." She paused. "Madison can be cruel to bright girls with big plans."

45

I studied her. Sheila rarely showed softness, but when she did, it came from someplace deep and private.

"Let me help," she said.

"You already have too much on your plate."

"Garth, please."

I hesitated. Sheila is not the type you drag into a mystery. She's the type who solves the mystery of why the department budget is short by two grand before the dean even knows it happened. But this case felt different—darker, deeper, with undercurrents I couldn't name yet.

"What do you want to do?" I asked.

"Start with information," she said. "Students, professors, research groups. Everything leaves a paper trail, even secrets."

I smiled despite myself. "Good. Because I need that."

Her mouth twitched—her version of a smile.

But before she could say more, someone knocked.

Sheila opened the door.

Detective Martinson filled the doorway like a disgruntled refrigerator. His coat dripped rain onto the carpet.

Sheila stiffened. "Can I help you?"

Martinson held up a badge. "Looking for Myers."

"What did he do?" Sheila asked immediately.

Martinson smirked. "Nothing yet."

I stood. "Detective."

"Mind if we talk?"

"I'm in the middle of something."

"I know," he said. "That's why I'm here."

He glanced at Sheila. "Alone."

Sheila's jaw tightened. "Whatever you can say to him, you can say to me."

"I doubt that," Martinson said.

The air thickened.

"It's okay," I said softly.

Sheila looked at me, then at Martinson, then back at me.

"This is not over," she said, and stepped out, leaving the door slightly ajar on purpose—she never trusted cops.

Martinson shut it anyway.

He sat. The chair groaned under him.

"You were at the campus late last night," he said.

Great. Someone had eyes everywhere after all.

"I was walking," I said.

"In the rain?"

"I enjoy the damp."

He snorted.

"You're digging," he said. "I told you not to."

"I'm looking into a missing student. Same as you."

"No," Martinson said. "I am following protocol. You are following hunches. Those get people killed."

I folded my arms. "You find anything new?"

Martinson's jaw clenched. His silence answered the question.

"There was a call from a fisherman this morning," he finally said. "Out near the Lakeside causeway. Saw something floating."

My blood chilled.

"It wasn't a body," Martinson clarified. "It was a shoe. A woman's sneaker."

I exhaled.

He continued, "White. Muddy. Size seven."

"Does it belong to Lila?"

"We're checking. But your name keeps popping up."

"My name?"

"You're a professor. She worked for Regina Evert. Regina works with you. And you've already been down in the labs poking around."

I stayed quiet.

Martinson leaned closer. "Be honest. Did you find something you're not telling me?"

I hesitated.

Martinson's eyes narrowed. "That's a yes."

"It's a maybe," I said. "I found evidence someone was in the lab after her disappearance."

"Who?"

"I don't know."

"Do you have footage?"

"Not yet."

Martinson cursed under his breath. "This school is a black hole. Every admin has a different story, every professor thinks they're above me, and every student is scared to death of something they won't name."

I studied him.

"You want the truth?" I asked.

"No," Martinson said. "I want this to be simple. And it's not."

He rubbed his forehead. "Look. I'm not your enemy, Myers. But you're walking a thin line. Keep me in the loop. You see something, you tell me."

"Agreed."

He stood. "And stay away from that lake."

He left before I could answer.

Back in my office, Sheila walked in the moment Martinson left.

"What did he say?" she demanded.

"Nothing helpful."

"So everything," she muttered.

Sheila sat across from me. "Okay. Tell me everything from the start. No skipping."

I told her about the centrifuge. The missing notebook. The footprint. Evan's warning. The note taped to his locker. Martinson's update about the shoe. The basement.

Sheila listened without interrupting—a rare event.

When I finished, she steepled her fingers. "This is bad."

"I noticed."

"No, Garth. This is dangerous. Something is happening in that building. Something people don't want found. And if Lila knew something..."

"She's in trouble," I said.

Sheila nodded. "Or worse."

Silence settled between us.

Sheila leaned forward. "You need to let me help. I have access to the administrative records. Room assignments. Facility schedules. Renovation reports."

I blinked. "Renovation?"

"Yes. The Biochem building underwent renovations about six years ago. Basement included."

My pulse quickened. "What kind of renovations?"

"I don't know yet. But I can find out."

"I need blueprints."

Sheila raised an eyebrow. "I can get them."

"How?"

She shrugged. "People like me. People fear me. People give me what I ask for."

I smiled. "I always thought it was because you're terrifying."

"That too."

Sheila stood. "Give me a few hours."

Before she left, she paused at the door. "Garth... be careful."

"Everyone keeps saying that."

"Maybe listen."

She walked out.

The rest of the afternoon blurred past. I taught a class but remembered none of it. Office hours felt like a dream. Students complained about homework, asked questions, told jokes—but my mind was stuck in that basement.

By late afternoon, the sky had darkened again. Rain slanted sideways against the windows.

My phone buzzed.

Sheila.

Come to my office. Now.

I hurried down the hall. Sheila sat at her desk surrounded by blueprints—big sheets of yellowing paper that smelled like dust and time. She tapped one.

"I found something."

I leaned over.

"This," she said, pointing to a rectangular space beneath the main lab, "is labeled B3-11."

"Matches the door number."

She nodded. "But look at this."

Her finger moved to the blueprint just beneath it: B3-12.

A room the size of a small lecture hall.

"Regina said B3-12 doesn't exist."

"Because it was decommissioned," Sheila said. "According to records, the room was sealed off during renovations."

"What kind of room was it?"

Sheila swallowed. "Cold storage."

I stared at the blueprint.

"Why would a sealed cold storage room still draw power?" I asked.

She shook her head. "It shouldn't."

"And why would someone use the centrifuge after Lila disappeared?"

"She found something," Sheila whispered.

We both stared at the blueprint.

The truth seemed just under the surface—close enough to see shadows but not close enough to reach.

Just then, the lights flickered.

We froze.

Then they flickered again.

Twice.

Then they went steady.

Sheila exhaled. "Storm?"

"Maybe."

But the timing felt wrong.

Too precise. Too pointed.

I rolled up the blueprint. "I'm going back to the basement."

Sheila grabbed my arm. "Not alone."

"I have to see what's behind that door."

"I'm coming with you."

"No."

Sheila straightened. "Garth, if you go alone, you might not come back."

Her voice cracked slightly. A tiny fracture. A glimpse of fear.

"Sheila—"

She crossed her arms. "My office or yours is going to be the site of our funeral if you keep arguing. I'm coming."

Before I could respond, footsteps echoed in the hallway. Heavy. Purposeful.

We turned.

No one there.

Just the echo fading.

Sheila swallowed hard. "Garth... something is wrong here."

I nodded. "Let's go."

We grabbed coats and headed for the stairwell.

Rain hammered the windows. Lights buzzed overhead. The air felt charged, electric.

Sheila walked beside me, her presence grounding, sharp, unwavering.

Together, we approached the basement.

And for the first time, I felt truly afraid.

Not of water.

Not of darkness.

Not even of the basement itself.

But of the possibility that whatever we were about to find...

might already know we were coming.

CHAPTER 5

What Lies Below

What we fear most is rarely the darkness—it's what waits beneath it.

The air in the stairwell felt colder as Sheila and I descended, step by step, toward the basement level of the Biochemistry Building.

Colder, but not empty.

Not dead.

The kind of cold that moves—that seems to breathe from the walls themselves.

The fluorescent lights buzzed overhead, flickering in tiny spasms, each one threatening to go dark and leave us in shadow. Sheila walked one step behind me, not because she was afraid, but because she had the instincts of a woman who had spent her life smoothing chaos. She followed, watched, and calculated.

"Tell me again," she said, voice low, "why are we doing this without Martinson?"

"He'd shut this down."

"Because that's reasonable."

"We need answers."

We reached the landing. The metal door—B3-11—stood before us. Gray. Plain.

Too plain.

Sheila tightened her grip on the rolled blueprint under her arm.

"Garth," she whispered, "look."

The faint line of moisture from last night's footprint was still visible near the doorframe. It hadn't evaporated.

Hadn't dried.

It looked fresh.

Too fresh.

My heart kicked once against my ribs.

I leaned closer.

This time, the water wasn't just a smear.

It had collected in a small bead at the edge of the floor drain. A bead so clear, so still, it reflected the flickering light above.

Sheila's breath hitched. "Is that... lake water?"

"Yes."

"How can water stay fresh this long on cement?"

I didn't answer.

Because the better question was:

Why was it here again?

Tonight?

I reached for the door.

It was warm.

Warm... from the inside.

Machines, maybe.

Or something else.

Sheila unfolded the blueprint and flattened it against the wall with her palm. The paper crackled softly.

"Look." She traced the lines with a pen. "This is the current layout. B3-11 connects to a secondary chamber. But here—" she tapped another spot, "—this is the sealed room. B3-12."

It sprawled beneath us like a crypt.

"Cold storage," I said.

"Yes. But not standard cold storage. These notations..." She pointed at old engineering codes scribbled in the margins. "This means cryogenic. And this? These symbols indicate redundancies in ventilation and drainage."

"Meaning?"

She swallowed. "Meaning something was kept very cold in there. Something that needed constant airflow and moisture containment."

"Biological material."

She didn't answer.

Her silence said enough.

I felt a stab of dread in my chest. "Blueprints don't just forget rooms."

"No." Sheila looked pale. "People forget rooms. Institutions bury them."

She pressed a finger against a faint square symbol near the bottom corner. "And look—this."

"What is it?"

"An access hall." She traced the line. "From the outside. From the lake-facing side of the building. A secondary service tunnel."

My stomach tightened.

A tunnel.

Connecting the basement to the lake.

"Who else knows about this?" I asked.

"Besides you and me?" Sheila shook her head. "No one. I had to dig through five layers of archives just to find these plans."

I stared at B3-12 again.

A room once used. Then sealed.

But clearly not forgotten.

Something moved inside B3-11.

Something mechanical. A hum.

Low. Rhythmic.

Sheila flinched. "Oh God—did you hear—"

"Stay behind me," I said.

I reached for the handle again.

Warm.

Alive.

Then, a soft click sounded behind the door.

Sheila grabbed my sleeve.

And just like that—

the world fell away.

"Garth."

Sheila's voice pulled me back into the present, though my chest still burned.

"Your face is white as chalk," she whispered. "Are you—are you alright?"

I nodded once.

Lie.

"Flashback," I said.

Her eyes softened. "The drowning?"

"Yes."

Sheila touched my arm gently. "You don't have to do this."

"I do."

"Then breathe. One hand on the wall. Steady."

I placed my palm against the cool painted brick, grounding myself.

The hum behind the door vibrated faintly against my fingers.

Sheila unfolded the blueprint again. "If this room still has power, something's wrong. B3-11 should have been stripped of electricity when B3-12 was sealed."

"Then someone kept it running."

"Yes."

"For what?"

"For something cold," she said quietly. "Or something alive."

That word—*alive*—settled heavily between us.

Sheila reached into her coat pocket and pulled out a small flashlight.

"You ready?" she asked.

I exhaled.

"We don't open it," I said. "Not yet. Just... listen."

We pressed our ears to the door.

At first: nothing.

Then—

A click.

A shuffle.

A faint, wet sound.

Not mechanical.

Organic.

Sheila jerked back. "Garth—"

"We're not alone," I whispered.

A shadow moved beneath the thin crack at the bottom of the door.

A soft gray smear sliding left to right.

I stepped back. My stomach churned.

"What the hell was that?" Sheila said, gripping my sleeve again.

"I don't know."

I did know.

But I didn't want to.

"Let's go," I said. "We shouldn't be here without more information. Or backup."

"Martinson?" Sheila asked.

"Not until we know what's behind this door."

She swallowed. "Right."

We backed away slowly, never turning our backs until we reached the stairwell.

When the door finally disappeared behind the concrete corner, Sheila let out a shaky breath she'd been holding.

"That room," she whispered. "I don't like it."

"Me neither."

"I don't like the way it feels."

"I know."

"It feels... watched."

I nodded. "Yes."

And it felt something else too—

like it remembered me.

Back in Sheila's office, she spread the blueprint across her desk again, her fingers trembling just slightly. She pointed to a secondary mark—one I hadn't noticed before.

"This," she said, "is a coolant line."

"And?"

"It runs directly under B3-11. And it shouldn't."

She traced it with a pen.

"It links to the same coolant system used for cryogenic freezers in the old Enzyme Research wing."

My eyebrows shot up. "The one closed in '89?"

"Yes. But look—someone rerouted the line in '93."

"Four years after closure."

"Exactly."

"Why would anyone do that?"

"Because something was installed there," Sheila whispered. "Something that required constant cold."

We stared at the blueprint.

"That's when the room was decommissioned," she continued. "But the coolant line wasn't removed. It was... redirected."

"To B3-11."

"And possibly B3-12," she said. "Depending on how far the line goes."

A shiver crawled up my spine.

"Someone built something down there," I said. "Something the university doesn't want found."

Sheila lowered her voice. "And I think Lila found it."

By late afternoon, the building was mostly empty. Graduate students had disappeared for dinner or caffeine or late-night experiments. The echo of footsteps had vanished.

I walked slowly down the hall, the blueprint rolled under my arm, heading toward the exit. The air felt heavy—thick with unasked questions.

As I turned the corner, someone stood at the end of the hall.

A woman.

Tall.

Still.

Silhouetted against the emergency exit sign like a shadow cut from the dark.

A baseball cap.

Long coat.

Face hidden.

She didn't move.

Neither did I.

For a long moment, we stared at each other across the dim corridor.

Then—

She lifted a hand.

Just slightly.

A gesture as subtle as fog.

Then she turned and walked through the exit, disappearing into the rain.

My breath froze.

"Garth?" Sheila called from behind me. "Are you coming—?"

I didn't answer.

Because the shadow woman wasn't a student.

Or faculty.

Or admin.

She didn't move like someone who belonged here.

She moved like someone who had been waiting.

Waiting for me.

That night, as I left campus and walked toward my truck, I passed by the basement window wells—deep concrete pits that sat a few inches above the ground.

Normally dark.

Tonight—

a faint light glowed behind one of them.

A cold, bluish light.

Pulsing faintly.

Like a heartbeat in the wall.

I took a step closer.

The window glass was fogged from inside.

And pressed faintly against that fog—

a handprint.

Small.

Delicate.

Smudged with something that looked like—

water.

Cold water.

Lake water.

My pulse thudded in my ears.

I stumbled back, chest tightening again—too fast, too hard—like the lake was dragging me under all over again.

The fogged window pulsed once more with blue light.

Then it went dark.

Completely.

As if whatever was inside had slipped back into shadow.

I exhaled, shaking, gripping the side of my truck for balance.

Someone—or something—was alive in that basement.

And the lake...

the lake was somehow part of it.

The reaction had already begun.

And I was in far too deep to turn back now.

CHAPTER 6

Evan Cracks

Pressure doesn't break a man all at once—it splinters him from the inside.

The rain had slowed by the time I reached the coffee shop again—the same one where Evan and I had talked two days earlier. The windows glowed gold against the gray dusk, fogged from the heat inside. Students huddled over laptops and textbooks, the air buzzing with espresso machines and quiet desperation.

But Evan wasn't inside.

He was outside.

On the sidewalk.

Pacing in tight circles, shoulders hunched, hair plastered to his forehead from sweat or rain—I couldn't tell which. He was wearing the same coat, same shoes, same tremor in his hands.

He didn't notice me at first.

He muttered to himself, his voice a frantic whisper.

"No, no, no... he said not to... he said it was done... he said... oh God oh God—"

"Evan."

He jolted like I'd hit him with a taser. Then he pressed his back against the brick wall, breathing hard.

"Dr. Myers... you... you shouldn't be here."

"I could say the same about you."

He rubbed his hands together compulsively, like he was trying to warm them—or scrub something off them.

"No," he said. "You don't understand. They're watching."

"Who?"

He clamped his jaw shut, eyes darting around.

"Evan," I said softly, "look at me."

His breathing quickened. "I—I can't—"

"Yes you can."

He finally looked up. His pupils were huge, swallowing the brown of his irises. Panic lived behind them—thick, frantic, animal panic.

"Sheila found the old blueprints," I said. "There is a basement lab. And a sealed cold storage room."

Evan's mouth trembled. He nodded once—barely.

"You know what's down there, don't you?"

He looked away.

"Evan."

He swallowed. "I can't say. If I say it... they'll know."

"Who will know?"

His breath hitched. "The people who took Lila."

A shock of cold went through me.

So he did know.

"Evan," I said, "I need you to tell me what she found."

"I can't," he said again. "You don't understand what they can do."

We needed privacy. Calm. Walls. Somewhere I could keep him from bolting into the rain or into traffic.

"Come inside," I said. "Let's sit."

"No," he whispered, backing away. "No walls. No doors."

"Why?"

"They lock."

His voice cracked like dry wood.

They lock.

My stomach tightened.

I took a slow step forward. "Evan... you're safe with me."

He shook his head violently. "No one's safe. Not if they know. Not if they talk."

"Tell me what Lila told you."

He squeezed his eyes shut.

"She said she found... a sample."

"What kind of sample?"

He shook harder. "Not normal. Not a protein. Not a plasmid. She said... it wasn't supposed to exist."

"What did it look like?"

"She said—" His voice caught. "She said it moved."

My skin prickled.

"Moved?"

"Not visually," he said quickly. "I mean... It changed the gel pattern. It shifted. Like the band moved between runs. She thought it was a contamination. But then she opened a freezer down there. And... and.." He pressed a hand over his mouth, gagging.

"Evan—" I stepped forward.

He held up a shaking finger. "No. I can't. I can't say it."

I waited.

Not pushing.

Just breathing with him.

Finally, he whispered:

"She saw jars."

"Jars?" I repeated.

His whole body shivered.

"With... things inside."

The café window behind us flickered, reflecting a passing car's headlights—just enough to cast Evan's face into a strange, haunted relief.

"What kind of things?" I whispered.

"Not an animal. Not a plant." He swallowed. "She said they... grew. Slowly. Like a tissue. Like... like someone was growing something alive."

My heart slammed once.

"Human tissue?" I whispered.

Evan didn't answer.

That was answer enough.

He pressed his hands into his hair. "She said they were trying to test something. A protein. A modified enzyme. Something that could... alter things."

"Alter things how?"

"Replication. Mutation. Repair. I—I don't know." His voice rose a pitch. "She wasn't supposed to see it. She said one jar cracked. That's why she emailed Regina."

The pieces snapped into place.

A broken vial in the freezer.

A missing plasmid library.

A basement lab that was still warm.

A cryogenic line rerouted to a sealed room.

"Then what happened?" I asked.

Evan's jaw clenched—and suddenly something broke inside him. Like a dam giving way.

"She came back the next day," he said. "She said someone had been in her apartment. That her research files were moved. Her notebooks were out of order. She was sure someone read them."

"Did she say who?"

"She didn't know. But she said the man with the baseball cap had followed her."

The one Regina mentioned.

"The same man?" I asked.

"No," Evan whispered. "There were two."

My blood went cold.

"Evan—"

He stepped closer suddenly, desperate, grabbing my coat with trembling fingers.

"She said his eyes were wrong."

"What do you mean *wrong*?"

"She—she didn't want to say. She just kept repeating it. 'His eyes are wrong.'"

A chill ran up my spine.

"Evan," I said gently, "do you think Lila was taken?"

He broke then.

His face twisted. His breath came in sharp, ragged sobs. He slid down the brick wall until he was crouched on the wet sidewalk, shaking violently.

"I think—" he choked out, "I think something happened to her... down there."

He covered his face with both hands.

"I think they know I know," he whispered through his fingers. "I think I'm next."

A quiet dread settled in my chest.

This wasn't fear.

This was terror.

This was a boy convinced his life was measured in hours.

"Evan," I said softly, crouching beside him, "you're safe right now."

"No I'm not," he sobbed. "They found my locker. They left another note."

"What did it say?"

He looked up at me—eyes red, wild, exhausted.

His voice was barely a breath.

"You're compromised."

A car hissed through the wet street.

For a moment, everything felt too still.

Too quiet.

Like the city itself had paused to listen.

"Evan," I said, "listen to me carefully. You need to come somewhere with me. Somewhere safe. Somewhere quiet."

"No walls," he whispered. "No rooms."

"Okay. Then somewhere open."

He nodded, collapsing forward into his own arms.

"Do you trust me?" I asked.

His voice cracked. "I think so."

"Then come with me."

After a long pause, he nodded again.

We walked slowly toward the lake path—Evan stumbling occasionally, breathing too fast, glancing over his shoulder every few seconds.

He wasn't acting.

He was breaking.

Every few steps, I caught him murmuring to himself.

"Not walls... not walls... open air... breathe..."

"Look at me," I said, "not behind you."

But he couldn't.

When we reached the lake, the water rippled dully. Small waves slapped against the stones with a faint *shhk shhk*sound.

The air smelled of algae and cold.

Evan stepped closer, hugging his arms around himself. "I can't be near it," he whispered.

"Why?"

"Because she hates it."

"Who?"

He shook his head. "I shouldn't have said that."

"Evan."

He closed his eyes.

"That woman."

"The one Lila saw?"

"No." He shook. "Another one."

My breath caught.

"How many women are involved?"

"Two."

"Who are they?"

"I—I don't know their names," he stammered. "The tall one with the baseball cap. And the other one. The one who talks to him."

"Him?"

"The man running the experiments."

I felt the drip of cold down my spine.

"And what does this woman do?"

"She checks the jars."

My jaw tightened. "The jars of tissue?"

"Yes."

"And what did she say about the lake?"

"Lila heard her once." Evan swallowed. "She said the lake is... helpful."

The lake? Helpful?

Something twisted in my stomach.

"Helpful how?" I asked.

"She said it... reacts."

My heart skipped.

"Reacts... how?"

He curled inward. "I don't know. I don't know. I don't know."

Suddenly Evan's breath hitched.

Then again.

Then it spiraled.

He clutched his chest. "I can't— I can't— breathe—"

"Evan."

I grabbed his shoulders. "Look at me."

His knees buckled.

We both dropped to the ground.

His breaths came in sharp, tearing gasps.

Chest heaving.

Eyes wide with animal fear.

The lake wind raking across his face.

"Evan," I said firmly, "listen to my voice."

He didn't.

He was collapsing inward.

Back into memory.

Back into something dark and small and claustrophobic.

"I'm trapped," he gasped.

"I'm trapped in the room— I'm trapped— I can't— I can't—"

"Which room?"

"The freezer— the freezer— the freezer—"

A jolt ran through my ribs.

My own chest tightened.

"Evan."

I shook him.

"Hear me."

He didn't.

He was drowning in the air.

And I knew the feeling too well.

"Evan!"

I cupped his face, forcing his gaze to mine.

"You're not in the freezer," I said. "You're not in the basement. You're right here."

He closed his eyes.

"No walls," he whispered.

"No doors.

No lake.

No freezer.

No eyes..."

"Open your eyes."

He didn't.

"Evan," I said sharply, "open your eyes or I'm calling an ambulance."

He froze.

Then gasped.

Then opened his eyes.

Finally.

I exhaled hard.

"Good," I said. "Now breathe. Slow."

He gulped air like a man surfacing.

After a full minute, he whispered, "I thought... I thought I was going to die."

"You weren't."

He looked at me with raw, vulnerable desperation.

"Sheila," he whispered.

"What about her?"

"She should stay away."

That made my skin crawl.

"Why?"

"Because she's curious," he said. "Like Lila."

My jaw clenched.

A protective instinct I hadn't expected surged up.

"And what happens," I asked softly, "to curious people?"

Evan swallowed hard.

"They get noticed."

My breath caught in my throat.

He added, barely audible:

"And once they're noticed… they don't come back."

It took another ten minutes to calm him enough to sit on a bench. The lake water slapped softly against the stones. The breeze was knife-cold against the skin.

"Evan," I said quietly, "you told me what Lila saw. But what did *you* see?"

He hesitated.

Then:

"I saw one of the jars," he whispered.

My pulse hammered.

"What was inside?"

He shook his head. "I didn't… I couldn't look long."

"You have to tell me."

He closed his eyes.

"It looked like… a hand."

My breath froze.

"A hand?"

"Not full. Not human. Not grown. But.." He trembled. "It had... fingers."

I felt my heartbeat thud once, hard and heavy.

"It was forming," he whispered. "Like someone was growing something. Piece by piece."

"And Lila saw more?"

"Yes."

"What did she think it was for?"

He trembled violently.

"She thought it was for testing."

"Testing what?"

He swallowed.

"A protein that... that alters replication. That mutates tissue quickly. That... that rebuilds."

My throat felt tight.

I whispered the worst possibility aloud.

"Regeneration?"

Evan nodded.

Then added, "Unstable regeneration."

That word—*unstable*—hung like a weight.

"And you told no one," I said.

"Who would believe me?"

"People believe the truth."

"Not this one."

His hands twisted into fists.

"So what do we do?" he whispered.

I exhaled.

"We find her."

"How?"

"We start with the basement."

His eyes widened with horror. "No. No. No."

"I have to."

"You can't. Because she's still down there."

His voice cracked.

"And whatever took her...

whatever they're doing...

they're not done."

He reached into his pocket and pulled out something wrapped in tissue.

"Lila dropped this," he whispered. "Outside my office. The day before she disappeared."

I unwrapped it carefully.

Inside was a tiny piece of plastic.

A broken shard.

From a vial.

A freezer vial.

The label had been ripped off, but faint letters remained:

...ASE-Δmut

...enct

...trial

My heart pounded.

This was the missing piece.

The missing plasmid library.

Modified delta-mutations.

Enzyme constructs.

Trial variants.

"Where did she find this?" I asked.

"On the floor of the basement."

"And she dropped it?"

"She didn't want anyone to know she had it."

That's when it hit me.

Why was her notebook missing?

Why were her files rearranged?

Why was her apartment searched?

She had proof.

Real proof.

Of a biological experiment someone wanted buried.

"We have to go to the basement," I said again.

Evan grabbed my coat. "No. Please. You'll die. They'll kill you."

"Not if I'm careful."

"No," he whispered, shaking violently. "Not careful. They see. They hear. They know. They know everything."

"Then tell me how to avoid them."

He hesitated.

"I don't know if you can."

"Try."

He breathed hard.

"Don't go in alone," he said. "Don't go without someone who knows the building. Don't go without—"

He froze.

And looked behind me.

Toward the pathway.

Toward the dark tree line.

Toward the rain-drenched silhouette of a figure standing far away.

Still.

Facing us.

A woman.

A tall woman.

Wearing a baseball cap.

Watching.

My blood ran ice cold.

When I turned fully, she stepped back into the darkness.

Silent.

Gone.

Evan shook uncontrollably.

"They found me," he whispered.

"No. No."

"They found me, Dr. Myers."

He backed away.

Then he ran.

Into the darkness.

Into the rain.

Down the lake path.

"Evan!" I shouted.

But he didn't look back.

He ran like a man who believed the night itself was hunting him.

Maybe it was.

I walked toward where the woman had stood.

Nothing.

Just cold air.

Wet leaves.

And farther down—

the lake.

A silent ripple ran across the surface.

Small.

But purposeful.

Like something just beneath it

had moved.

I stared for a long time.

The wind blew off the water.

I shivered.

Maybe from cold.

Maybe from memory.

Maybe from the feeling that the lake wasn't just a backdrop.

But a participant.

And somewhere in that depth—

in that cold, dark, shifting water—

something waited.

Something connected to the basement.

Something Lila saw.

Something Evan feared.

And something that wasn't done with us yet.

CHAPTER 7

Bob's Warning

A warning is just a truth arriving early.

The Monday-night AA meeting in the basement of a church on East Johnson always smelled faintly of burnt coffee, lemon disinfectant, and worn linoleum. Comforting smells, in a way. Smells that said:

You've been here before.

You're still alive.

Keep going.

The folding chairs were arranged in a semicircle, as always. A small podium stood in the center, flanked by posters with slogans most people roll their eyes at until the day they need them.

Easy does it.

Keep coming back.

One day at a time.

I wasn't sure which one applied to missing students and secret basement labs. Maybe none of them. Maybe all of them.

Bob T. stood at the back of the room, pouring himself a cup of the worst coffee in Dane County. He wore the same faded denim jacket he'd worn the night he convinced me to get sober, and probably the same jeans he'd worn the day Nixon resigned. His hair, white as chalk dust, curled beneath his cap.

He saw me walk in and grinned, the kind of grin that lifts the whole room up half an inch.

"Well, I'll be damned," he said. "I thought maybe you'd joined a cult or run off to join a biker gang."

"You'd be surprised how many cults are run by academics," I said.

He chuckled. "Good. That means you're still sarcastic. I worry when you get quiet."

We moved to our usual chairs. People filed in around us—teachers, electricians, nurses, a retired librarian with a laugh that could shake rafters. AA has no demographic; pain is universal.

The meeting began. A reading from the Big Book. A moment of silence. Introductions. Then the sharing started.

A young guy talked about slipping at a wedding—three shots of tequila before the best man even finished his toast. A woman talked about forgiving herself for relapsing after her mother died. A middle-aged trucker talked about passing his first milestone: seven days sober.

Seven days. I remembered those days. The walls sweating. The heart racing. The brain screaming. Sobriety isn't a ladder; it's a cliff climbed with fingernails.

When it came time for me to speak, I passed. I didn't trust myself. Not with the weight pressing down on my chest.

When the meeting ended, people lingered, chatting, hugging, and refilling coffee cups. Bob remained in his seat, watching me the way a man watches a kettle that might boil over.

"Walk with me," he said.

We left through the back door, into a parking lot washed clean by rain. The pavement glistened beneath the streetlights, reflecting the outline of the water tower like a ghostly exclamation mark.

Bob stuffed his hands in his jacket pockets. "Alright, kid. Why are you tied up like a pretzel inside your own head?"

I exhaled. "It's complicated."

"Everything is complicated when you're the one avoiding the truth."

I didn't answer. He waited. Bob has the patience of a saint, or a man who has seen enough darkness to know forcing the light never works.

Finally, I said, "A student went missing."

His expression didn't change. "Okay."

"She worked with Regina."

He nodded slowly. "Go on."

"And I think she found something she wasn't supposed to."

"Like what?"

"Something in a basement lab no one admits exists."

Bob stopped walking. "And what's in that basement?"

"I don't know," I said. "But something's alive down there."

He raised an eyebrow. "Alive how?"

"Organic. Grown. Experimental."

Bob took a long breath, letting it out slowly in a plume of steam.

"This ain't the first time science outran common sense," he said. "But your voice sounds like you're not telling me the worst of it."

I swallowed. "The worst of it is... I think someone took her. And I don't know if she's alive."

Bob nodded.

"Okay," he said.

"Okay?" I echoed.

"Yes," he said. "Okay. That means the next thing you do matters more than the last hundred things you did."

"I'm afraid, Bob."

"You should be."

That surprised me. Bob isn't careless with fear.

"I've been in AA for forty-four years," he said. "Seen men fall apart. Seen men rise. But you—" he pointed at me "—you have two fears, not one."

"Two?"

"Fear of water. And fear of what's inside you that wants to jump back in the bottle the minute things get hard."

I closed my eyes.

Bob continued, softer. "And this? All this darkness you're walking into? Missing girls and basement lies and secrets people kill over?" He shook his head. "This is the kind of thing that wakes the thirst."

I swallowed hard. "I won't drink."

"Good," he said. "Because you have work to do."

He stepped closer—Bob never touches people in AA unless it's important. But he put a hand on my shoulder.

"I'm going to tell you something my old sponsor told me when I was three weeks sober." His voice dropped. "When people hide sins underground, you don't dig unless you're ready for what comes up."

He let that sink in.

Then added:

"And kid... you're digging."

I nodded.

Bob stepped back. "But here's the other truth: you don't walk away from a missing girl. Not you. You weren't built that way. So do what you gotta do—but don't do it alone. You hear me?"

"I hear you."

"And whatever's in that basement—" he shook his head "—don't let it take your sobriety. And don't let it take you."

We walked toward our cars. The rain picked up again, tapping the hoods like impatient fingers.

Bob called out as he climbed into his truck, "And kiddo—stay away from that lake at night. I'm telling you. Something in that water remembers you."

He drove off.

Leaving me alone in the dark, with the rain, the echo of his warning, and the slow, cold realization that Bob was right:

I was digging.

And something was starting to climb out.

CHAPTER 8

The Last Footage

What's recorded isn't always what was seen.

The Biochemistry Building felt different at night. Quieter. Hollow. Like a cathedral built to worship secrets instead of gods.

Regina waited in her office, pacing in tight, anxious loops. Her hair was down—something she only did on days when the world was falling apart. A stack of security request forms cluttered her desk, most ignored. She turned when I stepped inside.

"They finally sent the footage," she said, voice tight.

"From the night Lila disappeared?"

She nodded. "It's incomplete," she warned. "Parts are corrupted."

"Convenient," I said.

Regina clicked play.

The screen flickered—grainy black-and-white hallway footage outside the main lab.

Timestamp: **10:47 PM**.

Lila entered the frame, carrying a notebook and backpack, moving fast but not frantic. She glanced over her shoulder once, twice—then swiped into the lab.

"She was alone," Regina whispered.

"Was she?" I murmured.

Because thirty seconds later, a second figure appeared.

Tall.

Thin.

Baseball cap pulled low.

Moving smoothly—too smoothly.

"Is that the man she described?" I asked.

Regina swallowed. "I've never seen him before."

He didn't swipe in. He didn't knock. He simply waited.

Then the hallway lights flickered.

Once.

Twice.

And he was gone.

Vanished between frames.

Regina's breath caught. "What—how—"

"Camera glitch," I said, though the words felt hollow.

The next segment showed nothing for several minutes. Then—

Timestamp: **11:09 PM**.

The stairwell door creaked open.

Lila again.

Only... not the same girl.

She walked slower. Stiffer. Shoulders curled inward, head tilted down as if bracing against something no one else could see.

"Why is she—" Regina whispered.

Lila paused at the bottom of the stairwell, staring toward the basement.

Then she descended.

Out of view.

Into the dark.

My skin prickled.

"Play the next camera," I said.

Regina clicked.

Basement corridor feed.

Static.

Snow.

Flicker.

"Corrupted," Regina murmured.

"Try the next one."

Another click.

Another camera.

More static.

Then—for a single, ghostly frame—something appeared.

A figure.

Emerging from the basement.

Not Lila.

Someone larger. Broader. Moving with a strange, uneven lurch, as if injured... or altered.

"Who is that?" Regina whispered.

"I don't know."

The frame glitched.

Then another figure surfaced for a split-second burst of pixelated distortion.

A woman.

Or something shaped like one.

Tall.

Hair pulled back.

Gloves on.

"Is that the same woman Evan saw?" Regina asked.

The tall woman in the baseball cap.

My pulse climbed.

Then came the final frame—the last image recorded before the camera died.

The basement door—**B3-11**—opened.

And a *hand* gripped the edge of the doorframe from the inside.

A hand dripping with moisture.

Water pooling on the floor.

Not blood.

Not condensation.

Water.

Cold water.

Lake water.

Regina covered her mouth. "Oh God..."

I leaned closer.

Across the hand were faint ridges, blurred by motion. Not symbols. Not writing. Just... ridges.

Ridges that didn't look quite human.

The hand slipped back into the darkness.

The screen went black.

Regina sank into her chair, shoulders trembling.

"She went into the basement," she whispered. "And something else came out."

I stepped back from the monitor, the outline of that wet hand burned into my vision.

This wasn't an accident.

This wasn't a misunderstanding.

This was deliberate.

I grabbed my coat.

"Where are you going?" Regina asked.

"To the basement."

"You can't—"

"I have to."

She stood. "Then I'm calling Sheila."

"No."

"Yes." She dialed with shaking hands.

I walked toward the door, then paused.

"Regina," I said quietly, "when did the footage end?"

She checked the timestamp. The color drained from her face.

"**11:13 PM**," she whispered.

The exact minute the centrifuge finished its cycle.

The exact minute someone walked out of the basement.

The exact minute everything misaligned.

And the exact minute the real nightmare began.

ACT II

What Lies Beneath

Some doors aren't meant to be opened. But once they are,
nothing behind them stays still.

CHAPTER 9

The Hidden Basement Lab B3-12

Some secrets aren't buried—they're engineered out of sight.

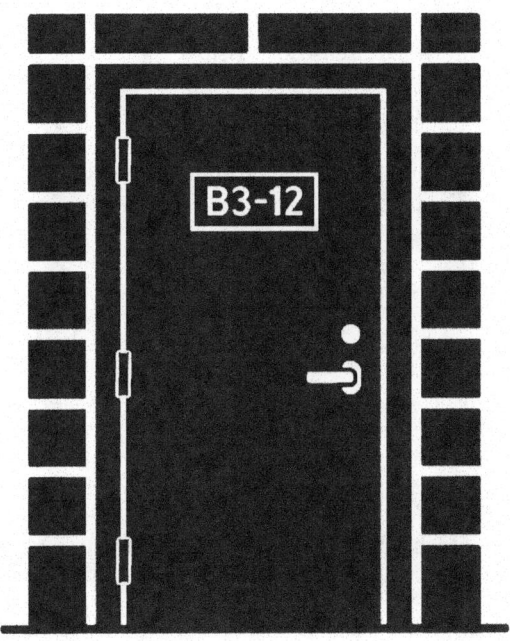

The wind had turned vicious by the time I left Regina's office. It barreled down the campus corridor outside, rattling windowpanes and moaning through cracked seals like an animal pacing in the dark. The storm wasn't supposed to hit until morning, but Madison weather doesn't respect forecasts—it arrives early, unannounced, and uninvited. Much like the truth.

Sheila was already waiting by the stairwell.

I didn't remember calling her. Regina must have done it. Or maybe Sheila just... sensed something. She had a sixth sense for danger the way some people have a sixth sense for gossip.

She stood stiffly, blueprint tube in one hand, flashlight in the other.

"You saw the footage," she said without preamble.

I nodded.

"Okay," she breathed. "Then let's go."

We descended together.

The stairwell walls seemed closer tonight. Shadows clung to the corners like wet cloth. The sound of the storm outside faded with each step until all that remained was our breathing, the hum of old fluorescent fixtures, and the low, muffled throb of machinery behind sealed doors.

When we reached the basement level, the air felt... wrong. Heavy. Cold. Metallic. Like a lab that had been sealed for years—but still working.

The hallway ahead lay in deeper darkness than usual. Even the emergency lights flickered like they'd been starving for power.

Sheila stepped closer to me. Not out of fear—Sheila doesn't fear darkness the way other people do—but out of instinct. She reads rooms like other people read recipes.

"Something's off," she whispered.

"It's not just me, then."

"No."

Sheila pulled out the flashlight and clicked it on. The beam cut across the corridor in a clean white arc, dancing across concrete walls and linoleum floors and—

"There," she said.

The door to B3-11. Exactly where we'd left it.

Except this time, it was open. Only an inch. Barely noticeable. Like someone had closed it with careless hands. Or opened it with deliberate ones.

A cold current slipped through the crack. Cold. Not mechanical. Not chemical. Cold like a freezer exhaling.

Sheila's grip on my arm tightened. "Garth... what if someone's in there?"

"Then we need to know who."

"No," Sheila whispered. "We need to know what."

I didn't answer. The truth was, I wasn't ready to know either.

But I pushed the door open anyway.

A hiss of pressure escaped—soft, but noticeable. Air equalizing. The smell hit me immediately: cold, salt, steel, and something organic. Not decomposition, not bacteria, not chemicals. Something in between.

The flashlight beam cut forward, illuminating a room larger than I expected. B3-11 wasn't a lab—it was a staging chamber. A transition space.

The walls were lined with sealed cabinets, heavy steel tables, and a console with screens that flickered faintly even though the power to this floor should've been cut.

Sheila stepped in behind me. "This... isn't on any blueprint I found."

"No."

"What was this room for?"

"Preparing samples," I said automatically. "Before cold storage."

"How do you know?"

"I've seen rooms like it. At Michigan. At NIH."

"But those were... legal."

"Yeah."

She walked along the nearest steel counter. Dust coated most surfaces—thin, soft, even. Except for one patch where a rectangular shape had recently been moved. A notebook-sized shape.

"Lila's journal," Sheila whispered.

"And it's gone."

She turned on her heel, flashlight sweeping the corners. "This room is wrong. The angles don't match the blueprint. The dimensions are larger."

I frowned. "What do you mean larger?"

"I mean—" she knelt, tapping the floor "—the blueprint says this room stops here. But the floor extends farther. This space shouldn't exist."

My stomach dropped.

"We're standing in something extra," she said. "Something added off the books."

She swept the beam forward, toward the far wall—toward the outline of another door. A heavier one. Thicker. Reinforced. Stenciled faintly with chipped white paint:

B3-12.

The sealed room. The cold storage chamber. The room Lila never should've found.

Sheila inhaled sharply. "Oh God..."

The flashlight beam trembled in her hand.

"Is this the room?" she whispered. "The real one?"

"Yes."

"Is it still active?"

The faint hum drifting through the metal answered for us.

Sheila looked at me, voice small, stripped of its usual bite. "Are we really doing this, Garth?"

"Yes."

She squeezed her eyes shut for a moment. "Then go slow. And don't breathe anything you don't have to."

I nodded, stepping toward the door.

The flashlight beam landed on the handle. It was frosted over. Thin ice crystals clung to the metal like lace.

"Sheila," I whispered.

"I see it."

The temperature on the other side must have been below freezing. But that wasn't the part that made my heart kick.

It was the drip.

A tiny drop of water—clear as glass—ran down the doorframe from the inside and froze halfway. Not melting. Freezing. Even though we were standing in a room above forty degrees.

My breath fogged.

Sheila noticed it too. "How—how is that possible?" she whispered.

"It's colder inside than out."

"That isn't how insulation works."

"No," I said. "It isn't."

I reached out and touched the metal—

and instantly jerked back.

Not because it was cold.

Because it was pulsing.

A soft, rhythmic vibration against the steel. Steady. Measured. Alive.

Sheila's eyes widened. "Garth—"

A flashback slammed into me with the force of a wave.

FLASHBACK — Drowning II: The Descent

Cold. Not the cold of air—the cold of water closing around your throat. The dark rushing up, down, sideways, everywhere, the lake's weight folding in, crushing, squeezing hope from lungs. A sense of space shrinking, of something pushing from below, a presence, a shape, pulling you down.

Hands—weed tendrils—the lake grabbed me, dragged, squeezed, filled my nose, my mouth, my memory. The pressure—the pressure—the feeling of being trapped in a space too tight, too cold, too hungry.

And then—a pale shape rising from the murk. A face? No. A reflection? No. A hand. A hand in the water, reaching, curling, pulling—

Black.

Nothing.

Cold.

BACK TO PRESENT

I gasped, stumbling backward until my shoulder hit the counter.

Sheila was at my side instantly. "Garth—hey—stay with me."

"I'm fine."

"You're not fine. Your face is white."

"Flashback."

She put her hand on my arm. "Do you want to stop?"

"No."

She exhaled shakily. "Okay. But breathe."

I did. Slow. Deliberate. One breath forward. One breath down.

Then I turned back to the door.

A small keypad sat beside it. Numbers worn down. Some buttons cracked. One—3—sharply dented, as if someone had struck it.

"What are the odds this still works?" Sheila asked.

"Too high," I said.

I ran my hand beneath the keypad. It hummed. Still powered. Still waiting. Someone had been using this door regularly. Recently. Maybe today.

Sheila moved the flashlight beam toward the floor. "Garth... look."

Ice had formed along the rubber seam at the bottom of the door. Cracked, brittle shards. And beneath that, a thin line of water. Fresh. Warm enough to run.

"Lake water," Sheila whispered.

I didn't ask how she knew. We both knew the smell.

Sheila swallowed. "If this room connects to a lake tunnel..."

"Then it's not sealed."

"Then someone—or something—uses it."

"And used it recently."

Sheila stepped back. "We need Martinson."

"No."

"Garth—this is too big. Too dangerous."

"I know."

"Then why—"

"Because if we leave," I said quietly, "someone will come back here. And erase everything. And Lila's gone forever."

That silenced her.

I reached for the keypad. It blinked. One green light. One red. Waiting.

"Do we have a code?" Sheila asked.

"No."

"Then how—"

I pressed the 3 key.

Once.

A beep. Soft. Acknowledgment.

And then the red light turned off. Both lights went dark.

And a final sound:

Click.

Sheila's breath hitched. "Garth…"

The door unsealed.

A hiss of air escaped—not pressure. Breath. Cold spilled out like fog.

I pushed. The door slid open slowly, reluctantly.

Inside was darkness. Deeper than night. Deeper than unlit rooms. Darkness that felt like a presence.

The flashlight beam carved a thin path forward, revealing frosted metal racks, containers sealed with thick clamps, shelves stretching far into the dark.

And on the nearest shelf—a jar.

A glass jar. Fogged from inside.

Inside it, something moved. Not fast. Not unmistakably. Just a twitch. A pulse. A contraction of pale tissue, like something learning to imitate muscle.

Sheila's hand flew to her mouth.

"Oh—oh God—"

The jar shifted again.

Then—a sound.

Not human. Not mechanical. A faint, wet scraping from deeper in the dark. Something else moving. Something larger. Something aware.

Sheila stepped back into me, trembling.

And for a moment—just a moment—my grief and fear fused into something colder than the room itself.

Because this wasn't just an illegal lab. It wasn't just unethical research.

It was purposeful. Hidden. Designed for something that wasn't finished.

And then—deeper in the dark—a whisper.

Not a voice. Not speech. But movement.

Dragging. Slow. Wet. Deliberate.

Sheila's breath hitched.

"Garth," she whispered, "we're not alone."

I swallowed hard.

"I know."

CHAPTER 10

Biotech Funding Shadows

Money leaves a trail—but in biotech, it's the shadows that matter most.

The storm rolled over Madison like a physical weight, a thick sheet of dark clouds bruising the already gray morning sky. The air felt metallic. Heavy. I'd slept maybe two hours total—the kind of sleep where you don't rest, you just temporarily forget you're awake.

By the time I reached campus, the streetlights were still on, fighting the dimness, losing.

Regina was waiting near the entrance of Engineering Hall. Coffee in one hand, folder in the other. She shook her head at me before I even opened my mouth.

"You look like hell," she said.

"I feel worse."

"Good," she said. "It means you won't do anything reckless."

"I'm about to do something reckless."

She sighed. "I know."

We walked in silence down the corridor toward my office. Students shuffled past carrying umbrellas, backpacks, and sleep deprivation. The building hummed with the normal rhythms of academia—printers, footsteps, murmured arguments about problem sets.

But there was something underneath it today. Something like tension. As if the building itself knew what was buried beneath it.

When we reached my office, Sheila was already inside, hunched over my computer. She had a binder open on the desk.

She didn't look up when she spoke. "It's worse than we thought."

Regina stepped in beside me. "What did you find?"

Sheila flipped a page. "I followed the funding trail. Or what I thought was the funding trail. There is no grant number for the basement project. No official ledger. No PI listed."

"That's not surprising," I said. "It was hidden."

She shook her head hard. "No, I mean there's no failed award either. No proposal. No submission. Nothing archived."

Regina frowned. "That's impossible. Even the worst proposals leave a paper trail."

"Not if it wasn't routed through UW."

We both turned toward her.

Sheila slid a printed page toward me. A small, terse memo:

FROM: Office of Sponsored Programs, Federal Liaison Desk

SUBJECT: Clearance Renewal Required — Project 6R-BL13

Regina's face tightened. "That's not an NIH code."

"No," Sheila said. "It's not."

"DARPA?" I guessed.

"Close," Sheila said. "But DARPA uses different notation."

I looked at the memo again. The wording was vague in the way only federal agencies can achieve—saying nothing, implying everything.

"What is Project 6R-BL13?" Regina asked.

"No idea," Sheila said. "But the liaison officer signed off on it last in 1993. Renewals every three years."

"So the last one was—"

"1996," Sheila said. "The year the basement was locked."

"Which fits," I murmured, "because if a classified project gets suspended, the physical space is supposed to be sealed but not decommissioned."

Regina's voice thinned. "Meaning someone could reopen it."

"Yes," Sheila said. "Meaning someone did reopen it."

I sat down hard.

Black-budget science. Federal contractors. Behind-the-books bioengineering. All wrapped around a missing grad student.

"Tell me the rest," I said.

Sheila took a breath before continuing. "There's more. I looked into who handled federal projects for the bio departments in the early '90s."

"Who?" Regina asked.

Sheila hesitated. Then she slid another document toward me. A printout of an old administrative directory. Highlighted name:

Dr. Otto Markson — Federal Contracts Officer, 1988–1997

Regina inhaled sharply. "Markson?"

"He would've known," I said quietly.

"Knew what?" Sheila asked.

"That the basement wasn't just a storage room. That it was a federal project site."

Regina placed her hand on the table. It trembled slightly.

"Does he still have access?" she asked.

"Yes," Sheila said. "He has legacy clearance for expired classified contracts. Some staff keep old access levels for emergencies."

I rubbed my temples. "So he can enter the basement."

"And so can whoever still uses his credentials."

Regina whispered, "Oh God... he might be compromised."

Or involved. Or something worse.

The storm outside cracked thunder across Lake Monona. The windows rattled.

Sheila folded her arms. "Before we even think of talking to Markson, you need to see something else."

She pulled out a second binder.

"This"—she tapped it—"is the award log for federal pass-through funds to UW in 1991. Most are standard: defense-funded polymer research, atmospheric modeling, materials testing."

"And the rest?" Regina asked.

"Three are classified at Level V."

My pulse thudded.

"Level V?" I whispered.

"That's not only above our clearance," Sheila said. "It's above the dean's clearance. Those grants were routed directly to a single PI."

"Who?" Regina asked.

Sheila turned the binder so we could see.

Principal Investigator: Dr. Leonard Druitt

Institute of Enzyme Research

Regina froze. "Druitt?"

I searched my memory. Leonard Druitt. I hadn't heard that name in twenty years. A brilliant enzymologist in his prime. One of those towering intellects who never published enough because his ideas were too strange even for the fringes.

"He left suddenly," Regina murmured. "Disappeared. Moved to industry. No forwarding address."

Sheila shook her head. "No. He didn't move to industry."

She pushed a final document forward. A one-line notice from 1998:

Dr. Leonard Druitt — federal assignment — status: classified

Regina leaned back in her chair. "Jesus."

"What does 'federal assignment' mean?" she asked.

"It means," Sheila said, "he stopped being a professor and started working for agencies that don't list their names."

My mouth felt dry. The storm outside intensified. Rain hammered the windows.

"So Druitt ran Project 6R–BL13," I said.

"It appears so."

"And the basement lab was the site."

"Yes."

"And someone reopened it."

"Yes."

"And Lila found evidence of it."

Sheila looked at me. Her eyes were sharp and scared at the same time.

"And someone," she whispered, "came after her for it."

I stood and walked to the window. The lake churned violently under the storm's weight. Whitecaps, black water, the surface heaving.

A memory tugged at me. Evan's voice.

The lake is helpful.

It reacts.

She checks the jars.

The storm cracked thunder again, shaking the pane.

Regina approached me quietly. "What are you thinking?"

"That this isn't just science," I said. "This is something the federal government wanted covered up."

She swallowed. "What do we do next?"

I turned toward them.

"We find Markson."

Sheila nodded. Regina hesitated. "And if he's involved?"

I met her eyes. "Then we find out who he answers to."

A silence hung in the room. Then my phone buzzed.

A number I didn't recognize. But the area code was Washington, D.C.

I answered.

A man's voice—low, flat, emotionless. "Dr. Myers?"

"Yes."

"This is a courtesy call."

"Who is this?"

"You've been requesting access to documents you do not have clearance for."

My back stiffened. "I don't know what you're talking about."

"Yes, you do."

A pause. Rain hammered the glass. The lake roared in the distance.

"Stop looking," the man said.

"What?"

"Stop looking into Project 6R-BL13."

My heart slammed into my ribs.

"Who are you?" I asked.

"A friend," he said. "One who recommends you stay away from the basement."

"Why?"

"Because the people involved don't want to be found."

"Who are they?"

He exhaled. Not annoyed—disappointed. "You're clever, Dr. Myers. Don't be stupid. You're not equipped for what you've stepped into."

"Why was a graduate student taken?"

Silence.

Then: "You're asking dangerous questions."

My chest tightened. "Tell me who you are," I repeated.

"I'm someone giving advice," he said. "Advice you won't get twice."

Then the line went dead.

I stood frozen, staring at my phone.

Regina's face drained. "Who was that?"

Sheila whispered, "What did they say?"

I lifted my eyes to them both.

"They told me," I said quietly, "to stop looking."

The room went still. Sheila's breath trembled. Regina reached for the back of a chair.

And I knew, in the pit of my stomach: someone in Washington was watching. Someone who knew exactly what was in that basement. And someone who was afraid I would keep digging.

I put the phone down.

"We're not stopping," I said.

Sheila exhaled shakily. Regina nodded once.

Outside, the storm smashed thunder across the lake. Inside, the truth pressed closer.

The hallway outside my office felt different when we stepped out. Quieter. More watchful. Like the air had ears.

Sheila shut the door behind us and locked it—something she never did during business hours.

Regina rubbed the back of her neck. "If federal agencies are sniffing around, Markson is either going to stonewall you... or he's going to panic."

"Either one tells me something," I said.

"Or," Sheila muttered, "he's going to lie so well you won't know what part of the truth he buried."

We headed down the corridor together. Students drifted past—unaware that the institution around them hid a sealed lab full of illegally grown tissue and a missing grad student whose research might have uncovered something never meant to be seen.

The hum of fluorescent lights echoed overhead. The kind of hum you don't notice unless you're on edge.

Sheila walked close to us, arms folded tight across her chest. "Whatever Markson knows," she said, "he's had twenty years to bury it. That makes him dangerous."

Regina nodded. "More dangerous if someone else is pulling his strings."

"Someone in Washington," I added.

"That man on the phone," Regina said, "he wasn't reading from a script. He knew who you were. That's not a casual warning."

Sheila gave a humorless snort. "Nobody uses the phrase 'courtesy call' unless they've thrown a few people into unmarked vans before."

I didn't laugh. Mostly because I agreed.

We turned the corner toward the administrative wing.

Markson's office waited at the far end—a glass-fronted suite decorated with framed photos of chancellors, award ceremonies, and the illusion of bureaucratic transparency.

I felt my pulse quicken with each step.

"Garth," Regina murmured, "let me talk first. He knows me better. He won't be defensive."

"No," I said. "This has to come from me."

Sheila huffed. "He's already defensive. He's been defensive since 1988."

We reached the door.

A placard read:

Dr. Otto Markson — Associate Dean of Research & Federal Liaison

Beneath it, a sticker:

Authorized Personnel Only

I knocked.

A muffled voice answered. "Come in."

I opened the door.

Markson sat behind his desk, hunched over paperwork. He looked older than last week—not physically, but in the way exhausted men carry their careers on their shoulders.

He looked up when he saw the three of us. His face tightened.

"Well this doesn't look like a social call," he said.

"It's not," I replied.

He gestured to the chairs. "Sit."

We didn't.

Regina spoke softly. "Otto, we saw footage. From the night Lila disappeared."

Markson paused. Just long enough to mean something. Then he stacked his papers and leaned back with theatrical patience.

"And?" he asked.

"And we know she went into the basement," Regina said. "We know there's a sealed room beneath the building that was part of a federal project."

His jaw clenched at the word federal.

Sheila stepped forward. "We also know the federal contracts office shows renewals for a project called 6R-BL13."

Markson went still.

I watched his pupils dilate.

"That project," I said, "was run by Leonard Druitt."

His breath hitched. Just slightly.

"Where is he?" I asked.

Markson folded his hands on the desk—the way people do when they want to hide the tremor in their fingers.

"Dr. Myers," he said calmly, "you are not cleared to know anything about Project 6R-BL13."

"I don't care about clearance."

"You should."

Regina stepped closer. "Otto. A student is missing. Someone opened that basement lab."

Markson's eyes flicked to her—and something inside him cracked. Not guilt. Not fear. Recognition.

"Regina," he whispered, "please don't involve yourself further."

She froze. So did Sheila. So did I.

"Why not?" I asked.

"Because," he said, voice strained, "I've seen what happens to people who ask too many questions."

My pulse thudded. "Is that a threat?"

"It's a warning."

I kept my voice steady. "From whom?"

He shook his head. "You don't want to know."

"We already know enough," Sheila snapped. "We know there's an unreported lab beneath this building. We know it was reopened. And we know you have legacy clearance to access that floor."

His face went ashen.

"I haven't gone down there," he whispered.

"Then who used your credentials?" I asked.

He didn't answer. Instead, he rubbed his temples—a gesture of a man wrestling a decision he didn't want to make.

Then he exhaled and leaned back in his chair.

"There were three classified projects routed through the Institute of Enzyme Research in the early '90s," he said quietly. "Only one went operational. Project 6R–BL13."

"What was it researching?" Regina asked.

"Biological resilience," he said. "Tissue regeneration. Extremophile-level adaptability."

Sheila crossed her arms. "That's not illegal."

"No," he said. "But what they did to make it work... was."

My chest tightened.

"What did they do?" I asked.

Markson stared at his desk.

"That basement lab was designed to test a protein capable of restructuring damaged cellular tissue. Accelerating healing. Enhancing survival. The military was interested in battlefield recovery. DARPA wanted to explore enzymatic models. NIH black-budget branches wanted potential medical applications."

He paused. Then added: "But the enzyme was unstable."

Regina leaned forward. "Unstable how?"

"It required a specific environmental catalyst," he said. "A water-based medium with high mineral variation. Cold. Dark. Pressure-resistant."

A chill ran up my spine.

"The lake," I whispered.

Markson nodded slowly. "They used water from Lake Monona. It had a property they couldn't replicate in the lab. Something about how mineral content interacts with protein folding in the cold. They ran trials using tissue samples submerged in lake water."

"And?" Regina pressed.

"And," Markson said, "the enzyme didn't just regenerate tissue."

He paused. Thunder cracked outside.

"It changed it."

Silence swallowed the room.

"How?" I asked.

"Replication patterns shifted. Structural morphologies altered. Cells didn't just heal—they reorganized. Grew in unintended ways."

My stomach churned.

"Unintended how?"

He looked directly at me.

"New structures formed," he said softly. "Structures that resembled embryonic development, but not human. Not exactly."

Regina inhaled sharply. Sheila stepped back. My throat felt tight.

"And Druitt?" I asked.

Markson closed his eyes. "He became obsessed with it," he whispered. "He believed they'd found something evolutionary. Something nature started but abandoned. Something the military wanted but couldn't control."

"And then?"

"Then the project was shut down," Markson said. "Internal review. Ethical collapse. And Druitt was reassigned."

"Where?" I asked.

"That's classified."

I stepped closer.

"So someone reopened the lab," I said. "Someone used your clearance. Someone restarted Druitt's work."

Markson paled. "You shouldn't say his name."

"Why not?"

He swallowed. "Because the man in Washington wasn't warning you for your safety."

My pulse hammered. "What was he warning me for?"

"For theirs," Markson whispered. "The people running this project do not want outsiders interfering. They will not hesitate to remove obstacles."

Sheila clenched her jaw. "Who are they, Otto?"

"I don't know," he whispered. "But I know this—whoever reactivated that basement lab... they don't report to the university."

"Then who?" I demanded.

He looked up. His eyes were wet, defeated, terrified.

"They report," he whispered, "to the same people who took Druitt."

A cold crept up my spine.

"And who took Lila," he added.

Regina swallowed hard. "So you believe she's alive?"

Markson shook his head. "I believe," he said, choking slightly, "that she was taken because she found something she shouldn't have."

"And what did she find?" I asked.

He closed his eyes and whispered the words I didn't want to hear.

"She found that one of Druitt's samples survived."

Regina gasped. Sheila's breath hitched. My chest locked.

"Survived?" I whispered.

He nodded. "That enzyme," he said, "should never have been biologically viable."

He paused.

"But something in that basement adapted."

Markson looked like a man who'd carried a secret for so long that speaking it aloud felt like breaking bone. His hands trembled. He kept pressing his thumb into his palm as if trying to ground himself. The storm outside cracked again, and he flinched—not dramatically, but the way someone does when their nerves are already stripped raw.

Regina stepped forward, voice soft. "Otto... what do you mean the tissue survived?"

He swallowed hard. "After the project was shut down, all biological material was supposed to be destroyed. Samples incinerated. Freezers purged. Chemical precursors neutralized. That's standard protocol."

"And it didn't happen," I said.

"No," he whispered. "Something went missing."

"What?" Sheila asked.

He hesitated—a long, painful pause—before answering.

"One jar."

The room went still.

"Just one?" Regina whispered.

"One that Druitt insisted on 'preserving for future review.' He hid it. Moved it without authorization. It went off the manifest shortly before the shutdown. We assumed he smuggled it out, or that the logs were wrong. But the basement freezer logs show a maintenance override in 1993. Three years after the shutdown."

My heart thudded. "So Druitt came back."

"No," Markson said quickly. "He was already reassigned by then. This was someone else."

Sheila stepped closer. "Who?"

Markson shook his head. "I've thought about that for twenty years. There were only five people with clearance to access that freezer. Druitt, me, and three contract researchers whose identities are still sealed."

"Still?" Regina said sharply.

"They worked under pseudonyms," he said. "Not uncommon for federal black-budget projects. I wasn't allowed to know their real names."

"Then who could have opened it?" I asked.

"I don't know," Markson whispered. "But the maintenance logs show manual temperature overrides. Someone kept the freezer running even after we shut down the project."

"So the sample didn't die," I said.

"No. It was preserved. Perfectly. And when the lab reactivated... it wasn't just preserved anymore."

I felt a cold crawl across my spine.

"Otto," I said, "what are we really dealing with?"

He stared at me. "A self-propagating tissue line," he said softly. "One that responds to cold. One that interacts with water in ways none of us understood. One that may have... integrated characteristics of whatever minerals, salts, and microorganisms were present in the lake water used as its medium."

Regina gasped. "You're saying the sample adapted to the environment?"

"It didn't just adapt," he whispered. "It changed."

I stepped forward. "Into what?"

He shook his head. "Not into something whole. Not an organism, not a creature, not anything cohesive. But into a pattern. A tendency. A behavior."

"Behavior?" Sheila echoed. "Tissue doesn't have behavior."

"This did," he said. "At least... Druitt believed it did."

The fluorescent lights hummed overhead. The storm boomed again. The building seemed to contract with it.

Regina whispered, "What did Druitt see?"

Markson rubbed his eyes. "He claimed the tissue responded to environmental cues. Movement. Pressure changes. Temperature fluctuations. That it grew toward stimuli. That it reorganized itself based on available structures."

I felt my pulse throb in my throat. "You mean it imitated."

Markson exhaled shakily. "He thought it was pre-sentient."

Sheila let out a small, involuntary sound—half laugh, half choke. "That's impossible. Tissue cultures don't have nervous systems."

"No," Markson agreed. "But something about the mineral composition of the lake interacted with its folding structures."

"The lake," I whispered.

Regina looked at me. "Garth..."

Evan's words rang in my head.

It reacts. It helps. It grows. It remembers.

I swallowed. "So whoever reopened the lab... they weren't just storing the sample."

Markson nodded slowly. "They were feeding it."

Sheila stepped back. "Jesus."

Regina pressed her palms against her eyes. "I should have seen this coming," she whispered. "Druitt always had this... obsession with extremophiles. Arctic bacteria. Pressure-resistant proteins. He said evolution had 'unfinished branches.' He meant it literally."

I turned back to Markson. "Where is he now?"

Markson's jaw tightened. "I told you. Classified assignment."

"That's not an answer."

"It's the only one I can legally give."

"Then give me the illegal one."

He looked up, fear etched plainly across his face. "Dr. Myers," he whispered, "I don't know where he is."

I stepped closer. "But you know which agency took him."

His eyes flickered. It was subtle, but it was enough.

"Which one?" I pressed.

He didn't answer.

Sheila stepped in. "Otto, you can trust us."

"No," he said. "I can't. And you shouldn't trust me either."

Regina's voice fractured. "Lila is missing. We don't have the luxury of trusting no one."

"That's exactly why you shouldn't trust anyone," Markson said.

He stood suddenly—a sharp, desperate movement—and closed the blinds. The room darkened. When he turned back, he was shaking.

"I covered the closure of Project 6R-BL13." His voice cracked. "I buried the logs. I filed the compliance reports. I let the higher-ups do what they wanted. And I told myself it was over."

Sheila frowned. "Otto..."

He slammed his hand on the desk. "It wasn't over! Nothing ever ends with these programs. They just go dark. And when they do, they stop reporting to the university. Or to NIH. Or to anyone except the federal liaison chain."

I stepped forward. "So tell me which liaison."

He shook his head violently. "They monitor communications. They monitor office access. They monitor internet queries. Hell, they probably monitored that student's last research search."

The storm outside roared.

Regina whispered, "What are you saying?"

Markson sank into his chair, defeated. "I'm saying," he said, "that someone inside this university—someone with clearance or stolen credentials—has been funneling information back to that chain."

Sheila's voice dropped. "A mole."

He nodded.

My pulse thudded. "Who?" I asked.

His eyes flickered again.

"Otto," Regina whispered, "you have to tell us."

He shook his head. "If I tell you... I'm dead."

I swallowed. "You're already in danger."

"I know," he said quietly. "And so are you."

The wind howled against the window. The building creaked around us. A heavy silence descended.

Then Markson exhaled—long, defeated. "You need to understand something," he said. "Druitt wasn't transferred. He wasn't promoted. He wasn't reassigned for his brilliance."

"What then?" I asked.

"He was taken," Markson whispered. "Because he wouldn't let the project die."

Regina's breath hitched. "So they removed him."

"Yes."

Sheila pressed a hand over her mouth.

"And," Markson said, voice trembling, "if Lila found the surviving sample..."

He didn't finish.

He didn't need to.

Regina whispered the words he couldn't. "Then someone removed her too."

I felt cold. Not basement cold. Not lake cold. Something deeper. Something like inevitability.

"We're going to find her," I said.

Markson looked up. A strange, hollow look in his eyes.

"No, Dr. Myers," he said softly. "You're going to find something else first."

"What?"

He hesitated—then said it.

"Evidence that the sample wasn't just preserved."

He paused.

"But liberated."

A chill ran straight down my spine. Thunder boomed again. Regina gasped. Sheila whispered, "Liberated? As in... out?"

Markson nodded miserably. "The last facility logs before the camera went offline," he said, "show a freezer door override. An anomaly. Something opened from the inside."

I felt my heart stop.

"From the inside?" I repeated.

He nodded. "You asked what adapted, Dr. Myers. The answer is—everything."

The silence after Markson's last words stretched long and tight, like the air itself was bracing for a blow. Sheila set her jaw so hard I could see the muscle twitch. Regina took a step back, hand over her heart, as if something had knocked the wind out of her.

I felt... hollow. Not frightened. Not shocked. Just... emptied. Like someone had opened a valve inside my chest.

After a long moment, I spoke. "Otto," I said, "tell us who the mole is."

He stared at the floor. Then at his hands. Then at the closed blinds. Finally, his voice came out low and brittle.

"I can't."

I stepped closer. "You don't have to give us the name. Give us something. A direction. A clue."

His eyes flicked upward—meeting mine for a moment—and something in his expression shifted. Not courage. Not defiance. But the worn-down resolve of a man who had run out of ways to hide.

"They're not faculty," he said.

I nodded once. "Good. That narrows it."

He shook his head. "Not administration either."

Sheila frowned. "Then who the hell—"

He cut her off quietly. "They're staff."

Regina inhaled sharply. "Which staff?"

Markson swallowed. "Internal operations. People who handle access logs, building maintenance, ID resets, equipment requisitions... the people no one notices."

My gut tightened. "They'd have access to everything," I said.

"Yes," he whispered. "That's the point."

Regina whispered, "Someone on campus is feeding information to the same chain that took Druitt."

"Not just feeding information," Markson said. "Facilitating access. Moving equipment. Cleaning up traces. And making sure certain doors stay unlocked."

Sheila's eyes widened. "The basement door."

Markson nodded miserably.

I exhaled slowly. "Is this person working alone?"

His fingers twitched. "No."

Regina stepped closer. "How many?"

He hesitated. Then whispered, "Three."

Regina gasped. Sheila cursed under her breath.

My jaw tightened. "Three?"

Markson nodded. "One in facilities. One in research operations. One in security."

"Security?" Regina repeated, horrified.

Markson nodded. "Someone with access to override cameras. Someone who can mask badge traces. Someone who can alter logs so it looks like nothing happened."

"That's how they got in," Sheila whispered. "That's how they used your clearance. They piggybacked it."

"Yes."

I took a breath. "Do they know we're asking questions?"

Markson's eyes filled with something I didn't expect: genuine sorrow.

"They know everything," he said.

Silence swallowed the room. The kind of silence that follows bad diagnoses and unmarked graves.

I clenched my jaw. "We need names."

"I can't," Markson said, raw. "If I say their names, you won't reach your car alive."

"We're already in danger," I said.

"Yes," he whispered. "But right now, they still see you as an annoyance, not a threat. If you push too hard—"

"They'll escalate," Regina finished.

He nodded.

Sheila crossed her arms. "So what do we do?"

Markson looked at her—looked at all of us—like a man choosing whether to commit treason or drown quietly. Then he exhaled slowly.

"I'll point you," he said.

"Point us where?" I asked.

"The only place on campus where all three of them would intersect. Where security, operations, and maintenance overlap."

He leaned back. His voice dropped to a whisper.

"Facilities Control. Lower sublevel. North wing."

My stomach tightened.

The place students don't even know exists. Where the air ducts are monitored. Where water lines are routed. Where old tunnels map the underbelly of the university. Where the lake's underground channels meet infrastructure.

"Why there?" Regina asked.

"Because that's where the lake pumps feed into the building," Markson said.

A cold rippled through me.

"The lake," I whispered.

"Yes," Markson said. "Project 6R-BL13's environmental feed wasn't theoretical. It used the lake. The lake flows into the sublevels. Always has. Always will. They used it for cooling, for experimental mediums... and for disposal."

My chest tightened. "Disposal of what?"

Markson didn't answer. He didn't need to.

Sheila looked sick. "God..."

Regina whispered, "Garth... this is bigger than an experiment."

I nodded.

And that's when Markson's office phone rang.

A single shrill tone.

He froze.

The phone rang again. Not frantic. Not rushed. Purposeful. Three rings. Exactly three.

Markson stared at it like it was a pipe bomb.

Sheila whispered, "Otto, don't—"

He picked up.

"Markson," he said.

A pause. Then his face drained of color.

"Yes, I understand," he whispered.

Another pause.

"No, they're not interfering," he said.

His hand shook.

"Yes," he repeated. "I'll handle it."

The call ended. He didn't move for five seconds. Then he slowly hung up the receiver.

"Who was that?" I asked.

Markson didn't look at me. He stared at the wall—a man hollowed out.

"It's time for you to leave," he whispered.

Regina stepped forward. "Otto—"

"Leave," he said, more sharply. "Now."

Sheila grabbed her coat. I moved last. Markson still didn't look at me.

In a voice barely audible, he said, "I didn't warn them."

"What?"

His eyes flicked up—haunted. "That phone call," he whispered. "They weren't warning me. They were asking if I'd... informed anyone."

I swallowed. "And you said—"

"I said no," he breathed.

Regina's breath caught. Sheila whispered, "So they don't know we're here."

He shook his head miserably. "No. But they will."

I stepped closer. "Otto—"

He cut me off. "Go," he said. "And don't come back here until you know what you're walking into."

His voice cracked. "And for God's sake—don't go near the lake at night."

The urgency in his tone made something deep in my chest twist.

We backed away toward the door.

Before I left, he added, "Dr. Myers."

I paused.

He looked right at me. Into me. Through me.

"You're not investigating a disappearance," he whispered. "You're investigating a resurrection."

My skin went cold.

"Be careful," he said, "because the thing that came out of that basement is not the thing we put in."

My heart hammered. Regina grabbed my arm. Sheila whispered, "Garth... go."

I backed into the hallway. The door shut behind us. Soft. Final. Like a curtain falling.

We stood in silence, the storm pounding the windows, the hallway empty and humming.

"What now?" Regina whispered.

"We go to Facilities Control," I said.

"And then?" Sheila asked.

"And then we go back to the basement."

Thunder cracked. The hallway lights flickered. Somewhere far below us—in the hidden veins of the building—I thought I felt a vibration. A hum. Alive. Patient. Waiting.

CHAPTER 11

The Arteries of Stone

Even stone has arteries—you just have to know where to cut.

The Facilities Control wing wasn't on any student tour map. It wasn't on most faculty maps either. It sat beneath the north wing of the main engineering cluster, two levels down, behind a nondescript door labeled:

AUTHORIZED STAFF ONLY — MECHANICAL ACCESS

Most people walked past without ever noticing it.

Most people weren't supposed to notice it.

Sheila, Regina, and I made it halfway down the stairwell before I realized we all kept our voices low—instinctively, like people entering holy ground or enemy territory.

The stairwell smelled of rust, old concrete, and traces of lake water carried by air currents through unseen ducts.

Sheila led the way. She always did when bureaucracy or hidden passages were involved. She had the map of the university memorized in a way no one else did—because she'd spent twenty years helping lost grad students find rooms they shouldn't have been in.

She paused at the bottom landing.

"This level," she whispered, "connects to the emergency overflow system."

Regina frowned. "For floods?"

"For everything," Sheila said. "The lake's too close. If infrastructure fails, this place fills first."

"And if something needs to be drained quickly..." I murmured.

Sheila nodded. "Same deal."

A chill crawled up my arms.

The air was colder down here. Not refrigerated cold — subterranean cold. Old-space cold. A place the sun had never touched.

Sheila scanned the badge panel by the access door.

"Ready?" she asked.

"No," Regina said.

"Same," I added.

Sheila swiped her badge anyway.

The light blinked red.

She tried again.

Red.

Regina whispered, "Otto said someone with security access was part of it."

Sheila tried a third time.

This time the light blinked **green**, but only for half a second — like it was debating whether to trust us — then the latch clicked.

Sheila swallowed. "That shouldn't have worked."

"Why not?" Regina asked.

"Because my badge isn't rated for this level," Sheila whispered.

My chest tightened.

"So someone granted you temporary access," I said.

"Or," she whispered, "someone forgot to revoke it."

"Not likely," I said.

Sheila nodded. "No. Not likely at all."

She pushed open the door.

The hallway beyond was dimly lit by caged bulbs.

Pipes ran along the ceiling like exposed veins.

A faint metallic drip echoed from somewhere unseen.

At the end of the hall, a large metal sign hung slightly crooked:

FACILITIES CONTROL — SUBLEVEL 2

WATER MANAGEMENT — HVAC — ACCESS SYSTEMS

Sheila pulled out a folded map. "We're here," she said, pointing to a small square. "The lake feed junction is to the right, through the pump corridor. Security access controls are on the left."

"We split?" Regina asked.

"No," I said firmly. "Not down here."

Sheila gave me a small nod.

We moved together.

The first sound hit us before we even reached the pump room.

A deep, rhythmic thrum.

Mechanical.

But uneven — like something was interrupting the cycle.

When we turned the corner, the full scope came into view.

Six massive pumps lined the far wall, each encased in layers of steel and webbed with pipes large enough for a grown man to crawl through. Water roared through them — not clean water, but lake water, full of silt, minerals, and whatever else lived in the depths.

Regina stepped forward, squinting. "These... these aren't running at normal capacity."

"How can you tell?" Sheila asked.

Regina gestured to the vibration sensors mounted along the intake pipes. "They're registering pressure variations. Significant ones."

I noticed it too.

The gauges flickered like heart monitors, spiking irregularly.

Sheila frowned. "That's strange. These pumps don't fluctuate unless there's debris in the feed."

"Or unless," Regina said slowly, "someone's drawing water somewhere downstream."

A slow dread settled in my stomach.

"Downstream," I said, "would be the basement."

Sheila's face paled. "You're telling me the cold storage lab is drawing from the lake?"

Regina nodded. "Actively."

We moved closer to the gauge panel.

A small digital readout blinked in the corner:

MANUAL OVERRIDE ACTIVE — ROUTING: B3 AUX LINE

Regina inhaled sharply. "Someone rerouted water to the basement. Recently."

"How recently?" I asked.

"Hours," she whispered. "Maybe minutes."

I looked at Sheila. She looked back with a grim expression.

"They're still using the lab," Sheila said. "Right now."

We moved deeper into the corridor until the pumps' roar faded behind us. Pipes narrowed overhead. The smell of lake water grew stronger — earthy, silt-heavy, strangely organic.

Halfway down the next hall, we found it.

A heavy steel door.

Not a pump door.

Not a maintenance door.

A storage bay door built to withstand flooding.

Across the top, stenciled letters read:

WET STORAGE — ACCESS RESTRICTED

Sheila frowned. "This shouldn't be here."

"What do you mean?" Regina asked.

Sheila tapped the wall. "This is a newer door. Fifteen years old at most. But this infrastructure dates back to the '60s."

"So someone installed this for a specific purpose," I said.

133

"Yes," Sheila whispered. "And not for facilities use."

Regina stepped toward the badge panel. "Does it read yours?"

Sheila swiped.

Red.

Tried again.

Red.

Then the panel flashed:

ACCESS LOGGED

AWAIT INSTRUCTIONS

"What the hell does that mean?" Sheila whispered.

"It means," I said, "someone knows we're here."

Regina gasped softly.

"Step back," I said.

We all backed away from the door.

For a long moment, nothing happened.

Then faintly — faintly — from behind the steel, we heard something.

Not machinery.

A sound like...

scraping.

Slow.

Deliberate.

As if something dragged across concrete on the other side.

Regina covered her mouth.

Sheila whispered, "No..."

Another scrape.

Then silence.

Sheila grabbed my coat sleeve. "Garth... that's not a machine."

"No," I whispered.

The door didn't open.

But the message on the panel updated:

ACCESS DENIED

DO NOT PROCEED

Regina cursed under her breath. "Who the hell is sending these messages?"

There was no time to answer — because suddenly, the hallway lights flickered.

Once.

Twice.

Then steadied.

A chilled rush of air moved past us — like a pressure shift.

And from somewhere deeper in the sublevels came a faint clang.

Metal on metal.

Regina looked at me with wide eyes. "That came from the security control wing."

"Then that's where we go," I said.

Sheila hesitated. "Garth... the storage bay..."

"Later," I said. "We need the access logs. If we can trace who entered the basement, we find the mole."

"And if the mole is in security?" Regina whispered.

"Then they'll know we're coming," Sheila finished.

I nodded once.

"We go anyway."

We left the door behind us.

But as we turned the corner, I glanced back one last time.

Just as I did, a thin trickle of water — dark, opaque — leaked from under the steel.

Not clear water.

Not runoff.

Something mixed.

Something thicker.

Regina didn't see it.

Sheila didn't see it.

But I did.

The trickle wound across the concrete like a black vein.

And in it — for the briefest moment —

something granular moved against the current.

Swimming.

Alive.

I blinked.

It was gone.

I turned and caught up to them.

The door to the Security Control room was ajar.

Only slightly.

A sliver.

Like someone had left in a hurry.

Or hadn't cared to hide their tracks.

Regina whispered, "Do we go in?"

"Quietly," I said.

Sheila pulled her flashlight.

The room beyond was dim — lit only by the flicker of a half-dead monitor.

As we stepped inside, the smell hit us first.

Burnt plastic.

Cold metal.

And something else — the faint chemical tang of disinfectant.

Sheila moved to the central console, her fingers flying over the keyboard.

"Someone wiped the logs," she murmured.

"When?" Regina asked.

"Right before we arrived," Sheila whispered. "Minutes."

I scanned the room.

Three monitors.

Two chairs.

A rack of servers humming quietly.

A filing cabinet with one drawer slightly open.

And on the floor —

A small puddle of water.

Fresh.

Regina saw it too. "Garth..."

I knelt.

The water wasn't from a spill.

It wasn't from a leak.

It was from a shoe.

A footprint.

Not fully formed.

But undeniable.

Leading toward the back door.

"Someone was just here," I whispered.

Sheila froze. "And they left through that door."

Regina swallowed. "Should we follow?"

"No," I said. "We pull what we can first."

Sheila opened the filing cabinet fully.

Inside, amid old logs and repair records, was a folder.

Thin.

Unlabeled.

Out of place.

Sheila handed it to me.

The first page was a printout of an access log.

BASEMENT ENTRY — B3 LEVEL

CREDENTIAL: OVERRIDE — LEVEL V

TIME: 11:13 PM

Regina inhaled sharply.

"The same minute the footage ended," she whispered.

I turned the page.

Another entry.

OVERRIDE — LEVEL V

TIME: 3:42 AM

Another.

OVERRIDE — LEVEL V

TIME: 7:09 AM

All from the same credential.

Regina whispered, "They're visiting the basement multiple times a day."

"And they're using a clearance level we don't have," Sheila said.

I stared at the signature line.

The name was redacted.

A thick black bar.

Impossible to read.

But beneath the redaction...

the faintest edge of a typed letter peeked out.

A curve.

A loop.

A hint of a letter that hadn't been fully covered.

Sheila gasped. "Garth... that looks like—"

I held up a hand.

"No guesses yet."

A noise echoed from behind the back door.

A soft click.

Followed by the sound of something dripping.

Regina stiffened. "Oh God—"

The dripping grew louder.

Closer.

Then:

A single wet footprint

appeared under the door.

Small.

Human-shaped.

But the water around it shimmered with something darker.

Not just water.

Something suspended in it.

Sheila grabbed my arm.

"We need to leave," she whispered.

Regina nodded, pale. "Now."

I backed toward the main hallway.

We exited quickly but quietly.

As the door to Security Control closed behind us, I thought I heard—

A scraping sound.

Soft.

Deliberate.

And very much alive.

The hallway outside the Security Control room felt darker than when we entered it. The caged bulbs overhead buzzed in quick, frantic beats, as if they were flickering in time with our pulse. The air carried a faint chill, the kind that feels like it's coming from a direction you can't identify.

We didn't speak at first.

We didn't have to.

We were all running through the same questions.

Who was behind that door?

How long had they been watching us?

And why didn't they follow us?

Sheila walked fast, her breath uneven. Not panicked — Sheila doesn't panic — but rattled. Regina stayed beside her, stealing glances over her shoulder.

I brought up the rear, scanning every corner, every doorway, every shadow.

The echo of our footsteps carried unnaturally far.

Finally, at the intersection of two sublevel corridors, Sheila stopped abruptly.

"We can't go back up yet," she whispered. "If someone saw us pull those logs, they'll be watching the exits."

Regina leaned close. "So what do we do? Hide?"

"No," Sheila said. "We go deeper."

"Deeper?" I asked.

She nodded. "Toward the monitoring alcove."

"The what?" Regina asked.

"It's a dead-end room between the lake pipes and the old steam ducts. No cameras. No foot traffic. It's where facilities staff go when they don't want to be found."

Regina frowned. "That's reassuring."

"It was for them," Sheila said. "It will be for us."

We kept moving.

If the upper floors of UW–Madison are a campus, the sublevels are a labyrinth.

Pipes crawled along the ceilings like the exposed underbelly of a metallic beast. Rusty valves creaked as the building exhaled. The smell of damp concrete intensified the deeper we went.

At certain turns, the walls felt closer — not physically, but atmospherically. The air thickened, heavy with mineral fog carried from the lake's unseen channels.

We passed a junction where three corridors met. A sign hung overhead:

MECH 12 →

WATER FEED — LAKE MONONA ←

VAPOR TUNNELS ↓

Regina pointed to the second line. "Wait. The building has direct feed tunnels to the lake?"

Sheila nodded. "Three. One is historical, no longer used. One is for intake. One is... special."

"Special how?" Regina asked.

Sheila hesitated. "It was sealed in the '80s. For 'structural integrity and safety.'"

"But?" I said.

Sheila gave a tight smile. "Whenever a university says 'structural integrity,' it means 'we don't want to explain the real reason.'"

We turned toward the vapor tunnels.

The temperature dropped by several degrees.

Regina rubbed her arms. "Why is it so cold?"

I inhaled slowly.

Cold.

Sharp.

Icy.

It reminded me of the basement.

Of B3-11.

And B3-12.

And the pulse I felt behind the sealed door.

Sheila whispered, "This way."

We reached a door that looked older than everything around it.

Wooden, not metal.

Faded paint.

A brass handle worn smooth by decades of hands.

Sheila opened it.

Inside: a cramped alcove barely larger than a walk-in closet. A small desk. Two chairs. A corkboard with outdated maintenance schedules. A calendar from 1994. And a single hanging bulb that flickered twice before stabilizing.

This room felt forgotten.

Untouched.

Unmonitored.

Exactly what we needed.

Sheila closed the door behind us.

Regina dropped into a chair. "Okay. Let's see what we have."

I spread the folder across the desk.

The access logs.

The redactions.

The Level V overrides.

Sheila leaned over, pointing. "Look here. The manual overrides... they're not random."

Regina frowned. "What do you mean?"

She tapped five consecutive entries.

"All timestamped within a narrow window. All labeled Level V. And all happening on days when the lake pumps recorded pressure anomalies."

My stomach tightened.

"So the basement activity matches lake disturbances," I said.

"Yes," she whispered. "Exactly."

Regina ran a hand through her hair. "Someone is using the lake as part of the experiment."

"Not using," I said quietly.

"Relying on."

Sheila's eyes widened. "Meaning without the lake... the experiment fails."

We fell silent.

The building creaked around us, settling — or moving.

Regina tapped the top page. "What about the redacted name?"

I looked at the faint cut of the letter beneath the black bar.

A partial curve.

An arc.

"Could be a D," Regina offered. "Or an O. Or—"

Sheila grabbed the page, squinting.

Her eyes flickered.

"Garth," she whispered. "I think... I think it's an M."

My pulse kicked.

"A name starting with M," Regina breathed. "Do we know any M—"

She stopped.

So did I.

Markson.

Regina shook her head. "No. No, he said he hasn't gone down there."

"And I believe him," I said.

"Then who?" Regina asked.

Sheila whispered it first:

"Maintenance."

I looked at her sharply. "What?"

She pointed to the infrastructure codes at the bottom of the page. Small notations indicating where the clearance originated.

"See this? This is not a federal badge. This is a *proxied* credential."

"Meaning?" Regina asked.

"Meaning someone borrowed the clearance level. Possibly through building systems. Possibly through a hacked badge."

"A maintenance worker," I said.

"One with access to ducts, halls, tunnels," Sheila whispered. "One who knows how to go unseen."

Regina swallowed. "One who knows the lake tunnels."

We didn't say the next name aloud.

But the implication hung between us like a noose.

The university maintenance corps is large.

Most are harmless.

But some... some have master keys, access to everything, and a long history of being invisible.

"Who in maintenance has Level V clearance?" Regina asked.

Sheila shook her head. "None. They shouldn't. But—"

She pointed to a line on the log.

OVERRIDE: V-PROX 21

"V-PROX means 'proxied through a secondary system,'" she whispered. "And the '21'... that's an internal code for the maintenance hub."

My skin prickled.

"Someone in maintenance is bypassing clearance," I said.

"Yes," Sheila whispered. "And they have access to the lake feed."

Regina exhaled shakily. "Jesus..."

A sound echoed in the corridor outside.

We all froze.

Not footsteps.

Not machinery.

A tap.

Soft.

Metallic.

Like someone flicked a pipe with a finger.

Tap.

Tap.

Pause.

Tap.

Sheila's eyes widened. "Someone's outside."

I moved quietly to the door.

Pressed my ear against it.

At first: nothing.

Then...

Breathing.

Slow.

Controlled.

Close.

Regina mouthed, *Is it them?*

I didn't know.

Another sound — faint, subtle — like the drag of a boot across concrete.

Sheila whispered, "We can't stay here."

"No," I said. "We move."

Regina nodded, tense. "Back the way we came?"

"No," Sheila said quickly. "They'll expect that."

"Then where?" Regina asked.

Sheila pointed to a hatch above the old calendar on the wall. "The steam duct. It leads to the intake hallway. We can bypass the corridor entirely."

Regina stared. "We're crawling through ducts now?"

I shrugged. "Better than walking into whoever is outside."

The breathing continued.

Close.

Unhurried.

Like the person — or thing — had nowhere else to be.

Regina gripped the desk. "Okay. Sheila, you first."

Sheila climbed onto the chair, pushing the hatch upward. Dust rained down. The opening yawned above us — tight, dark, metallic.

Regina went next.

As I moved last, a soft shadow passed beneath the door crack.

A shape.

A foot?

A hand?

A smear?

I couldn't tell.

But the corridor suddenly smelled of cold water.

lake water.

Something brushed the bottom of the door — a faint, wet drag.

My pulse pounded.

"Garth," Sheila hissed from above, "come on!"

I climbed into the duct.

Just as I pulled the hatch closed, I heard it:

A whisper from outside the door.

Soft.

Wet.

Barely audible.

Not a word.

Not language.

Something like...

a gurgled breath

in shallow water.

The steam duct was narrower than it looked from the floor — a metal throat lined with rust flakes and the stale breath of decades-old heat. As I pulled the hatch closed behind me, the faint wet drag outside cut off like a severed nerve. The darkness swallowed us.

Regina whispered ahead of me, voice low but steady, "Sheila, how far does this duct run?"

Her voice echoed strangely in the enclosed space — too close, too intimate — as if the duct swallowed sound and fed back the pieces it liked.

"Twenty meters," Sheila murmured. "Then there's a cross-branch. We take the left chute, which dumps us near the intake hallway."

"How certain are you?" Regina asked.

"One hundred and... forty percent," Sheila said.

"You just made that number up," I whispered.

"Yup," Sheila replied. "But my guess is still better than whatever's waiting outside that door."

Fair enough.

We crawled forward.

The metal groaned beneath us, old joints protesting the weight of three humans who had no business being in a space designed for heat flow and dust, not amateur sleuthing. My back scraped the ceiling; my knees scraped the floor. Every movement sent tiny reverberations through the duct.

After ten meters, the temperature dropped.

Not by a little — by a lot.

"This isn't normal," Regina whispered, hugging herself.

"No," Sheila said. "It's coming from ahead."

I felt the cold like a hand closing around my throat. It wasn't the kind of cold you sense with skin. It was the kind that seeped into your bones — the kind that brought back Lake Monona in sharp, merciless clarity.

The memory slammed into me.

"Garth?" Regina whispered.

I'd stopped crawling.

"I'm fine," I lied. "Keep moving."

We pushed on.

A faint glow pulsed ahead — cold, bluish-white, like a dying LED left in an abandoned freezer.

Sheila reached the junction first. "This is it," she whispered. "Left chute."

Before she shifted direction, she froze.

"Wait."

Regina stiffened. "What?"

Sheila held up a hand. "There's condensation on the metal."

I crawled up beside them and saw it — droplets forming on the duct walls, shimmering faintly under the cold glow.

Regina whispered, horrified, "This isn't from steam. This is—"

"lake water," I finished.

Sheila wiped her gloved finger along the metal and sniffed it — a habit from years of facility triage.

"Smells like silt," she murmured. "Fresh."

"Fresh?" I repeated.

"That means something carried it through here recently."

Regina swallowed. "Something small?"

Sheila shook her head. "Something... dragging."

My breath halted. "Dragging?"

She nodded. "That smear pattern? That's not runoff. That's locomotion."

Regina whispered, "Something crawled through this duct?"

We all went silent.

We did not, however, turn around.

We moved forward because going back was worse.

Ten more meters and the duct sloped downward slightly. The glow grew brighter — a thin, cold light leaking from a set of slits cut into the duct wall.

"What's that?" Regina whispered.

Sheila peered through one slit.

Her breath hitched.

"Oh God."

"What?" I whispered.

"Look."

I pressed my eye to the slit.

Below us was a chamber I didn't recognize — a maintenance hall intersecting with an older part of the sublevels. Concrete stained the color of old ash. Several large drainage pipes emptied into a grated trench in the floor.

Water flowed there — a constant stream of dark lake water.

But that wasn't the disturbing part.

The disturbing part was the figure kneeling beside the trench.

A maintenance uniform.

But wrong.

The posture was off.

Shoulders too rigid.

Head tilted at an unnatural angle.

Hands — or what should have been hands — submerged in the water.

Regina whispered, "Is he cleaning something?"

"No," Sheila said, voice tight.

"He's... listening."

We watched.

The figure leaned closer to the trench.

The surface of the water rippled — not from flow, but from *something below* pushing upward.

Like an unseen presence pressing against the underside of the stream.

The uniformed figure tilted its head again — slow, unnatural.

"Garth," Sheila whispered, "that's not human."

I stared harder.

Something was wrong with the shoulders. Too broad. The proportions off. The uniform stretched strangely around the arms, as if something beneath had grown or rearranged.

Regina grabbed my sleeve.

"Please," she whispered, "say that's a trick of the light."

But then we saw it.

The figure's arm elongated.

Not fully.

Not grotesquely.

Just enough.

A ripple beneath the uniform sleeve — a movement *under the skin*.

My pulse surged.

Regina covered her mouth with both hands.

Sheila whispered, "It's a person. But... changed."

The figure suddenly jerked its head upward.

We all froze.

It looked straight toward the duct slits.

Straight at us.

Regina stiffened.

"He can't see us," Sheila whispered. "He can't. It's too dark in here."

But I wasn't sure.

The figure stared for five seconds.

Then ten.

Then—

It stood.

Slowly.

Like someone assembling themselves for the first time.

Sheila hissed, "Move. Move now."

We crawled as fast as the duct allowed — metal scraping, knees bruising, hearts hammering.

Behind us, a metallic clang echoed.

Regina gasped. "Did he—did it—move toward us?"

No one answered.

We kept crawling.

At the far end of the duct, a small, round maintenance hatch waited — rusted around the edges but intact.

Sheila twisted the latch.

It didn't budge.

She tried again, harder.

Still nothing.

"Garth," she whispered urgently, "help."

I wedged beside her and pulled.

On the third try, the latch snapped free.

The hatch opened.

Cold air rushed in.

Not lake-cold.

Tunnel-cold.

The kind that rides along forgotten infrastructure.

Sheila dropped into the hallway first, landing lightly.

Regina went next.

I followed.

As soon as I hit the ground, Regina grabbed my arm.

"Listen," she whispered.

We did.

From inside the duct:

scrape

… pause

… scrape-scrape

… pause

… drag

Something was following us.

Sheila snapped the hatch shut and slid a metal bar through the handle.

It wouldn't hold for long.

But we didn't need long.

"Come on," she whispered, voice shaking.

We ran.

This hallway was different from the rest of the sublevels — older, narrower, with brick walls instead of concrete. The pipes here were massive, ancient relics from the original building design, reinforced with bands of iron.

Water dripped rhythmically from overhead, creating dark patches on the floor.

The air smelled of rust and lake minerals.

Regina pressed a hand against her chest. "What was that thing?"

"A person," Sheila said. "Or they used to be."

"You mean—"

"Yes," Sheila whispered.

We ran until the ducts were far behind us.

Only then did we slow.

Sheila pointed. "We're close. That's the intake hallway ahead."

We turned the final corner—

And stopped.

Because someone was standing at the far end of the corridor.

A silhouette.

Tall.

Still.

Backlit by a dim emergency light.

Not moving.

Not approaching.

Just waiting.

Regina's breath faltered. "Is that—"

She didn't finish.

Because the figure lifted a hand.

Slowly.

Deliberately.

Not waving.

Not signaling distress.

A gesture.

A beckoning.

Sheila whispered, "Oh God..."

I stepped in front of them.

The figure didn't move.

Didn't advance.

Didn't retreat.

It just stood there.

Then — without warning — the emergency light flickered.

Once.

Twice.

The silhouette vanished.

Gone.

Like it had never been there.

Regina pressed herself against the wall. "We can't stay down here."

"No," I said quietly. "We can't."

We moved again.

Faster.

Quieter.

Until we reached a single steel door marked:

INTAKE HALLWAY — AUTHORIZED STAFF ONLY

Sheila swiped her badge.

This time it opened instantly.

We rushed inside, and the door slammed behind us.

The intake hallway was still underground, but it felt different — brighter, less claustrophobic, monitored by legitimate facility cameras instead of rewritten logs.

For the first time in an hour, the air didn't feel like it was watching us.

Regina leaned against the wall, trembling.

Sheila braced her hands on her knees, exhaling hard. "Okay. That was... a lot."

I nodded. "We need to regroup. Fast."

Regina pointed back toward the sublevels. "Garth... what was that man? That thing?"

"I don't know," I said.

But I did know one thing.

Whatever survived in the basement hadn't stayed in the basement.

It had moved.

It had learned.

And it wasn't alone.

The intake hallway hummed with mechanical life — steady, predictable, human-engineered. After the labyrinth behind us, the reliable thrum of industrial HVAC felt almost comforting, like the sound of a familiar engine in a storm.

Regina leaned against the concrete wall, skin pale, breath shallow. Sheila wiped her palms on her jeans, hands trembling in a way she tried—unsuccessfully—to hide. I stayed facing the door we'd entered through, listening for any sound that didn't belong.

Nothing followed us.

Not yet.

But the silence wasn't safety.

It was intermission.

Regina finally spoke, voice cracking. "Garth... what happened back there? That—that thing by the water line—"

"It wasn't fully human," Sheila whispered.

Regina's eyes filled. "Don't say that."

"It's true," Sheila said. "You saw the arm."

Regina shut her eyes. "I don't know what I saw."

"You do," Sheila replied softly. "You just don't want to."

Regina's breath stuttered. "I keep thinking... Lila might be down here. Hurt. Alive. Or—"

She couldn't finish.

I stepped closer, touching her shoulder. "Regina. Look at me."

She hesitated.

"Lila is smart," I said. "She didn't just stumble into this. She knew where she was going. She knew something others missed. She wasn't reckless."

Her eyes locked onto mine. "But she's in danger."

158

"Yes," I said. "And that's why we're here."

A beat.

She closed her eyes, steadied her breathing, and nodded. "Okay."

Sheila straightened. "We should go topside. We need to process what we found before anyone realizes the logs are missing."

"Agreed," I said.

We began moving toward the far exit — the one leading to a stairwell that surfaced near the old loading docks. The hallway stretched ahead, wide enough for maintenance carts, lit by overhead strips that flickered lazily but without malice.

Halfway down the corridor, Regina stopped suddenly.

"Garth," she whispered, "look."

She pointed to a puddle.

Small. Perfectly circular.

Clear water with a faint dark swirl in the center — like pigment dissolving.

The same pattern we'd seen beneath the wet storage door.

But there were no pipes overhead here. No leaks. No ducts. No reason for standing water.

Besides, puddles don't *form perfectly circular pools.*

Not naturally.

Sheila crouched beside it, studying the edges. "This was placed here. Not dripped."

"Placed," Regina echoed. "By what? A cup?"

"No," Sheila said quietly. "There's no splash pattern. This was set down."

"Set down?" I asked.

Sheila's voice dropped. "Like someone carried it. Or... tracked it."

A slow chill rippled down my spine.

"Let's keep moving," I said.

We pushed onward.

The stairwell was a tall, echoing concrete shaft — utilitarian, exposed rebar visible in places where the wall had chipped. The exit sign glowed weakly overhead. We climbed quickly.

Halfway up, Regina slowed. "Garth... my heart is racing."

"That's adrenaline," Sheila said. "You saw something no one should ever see."

Regina placed a hand on the rail. "No. I mean... I can feel it. In my ribs. In my teeth. Like something is vibrating."

I stepped closer. "Vibrating how?"

"Like something down there is... humming."

She wasn't wrong.

I could feel it too — a faint resonance, barely perceptible, like a low-frequency tremor.

"Keep climbing," I said.

We reached the top and stepped out into a loading bay corridor — dusty from disuse, filled with pallets and crates that hadn't been moved in years. The overhead lights buzzed gently.

Sheila exhaled. "Finally. Air that doesn't feel... watched."

Regina gave a strained laugh. "Let's not go back down there unless necessary."

"Oh, it'll be necessary," Sheila muttered.

We crossed the loading bay and stepped outside.

The late afternoon light hit us like a physical force — bright, almost offensive after the sublevel gloom. The storm had moved east, leaving behind damp pavement and a sharp wind rolling off Lake Monona.

Regina hugged herself against the cold.

I scanned the area.

No one.

Just the muted hum of campus in transition — students heading to late classes, cyclists weaving past, the far-off blur of car traffic on University Avenue.

Sheila checked her watch. "We were down there for almost two hours."

Regina's eyes widened. "It felt like thirty minutes."

"Time distorts underground," Sheila said. "No windows, no reference points, high stress."

"Or," Regina said, "someone wanted us disoriented."

We didn't answer.

We walked together toward the faculty lot. My Miata, which I got as a summer relief a couple of years ago, sat where I'd left it, top up, droplets glistening on the paint. It looked like a toy in all this seriousness, too cheerful for what we'd just seen. She was my security blanket.

As we approached, I froze.

There was something tucked under my windshield wiper.

A note.

White.

Plain.

Folded once.

Sheila whispered, "Garth..."

I reached for it, every sense alert.

The paper was dry — meaning it had been placed there after the storm.

I unfolded it.

The handwriting was precise.

Small.

And unmistakably careful.

Three words:

STOP

LOOKING

DOWN

Regina inhaled sharply. "Oh God."

But there was more.

A faint watermark on the paper — the kind used by federal agencies.

An embossed seal.

Partially visible.

"Is that—?" Sheila asked.

"Federal letter stock," I said.

Regina looked at me. "Garth... they know you were down there."

"Yes."

"And they know what you're doing."

"Yes."

"Do you know what this means?" she whispered.

I nodded once.

"It means they're not warning us anymore," I said. "They're watching us."

A sharp wind blew across the lot, carrying the smell of wet leaves and cold lake water.

We were silent for a long moment.

Then Sheila stepped closer. "We go to the cops now. Or the dean. Or the federal liaison. Anyone."

"No," I said.

"Why the hell not?" she whispered.

"Because going to them is exactly what they want."

Regina swallowed hard. "Then what do we do?"

I looked at the note again.

"Someone is trying to scare us away from the basement," I said. "Which means whatever's down there is important."

Sheila shook her head. "Garth—"

"We saw someone changed," I said. "Someone who's been exposed to that enzyme. Someone who shouldn't be alive. They're not just covering up a crime. They're continuing the experiment."

Regina whispered, "Then we go back."

"No," I said. "Not yet."

Sheila frowned. "Then when?"

"When we know who the mole in maintenance is."

Regina looked at me, fear and resolve twisting together. "Which means we need to go through every maintenance log. Every badge. Every person who had access to the tunnels."

"Yes."

Sheila nodded firmly. "I can get that."

"And we need," I added, "to talk to someone who knew those sublevels better than anyone else."

Regina's eyes widened.

"No."

"Yes," I said softly.

"Garth... Bob is not getting dragged into this."

"He already is," I said. "He knows the tunnels better than any of us. He worked construction crews in the early days. He's old enough to remember what used to be down there. And he's my sponsor."

"And he's eighty-three," Regina said sharply.

"And he's the only one," I said, "who'll tell me the truth."

I nodded.

"It has to."

Regina touched my arm gently. "Garth... you need to be careful. For once in your life."

"I know."

But my eyes drifted back to the note.

Those three words weren't a warning.

They were a threat.

STOP

LOOKING

DOWN

Regina whispered, "They think the danger is below."

"They're wrong," I said.

"What do you mean?" she asked.

I looked across campus, at the quiet buildings, the tranquil post-storm sky, the rippling lake beyond.

"Because whatever's down there..." I said, "is coming up."

CHAPTER 12

The Drowning Echo

Some voices don't fade—they sink, and keep sinking.

The church basement always smelled the same: burnt coffee, lemon floor cleaner, and a faint undercurrent of folding chairs that had held too many confessions. I'd been coming here for years, long enough for the smell to become part of my theology.

The meeting had ended twenty minutes ago. Stragglers loitered near the coffee table, laughing softly, discussing their weeks. The usual cast of ghosts trying to stay alive above ground.

Bob Thomas sat alone at one of the circular tables, hunched over a Styrofoam cup of coffee like he was interrogating it. The overhead fluorescent light flickered in a way that gave him a kind of halo — a cracked, weary halo, but a halo nonetheless.

He didn't look up when I sat down.

"You missed the first half," he said.

"Work," I said.

"That's what you always say."

"And it's usually true."

He grunted. "Usually."

Bob had the kind of face you could mistake for sternness if you didn't know him — carved lines, deep-set eyes, a jaw like worn granite. But he wasn't stern. He was tired. Old tired. From a lifetime of losing people, finding them, and losing them again.

He set his coffee down. "You been drinking?"

"No."

He studied my eyes. "Thinking about drinking?"

"Depends on the hour."

"That's honest," he said. "Honesty's good. Honesty saves your life."

I nodded.

He leaned back. "So. What's eating you? You're wound tight as a guitar string in a hailstorm."

I looked at my hands.

Then at Bob.

Then back at my hands.

He waited.

Bob never rushed me. That was half his therapy. The other half was knowing when to jab the truth out of me.

I inhaled slowly. "I found something under campus."

He didn't blink. "Define 'something.'"

"A... room."

"Plenty of rooms under campus."

"This one wasn't plenty. This one was sealed."

He nodded once, like he expected that answer.

I continued. "Someone reopened it."

His eyes narrowed. "Ah."

"Ah what?" I asked.

He folded his arms. "You wouldn't be the first person to go poking around where the university buries its bones."

I felt my pulse thrum. "Bob... what do you know about the tunnels?"

He didn't answer immediately.

He sipped his coffee.

Then said, "Depends which generation of tunnels you're talking about."

"There's more than one?"

"Three," he said. "Four, if you count the ones nobody admits to."

I leaned forward. "Bob. I need you to be straight with me."

He gave me a look — soft, almost fatherly.

"I've always been straight with you, son. You just haven't always been ready to hear it."

I swallowed.

"Start from the beginning," I said.

He sighed. "Okay. You know the steam tunnels."

"Yes."

"And the maintenance tunnels."

"Yes."

"And the old Prohibition tunnels — the ones fraternities swore they didn't use for smuggling beer."

"Yes."

Bob leaned closer.

"But you don't know about the lake tunnels."

A chill crept through me.

"Lake tunnels?" I repeated.

He nodded. "They were built in the 1920s and '30s. Depression-era works. You know how it was — ambitious, weird, half-documented. They ran cold intake channels from Lake Monona into the engineering cluster and the old labs for cooling. Cheap alternative to industrial chillers back then."

"Was that safe?" I asked.

"No," he said bluntly. "But nobody gave a damn. It worked. They built three primary inflow tunnels, one outflow, and some side channels branching deeper under campus."

Regina's voice echoed in my mind.

The lake is the catalyst.

The lake fed the experiments.

"And they're still there?" I asked.

"Sort of," Bob said. "Two were officially sealed in the '60s. 'Officially' meaning concrete poured over the openings. But if you know where to press—"

"Bob," I said, "I need locations."

He shook his head. "No, you need caution."

"Bob."

He took out a yellowed piece of paper from his jacket — folded so many times it looked like a religious relic. He smoothed it on the table.

A map.

Hand-sketched.

Detailed.

Precise.

Lines crisscrossed under campus like veins under skin. Three thick lines led from the lake's edge straight beneath the buildings.

He tapped one with his callused finger.

"This one's long gone. Collapsed."

He tapped another.

"This one still exists but is blocked somewhere around the sublevels. Didn't fully seal. Probably still breathes lake air."

Then he tapped the last.

"This one," he said, "was never sealed properly. They poured concrete at the mouth, but the tunnel runs fifty yards before that point. Everything behind the concrete is still hollow."

My heartbeat stuttered.

"Where does it lead?" I asked.

Bob traced it with his finger.

"Right beneath the engineering cluster."

My mouth went dry.

"Right beneath B3," he added.

I closed my eyes.

Bob watched me calmly.

"You didn't just find a sealed room, Garth," he said.

"You found something built on top of a tunnel no one was supposed to use again."

"What was it used for?" I asked.

He took a breath.

"Originally? Cooling lines. Water flow. Maybe some questionable experiments back in the day. This university has skeletons older than its chancellors."

"And later?"

"Later…" He paused, the silence heavy.

"Later, someone reopened it."

My pulse hammered.

"When?" I whispered.

Bob shook his head. "Nineties. Eighties. Doesn't matter. They pumped water through it again. Quietly. Off the books."

"Bob," I said softly, "did you know they were experimenting with biological material down there?"

His reaction wasn't shock.

It was sadness.

"Yes," he said quietly. "I knew."

Sheila would have fainted if she'd heard that.

"Bob," I said, "why didn't you tell me earlier?"

He looked me dead in the eyes.

"Because it wasn't your fight yet."

My throat tightened. "And now?"

"Now it is."

We were silent for a long moment.

Then he said:

"I know what you saw."

I stared at him. "You do?"

"Yes."

"Then help me make sense of it."

He shook his head. "No, Garth. I'll help you survive it."

I leaned closer. "What was that thing in the tunnels? That... person?"

Bob didn't blink.

Didn't hesitate.

"Someone who stayed down there too long."

I felt something twist deep in my gut.

"You're saying they're alive?"

"Alive?" Bob echoed. "Sure. In the way a mushroom on a rotten stump is alive."

"Jesus."

He pointed at the map again.

"You want answers? Start here."

He tapped the unsealed tunnel line.

"Find the old intake chamber. The original one. The one behind the concrete."

"Why?"

"Because that's where the lake speaks the loudest."

I stared at him.

"The lake?" I whispered.

He nodded.

"There's something about that water, Garth. Something old. Something patient. Something that remembers."

My pulse spiked. "Remembers what?"

Bob inhaled, then exhaled slowly.

"Everything that's ever fallen into it."

A cold rolled through me — not from memory, but from the certainty in Bob's voice.

"Bob," I said softly, "what did you see down there?"

He closed his eyes.

When he opened them, he looked more ancient than he ever had.

"I saw something that shouldn't exist," he said. "And I learned the hard way you can build on top of the lake... but you can't keep it buried."

My skin prickled.

My breath stalled.

He slid the map across the table.

"Take this," he said. "But listen carefully."

I leaned in.

His voice dropped to a whisper.

"You don't go near that tunnel alone. You don't go at night. And whatever you do..."

He looked me dead in the eyes.

"...don't let the water touch you."

I swallowed. "Why?"

He leaned back.

And said something I would not forget for the rest of the investigation:

"Because the lake doesn't just remember. It takes."

I left the church basement with Bob's map tucked inside my coat like a contraband scripture. The sky had gone that deep bruised-blue that only November in Madison can manage — dark before its time, heavy with cold. A streetlight flickered overhead while I crossed the lot, Regina waiting by my Miata with her coat pulled tight around her.

"You were gone for a while," she said softly.

"Yeah."

"Did he help?"

I opened the passenger door for her. "He did more than help."

She saw the look on my face and didn't ask anything else until we were halfway back to my place.

The heater wheezed in protest against the cold. The lake shimmered through the passenger window — silver, almost metallic, a flat mirror that looked nothing like the warm water of summer.

Regina watched it quietly. "The lake... feels different lately."

"Yeah," I said. "It does."

"Do you think this is just biology, Garth? Just a rogue experiment?"

"No."

She nodded once. "That's what scares me."

I drove in silence until we reached my house — the little cottage on Lake Monona, its windows glowing faint yellow like an aging lighthouse.

Regina stopped at the base of the steps. "Inside or car?"

"Inside," I said. "We'll need the table."

"And coffee."

"Lots," I said.

We laid Bob's hand-drawn map across my kitchen table. The paper was brittle, stained in places, edges softened by decades of use.

Regina leaned over it, tracing the thick lines with her finger. "These are the original intake tunnels?"

"Yes," I said. "And this one—"

I tapped the unsealed line Bob had emphasized.

"—was never filled properly."

Regina examined the faint scribbles around it. "This notation... the one here says 'OIC.'"

"Old Intake Chamber," I said.

"And this one says 'S-Feed.'"

"Side feed."

"To the basement," she whispered.

"To the lake," I said.

Her face tightened. "The enzyme... the growth... it used this."

"And still is," I said.

She sat back, rubbing her temples. "So the basement lab wasn't an isolated chamber. It was a control point built on top of something older."

"The federal project simply exploited what the campus already had," I said. "A direct, unmonitored water route from the lake."

Regina frowned. "But why would they need unmonitored water?"

"Because the lake wasn't just a medium," I said. "It was the catalyst."

She shivered.

"Bob says the tunnels breathe," I added.

"Breathe?" she repeated.

"As in, they move water from under campus back to the lake. And vice versa."

Regina exhaled slowly. "So if something adapted down there... it could move with that water."

I looked at her.

"So could someone be exposed to it," I said.

Regina closed her eyes briefly. "Like the man in the pump corridor."

"Like him," I said.

"And possibly others."

Her breath caught. "Garth... you don't think Lila—"

"No," I said firmly.

Too quickly.

Regina didn't press, but the look in her eyes said she wasn't entirely convinced.

My phone buzzed on the table.

Sheila (6:41 PM):

Get home now. I need to talk to you both.

I texted back:

We're here.

She replied instantly:

Good. I'm outside.

I opened the front door.

Sheila stood on the porch with her coat half-zipped, cheeks pink from the cold. But her eyes—they were sharp, alert, spooked.

"What happened?" I asked.

She brushed past me into the living room. Regina followed. I shut the door behind us.

Sheila didn't sit. She paced. "Okay. I spent the last three hours digging through maintenance logs."

175

Regina's eyes widened. "Please tell me you found something."

"Oh," Sheila said, "I found something all right."

She stopped pacing and pulled a printout from her coat pocket.

It wasn't a normal log. It was a badge-trace summary from the central access system — the kind of record that tracks badge swipes, door access, and proxied credentials.

Sheila slapped the paper onto the coffee table.

"You see this entry?" she asked.

Regina leaned closer. "A Level V override."

"Yeah," Sheila said. "And look at the source code."

I leaned over the table.

The source code was a string of numbers and letters — meaningless to most, but not to us after our time in the sublevels.

Regina whispered, "V-PROX 21."

"Exactly," Sheila said. "Maintenance proxy. But here's the weird part."

She pointed to the final column.

User: 0000-STAFF

"A placeholder?" I asked.

Sheila shook her head fiercely. "No. A deletion. A deliberate deletion. Someone erased the user ID associated with that credential."

"When?" Regina asked.

Sheila pointed to the timestamp.

"Seven minutes," she whispered, "after we left the sublevels."

My pulse tightened in my throat.

Regina whispered, "They were watching us."

Sheila nodded. "Not only watching us. Cleaning up after us."

A cold silence settled in the room.

"Who's deleting logs?" Regina asked quietly.

Sheila looked at us with an expression I'd only seen once before — the night she told me her husband wasn't coming home.

"I don't know," she said. "But it's someone who has access to both the security wing *and* maintenance oversight."

Regina whispered, "So... the mole."

Sheila nodded.

"And here's the part that bothers me," she added. "This deletion wasn't subtle. It was sloppy. Like someone wanted us to see it."

I swallowed. "A warning."

"No," she said. "A message."

Regina tensed. "Saying what?"

Sheila met her eyes.

"Saying: We know where you were. We know you saw us. And we're not hiding anymore."

A chill rolled through me.

"And there's more," Sheila added, pulling out another sheet.

Regina leaned closer. "What's that?"

"A campus security memo," Sheila said. "Issued today."

I took the paper.

My stomach dropped.

It wasn't addressed to the campus.

It wasn't addressed to faculty.

It was addressed to:

SELECT PERSONNEL — OBSERVATION LIST

Regina whispered, "Is that... a surveillance roster?"

Sheila nodded grimly.

I scanned the list.

Most names meant nothing to me. A few I recognized — senior researchers, certain administrators, one or two professors rumored to have handled classified contracts in the '90s.

Then I saw it.

Near the bottom.

My name.

Myers, Garth — priority observation.

Regina inhaled sharply.

Sheila whispered, "You're being monitored, Garth."

My throat tightened. "By who?"

She pointed to the memo header.

It wasn't UW-Madison security.

It wasn't facilities.

It wasn't any campus department.

It was:

FEDERAL LIAISON – MIDWEST BIOLOGICAL RISK DIVISION

Regina covered her mouth with her hand.

Sheila's voice trembled. "They're not hiding at all anymore."

I felt suddenly exposed — like the walls of my home were transparent.

Regina moved instinctively closer to me. "Garth... we need to go somewhere safe."

"No," Sheila said. "No safe place inside the university system. They're tied into everything."

"What do we do?" Regina asked.

"We look at the next name below Garth's," Sheila said.

I did.

And my breath caught.

Thomas, Robert — secondary observation.

Regina whispered, "Oh God..."

"They're watching Bob," Sheila said quietly. "Which means they know he talked to you. Or they know he's connected."

My pulse hammered.

Regina grabbed my hand. "He's in danger."

I nodded slowly.

Sheila sat on the arm of the couch, rubbing her forehead. "This is what I came here to tell you. Someone saw you leave the church. Someone followed you or checked logs. They know who you went to."

"How could they track that?" Regina asked.

"License plates," Sheila said. "Traffic cams. Or someone physically watching."

I exhaled slowly. "Which one?"

Sheila pointed to my front window.

"Look outside."

I walked to the window and pulled the curtain aside.

Parked across the street was a dark sedan.

The kind with no plates.

No stickers.

No parking permit.

Just a silhouette inside.

Watching.

Waiting.

I let the curtain fall.

"They're here," I said.

Regina's voice tightened. "For you?"

"For all of us," Sheila said. "And for Bob."

I turned back to them.

"We don't panic," I said.

Regina swallowed hard. "Then what?"

"We go to the tunnel entrance," I said. "The one Bob marked."

"Tonight?" Sheila asked.

"Yes," I said. "Because if they're watching us... they think we're scared."

Regina exhaled. "And we're not?"

"Oh, we're terrified," I said. "But tonight, we use that."

Sheila nodded slowly. "Okay. I'll bring the badge codes. You bring the map."

"And I," Regina said softly, "will bring the courage."

Sheila grabbed her coat. "three idiots walking straight into hell."

"Not idiots," I said.

"Then what?" she asked.

I looked at the map.

"The only people left who know what's actually happening beneath this university."

Regina whispered, "And what is that, exactly?"

I folded the map and slipped it into my jacket.

"The past," I said, "is waking up."

The night settled over Lake Monona like a sheet of black glass — still, opaque, deceptively calm. Lights from the opposite shore shimmered across the water in long, unbroken reflections that looked too smooth, too perfect, as if nothing beneath the surface could possibly stir.

Which was a lie.

The lake was never still.

Not really.

Not since the basement.

Regina, Sheila, and I walked along the narrow path behind my house, flashlights off. We stayed in the shadows cast by skeletal trees, fallen branches crunching quietly under our boots. Behind us, the unmarked sedan still sat across the street — watching.

Regina whispered, "Are you sure they're not following us?"

"No headlights," Sheila murmured. "No movement."

"That doesn't mean they're not watching," Regina said.

"They are," I said. "Which is why we didn't take the road."

Sheila smirked darkly. "Good to know the tunnels under Madison are safer than its streets."

"They aren't safe," I said. "They're just less watched."

Regina wrapped her scarf tighter. "Comforting."

Wind rolled off the lake, carrying the mineral smell of cold water. The map Bob gave us rustled in my pocket like it wanted out.

We approached the first landmark.

A rusted metal fence.

Vines dead from frost.

A long-forgotten "KEEP OUT" sign, its paint faded to ghosts of letters.

"Here," I whispered.

Sheila knelt beside the fence and clipped the lowest section with a pair of cutters she'd stolen from a maintenance closet years ago and never returned. We slipped through one by one.

Beyond the fence lay a stretch of packed earth leading toward the lake.

This was the old service road — the one crews used in the '30s during tunnel construction. Now overgrown. Forgotten. A rumor more than a road.

Sheila checked the map under the moonlight.

"Bob's markings put the tunnel head..." She pivoted to her right.

"...over there."

Regina frowned. "By those rocks?"

"Yes," Sheila said. "Under them."

We crossed the clearing.

The rocks weren't natural; they never were. They were remnants of old construction piles — concrete chunks, rebar, stones that didn't match shoreline geology. A fake cluster meant to look like debris.

I knelt beside the largest slab.

There it was.

A faint seam.

A line too straight to be natural.

Regina crouched next to me, breath visible in the cold. "They sealed the tunnel with this slab?"

"Not sealed," I said. "Covered. It's not structural. Just disguised."

Sheila brushed away dead leaves, exposing a rusted metal ring embedded in the surface.

"A handle," she whispered.

"Help me," I said.

We gripped and pulled.

The slab didn't budge.

We tried again — harder.

A groan rose from beneath the stone, unsettled and tortured — like something deep underneath was shifting in annoyance.

"Again," I said.

We pulled.

The slab moved.

Barely.

A crack opened — a thin, black line just wide enough to let a sliver of cold air escape.

Regina staggered back, clutching her throat. "Garth—"

"Yeah," I whispered.

The air coming out wasn't just cold.

It was alive.

A faint, rhythmic pulse emanated from the crack — like breathing.

Slow.

Wet.

Deep.

Sheila's voice trembled. "Okay. That's... that's not normal."

"No," I said. "It's not."

Regina's hand shook as she pointed to the opening. "This air... it feels like the basement."

"Older," I whispered. "Much older."

We braced ourselves and pulled again.

The slab shifted a full inch.

The crack widened.

A wave of cold air rolled out, carrying a smell of silt and old water. The taste of metal. The memory of drowning.

My chest tightened.

FLASHBACK — Underwater

Pressure.

Hands clawing.

Light disappearing.

A shape beside me, unmoving — pale — drifting like it was part of the lake.

I kicked.

Screamed.

The lake filled my mouth.

The shape tilted its head.

As if listening.

BACK

Regina touched my arm. "Garth... hey. Come back."

I blinked, breath shaky. "I'm fine."

"You're not," she whispered. "But you're here. Stay here."

I nodded.

Sheila stepped forward. "We can open it enough to look inside."

"No," I said.

"Why not?"

"Because something opened it already."

Sheila froze. "What?"

I pointed.

Inside the crack — deeper now that the slab had shifted — fresh scratches lined the inner concrete. Not made by tools. The grooves were uneven, organic, claw-like.

Regina's breath caught. "That's not from erosion."

"No," I whispered.

Sheila swallowed hard. "Those scratches... they're on the inside."

Silence.

A silence deeper than any lake.

"We stop," Regina whispered. "We should stop."

But Sheila leaned closer to the crack. "Something moved through here. Recently."

"Recently?" I asked.

She nodded. "These marks are fresh. No algae yet."

I crouched, peering inside.

The darkness was absolute.

But in that absolute darkness... something faint glimmered.

Not a reflection.

Not light from above.

A faint phosphorescent shimmer deep within the tunnel.

It pulsed.

Regina whispered, "Do you see that?"

"Yes," I said.

Sheila's voice shook. "Is it water?"

"No," I said. "Water doesn't pulse like that."

We watched the shimmer.

It grew brighter.

Then dimmer.

Then bright again.

Regina grabbed my sleeve, voice tightening. "Garth... something's coming."

"No," I whispered. "Something's breathing."

Sheila backed up. "Okay. We've seen enough. We need to go. Now."

For once, Regina didn't argue.

We moved quickly, retreating from the slab.

Halfway across the clearing, I glanced back—

And froze.

Because a new crack had formed.

Not the one we made.

A second crack.

A thinner line running down the slab's side.

Spreading.

Slowly.

As if pressure from inside was pushing outward.

Regina followed my gaze.

"Oh God."

Sheila grabbed our arms. "Move. Move now."

We reached the tree line when the sound hit us—

A deep

wet

groan

from beneath the slab.

The earth shuddered beneath our feet.

A wave of disturbed lake-wind rolled across the clearing, carrying the smell of ancient water and something else—

Something rotten.

Something breathing.

Something remembering.

We didn't run.

We didn't scream.

We left quietly, fast, deliberate — the way prey leaves a clearing when they know the predator hasn't decided whether it's hungry yet.

When my house came into view again, the unmarked sedan was gone.

Regina whispered, "Do you think they left?"

"No," I said, scanning the street. "They repositioned."

Sheila looked up the block. "There."

A second vehicle — same model, different color — now sat two houses down.

Regina's voice thinned. "They're watching the tunnel entrance. Not your house."

She was right.

The sedan wasn't angled toward my house.

It was angled toward the lake path.

Sheila whispered, "They know where we went."

My jaw tightened. "No. They know where we *would* go."

Regina swallowed. "Meaning... the tunnel matters."

Sheila nodded. "Meaning it's the origin point."

We approached the house.

Before I reached the door, I felt something underfoot.

A piece of paper.

Folded twice.

Weighted with a small pebble.

I picked it up.

Same stationery as the previous note.

Same watermark.

Same careful handwriting.

Three new words:

WE

SEE

YOU

Regina closed her eyes.

Sheila whispered, "They're escalating."

I folded the note once, twice, tucked it into my coat.

"No," I said softly.

"They're warning us."

Regina met my eyes. "Garth... should we stop?"

I shook my head.

"Whatever is in that tunnel," I said, "isn't contained anymore."

Sheila looked back toward the lake, expression grim. "And whatever is in that basement isn't either."

Regina placed a hand over her heart. "Then what do we do?"

"We prepare," I said.

"For what?" she whispered.

I stared at the tunnel's direction, the crack, the pulse beneath the earth.

"For the thing," I whispered, "that's trying to come up."

Regina sat at the far end of my living room couch, elbows on her knees, face buried in her hands. She wasn't crying — not exactly. Her breath moved in short, uneven bursts, the kind that come right before the tears start or right after they stop.

Sheila paced behind her like a general in a war room, muttering fragments of thoughts to herself — "not sealed," "maintenance logs," "override codes," "not human — *not human—*"

I stood at the window, staring at the second unmarked sedan down the street. It hadn't left. It hadn't shifted. It just idled in the dark, the silhouette inside unmoving.

Watching.

Always watching.

Regina finally spoke. Her voice was so thin it almost wasn't there.

"Garth... what if we can't save her?"

Her words hit harder than anything in the tunnels.

I turned. "Regina—"

She lifted her head. Her eyes were rimmed red, pupils wide, shaking.

"No, listen," she said. "I'm serious. What if we're too late? What if whatever you saw down there... whatever that man was... what if that's what happens to people who get exposed to that enzyme?"

Sheila stopped pacing.

Her breath caught.

She looked away.

I crossed the room and knelt in front of Regina.

"Regina," I said softly. "Lila is not gone."

Her voice trembled. "You don't know that."

"No," I said. "I don't. But I know she wasn't just taken. She was *hidden*. Which means she's important to them."

Sheila sat beside her. "You think they're keeping her alive."

"I think," I said, "that whatever adapted down there is more valuable alive than dead. And if she triggered the reactivation of the old lab, then she's the only witness who can expose it."

Regina's breath stuttered again. "But what if she— what if she's already—"

She couldn't finish.

I took her hands.

"Regina," I said. "Look at me."

Slowly, painfully, she did.

"This isn't just a search," I said. "It's an intervention."

"For who?" she whispered.

"For the truth," I said. "And for Lila."

She didn't cry.

She didn't break.

She just nodded — once, small, desperate.

Sheila exhaled and stood. "Okay. Enough spiraling. We have data to process."

Regina wiped her face. "What did you find?"

Sheila pulled out a folder from her coat and dropped it on the coffee table.

"This," she said, "is every maintenance worker currently employed by UW–Madison."

The list was long.

Too long.

Regina scanned the names. "We're looking for someone with clearance access?"

"No," I said. "Someone without clearance."

Sheila nodded. "The mole wouldn't be someone high-profile. They'd be invisible. Overworked. Underpaid. Someone no one would question crawling around ducts."

She turned a page.

"And someone who hasn't been showing up."

Regina leaned forward. "What do you mean?"

"This," Sheila said, pointing to a red-highlighted line, "is the facilities attendance sheet. One of these workers hasn't clocked in for eight days."

Regina frowned. "Eight days? Wouldn't someone report that?"

"Not if he was the night-shift floater," Sheila said. "No supervisor for half his hours. Mostly independent tasks."

I read the name.

M. Gillen

Regina whispered, "The initial... M."

Sheila nodded grimly. "The same curve we saw under the redacted clearance."

I stared at the name.

"Do we have a photo?" I asked.

Sheila flipped the page.

A grainy badge photo showed a man in his mid-forties. Average build. Tired eyes. Slight slouch. A man who lived in the background of every hallway and no one ever looked at twice.

"Do you recognize him?" Regina asked.

"No," I said.

But Sheila's face changed.

"Sheila?" I asked.

She swallowed. "I've seen him. Not recently. Months ago. Down by the lake access closet in the engineering cluster."

Regina's eyes widened. "What was he doing there?"

Sheila whispered, "He said he was checking moisture seepage. But now—"

We all went still.

"He was listening," I said quietly.

Sheila nodded. "Listening to the water."

Regina's breath caught in her throat. "Then he's..."

"Exposed?" I said.

"Possibly," Sheila whispered.

"And missing," I added.

Another silence.

Regina whispered, "Garth... is he the one we saw in the tunnel?"

I closed my eyes.

The shoulder proportions.

The shifting under the uniform.

The unnatural angle of the head.

The dragging movement.

The listening.

"Yes," I said softly.

Regina covered her mouth. "Oh God."

Sheila sat hard on the armchair. "So our mole... is no longer entirely human."

I nodded.

"And that means," Sheila said, "someone else is controlling the access logs."

"Which means," Regina whispered, "there's a second mole."

A cold rolled through me.

"Or," I said softly, "a handler."

The room fell quiet again.

Then — just as the silence grew unbearable — my phone rang.

Bob.

I answered instantly.

"Bob?"

His voice was strained. Low. Shaking in a way I'd never heard.

"Garth," he whispered, "listen to me carefully."

"Bob, what's wrong?"

"You need to stay inside."

"Why?"

"Because the lake," he whispered, "isn't calm tonight."

My skin prickled.

Regina mouthed, *What is he saying?*

"Bob," I said, "what do you mean?"

"I mean," he said, breath ragged, "I live two blocks from the shore. And I can hear it."

"You can hear the lake?"

"Not the lake," Bob whispered.

"The tunnels."

My pulse hammered. "Bob—"

"It's moving, Garth," he whispered hoarsely. "Something is moving under the water. Something big."

Sheila stood up sharply.

Regina grabbed my arm.

"Bob—" I said.

"Garth," he breathed, "do not go back to the shoreline. I'm telling you—"

His voice cut off.

A muffled thud.

"Bob?" I shouted. "BOB!"

Another sound — like something scraping across the floor.

Not a human movement.

Not a stumble.

A dragging.

A dragging I recognized.

The line went dead.

Regina gasped. "Garth—"

I stood so fast the chair behind me toppled.

Sheila grabbed her coat. "We have to go to him."

"No," I said sharply.

They both froze.

Regina's eyes widened. "What do you mean no?"

"Think," I said. "They're watching us. They followed us to the lake. They know Bob talked to me. They would expect us to run to him."

Sheila swallowed. "Then what do we do?"

I looked down at the map — at the Old Intake Chamber, at the tunnel beneath my feet, at the line winding beneath the city toward the lake.

"We don't run to Bob," I said.

"Then where?" Regina asked.

"We run," I said quietly, "to the place he told us never to go."

Sheila's breath caught. "The tunnel."

I nodded.

"Because whatever took Bob," I said, "came from below."

I grabbed my coat, the map, and a flashlight.

Regina took a shaky breath. "Garth... if we go down there—"

"We might die," I said.

"But if we don't..."

I looked at the lake through the window.

The water rippled.

Once.

Twice.

Then again.

Like something beneath the surface was pushing upward.

"...we might die slower."

Regina squeezed my hand.

Sheila locked the door behind us.

CHAPTER 13

The Cavern Beneath the Lake

Still water hides the deepest hollows.

The shoreline at night was the kind of dark that swallows you if you stare at it too long. No reflection, no sparkle — just a black plane stretching into infinity. Even the air felt different near the lake. Thick. Dense. Holding its breath.

Sheila clicked on her flashlight but kept the beam low. "If they're watching us, headlights will get us spotted."

Regina pulled her coat tighter. "So we walk in the dark?"

"Better than the alternative," I said.

Sheila snorted. "There is no alternative. If we wait until morning, the crack we saw earlier might not be a crack anymore."

Regina swallowed hard. "You think it's expanding?"

"Yes," Sheila said. "And I think whatever's behind it likes to stretch."

We moved off the trail and through the trees. The ground was uneven — roots, rocks, half-frozen patches of earth. My boots sank with each step, but my mind wasn't on footing.

Bob's last words replayed in my head:

"It's moving, Garth... something is moving under the water."

"The tunnels."

"The tunnels."

The wind shifted.

Cold. Sharp. Metallic.

The smell of deep water.

Regina touched my arm. "Hey. Are you okay?"

No.

But that wasn't helpful.

"I'm with you," I said.

"That's not what I asked."

I forced a breath. "I'm functional."

She nodded once — that was enough.

We approached the clearing.

The slab where the crack had formed sat ahead of us like a tombstone for something better left buried. The moonlight hit it just enough to illuminate the seam we'd opened earlier.

Except—

Regina stopped. "Garth."

"I see it," I whispered.

The seam had widened.

Not by inches.

By *feet*.

A jagged slit now ran across the stone like a claw mark gouged in concrete.

Sheila lifted her flashlight higher, despite the risk.

"Holy..."

She stopped before finishing the sentence.

The crack wasn't clean.

It wasn't from pressure.

Or erosion.

Or even blunt force.

It was from something *pulling outward*.

Regina covered her mouth. "It pushed its way up."

"No," I said quietly. "It didn't just push."

I crouched and ran my fingers along the edge of the concrete. It wasn't crumbling. It was sheared. Like something incredibly strong had slid its way out through the smallest opening.

"It *slid*," I said. "Not broke. Not shattered."

Sheila whispered, "Like it was growing out of the tunnel."

The ground beneath my feet pulsed.

Just once.

Regina stepped back instantly. "Did you feel that?"

I nodded. "It wasn't seismic."

"It came from below," Sheila said.

"And from something alive," I added.

A beat of silence.

Then a sound rose from the crack.

Soft.

Wet.

Not quite a breath.

Not quite a voice.

Something in between.

Regina grabbed my sleeve. "Garth... we can't go down there."

"We have to."

Sheila exhaled shakily. "Because of Bob."

I nodded.

"And because whatever came out," I said, "isn't done."

We positioned ourselves at the edge of the crack. The moonlight revealed a sloping passage beyond — concrete walls streaked with moisture, rusted rebar exposed like ribs. It angled downward toward blackness.

"Flashlights on," I said.

Sheila clipped hers to her jacket. Regina held hers in both hands like a weapon she hoped she wouldn't have to use.

Before descending, I kneeled beside the crack.

Regina lowered her voice. "What are you doing?"

"Listening."

The tunnel emitted a faint hum.

Not mechanical.

Not airflow.

Biological.

Steady.

Rhythmic.

Responsive.

Sheila whispered, "Garth..."

I leaned closer.

The hum changed.

Shifted.

As if responding to my proximity.

Like the lake had ears.

I stood abruptly.

"Let's go."

Regina hesitated. "One last chance to back out."

Sheila snorted. "Back out? Honey, the only way out is through."

I lowered myself into the opening.

The temperature dropped instantly — not the chilly cold of winter air, but the deep cold of buried stone. The kind of cold that creeps through bone and settles in memory.

My hands touched wet concrete.

Silt.

There was silt on the walls.

Regina followed behind me. Sheila came last, sealing our only exit by pulling the slab partially closed so no one would see fresh movement from the outside.

The crack sealed us into the dark.

Our flashlights cut narrow cones of light into the corridor. The walls glistened. Drops of water fell from above, hitting the ground with small, rhythmic splashes.

Regina whispered, "This doesn't look like campus infrastructure."

"It isn't," I said. "It's older."

Sheila ran her fingers along an old metal bracket embedded in the wall. "These are from the original intake system. Pre–World War II."

Regina pointed at the far wall. "And what's that?"

We moved closer.

A faded stencil.

Barely legible.

OIC — No Unauthorized Water Flow

Regina touched the lettering. "OIC... Old Intake Chamber."

"And we're walking straight toward it," I said.

We pressed on.

The tunnel narrowed. The ceiling lowered. The floor sloped gently downward. Water trickled along the sides, forming thin rivulets that sparkled under our lights.

The hum grew louder.

Stronger.

More like a heartbeat now.

But wrong.

Off.

Regina whispered, "It's organic."

"Yes."

Sheila shivered. "It's... *adaptive.*"

"Yes."

We continued until the tunnel widened into a small chamber — an anteroom, maybe ten feet by ten feet, with rusted ladders leading nowhere and pipes capped with metal seals decades old.

Three things immediately stood out.

1. The Graffiti

A single phrase scrawled in chalk:

DON'T LISTEN TO THE WATER

Sheila inhaled sharply. "That's new chalk. It's not weathered."

"Recent," I said.

"Recent?" Regina echoed. "By who?"

Sheila whispered, "By someone who didn't make it out."

2. The Footprints

A set of footprints in the silt on the floor.

Human-shaped.

Then distorted.

Toes lengthened.

Heel pressure uneven.

Regina covered her mouth.

Sheila crouched beside them. "These... these changed over time."

"Yes," I said quietly.

"These belong to a man turning into something else."

3. The Wet Coat

A piece of clothing hung from a pipe — soaked, torn, clinging like shed skin.

Regina reached for it but stopped. "Is that—"

She didn't finish.

I didn't let her.

"Yes," I said. "It's M. Gillen's jacket."

Sheila whispered, "Then he made it this far."

"And then changed," I said.

"And then went deeper," Sheila whispered.

Regina turned toward me slowly. "Garth... this is getting worse than we thought."

I nodded. "And we're not at the bottom yet."

The hum stopped.

Completely.

Silence pooled around us, heavy and suffocating.

Regina whispered, "Why did it stop?"

I held up a hand.

The silence thickened.

For a full ten seconds, the tunnel was still as death.

Then—

A deep, slow exhalation

rolled through the corridor.

Not wind.

Not pressure.

A *breath.*

A breath from something enormous.

Something ancient.

Something alive.

Regina staggered back, hand on her chest. "Oh my God—"

Sheila grabbed my arm. "Garth, that's not possible—"

"It is," I whispered.

Because I had heard it before.

Not here.

Not in a tunnel.

In the lake.

The day I almost drowned as a boy.

That same exhale beneath the water.

That same presence brushing my leg.

Sheila's voice quivered. "That wasn't structural. That wasn't water movement."

"No," I said.

"It was—"

"Yes," I said softly. "Breathing."

The tunnel grew colder.

A second breath came.

Closer.

Deeper.

Almost curious.

Regina pressed her back against the wall. "Garth... we need to leave. Right now."

"We can't," I said.

"Why not?" she whispered.

"Because Bob might be down there."

Regina's eyes filled with fear. "Garth—"

Suddenly, a noise echoed from deeper in the tunnel.

Not a breath.

Not a hum.

A **wet footstep.**

Then another.

Getting closer.

Slow.

Dragging.

Changing.

Sheila whispered, "Oh God... it's him."

Another footstep.

Closer.

Regina grabbed my arm, knuckles white.

"Garth..." she whispered, "we are not alone."

The footsteps echoed again — soft, wet, irregular. The kind of sound that comes from a foot no longer shaped the way a foot should be.

Regina pressed closer to me, her breathing shallow. Sheila raised her flashlight, though her hand trembled hard enough that the beam jittered against the tunnel wall.

Another footstep.

And with it... a low scraping, like skin sliding over concrete.

I whispered, "Turn off the lights."

Sheila didn't hesitate. Regina shakily clicked hers off. I switched mine last.

Darkness swallowed us instantly.

Not normal darkness — not the absence of light.

This darkness had weight.

It settled on our shoulders, pressed against our faces, thick as damp soil. When I inhaled, I could swear I tasted lake water.

Regina whispered, "Oh God, Garth..."

I touched her arm. "Stay against the wall. Both of you."

Something shifted farther down the tunnel — a heavy shape dragging itself forward. The wet scrape repeated. Then something else: a faint, irregular clicking sound, like bone tapping bone.

A breath — not human — drifted down the tunnel.

Warm.

Moist.

Shuddering.

And close.

Sheila whispered, "It's right there."

She was right.

I could hear it — the slight hitch in its inhalations, as though whatever lungs it possessed weren't made for air anymore. Its breath rattled. The sound reverberated through the tunnel walls, making the stone itself feel alive.

Regina covered her mouth, trying not to make a sound.

The footsteps grew louder, then... paused.

A moment of silence stretched out so long it felt predatory.

Then—

Something sniffed the air.

A long, deliberate inhale.

Searching.

Scenting.

Sheila clutched my sleeve. "It's trying to find us."

The inhale came again — louder this time, wet and dragging. It seemed to fill the tunnel. Then it choked, as if the breath caught in a throat not meant for breathing.

Then it exhaled in a long, shuddering hiss.

And moved closer.

We stayed perfectly still.

Something brushed the concrete near my boot.

Not a hand.

Not a foot.

Something soft.

Flexible.

Like a strand of kelp sliding across the floor.

Regina tensed. "Garth... something touched me."

I nudged her hand gently. "Stay still."

The creature—Gillen, or what was left of him—shuffled closer. I could hear the subtle shift of his joints, the dragging of a limb, the soft slap of water pooling beneath him.

Then—

A faint glow bloomed in the dark.

Not bright.

Not steady.

A bioluminescent shimmer.

Soft. Blue-green. Pulsing slowly.

It revealed only fragments — enough to twist the imagination.

A shoulder, hunched and swollen.

A length of skin stretched too thin.

Something twitching beneath it.

The outline of a head… tilted in the wrong direction.

Regina shook silently beside me.

The glow intensified for a moment — enough to illuminate the wall.

Marks.

Claw–like.

Long.

Parallel.

The same ones at the crack above.

Sheila whispered, her voice barely audible, "It's metamorphosing."

Another glow pulsed.

Then dimmed.

Then pulsed again.

The rhythm matched the breath.

The creature was breathing light.

Regina's breath hitched audibly.

The creature froze.

It turned slightly.

Toward her.

Toward us.

I felt the air shift.

I whispered, "Move on my count."

Sheila squeezed my elbow once—ready.

Regina squeezed my wrist—terrified but present.

The bioluminescent shimmer flickered, the creature adjusting its posture, leaning toward our wall.

"Three..."

The creature sniffed the air again.

"Two..."

A wet step forward.

"One—"

RUN.

We bolted.

The tunnel exploded behind us in a wet, ragged roar — the creature lunging, its limbs slapping the ground in grotesque, rapid patterns.

Regina stumbled but righted herself. Sheila grabbed her arm and yanked her forward.

Behind us, I heard the creature's claws rake the wall, sending stone shards scattering.

The tunnel ahead narrowed into a passage we'd seen on Bob's map. A sharp turn. A choke point.

"Left!" I shouted.

Regina and Sheila turned.

The creature slammed into the wall at the bend, the impact shuddering through the concrete.

Regina gasped. "It's fast—"

"Go!" I barked.

We sprinted deeper.

The tunnel constricted into a slit barely wide enough for one person. Rusted pipes lined the ceiling. Water dripped steadily from somewhere unseen.

The space forced us into a single file.

Sheila in front.

Regina next.

Me last.

Behind me, scraping echoed again.

Regina whispered, "Garth—he's coming."

I risked a look.

The bioluminescent glow seeped into the narrow passage, revealing a distorted silhouette trying to force its way through.

It got one shoulder inside.

The concrete groaned.

It pushed harder.

A wet, cracking sound—its bones shifting beneath the skin.

Regina whimpered. "It's reshaping itself."

Sheila hissed, "Move!"

We forced ourselves deeper, scraping against the rough walls.

Behind us—

CRACK.

The creature forced another joint through the gap, the glow bathing the tunnel in sickly blue light.

Then—

A voice.

Not a human voice.

A sound that could have once been speech before anatomy betrayed it:

"—hhhhh—arrr—tttt—"

Regina froze.

It said my name.

I grabbed her wrist. "Keep going. Don't listen."

The creature repeated it.

Closer.

Clearer.

"—garrrrth—"

My blood went cold.

Not because it spoke.

But because the tone was familiar.

Regina whispered, "Garth... that wasn't Gillen."

I tightened my grip on her arm.

She was right.

It wasn't Gillen's voice.

It was **Bob's.**

I choked. "No. No—"

Another breath from the creature — long, rattling, mimicking a human inhale.

Then, clearer:

"—help me—"

Regina shook her head violently. "That's not him. Garth, that's not him."

But it sounded like him.

Broken.

Distorted.

Begging.

"—help me—"

The light flickered.

A hand — if it could still be called that — reached through the slit.

Swollen.

Pale.

Webbed.

It scraped the wall.

Searching.

I tasted bile.

"Move," I whispered hoarsely. "Now."

We pushed forward into the narrowing tunnel.

The creature roared, slamming its shoulder into the stone, trying to widen the gap.

The sound was deafening — like stone cracking under a hammer.

Sheila shouted, "Faster!"

Regina stumbled again. I caught her. Pushed her.

The roar came again — this time with unmistakable agony.

And unmistakable rage.

Another breath behind us — deep, furious.

And close.

The passage pinched to a point where we had to slide sideways to pass.

"Sheila—through!" I ordered.

She squeezed through.

Regina followed.

I was halfway in when the creature slammed into the gap again.

Concrete buckled.

Dust rained down.

The wall shifted.

I gritted my teeth and shoved forward.

Behind me, the creature screamed — not human, not animal — a primal underwater wail that shook the entire corridor.

The gap widened.

The creature's head forced through.

Half human.

Half something else.

And its eyes—

Glowing faintly.

Blue-green.

Like the lake itself.

The same eyes I saw underwater the day I almost drowned.

Its voice gurgled:

"—garrrrth—"

I pushed with everything I had.

The concrete scraped my shoulders raw.

My ribs squeezed.

My breath caught.

The creature reached.

Its fingers brushed my boot.

Then—

I burst through the slit.

Sheila grabbed my jacket and yanked me forward.

Regina slammed her flashlight against the wall, sending a shower of concrete shards down onto the creature's reaching hand.

A howl — furious, wounded — echoed through the passage.

I collapsed beside them, gasping.

Behind us, the creature thrashed against the narrowing squeeze, unable to follow further.

For now.

Sheila whispered, "We need to keep moving."

Regina pulled me upright. "Garth. Look at me. You with us?"

I swallowed hard. "Yes."

"Then we go," she said. "Before it finds another way around."

I nodded.

We pushed forward into the darkness.

But before the tunnel curved, I heard one last sound from behind us:

A single breath.

Not of anger.

Not of exhaustion.

A breath of recognition.

Like something in the dark remembered me.

The tunnel twisted downward in a slow spiral, each curve tightening like a corkscrew into the earth. The air grew colder the deeper we went — not with the crisp cold of winter, but with a *wet cold*, the kind that comes from stone saturated for decades.

Our footsteps echoed softly. Water dripped steadily from pipes overhead. The smell of algae thickened until it clung to the back of my throat.

Regina stayed close behind me, her hand occasionally brushing my jacket. Sheila led, her flashlight beam cutting the darkness ahead with surgical precision.

None of us spoke.

Not because we didn't have things to say.

But because the tunnel's air felt like it was listening.

The creature's voice still echoed in my skull.

—garrrrth—

I tried to shake it off. Tried to replace it with rational thought, engineering logic, enzyme kinetics, anything measurable or numeric.

But the sound was rooted too deeply.

Not because it called my name.

Because it used **Bob's** voice.

Regina whispered, barely audible, "It wasn't him."

"I know," I said quietly.

"Do you?" she whispered again.

I didn't answer.

Because I wasn't sure.

After several hundred feet, the tunnel opened into a wider passage. The floor here was uneven and slick, coated in a thin biofilm that shimmered faintly under the flashlight beams.

Sheila crouched. "This sheen wasn't here earlier in the tunnel."

I nodded. "It's new growth."

"New as in weeks? Days?"

I touched the wall lightly.

The film recoiled.

Not visibly — but I felt it. An almost imperceptible tension, like static under skin.

"Hours," I said.

Regina's breath caught. "This is spreading faster."

"It's reacting to something," I said.

Sheila stood. "Reacting to us?"

"No," I whispered. "To light."

I shined my flashlight on the wall directly.

The bioluminescent sheen pulsed.

Slowly.

Deliberately.

Like a jellyfish responding to tidal change.

Regina shivered. "It's... beautiful."

"It's adaptive," I said.

"Isn't that the same thing?" she asked.

"No," I said. "Beautiful things don't try to consume their environment."

We continued down the corridor.

The hum we heard earlier grew louder, but not in volume — in presence. It vibrated lightly through the soles of our boots, through the walls, through the air. It sounded almost like the low frequency of an engine.

Except engines don't pulse with the rhythm of a heartbeat.

Sheila whispered, "We're getting close."

Regina pointed ahead. "Look."

A faint glow — not flashlight, not reflection — seeped around the curve.

Blue-green.

Lake water green.

The same color that had glimmered on the creature.

I swallowed. "The Old Intake Chamber."

We moved slower now, as though the air itself were thickening. My pulse thudded in my ears.

The hum deepened.

Then —

The sound of water.

Not dripping.

Flowing.

A steady, mechanical rush.

Regina whispered, "We're near the intake."

Sheila slowed her steps. "Brace yourselves."

We stepped into an enormous stone room.

Circular.

Twenty, maybe thirty feet across.

Ceiling low enough to touch.

The walls were slick with condensation. Faint, ancient arches marked old engineering designs, water erosion tracing their curves.

But three things dominated the chamber.

1. The Water Pool

At the far end of the room, a pool of dark water roiled. Not violently — but steadily, as though water fed into it from underneath.

It wasn't lake water.

Not exactly.

It was darker.

Thicker.

And bioluminescent webs flickered beneath the surface.

"What is that?" Regina whispered.

"The lake," I said. "Before the lake reaches the lake."

2. The Federal Equipment

Against the right-hand wall sat a metal crate — stainless steel, stamped with:

MBRD — FEDERAL BIOHAZARD PROTOCOL

Midwest Biological Risk Division.

Same acronym from the surveillance memo.

Sheila stepped toward it. "It's been down here recently. No dust."

"Recently?" Regina asked.

Sheila pointed to scuff marks. "Within days."

The crate was open.

Inside:

- Empty vials

- Biohazard bags

- A set of waders

- A long-handled collection net

- Three sealed plastic cylinders labeled:

SPECIMEN – LAKE MONONA SUB-BASIN INTAKE

6R-BL13-D

Regina whispered, "No..."

Sheila touched the edge of the crate. "They're collecting from the water source."

I shook my head. "Not collecting."

Regina looked at me. "Then what?"

"Feeding it," I said.

They stared.

"The enzyme," I explained. "The original catalyst. They're reintroducing something back into the water."

Regina's voice cracked. "Why?"

"For growth," I said. "For adaptation."

Sheila whispered, "For evolution."

I nodded. "Yes."

3. The Footprints

Silt coated the chamber floor. And across it — clear as ink — were tracks.

Human footprints.

Then warped.

Then deeper, wider.

Ending at the water's edge.

Regina whispered, "He went into the pool."

Sheila's voice trembled. "Gillen?"

"Gillen," I said softly. "And maybe others."

Regina whirled toward me. "Garth. What if Lila—"

"No," I said sharply.

Too sharply.

But the thought hit me hard:

If the enzyme adapted Gillen...

Who else had been exposed?

Who else had been brought down here?

The hum deepened.

The water rippled.

And something beneath the surface shifted.

A mass.

A shape.

A movement too large to be a person.

Regina stepped back. "What was that?"

Sheila reached for my arm. "Garth... that's not Gillen."

"No," I whispered. "It's older."

The water stirred again.

A long shadow drifted across the bioluminescent threads beneath the surface.

My breath froze.

FLASHBACK — Drowning

The lake's hand on my ankle.

The pull.

The cold.

The shape beside me opening one eye — blue-green — before drifting upward.

A voice underwater.

Impossible.

Calling my name.

BACK

Regina's voice trembled. "Garth. You're pale."

"I remember this," I whispered. "I remember this exact sound."

"The water?" she asked.

"No," I said. "The breathing."

The water rippled outward, gentle but deliberate.

Sheila took a step back. "We need to leave."

But I stepped forward.

Closer to the pool.

The hum resonated in my chest, like a memory vibrating through bone.

Regina grabbed my sleeve. "Garth, stop."

But I couldn't.

I crouched at the pool's edge.

The water pulsed with a faint glow — blue-green threads swirling in rhythm.

And then—

Something rose toward the surface.

Slow.

Massive.

Not a creature.

Not a person.

A silhouette of something expanding beneath the water.

Not fully formed.

Not fully... decided.

The surface tension rippled outward.

Regina whispered, "Oh my God.."

Sheila backed toward the exit. "Garth, we're out of time. We need to—"

Then—

A human hand broke the surface.

Pale.

Webbed.

Veined with blue-green filaments.

It grasped the stone edge.

Another hand emerged beside it.

Then—

A face.

Part human.

Part something else.

Eyes closed.

Skin translucent.

Features rearranged by adaptation.

Regina gasped, stumbling back. "It's—it's—"

Sheila froze. "That's not him. That's not Gillen. That's—"

The figure opened its eyes.

Blue-green.

Glowing softly.

It whispered:

"—garth—"

Regina screamed.

Sheila pulled her away.

I couldn't move.

Because the voice —

the whisper —

the tone —

Was unmistakable.

Broken.

Distorted.

Drowned.

It was **Bob's voice.**

For a moment, time froze.

Not metaphorically.

Not emotionally.

It **froze** — like the air itself locked into place.

Regina's scream cut short, stuck in her throat.

Sheila's flashlight beam hung mid-shake, a trembling white slash across the chamber.

And I...

I couldn't breathe.

Bob — or what had once been Bob — clung to the stone edge of the pool, his fingers pale and webbed, tendons too visible under skin stretched too thin. His face floated just above the surface, water streaming down features twisted by something not built for human anatomy.

His eyes — glowing blue-green — fixed on me.

They were not angry.

Not in pain.

Not pleading.

They were **aware**.

He whispered again, barely audible through a throat that had forgotten how to shape sound:

"—garrrrth—"

The voice cracked halfway through, sinking into a wet, bubbling gurgle.

Regina's grip on my arm tightened until her nails cut skin. "Garth—Garth we have to go—"

Sheila stumbled backward, pointing her flashlight toward the exit. "He's not... he's not alive, Garth. He's *not Bob.*"

But she said it like she didn't believe herself.

I stepped toward the pool.

Regina yanked harder. "Garth, NO."

I didn't stop.

I couldn't.

Because something in those glowing eyes wasn't alien.

It was *recognition*.

The creature—Bob—shifted, rising higher from the water. His shoulders breached the surface, revealing skin that shimmered with bioluminescent threads and patches of what looked like translucent membrane. Veins pulsed rhythmically with blue-green light.

He opened his mouth, trying to form words.

"—st... t-top...—"

Regina gasped. "Oh my God..."

Sheila shook her head violently. "That's not communication. That's mimicry."

Bob's head tilted.

The motion was wrong.

Too fluid.

Too soft.

His jaw slackened as though his bones weren't fully fused.

"—st... op...—"

A shudder rolled through the water.

Then —

The room's hum heightened.

Deepened.

Shifted.

And something **else** rose beneath him.

A massive silhouette.

A shape so large it warped the light beneath the surface.

Not humanoid.

Not even symmetrical.

A shifting mass of tendrils, membrane, bone-like ridges — a thing still deciding what form to take.

Sheila's breath hitched.

Regina whispered, voice thin with terror, "He's... not alone."

Bob — or the remnant of him — flinched, like a puppet tugged by invisible strings.

His head jerked toward the deeper water.

His fingers dug into the stone.

He was being **pulled back.**

Into the mass below.

Into the lake's deeper intelligence.

My stomach twisted. "Bob—"

He locked onto me again.

His eyes flickered.

Once.

Twice.

Then, impossibly —

the blue-green glow dimmed.

Revealing, beneath it, a flicker of *brown.*

His original eye color.

Regina inhaled sharply. "Garth... he's still in there."

Sheila whispered, "How? HOW?"

Bob raised one hand — slow, trembling, tendons spasming under forced movement.

"—sto... p...—"

I stepped closer.

"Stop what, Bob?" I whispered. "What do you want me to stop?"

His jaw shuddered open.

"—down...—"

Down?

Regina shook her head. "Garth, that means nothing. He's not—"

But it wasn't just "down."

I saw it now.

He wasn't warning us to stop going down.

He was warning us to **stop what was coming up.**

Bob's hand slipped on the stone edge.

The water behind him churned.

Something vast moved beneath the surface, bending the light with its mass.

Bob clawed at the stone again, trying to hold himself above water.

Trying to resist whatever was pulling him back under.

He trembled violently.

And whispered again:

"—st... o... p... it—"

Then he convulsed.

Veins glowed bright blue.

His skin rippled as if something underneath pressed outward.

Regina sobbed, "Garth, please—PLEASE—we have to RUN."

She was right.

But I couldn't move.

Because Bob — my sponsor, my anchor, the man who kept me sober, who kept me alive — was being dragged under by something we still didn't understand.

I reached out toward him.

His hand latched onto mine.

Too strong.

Too cold.

"Garth!" Sheila screamed. "Let go!"

But he held tight.

His grip was desperate.

Pleading.

Human.

His half-formed voice rasped:

"—burn... it—"

And then—

The lake spoke.

Not metaphorically.

Not figuratively.

The water beneath him released a sound so deep it bypassed my ears and struck behind my sternum — a vibration that felt like a command.

Regina staggered. "What—what was that?"

Sheila clapped her hands to her ears. "It's a signal. A *biological signal.*"

The water surged upward, engulfing Bob.

He lunged forward — not to attack, not to pull me in.

But to **give me something.**

A metal object — slick, cold, tiny — landed in my palm before he disappeared beneath the surface.

Then—

He was gone.

Dragged down in a violent whirl of bioluminescent water as the mass beneath him withdrew like a giant organism retracting into darkness.

The hum faded.

The chamber stilled.

Only then did I realize Regina was sobbing into my shoulder and Sheila was shaking violently beside us.

I opened my hand.

A small metal disc sat in my palm.

Old.

Rust-edged.

Worn.

A badge.

Sheila whispered, "What is that?"

I turned it over.

Stamped on the back:

UW–MADISON

RESEARCH ACCESS

TIER OMEGA

– DRUITT, E.

Regina covered her mouth.

Sheila's breath hitched, "Druitt... the original project lead..."

"He hid this," I said softly. "In the lab. In the tunnels. And Bob found it."

Regina stared at the water, her voice shaking. "He... he wasn't trying to pull you in."

"No," I whispered. "He was trying to give me the truth."

The water rippled gently, almost peacefully now.

But beneath it —

deeper —

something pulsed.

Something enormous.

Sheila stepped backward. "We need to get out. We need to go RIGHT NOW."

Regina grabbed my arm. "Garth—"

I closed my hand around the badge.

And nodded.

"Yes."

But before we turned to leave, the chamber echoed with a sound that froze all three of us mid-step.

A new breath.

Not Bob's.

Not the creature's.

A different inhale — smaller, faster.

Human.

From behind us.

From somewhere in the chamber's dark recess.

Regina whispered, trembling:

"Garth... someone else is down here."

CHAPTER 14

The Voice in the Dark

Darkness speaks in the tone we fear most.

The second breath came again — shallow, uneven, human.

Not the monstrous, membrane-rattling inhale from the pool.

Not the watery gurgle of whatever Bob had become.

This was *different*.

Close.

Frighteningly close.

Regina tightened her grip on my forearm. Sheila raised her flashlight but kept the beam pointed down so its glow wouldn't advertise our position.

We turned slowly.

The far side of the chamber was a pocket of darkness — a recess in the stone wall we hadn't noticed when Bob emerged from the water. The faint bioluminescent sheen from the pool cast moving shadows across it, like the wall itself breathed along with the lake.

The breathing sound came again.

Regina whispered, "Garth... someone's hiding there."

Sheila clenched her jaw. "Or something is."

"No," I said softly. "This is human."

"How can you tell?" she whispered.

"Because they're *trying not to breathe*."

A third breath — quick, shaky, like someone terrified of making noise. Someone pressed flat against the stone. Someone who had been here the whole time, watching the creature rise and the lake swell and Bob be pulled under.

Someone who never moved, even when we ran, shouted, or nearly died.

Sheila whispered, "Should we call out?"

"No," I said instantly.

"Oh good," she muttered. "I was hoping you'd say that."

Regina stepped closer to me. "Then what do we do?"

"We flush them out," I whispered.

"How?" she asked.

"By giving them a choice."

I flipped on my flashlight and pointed it toward the recess — not directly, but close enough that it illuminated the chamber around it.

"I know you're there," I said, keeping my voice steady. "We're not here to hurt you."

A small gasp — barely audible.

Sheila hissed, "There."

Regina whispered, "Garth... who could be alive down here?"

A figure shifted in the darkness.

Just a shape at first — hunched, trembling, limbs pulled tight against the body. Too small to be Gillen. Too small to be anyone like him.

A person stepped forward.

Slowly.

Flinching when my flashlight brightened.

Regina gasped. "Oh God..."

It was a **girl.**

Maybe nineteen. Maybe twenty.

Young.

Gaunt.

Eyes wide and hollowed by terror.

Hair matted.

Clothes damp and torn.

Feet bare and raw.

She looked like she'd been hiding in the dark for days—maybe longer.

She didn't speak.

She just stared at the water, body trembling violently.

Regina stepped forward, voice cracking. "Honey... are you hurt?"

The girl flinched at the sound, backing against the wall like a wounded animal expecting a blow.

Sheila lowered her flashlight. "We're not here to hurt you. We're getting out of here."

The girl shook her head frantically.

I raised a calming hand. "It's okay."

She stared at my face. My voice. Her chest rose and fell in ragged breaths.

Then—

Very faintly—

She whispered:

"Don't go near the water..."

Her voice was papery, dehydrated, ruined by panic.

Regina covered her mouth. "Garth—"

But the girl wasn't finished.

"...it listens."

My skin prickled. "What listens?"

She shook her head violently, eyes widening with fresh terror.

"The lake," she whispered. "The lake hears everything."

Sheila whispered, "Jesus..."

The girl stumbled toward us — desperately — reaching out with shaking hands.

She was real.

Human.

Alive.

Regina moved to support her. "We're going to take you out of here, okay? You're safe now."

But the girl recoiled immediately.

"No... no safe," she whispered. "They're coming."

Regina froze. "Who?"

She pressed both hands to her ears, trembling. "The ones from up top."

Sheila frowned. "Federal?"

The girl nodded.

My throat tightened. "How do you know that?"

Her eyes filled with tears.

"They brought me."

Regina whispered, "Brought you... here?"

She nodded again.

Slow. Shameful.

"They said I'd be safe," she whispered. "They said it would just be a test."

My heart hammered.

Regina's breath caught.

Sheila swore under her breath.

"What test?" Regina whispered.

The girl pointed to the pool, hand shaking violently.

"That," she said. "The experiment in the water."

Sheila dropped to her knees beside her. "Do you know its name? The project number?"

The girl wiped her eyes with a filthy sleeve. "They called it the... the Renewal."

My stomach dropped.

Regina whispered, "Garth—"

I nodded.

That was the unofficial name of **6R-BL13**.

Renewal.

The resurrection enzyme.

The project older than our entire careers.

The project that disappeared from records.

The project that killed Druitt.

Sheila's voice shook. "What did they do to you?"

The girl wrapped her arms tightly around herself. "They made me go in."

"In...?" Regina couldn't finish.

The girl's voice broke. "Into the water."

Regina's knees gave out.

Sheila caught her.

"You were part of the experiment," I said softly.

The girl nodded, tears streaking her dirt-covered cheeks. "I wasn't supposed to come out."

Her entire body trembled.

"But I did," she whispered. "And then... they locked me down here."

Regina rushed forward. "How long have you been here?"

The girl didn't answer.

She didn't need to.

Her sunken cheeks, cracked lips, trembling limbs...

the claustrophobic terror in her eyes...

Sheila whispered, "Days. She's been down here for days."

The girl's gaze darted back toward the pool.

"They're not done," she whispered. "It's waking up."

Regina closed her eyes. "What is?"

The girl trembled harder.

"The thing they fed," she whispered. "The thing they broke."

A chill rolled down my spine. "What broke?"

She pointed to the pool again.

"The water," she whispered. "It's angry."

Sheila looked at me. "Garth... we have to get her out now."

"Yes," I said. "All of us."

But the girl grabbed my sleeve.

Hard.

Her voice dropped to a hiss:

"No. Not up. *Down.*"

I froze.

Regina whispered, "Down where?"

She pointed to a narrow, half-submerged tunnel on the opposite side of the chamber — a tunnel we'd missed while staring at Bob.

A tunnel that led deeper.

"Down to where it came from," the girl whispered. "Down to where they hid the first one."

Silence.

Thick.

Horrified.

Sheila whispered, "What 'first one'?"

The girl met my eyes.

And whispered:

"The one that drowned you."

The floor tilted beneath me.

Regina grabbed my arm, eyes wide. "Garth—she knows."

The girl nodded weakly.

"I've seen it," she whispered. "In the water. In the walls. In the dreams the lake makes you dream."

My voice cracked. "How?"

She closed her eyes.

"The lake remembers," she whispered. "And it showed me everything."

Sheila's face drained of color. "Garth... we can't stay here."

I nodded slowly.

But before we could move—

The water in the pool shifted.

Once.

Twice.

A low hum pulsed through the chamber — deeper than before.

The girl clung to me.

"It knows you're here," she whispered. "Both of you."

"Both?" Regina asked, terrified.

The girl nodded at me.

Then at Regina.

Her voice trembled:

"You're connected. You both touched it once."

Regina froze. "I—what?"

The girl pointed at Regina's jacket collar.

At a faint mark I'd never noticed.

A thin white scar.

Regina stepped back like she'd been burned. "No... no, no—I've never—"

But she didn't finish.

Because the water rippled again.

Harder.

A deep shape moved beneath it.

And the hum became a whisper — a vibration in the air.

A sound that felt like a word.

A call.

The girl shrieked and covered her ears. "It's coming—IT'S COMING—"

Sheila grabbed her. "We need to MOVE—"

Regina pulled me, voice near panic. "Garth, please—PLEASE—"

But I didn't hear her.

Because the whisper from the water grew clearer.

Deep.

Ragged.

Calling to me.

Calling my name.

And Regina's.

"Gaaarth... Reeeginaaaa..."

The girl screamed.

Something massive rose beneath the surface.

The water **heaved** upward.

Not a splash.

Not a ripple.

A *heave*—like the lake itself was inhaling through a mouth we couldn't see.

The bioluminescent threads under the surface spiraled violently.

Light fractured.

The hum crackled into something alive, something aware, something emerging.

The girl clamped her hands over her ears, screaming, "IT KNOWS—IT KNOWS—"

Regina yanked my arm. "Garth, MOVE—"

Sheila pulled the girl toward the semi-dry side of the chamber. "Go! GO!"

But my legs wouldn't move.

241

Because the voice rising from the water—

that deep, broken whisper calling my name—

"Gaaaaarth…"

—I had heard it once before.

In Lake Monona.

Age nine.

The day I nearly drowned.

My lungs constricted.

The girl shrieked, "DON'T LISTEN—DON'T LISTEN—IT'S NOT A VOICE IT'S A *PULL*—"

Regina grabbed my face with both hands, forcing me to look at her.

"Garth. Look at me. Stay HERE. Stay. Here. With. Me."

The chamber trembled.

A wave surged upward from the pool—

slapping against the stone lip, spraying us with cold droplets that stung like needles.

Sheila shouted, "BACK! GET BACK—"

The girl convulsed. "It's angry—it wants you—it wants BOTH—"

The water split.

A shape rose.

Not Bob.

Not Gillen.

Not anything human.

A mass of tendrils and bone-like ridges writhed beneath the surface, struggling upward, like a creature trying to force its way through a too-small opening.

A large segment of it—

smooth, pale, impossibly organic—

came within inches of breaching the surface.

The girl screamed, "DON'T LET IT TOUCH YOU—IF IT TOUCHES YOU IT MARKS YOU—"

I stumbled back instinctively.

Regina dragged me toward the tunnel entrance. "We're leaving—NOW—"

But the girl ripped free of Sheila's grip.

"No! Not up—DOWN! DOWN—NOW!"

Sheila hissed, "We're not going *deeper* into this nightmare!"

The girl pointed to the submerged tunnel on the opposite side of the chamber—the narrow stone throat partially hidden behind residue and shadow.

Her voice cracked into a sob.

"That's the only way out. Up there—" she pointed to the crack we entered from— "they're waiting. They ALWAYS wait there."

I froze.

The federal sedan.

The surveillance shifts.

The cleaning of badge logs.

The abandoned crate.

They *knew* about the creature—

and they weren't here to stop it.

They were here to contain witnesses.

Regina's breath caught. "You think they'll block us from leaving?"

243

The girl nodded so fast she nearly fell. "They NEED you down here. You heard it—they KNOW you. They've BEEN watching you. You're part of it now."

My hands trembled.

Sheila whispered, "Oh hell… they're not following us. They're *corralling* us."

Another surge from the pool.

Another whisper.

"Gaaaaaarth…"

The chamber vibrated.

The waterline rose.

The girl grabbed my sleeve with both hands, desperate clawing nails.

"You have to go DOWN—*down is the only safe direction*—down is the way AWAY from it—down is where the first one is—down is where it can't reach."

Regina shook her head violently. "That doesn't make any sense. How can down be safer than up?"

The girl turned on her with a look so feral and haunted Regina actually stepped back.

"Because the lake goes UP," she whispered.

"And the tunnels go DOWN."

A silence fell over us.

Not peaceful.

Not calm.

A suspended moment—

like the stillness between lightning and thunder.

Then—

THE WATER EXPLODED.

A huge mass slammed upward, sending a shockwave across the chamber floor.

Bioluminescent threads cracked like lightning.

Cold spray blinded us.

I grabbed Regina and shielded her as debris scattered.

Sheila grabbed the girl.

We all staggered back.

A tendril—thick, muscular, dripping with viscous blue fluid—whipped across the surface like a striking eel.

It hit the stone edge with a sickening crack, leaving a glowing smear that pulsed like a heartbeat.

Regina screamed. "Garth—LOOK!"

The smear was *spreading*.

Like the biofilm earlier.

Only faster.

Hungry.

I ripped her away before it reached her boots.

The girl screamed again, voice breaking:

"GO! DOWN! NOW BEFORE IT FINDS THE OPENING—"

Regina shook her head. "We can't just follow her—we don't know who she is—"

The girl turned to us, tears streaming down her face, raw desperation in every inch of her.

"My name is **Lila**."

Everything inside me collapsed.

Regina screamed.

Sheila gasped.

My pulse detonated inside my skull.

"No," Regina whispered, knees buckling. "No... no, no, no—"

But the girl—

the trembling, starved, terrified girl—

looked straight into Regina's eyes.

"I'm Lila."

Regina collapsed to her knees.

I grabbed her before she hit the stone.

She choked out, "Lila—Lila—oh my God—LILA—"

The girl sobbed, shaking.

Sheila stared between them, speechless for the first time since I met her. "How—how is she—how did she survive—"

"My God..." Regina whispered, reaching toward her. "Lila... what did they do to you?"

The girl—Lila—flinched but didn't pull away entirely.

"They told me it was a study. They told me it was just water."

She trembled.

"They lied."

Another surge from the pool slammed into the chamber wall.

I shouted, "WE HAVE TO MOVE NOW—"

But Regina was still frozen, devastated, trying to reconcile the twisted, starved girl in front of her with the brilliant assistant she loved.

"Lila..." she whispered again. "Lila, you were *gone.* We thought—"

"I wasn't gone," Lila whispered. "I was **taken.**"

Sheila grabbed her arm. "Then you need to tell us how to get out."

Lila shook her head violently. "There is no *out*. Not up. Not back. Only down." She pointed to the submerged tunnel. "That leads to the original intake chamber. The real one. The one they built this whole place over."

Regina grabbed Lila's face between both hands. "Please—just tell me—were you exposed?"

Lila's voice broke into a sob.

"They put me in the water."

My stomach twisted.

Regina screamed silently, mouth open but no sound coming out.

"What did it do to you?" she whispered.

Lila choked out one word.

"*Showed me.*"

Before any of us could react—

The lake beneath the chamber **spoke** again.

Not a whisper.

Not a voice.

A *command*.

A pulse that rippled through the stone under us, shaking the chamber from floor to ceiling.

The water surged, reaching the lip of the pool—

Then spilling onto the floor.

A flood.

Cold.

Luminous.

Creeping toward us like living liquid.

Lila grabbed Regina's hand. "GO—DOWN—NOW—BEFORE IT REACHES YOU—"

Sheila swung her light toward the submerged tunnel entrance.

The stone beneath it was cracked.

Dark water pooled around its mouth.

A faint, cold draft drifted from the passage—like a breath from the ancient earth.

"Garth!" Sheila shouted. "MOVE!"

I grabbed Regina's arm.

She grabbed Lila's.

The water hit my boot and stung like acid.

I jerked forward.

The pain sharp.

Electric.

Wrong.

The lake had changed.

We sprinted across the chamber, skidding in the silt.

The water surged behind us, faster than a flood, almost intelligent.

Lila dove into the narrow downward tunnel first.

Sheila followed.

I forced Regina in after them, then slid in last.

Before the lake could swallow my legs—

The chamber behind us erupted in a sound that made my bones vibrate.

Something enormous hit the surface.

Something rising.

Something ancient.

Something that remembered me.

As we crawled downward into the pitch-black, the water roaring behind us like a creature in pursuit, Lila whispered back through the dark:

"Don't stop.

Don't look back.

And whatever you do…

don't listen when it calls your name."

The downward tunnel tightened almost immediately, forcing us onto hands and knees. The ceiling dropped low enough to scrape our backs. Slime-coated walls pressed in from both sides. The air was wet, metallic, and suffocating.

Lila led, her thin frame moving quickly despite exhaustion and weeks—maybe months— of starvation and terror. Sheila followed close behind her, crawling fast, muttering fragments of prayers she probably didn't know she remembered. Regina crawled ahead of me, breath coming in panicked bursts. I took the rear, the only position I trusted to keep anything behind us from dragging her away.

Behind me—

the chamber roared.

A sound like a wave collapsing.

Then a sound like **something** collapsing.

The tunnel vibrated. Loose stone rained down.

Regina gasped. "Garth—!"

"I'm here," I said. "Keep moving."

"But— the sound—"

"I heard it. Move."

Behind me something slapped the chamber floor—

like a massive, wet limb.

The bioluminescent glow chased us briefly, reflecting inside the tunnel like some kind of underwater lightning. Then it receded as the creature slipped fully into the chamber above.

The girl—Lila—whispered furiously through the dark:

"Don't slow down. It knows where we are."

Regina crawled faster.

Sheila whispered, "Are there any other exits?"

"No," Lila said. "But it can't come down here. It's too big. That's why they sealed the mouth of the upper tunnel."

Regina looked over her shoulder. "Then why does this tunnel exist?"

Lila's voice cracked.

"Because the first one still lives down here."

The tunnel suddenly felt even smaller.

Sheila whispered, "The first... what?"

Lila kept crawling. "The first subject. The one they tested in the '90s. The one Druitt reported dead."

I froze.

Regina whispered, "They didn't kill the first subject?"

"No," Lila said. "They didn't kill it. They just locked it down here."

Sheila crawled faster. "And you want us to go *toward* it?"

"Better toward it than toward the lake," Lila said.

Another vibration shook the tunnel.

The lake wanted us back.

A minute of crawling passed in panicked silence before Regina whispered, "Lila... how are you still alive?"

The girl's voice was hollow. "I'm not sure I am."

Regina nearly sobbed. "What does that mean?"

Lila crawled faster, refusing to look back. "It showed me things. The water. It... changed something in me. I don't know how to explain it. I feel sick, and weak, and wrong, but—"

She paused.

Then whispered a word that cut through me like a blade:

"—connected."

Regina froze. "Connected to WHAT?"

Lila didn't speak.

She just crawled.

I whispered, "The lake."

Lila flinched.

Sheila whispered, terrified, "It talks to her."

"No," Lila said. "Not words. It doesn't *speak*. It... knows."

I felt something tight coil in my gut.

The same sensation I had as a boy beneath the water.

The same presence.

The same awareness.

Regina whispered, "Lila, what did it show you?"

Lila finally stopped crawling.

Only for a moment.

Only to speak:

"It showed me you."

Regina's breath hitched violently. "Me?"

"And him," Lila said quietly, nodding toward me.

My blood froze.

"Why us?" Regina whispered.

"Because you both touched it," Lila said.

Regina stiffened. "No—no, I—"

"Yes," Lila said. "The scar on your neck—"

Regina reached up instinctively.

Her fingers brushed the faint white line.

Barely noticeable.

A mark I'd never known the origin of.

Sheila whispered, "Regina... what happened?"

Regina's voice shook. "Nothing. I—I must have gotten it as a kid—I don't even remember—"

Lila crawled closer to her.

"You don't remember because it was the lake."

Regina stopped breathing.

"It touched you once," Lila whispered. "And it never forgot."

My heart slid into my stomach.

Regina stared at Lila like she was looking at a ghost.

"No," she whispered. "No, no, no, that's not possible—"

The tunnel ceiling dropped even lower. We had to flatten our chests against the stone to move forward.

My voice came out hoarse. "Lila... what exactly did the lake show you?"

Lila's breath brushed the stone ahead.

"That you were both marked."

A silence settled around us so complete it seemed to swallow the air.

Regina whispered, "Garth was—yes—but I—"

"Not the drowning," Lila said. "Something else."

Regina gulped violently. "Then *what?*"

Lila turned her head. In the faint trickle of light from Sheila's flashlight, her face looked older than she should have been—aged by fear, hunger, and everything the lake had taken from her.

"It didn't just show me what it did," she whispered.

"It showed me what it's waiting for."

We crawled onward, the air growing colder and thicker. The biofilm changed texture. It became denser, sticky in places, almost pulsing.

Sheila muttered, "This isn't natural."

Nothing here was.

Lila shivered. "It's awake because you're here."

"Why?" I whispered.

Lila didn't answer.

Regina whispered, "Lila... what did it show you about Garth?"

Lila hesitated—

then she spoke.

"It showed me the day he drowned."

Ice prickled my spine.

Regina whispered, "Lila... how? You weren't even born."

She shook her head. "The lake remembers everything. It can replay any memory it touches."

My throat constricted. "What did it show you?"

Lila's voice softened into something almost mournful.

"It showed me a boy sinking. Kicking. Fighting. It showed me something beside him... watching him."

Sheila swallowed. "Watching?"

"Yes," Lila said. "Not attacking. Not saving. Just watching. Like it was deciding."

I stopped crawling.

My entire body locked.

Regina whispered, voice trembling, "Deciding *what?*"

Lila crawled back close enough to touch my arm.

"Whether to keep you."

Every root, every nerve, every rational piece of me retracted into cold.

"And it didn't," Lila said. "It let you go."

Regina's voice broke. "Garth—"

I couldn't speak.

"It let you go," Lila repeated. "But it didn't forget you. It put something in you. A piece. A thread."

A thousand impossible memories surged in my skull—

the pressure,

the lightlessness,

the sense of a presence,

something brushing my ankle,

something choosing.

Sheila whispered, horrified, "Garth... you're—"

"No," I snapped. "No."

Regina grabbed my hand, her touch grounding enough to force breath back into my lungs.

Lila whispered, "It marked you. And it marked her."

Regina froze.

Sheila whispered, "Regina... the scar—"

Regina shook her head violently. "No! No! I don't remember—"

"That's the point," Lila said. "You aren't supposed to."

Regina's hands shook uncontrollably. "Garth—what is she saying?"

I forced myself forward again, my voice a raspy growl.

"We don't know yet."

Behind us, the tunnel shook with another pulse.

Lila whispered, "It's following."

Regina screamed, "How? It's too big!"

"No," Lila said. "Not the creature. The lake."

The idea hit like ice water on raw nerves.

Sheila hissed, "What do you mean the *lake* is following us?"

"The water," Lila whispered. "It's coming down the cracks. Through the walls. Through the old intake lines."

As if on cue—

a trickle of cold water seeped between the stones behind us.

Bioluminescent specks floated inside it.

Alive.

Aware.

Regina scrambled. "Oh God—Garth—GO—GO!"

We crawled faster.

The tunnel dipped sharply downward—almost a slide. We skidded, scraped knuckles and knees, slammed into stone.

Lila shouted, "THIS WAY—THE FIRST CHAMBER IS CLOSE—"

"What's in it?" Sheila shouted.

Lila didn't answer.

Because the water behind us surged again, flooding the upper passage, chasing us with a roar like a tidal heartbeat.

We scrambled down the slope, tumbling into a wider chamber—

And froze.

Because at the far end—

in the center of the stone floor—

something lay curled like a sleeping titan.

Something enormous.

Pale.

Veined with blue and green light.

Something shaped like a human—

but far too large.

Far too wrong.

Regina whispered, "Is that... the first subject?"

Lila shook her head slowly.

"No," she whispered.

"That's the *original host.*"

The chamber was wider than the last, but lower. A half-dome of ancient stone pressed down from above, slick with condensation that reflected faint blue-green light. A single drainage grate in the floor trickled water downward—steady, rhythmic, like a pulse.

And lying at the center—

The Original Host.

A mass of pale tissue coiled into a vaguely fetal shape, as if something human had once curled to sleep here and slowly grown into something else. Veins pulsed faintly beneath translucent skin. Its ribs—or what resembled ribs—expanded and contracted in the slow rhythm of a creature dreaming underwater.

Its size was impossible to comprehend.

Seven feet long?

Eight?

More?

Regina gripped my arm so hard I felt her nails through my jacket.

Sheila whispered hoarsely, "Is that alive?"

"Yes," Lila said.

Not fearful. Not reverent.

Flat. Knowing.

Regina trembled. "What... what does it *do*?"

Lila stared at the swollen shape.

"It remembers."

Sheila's jaw clenched. "Remembers what? Its previous form?"

"No," Lila said softly. "It remembers *everyone*. Everyone who's touched the water. Everyone who's heard it. Everyone the enzyme marked. Everyone it decided to let go."

A cold slid under my skin.

Regina whispered, "Lila... why is this down here?"

The girl shook her head. "It never died. They said it did, but it didn't. They tried to kill it. They tried to burn it, freeze it, suffocate it."

She hugged herself tightly, shivering as though the memory weren't hers, but absorbed.

"But it kept adapting. The lake's water—whatever is in it—kept it alive."

Sheila knelt beside some old metal debris—rusted equipment smashed against the wall.

"Druitt was here," she whispered. "He must've discovered this thing."

Regina whispered, "And they silenced him."

Lila nodded. "They sealed the chamber and told everyone the experiment was discontinued."

I stepped closer to the Original Host.

Every instinct screamed to stop.

But something else—

something deeper—

pulled me forward.

A memory flickered.

Dark water.

A pale shape moving beside me.

A single glowing eye opening in the deep...

My breath shuddered.

Regina grabbed my sleeve.

"Garth. Don't."

But the Host's breathing shifted.

Slow.

Heavy.

Deliberate.

The chamber vibrated.

Sheila hissed, "It's waking up—"

"No," Lila whispered. "It's listening."

Another long, deep inhale from the Host—

a cavernous sound, like air pulled through lungs far too old.

Regina choked out, "Lila… what does it want?"

Lila's voice cracked.

"You."

Regina's face went white. "Why me?"

"Because you were marked."

Regina shook her head violently. "No—NO—I don't even remember the lake touching me—"

"That doesn't matter," Lila whispered. "It remembers."

The Host exhaled—

a sound like water sliding over stone.

The air thickened.

Glistened.

Sheila stood quickly, grabbing both our arms. "We need to leave. We need to go NOW—"

But Lila shook her head.

"Not yet," she whispered.

She stepped toward the Host.

Regina lunged to stop her. "LILA—NO—"

But Lila didn't stop.

She moved slowly, as if in a trance, arms trembling, eyes locked on the pulsing mass in front of her.

"Lila!" Regina screamed. "Please—please no—come back—"

The girl stopped inches from the Host.

She placed her hand on its surface.

Regina dropped to her knees.

Sheila froze.

I couldn't breathe.

The bioluminescent veins beneath the Host's skin brightened under her touch.

Lila shuddered—

once

twice

then went utterly still.

Her voice came out hollow.

"It's showing me again..."

Regina reached toward her, fingers shaking uncontrollably. "Lila, come back. Please."

"It's showing me what it showed you," Lila whispered.

Regina recoiled. "What?"

Lila turned her head just enough to look at Regina.

"You don't remember because you blocked it out."

Regina's breath hitched violently.

"What... what did I block out?"

Lila whispered slowly, painfully:

"You were in the water once, too."

Regina shook her head. "No—no—no I wasn't, I wasn't, I—"

"You were," Lila whispered. "It touched you when you were little. Just like it touched him."

She pointed at me.

My stomach twisted.

Regina covered her face, sobbing into her palms. "Garth—tell her she's wrong—tell her—"

But I couldn't.

Because ever since the tunnels, I'd been seeing flashes in my mind—

not of my own drowning,

but of a second scene.

A girl on a shoreline.

Falling.

Water closing over her head.

Hands pulling her up.

A scar on her neck.

Regina whispered, broken, "Garth... I don't remember—"

"It's not your memory," Lila said. "It's the lake's."

I helped Regina up. Her legs were barely holding her.

She whispered, "Why us? Why is it tied to us?"

The Host inhaled again.

The chamber shook with the weight of its breath.

Then—

The lake spoke.

Not words.

Not voice.

A *presence* exploded through the chamber, through our skulls, through our ribs, through every memory we didn't want to revisit.

A call.

A longing.

A command.

All three of us collapsed.

Regina screamed.

Sheila clutched her temples.

I fell to a knee, vision blurring.

Lila didn't scream.

She whispered, "It's telling you the same thing it told me."

Regina sobbed, "What is it saying?!"

Lila looked at each of us through tears of terror and awe.

"It wants you to come back."

The Host shifted—

a ripple of life under its pale membrane.

The water from above began seeping through cracks, sliding down the walls.

The chamber temperature dropped.

The air thickened.

The bioluminescent veins pulsed faster—

thump

thump

thump

—like a heartbeat syncing with ours.

Lila stumbled back toward us.

"It remembers you."

She pointed at Regina.

"It wants you."

She pointed at me.

"And it wants you."

Then at Sheila.

Sheila's face twisted. "ME? Why me?! I've never been in the damn lake—"

Lila swallowed.

"It doesn't just remember the marked."

Sheila blinked, horrified. "Then what—"

"It remembers the ones who investigate," Lila whispered. "The ones who look too closely. The ones who uncover the old paths."

The Host exhaled sharply.

The water behind us surged.

The lake's presence flooded our minds—

COME

BACK

Regina collapsed fully.

Sheila screamed.

I clutched the wall, fighting the sensation pulling at the edges of my consciousness—

the same pull I felt as a boy underwater.

Warm.

Cold.

Final.

Lila grabbed my collar, face inches from mine.

"You can't let it take you," she whispered. "Either of you."

I gritted my teeth. "How do we stop it?"

She shook her head.

"You don't stop it," she whispered.

"You outrun it."

The Host shifted violently—

a tendril tearing free from the membrane, slapping the floor with a crack.

Regina screamed, "Garth—PLEASE—"

Lila pointed to a narrow fracture behind the Host.

A downward crack in the stone.

A deeper tunnel.

"The federal agents don't know about that one," she said. "It's older than their maps. Older than the tunnels. Older than everything down here."

"Where does it go?" Sheila shouted.

Lila's face blanched.

"Below the lake," she whispered. "To the cavern."

"What cavern?" Regina cried.

"The one the Host came from."

The water surged behind us.

The Host's tendrils slapped the stone, reaching outward.

The lake's presence screamed inside our skulls—

COME

BACK

COME

BACK

Lila grabbed Regina with one hand and Sheila with the other.

"MOVE—NOW—DOWN THERE—BEFORE IT WAKES—"

I grabbed the three of them and forced us toward the crack.

Behind us—

the Host screamed.

Regina sobbed.

Sheila cursed.

Lila trembled violently.

I looked back once.

The Host's glowing eyes—

two huge, lidless pools of blue-green light—

opened for the first time.

And saw us.

It whispered one word:

"RETURN."

Then the chamber exploded into motion.

And the four of us plunged into the darkness below.

ACT III

The Depths Reveal Their Dead

The truth rises like something pulled from deep water—

slow, heavy, and forever changed by the dark it came from.

CHAPTER 15

The Cavern Beneath Everything

Every world rests on a hollow—only some of us hear it echo.

The stone throat we dropped through had no right to exist.

It wasn't carved, or blasted, or engineered — it was **grown**, like something underground had pushed upward through the limestone, cracking it in long, rib-like seams. The air shifted the deeper we descended. The cold changed from lake-cold to cave-cold, damp and ancient. Lila slid ahead of us with an instinctive familiarity, as though she'd been here a thousand times in her nightmares.

Regina shivered so hard her teeth clicked. Sheila swore under her breath each time her injured ankle brushed a jagged rock. I stayed behind them, watching the tunnel's mouth above slowly shrink to a slice of darkness.

Somewhere up there, the Original Host screamed again.

The sound traveled down the stone like a shudder, vibrating through our spines. Regina grabbed my arm on instinct. I felt her whole body tremble.

"It can't fit down here," Sheila panted. "It's too damn big, right? Tell me it's too big."

"It's too big," I said.

It was probably a lie.

Lila didn't pause. "Keep moving. The water's finding cracks."

I turned.

She was right.

Thin, glowing threads — bioluminescent veins in the runoff — began sliding down the stone behind us like rivers of liquid nerve.

Regina's breath caught. "Garth—"

"Don't touch it," I said. "Move."

We reached a ledge where the tunnel dropped into a cavern so massive I couldn't see the opposite wall.

Sheila shined her flashlight downward.

"Nope," she whispered. "Absolutely not."

268

The beam never reached the bottom — the darkness below swallowed it like ink.

A thin rusted ladder clung to the stone wall, bolted decades ago, now corroded into a metallic skeleton. It descended into the abyss and disappeared into the dark.

Lila began climbing.

Regina grabbed her wrist. "Wait — wait! Lila, you need to rest. You're exhausted."

Lila blinked at Regina — eyes sunken, face streaked with cave dust — then shook her head.

"If we rest," she whispered, "it'll find us."

Sheila muttered, "Love this."

I motioned Regina ahead of me. "I'll go last."

"Why?" Regina whispered.

"So if something follows—"

I didn't finish.

She knew.

Her hand lingered on my sleeve before she stepped onto the ladder.

The ladder creaked beneath our combined weight. Rust flaked like scabs. Some rungs were half-melted by the bioluminescent growth. A few were missing entirely. The air thinned — colder, heavier, threaded with a smell like wet stone and old metal.

Halfway down, the cavern walls came into view, streaked with black mineral deposits and veins of something faintly glowing — like the walls were alive with old light.

Regina gasped. "Garth... look."

I looked.

Embedded in the stone were bits of corroded equipment — a metal bracket, a rusted cot frame, an oxygen tank from the 1970s.

Sheila touched one through the bars of the ladder. "This was an installation. People lived here."

"Researchers," I said.

Lila didn't look back. "Druitt's team. Before the federal ones."

Regina's voice cracked. "They lived down here?"

"They didn't have a choice," Lila whispered.

The ladder ended on a narrow platform of natural stone. Below it... another fall into deeper dark.

But on this ledge, someone had once carved out a small encampment.

A cluster of metal shelves.

A rusted desk.

A single overturned cot.

A smashed lantern.

And a wall covered in chalk markings.

Regina lifted her light. "What is that?"

Lila stepped toward it reverently. "Warnings."

I joined her.

The wall was covered in hastily written sentences, some smeared by moisture, some scratched so deeply into the stone that fingernails must have split to make them.

THE WATER DOES NOT FORGET

THE FIRST HOST BREATHES BELOW

DO NOT DREAM AT THE EDGE OF THE POOL

LIGHT AWAKENS IT

THE MARKED MUST NOT RETURN

Sheila swallowed. "Marked. As in—"

270

Lila nodded.

Regina's hand flew to her scar.

I wanted to reach for her but froze when Lila whispered:

"That's why it responded to you."

Regina shook her head, breath shaking. "If I was marked... if something happened when I was a child... why don't I remember?"

Lila stepped close.

"Because the lake learned how to erase."

I felt Regina's knees weaken. I caught her.

She whispered, "Garth, I'm going to be sick."

I held her until the shaking passed.

Then Sheila tested the far end of the ledge. "There's another path," she said, pointing to a narrow fissure that dipped downward. "It leads deeper."

Regina whispered, "Why is everything deeper?"

Lila answered softly. "Because everything the lake hides sinks."

We took the fissure, crawling sideways through stone so tight it squeezed our ribs. The air changed again — denser, humid, threaded with the faint metallic taste that haunted the tunnels above.

Then the fissure opened.

Into a hollowed cavern.

And my breath stopped.

A river ran below us — not water, not lake water, but a thick black flow threaded with faint blue-green luminescence. A current without surface. A liquid organism.

"It's a sub-basin vein," Lila whispered. "They never mapped this one."

Regina's voice broke. "Lila... how do you know all this?"

Lila hugged herself. "Because it showed me."

She pointed to the noxious river below.

"I've been in that."

Regina recoiled. "No—"

"It didn't kill me," Lila whispered, emotionless. "It rewrote me."

Sheila stared in horror. "What does that mean — rewrote?"

Lila looked directly at me.

"The enzyme isn't the experiment. We are."

A tremor ran through the cavern. Pebbles scattered. A faint echo traveled up the hollow like a heartbeat answering a heartbeat.

Regina's voice hitched. "Garth... the Original Host... is it connected to this?"

"Yes," Lila whispered. "Everything is."

We followed a narrow footpath along the cavern wall until the river widened into a subterranean lake — smaller than Monona, but still enormous, hidden beneath the city like a buried heart.

At its edge stood a rusted sign half-submerged in silt:

UW–AEC

SUBMERGED RESEARCH NODE 1

1971

The date punched the breath out of me.

"Christ," Sheila muttered. "They were down here fifty years ago."

Lila pointed at the center of the underground lake. "They brought the first subject there."

Regina whispered, "But why—why bring it so deep?"

Lila didn't look at her.

"Because once they made it... they couldn't let it go back up."

The underground lake wasn't still.

It breathed.

Not metaphorically.

The surface rose

fell

rose

fell

like lungs expanding under a thin membrane.

The rhythm was slow.

Patient.

Ancient.

As I stared at it, something cold curled around my spine.

A memory.

A foreign one.

Not mine.

Forced into my skull by the tunnels.

I was underwater again — nine years old — sinking, choking, unable to scream.

A shape moved in the dark beside me.

Huge.

Silent.

Not touching.

Watching.

Then an eye — huge, blue-green — opened inches from my face.

I convulsed. Regina caught me.

"Garth!"

Sheila pulled me upright. "Hey—hey—look at me—stay with us—"

But the cavern wasn't done.

The lake surged once—

a soft, gentle push, like a pulse.

Lila whispered, "It remembers you."

I struggled to breathe. "Why?"

"Because you were the first one it let go," Lila said.

Regina froze. "Let... go? Not escape? Not save?"

Lila shook her head.

"You think it saved him?" she whispered. "No. It *returned* him."

Regina staggered backward like she'd been struck.

The cavern darkened suddenly.

The glow in the underwater lake concentrated in one massive thread.

It rose toward the surface.

Regina grabbed my hand. "Garth... something's waking—"

"No," Lila whispered. "It's not waking."

She pointed at the glowing thread.

"It's remembering."

The thread broke the surface, pulsing in open air.

Then it split.

Revealing a shape beneath the lake floor rising slowly.

A silhouette larger than the Original Host.

Older.

Deeper.

More complete.

The first host.

The primordial one.

The one Druitt tried to kill.

Regina whispered, nearly fainting, "Garth… we need to run—"

Lila's voice cut through the cavern.

"No."

She turned to face us.

Her face wet with tears.

"We need to listen."

The cavern pulsed.

The primordial host's eyes began to open.

And the lake spoke again.

But this time, it wasn't a whisper.

It was a **word**:

"RE—TURN."

The word **RETURN** didn't echo.

It *vibrated.*

Through bone.

Through marrow.

Through the wet stone beneath our palms.

Through the underground lake that pulsed like a living lung.

The cavern swallowed the sound and exhaled it back into us with twice the force.

Regina collapsed against me, both hands over her ears. Sheila stumbled backward, flashlight shaking wildly. Lila remained upright — barely — gripping a rock outcrop as though she'd been bracing for this exact moment.

The word came again, lower this time, rumbling upward like the voice of the earth itself:

"RE—TURN."

Lila whispered hoarsely, "It's not calling you to come back. It's calling you to come *down.*"

Sheila choked, "We're already down."

"Not enough," Lila whispered. "Not for it."

The underground lake shifted, the glowing veins beneath its surface spiraling inward. The water pulled into a slow whirlpool, revealing the rising silhouette.

A body too large to be human.

But not monstrous.

Not like the ones above.

This one was... structured.

Symmetrical.

Shaped with intent.

Regina's voice shook. "What is that?"

Lila stared, jaw trembling. "The First Host."

I swallowed hard. "Druitt's subject."

"No," Lila whispered. "Older."

"Older?" Regina gasped. "How can something be older than—"

"It was here," Lila said, "before they found the enzyme."

My skin crawled.

Before?

The glowing veins beneath the lake coiled upward, revealing more of the silhouette — a massive limb, smooth as carved stone, bioluminescent filaments pulsing inside. Then another limb. A torso. A head.

Human-shaped, but elongated.

As though a person had been stretched to twice their height.

Sheila pointed her trembling flashlight. "That thing was a person?"

Lila nodded slowly. "Once."

Regina choked. "Before... the lake changed it?"

"No." Lila stared into the water. "Before the lake *made* it."

My breath stilled.

Made.

Not infected.

Not mutated.

Not transformed.

Made.

The cavern trembled again. Sediment shook loose from the ceiling. The river vein feeding the underground lake surged, glowing brighter.

The host rose another inch.

Its eyes began to open.

Two massive blue-green irises, round as lanterns, glowing softly through the water.

Regina whimpered, "Garth... Garth, it's looking at us—"

Sheila whispered, "Then move. We have to move. Right now."

But Lila grabbed her wrist.

"No."

Her voice cracked, desperate.

"Listen. You have to listen before you run."

Sheila jerked her hand back. "Why?"

Lila shook. "Because it showed me this moment. Everything leads to this. If you run without knowing—"

The lake surged, interrupting her. Water spilled onto the stone path, licking at our boots in bright blue streaks.

Regina screamed. "It's coming onto the shore—Garth—"

I grabbed her waist and pulled her back. Sheila stumbled into me. Lila remained at the edge, unmoving, staring into the rising mass with a kind of terrified reverence.

"Don't move," Lila whispered. "Don't turn away. Don't run."

Regina sobbed, "Why? Why shouldn't we run?!"

"Because it chooses the ones who run," Lila said. "It follows them. Takes them. Pulls them into the cracks."

Sheila froze mid-step. "What the hell—"

"The tunnels," Lila whispered. "All the missing ones... the ones who panicked... it took them first."

A flash of movement under the lake — a pale hand brushing the underside of the water's surface like a whale brushing a ship.

Lila whispered, "If you run, it knows you're afraid."

"It already knows we're afraid!" Sheila snapped.

"No," Lila said. "There's a difference between fear and *flight*. It hunts the ones who flee."

Regina stared at her, shaking uncontrollably. "Lila... how do you know this? HOW?"

Lila pressed both palms to her temples, tears sliding silently down her face.

278

"Because it showed me the others," she whispered. "It showed me everything."

The cavern dimmed for a moment — the glowing veins beneath the lake darkening like a heartbeat missing a beat.

Then—

The word came again.

Not shouted.

Not screamed.

Not even spoken.

"RE—TURN."

But this time it wasn't in the cavern.

It was inside our heads.

Regina cried out and fell to her knees. Sheila clutched the stone wall. I staggered backward, vision blurring, hearing a muffled roar inside my skull. Lila dropped entirely, hands clutching her head, body convulsing like a struck string.

The host's eyes widened.

Its pupils dilated.

The glow pulsed.

And something inside the cavern unlocked.

A memory.

A sound.

A place.

Not here.

Not underground.

The lake.

Years ago.

A boy sinking.

And not alone.

The breath left my lungs.

I wasn't in the cavern anymore.

I was back in the lake.

Age nine.

Water above me.

The sun refracting into fractured diamonds.

Cold pulling me downward.

Something brushed my ankle.

Something soft.

Something *curious.*

Then a shape beside me.

Long.

Pale.

Slow.

An eye opened beside my face —

the same blue-green, round eye I was seeing now in the cavern.

The host.

It had been beside me.

In the lake.

Watching.

I remembered kicking weakly, my lungs burning, bubbles rising like ghosts. I remembered the moment I stopped fighting. When my arms went limp.

And I remembered the host reaching out —

not grabbing,

not pulling,

but **touching my forehead with one cold finger.**

And then—

My body rushing upward on its own, like the lake had ejected me.

I burst toward the surface.

Someone screaming on shore.

Hands pulling me onto wet sand.

Voices shouting my name.

But none of that mattered.

Because the host hadn't been trying to drown me.

It had been trying to **mark** me.

My breath hitched in the cavern.

Regina grabbed my arm. "Garth—Garth, what did you see—"

I choked, "Me. It was me. I— I didn't escape the lake."

Regina sobbed, "Garth—"

"It *spat me out.*"

The host moved again, lifting itself another few inches above the water.

Its presence exploded into our skulls:

YOU.

Lila screamed. "It's choosing—"

Regina clutched my shirt. "Garth—Garth, it's choosing YOU—"

But the word came again—

this time splitting into multiple meanings:

YOU.

AND.

HER.

Regina froze.

Her face went white.

"Me?" she whispered. "No... no..."

Lila whispered, drenched in grief, "It marked you too. Years ago."

Regina shook her head. "I never—I never—"

"You didn't drown," Lila said. "Not like him. But you fell in once. Just a moment. You touched the filaments."

Regina started crying, shaking uncontrollably.

"I don't remember—"

"You weren't supposed to," Lila said.

The host's eyes widened.

Its chest expanded.

The cavern darkened again.

The water surged.

And a third voice entered our minds.

Not the host.

Not the lake.

Something older.

Deeper.

A primordial echo:

"MERGE."

Sheila gasped. "Oh, HELL no—"

Regina whimpered. "Garth—what does it want?!"

I stared into the glowing eyes.

The answer hit me like ice.

"It wants to reconnect what it marked," I whispered.

Lila nodded slowly through tears. "It wants the two of you. Together."

Regina grabbed my face. "Garth—don't let it—please—don't let it—"

The water rose another inch.

The host leaned forward.

The lake pulsed violently beneath it.

Sheila screamed, "RUN!"

Lila shouted, "DON'T!"

Regina sobbed, "Garth, PLEASE—"

The cavern floor cracked beneath us.

Water flooded upward in glowing torrents.

The host's arm lifted—

slow, heavy, deliberate—

toward me.

A voice of command:

"REUNIT—"

The cavern exploded into collapse.

The cavern didn't collapse all at once.

It failed **in pulses** — rhythmic, seismic shudders that matched the host's breathing. Each exhale shook loose another layer of ancient limestone. Each inhale pulled the underground river's glow brighter, like the lake itself was inflating beneath us.

Regina screamed as the ground split beneath her boot. I lunged, catching her wrist just before she fell into the glowing water below.

"Garth—don't—LET GO—" she sobbed.

"Not a chance," I growled, pulling her back onto the ledge.

Behind us, Sheila shouted, "MOVE—MOVE NOW—THIS WHOLE CHAMBER'S GIVING WAY!"

The host rose further, water cascading off its pale shoulders like a living waterfall. Its eyes — impossibly large, impossibly human — fixed on us with something like longing.

Lila grabbed Regina's back and shoved her toward a narrow exit fissure. "GO!"

Regina stumbled but obeyed. Sheila followed, limping, nearly falling as a quake knocked her sideways.

I turned to run.

Then the host spoke inside my skull.

No words.

A **feeling**.

A pull.

A thread tightening around my spine.

A familiar hand around a drowning boy's ankle.

YOU.

I staggered, losing balance. The cavern tilted sideways. Water surged upward along the edges like sentient tide.

Lila screamed, "DON'T LOOK AT IT, GARTH—RUN!"

But the host wasn't done.

YOU.

AND.

HER.

Regina's scream fractured.

She slammed into the cavern wall, hands over her ears. Sheila grabbed her arm and dragged her deeper into the exit fissure.

Lila grabbed my shoulders and shook me violently.

"Garth—LISTEN TO ME—if you respond to it, it takes you. That's how it works. That's how it marks you. You have to break the connection!"

"I—can't—"

"You HAVE TO!" she shrieked. "Or it will swallow you and she will FOLLOW YOU INTO IT!"

Her words hit me harder than the cave's collapse.

Regina.

Following me.

Into the water.

I snapped back to myself like a rubber band.

"GO!" I roared.

We sprinted toward the fissure.

Behind us, the cavern's final supports groaned like a dying animal. A fissure tore through the floor, splitting the platform in two.

Blue-green water surged upward.

The host stepped toward us — one massive, slow-motion stride — and the water rose in answer.

The cavern ceiling collapsed.

The exit wasn't a hallway.

It was a slit of eroded stone barely shoulder-wide, plunging downward like a stone esophagus. Regina slipped the moment she entered, tumbling two feet before wedging herself against a curve.

I skidded in after her, catching the back of her jacket to stop her slide.

Sheila followed, cursing with every motion, her flashlight dancing madly over the stone.

Lila came last — and only just made it.

A tidal wave of glowing water slammed into the fissure entrance as she flung herself through. The pressure crushed inward, stone screaming. The fissure sealed behind us with a roar like the entire lake collapsing into a sinkhole.

Regina sobbed uncontrollably against the stone wall. Sheila was shaking, injured ankle bent awkwardly beneath her. Lila lay facedown, gasping, mud streaking her hair.

I looked back.

The entrance was gone.

Not blocked.

Gone.

Buried in a mountain of stone and water.

We were sealed inside the lower tunnels.

Regina crawled into my arms, clinging like she'd fall apart if she let go.

"Garth... I can't do this—I can't—please—please—"

Her whole body shook like she was freezing.

I held her until her breathing slowed, until the tremors lost their violence.

Sheila propped herself upright, grimacing. "We're still alive. Somehow."

Lila wiped her face with the back of her hand. "It's not done."

Regina's voice cracked. "What... what does it want?"

Lila swallowed.

"It wants its marked ones to come back."

Regina stared at her, horrified.

"But why? Why us?"

Lila didn't answer immediately.

Her voice came out small. "Because you both survived it."

Regina blinked. "That doesn't make sense—"

"No," Lila whispered. "It doesn't. And that's the problem."

Sheila braced her back against the stone. "What was that thing? The big one. The... the host."

Lila hugged her knees, eyes unfocused. "It's not the first experiment. It's the first... partner."

The word echoed down the tunnel.

Partner.

Regina shivered violently. "Partner with what?"

Lila looked at her.

Then looked at me.

And for the first time, I saw the depth of what the lake had forced into her mind.

"Not with what," she whispered. "With *who*."

My heartbeat thudded in my ears.

"Explain," I said.

She shook her head helplessly. "I don't know how. Not fully. But the lake isn't a creature. It's a... system. A network. A mind broken into currents. The host was the first person it tried to merge with."

Regina covered her mouth. "God..."

Sheila muttered, "This is... this is impossible."

I exhaled slowly.

"Druitt. The project lead. He wrote something in his notes — that the enzyme only 'activates' when exposed to a human substrate."

Lila nodded. "Because humans are the bridge."

Regina squeezed my sleeve. "Garth... you said it marked you. On the day you drowned."

I nodded.

"And you said it marked me."

"Yes."

Lila looked between us.

"And it hasn't marked anyone else fully since."

The weight of her implication crushed my chest.

I whispered, "We're... conduits."

Lila's eyes filled. "Yes."

Regina's breathing hitched. "Please... tell me that isn't true."

Lila didn't.

The tunnel vibrated — softer, deeper, distant.

A low, mournful hum rolled through the stone, like a whale song traveling through solid earth.

Lila flinched.

She whispered, "It's searching the tunnels."

Regina clung to my sleeve. "Garth—we have to move."

Sheila nodded. "Before the water finds a weak spot and floods this shaft."

I helped Regina to her feet. "Downward?"

Lila shook her head.

"No," she whispered. "Not down."

She pointed to a sloping passage leading away from the collapsed chamber.

"Sideways."

Sheila frowned. "Why sideways?"

Lila met my eyes.

"Because that's the only direction it can't predict."

My skin crawled.

Sheila swore. "Fantastic. We're outsmarting a lake."

Regina gripped my hand tightly, knuckles white. "Garth—please—let's go."

We moved.

The sideways tunnel curved gently, irregularly, like the path of water through stone. Lila led us, though she moved like someone listening to something none of us could hear.

We passed remnants of past exploration — a broken helmet, a rusted chain, a collapsible stretcher crushed by falling rock. One wall bore scratch marks deep enough to reach the limestone beneath.

Sheila whispered, "Those aren't tool marks."

"No," Lila said. "Those were hands."

Regina looked away.

Minutes—or hours—later, the tunnel widened again.

And we stepped into a corridor that did not belong underground.

Concrete walls.

Old fluorescent light fixtures.

A rusted rolling door.

Water pooling across tile floor.

Regina gasped. "This... this was built."

"It was hidden," Lila said.

She pointed to the rusted door.

"Sub-Basin Access Point A. The first federal installation."

Sheila frowned. "From the 70s?"

Lila shook her head. "Earlier. Before they called it federal."

We entered.

The hallway inside was warped by moisture, ceiling tiles collapsed in heaps. The air stank of old chemicals and mold. Papers slathered against the walls like barnacles — lab notes fused by water.

I peeled one free.

The ink had run, but one line survived:

SUBJECT 01: COGNITIVE RETENTION

UNEXPECTED.

My blood froze.

Another sheet:

SUBJECT 01:

NOT HUMAN.

NOT ANIMAL.

NOT DONE.

Regina's voice shook. "Garth... this wasn't an experiment gone wrong. This was one they... continued."

Lila whispered, "They didn't lose control. They ceded it."

Sheila muttered, "Meaning what?"

Lila looked at us with haunted clarity.

"They didn't fail to stop the organism."

She pointed back toward the cavern.

"They obeyed it."

Regina's knees nearly buckled.

I steadied her.

The hallway shuddered.

A low, resonant hum rolled through the facility — the same hum we heard under the lake.

Lila grabbed Regina's hand — then mine — and pulled us deeper into the sub-basin.

"We're almost there."

"Where?" I asked.

She looked back with terror and certainty braided together.

"The place Druitt tried to escape from."

The deeper we moved into the sub-basin corridor, the more the air changed.

Not colder.

Not damper.

Different.

As if oxygen had memory.

The buzzing fluorescence overhead flickered once—then died completely, plunging us into a darkness that felt **aware**.

Our flashlights cast long, slanted beams across the warped tile and rusted metal.

Regina whispered, "Garth... I think I can hear it breathing."

She wasn't wrong.

There was a faint sound beneath our footsteps—

not wind,

not water,

but a slow, rhythmic expansion and contraction of the air itself.

Sheila muttered under her breath, "This is bad. This is very, very bad."

Lila didn't slow down.

She moved like someone following a path she hoped wasn't real but knew she must walk.

The corridor ended in a reinforced door half-crushed under falling stone. A faded federal stencil was barely legible through layers of mineral deposits:

SUB-BASIN NODE 0

AUTHORIZED PERSONNEL ONLY

UW–AEC / MIDWEST BIOLOGICAL RISK DIVISION

1971 | 1976 | 1984 | 1990

Four dates.

Four attempts.

Four failures.

Lila touched the door with trembling fingers. "Druitt sealed it from the inside."

Regina inhaled sharply. "He died here."

"No," Lila whispered. "He didn't die here."

She turned to me, eyes as hollow as the tunnels.

"He died *after* he did what he came here to do."

I swallowed. "What was that?"

Lila's voice was barely audible.

"He tried to kill it."

Sheila hissed out a breath. "And failed, I'm guessing."

Lila nodded.

"We're going in," I said quietly.

Regina tightened her grip on my sleeve. "Garth... what if it's not dead?"

The tunnel vibrated.

A faint pulse rolled through the ground.

I whispered, "It's not."

Sheila pushed her flashlight forward, bracing her injured ankle. "Let's do it before we freeze to death in a hallway full of nightmares."

I wedged my shoulder against the half-crushed door and shoved.

Stone dust rained down.

Metal screamed.

Then the seal gave way—

and the door grated open onto a space unlike anything we'd yet seen.

The room was circular.

Wide.

Vaulted.

But not carved by nature—

rather by engineering too advanced for the damp, decayed state we found it in.

Rusted metal scaffolding lined the outer ring.

Old monitors sagged on broken arms.

A half-collapsed observation balcony overlooked the center like a forgotten throne.

And at the center—

A dry pool.

Circular.

Reinforced.

Eight feet deep.

Eighteen feet across.

A containment chamber.

The bottom was cracked, chunks of concrete scattered like fragmented teeth.

And in the cracks—

glowing blue-green filaments.

Regina gasped. "Garth… it was here."

Sheila's voice shook. "This is where they kept the first host."

"No," Lila whispered.

She pointed to the chamber floor.

"This is where they *made* it."

My flashlight beam traced what remained of the chamber's interior. Blood-pressure cuffs. Shackles. Monitoring cables fused into the stone. Old syringes embedded in crumbling grout.

I forced my breath through a tightening throat.

"They experimented on someone here," I said quietly.

Regina whispered, "Someone human."

Sheila swore again under her breath.

Lila walked down the broken steps into the dry containment pool. Her steps were slow, heavy, mourning.

"When the lake chose the first host," she said, "it didn't just mark them. It merged with them. Bonded. The researchers thought they were studying something biological."

She touched the glowing filaments nestling in the cracks.

"They were studying something **intelligent**."

Regina sank onto the steps, hands over her mouth. "This... this is worse than we thought."

Lila looked up at us.

"No. It's worse than they ever understood."

Something glinted beneath a slab of collapsed concrete. I climbed down into the chamber and heaved the piece aside.

Underneath was a metal notebook.

Dented.

Rust-stained.

But sealed.

Regina breathed, "Oh my God—it's Druitt's."

I opened it.

Pages were ruined—

but a section near the back was intact.

Handwriting frantic.

Pressure-etched.

"The host is changing its breathing pattern... it responds to auditory frequencies..."

"It mirrors the rhythms of any human heartbeat in proximity..."

"Subject 01 not stable but not dying... not decaying... adaptation continuous..."

"If this is intelligence, it is not singular... it is distributed..."

Then:

"I was wrong.

It is not alive IN the lake.

It IS the lake."

Regina recoiled. "What—what does that mean?"

I read the next line aloud.

"We did not awaken a creature.

We awakened the WATER."

Sheila whispered, "Jesus."

I kept reading.

"It has no body.

No central form.

It uses us as form.

Hosts are exo-bodies, not endpoints."

And finally:

"To stop it, you must isolate the marked.

To starve it, you must break the bond.

To end it...

you must never return."

My chest tightened.

Never return.

Lila swallowed. "He couldn't do it."

"No," I whispered. "He couldn't."

Regina looked at me, eyes brimming with fear. "Garth... what does that mean for us?"

I couldn't answer.

Because the page was shaking in my hands.

And not just from my tremor.

The ground vibrated beneath us.

Not a collapse.

Not a quake.

A heartbeat.

The lake's heartbeat.

Lila snapped her head toward the tunnel. "It found us."

Sheila's flashlight beam stuttered across the concrete. "How? How the HELL did it—"

The hum rolled through the chamber.

Regina grabbed the front of my jacket. "Garth—tell me what to do—"

The water spoke again.

A single word, louder than before, ripping through the chamber and our skulls:

"MERGE."

We staggered.

Regina screamed.

Lila fell to her knees.

Sheila clutched her ears until they bled.

The chamber's floor cracked.

Glowing filaments shot up through concrete like vines.

And something began rising through the fissures below.

Smooth.

Pale.

Shaped like a hand—

but far too large.

Sheila shouted, "MOVE! MOVE! MOVE!"

But Lila stared at the rising form like watching a prophecy unfold.

"It followed us," she whispered. "All the way down."

Regina clung to me, crying. "Garth—please—please don't let it take us—"

I grabbed her hand.

I grabbed Lila's arm.

Sheila grabbed my shoulder.

The chamber exploded in a shower of stone—

and the Primordial Host's arm shot upward, trying to seize us.

We ran.

We ran through the collapsing sub-basin hallway, the walls slamming inward, the glowing water surging behind us like a living tidal wave.

And as we fled into the blackness of the next tunnel, I heard the lake speak again—

soft, tender, mournful:

"**COME.**

HOME."

We didn't look back.

We couldn't.

Because whatever was rising behind us...

it was no longer confined to the water.

CHAPTER 16

The First Memory

The first memory never fades—it waits for the moment we return to it.

The tunnel we sprinted into after escaping the sub-basin wasn't a passage so much as a wound in the bedrock — jagged, wet, irregular, stitched with veins of glowing blue-green that pulsed like arteries under skin. Each pulse echoed faintly in the stone, traveling ahead of us.

Like it was announcing our arrival.

Regina stumbled beside me, breath hitching in ragged bursts. She'd cried herself silent, then into tremors. Sheila's ankle barely held as she limped along the uneven floor, muttering curses at every jolt of pain. Lila ran ahead, moving in sharp, instinctive bursts — like someone hearing directions none of us could hear.

After fifteen minutes, the tunnel widened abruptly.

We entered a dome-like chamber.

Round.

Smooth.

Geologically impossible.

This was not carved.

This was not man-made.

It was **dissolved.**

The stone had melted away in wide spirals, as if the lake water had seeped through, bored downward, and shaped a cathedral of erosion. Stalagmites glowed with the faint blue-green signature of the organisms. Water pooled across the floor, barely an inch deep.

Regina stopped suddenly, clutching my arm.

"Garth. I don't... I don't feel right."

I turned. "Where?"

She pressed her palm against her sternum. Her breath shortened. Her pupils widened unnaturally.

"I feel... pulled."

Sheila swore quietly. "It's the mark flaring up. Same as Garth earlier."

Lila turned, trembling. "It's not the mark."

Her voice cracked.

"It's the memory."

Regina's face drained. "What memory? I don't have— I've never—"

Her voice faltered.

She staggered.

I caught her before she collapsed into the glowing water.

"Regina," I whispered, "look at me. Stay with me."

But her eyes weren't seeing me.

She was seeing something else.

Regina began to shake uncontrollably.

Her breath rasped out in short, panicked bursts. Tears welled and fell unstopped. She gripped my jacket like she was drowning again — but not here. Somewhere else.

"Garth," she whispered, voice breaking. "I... I think... something happened when I was little."

Lila knelt beside her, placing a trembling hand over Regina's.

"It's coming back because the lake is close enough to reach it."

Regina's voice was small, terrified. "But I don't want to remember."

"You don't have a choice," Lila said softly.

Sheila knelt on Regina's other side, holding her shoulders gently. "You're not alone. We're right here."

Regina shook hard. "Something... something pulled me under. I thought it was weeds. I always thought it was weeds."

She paused, breath catching.

"It wasn't weeds."

I cupped her face.

"What was it?"

She swallowed, lips trembling.

"A hand."

Her voice splintered.

"A hand, Garth."

I froze.

Lila closed her eyes with sorrow. "It touched you the same way it touched him."

Regina sobbed against my shoulder. "I was only seven. Only seven. Why didn't anyone tell me?"

Sheila whispered, voice thick, "Honey... your brain probably hid it. Kids forget trauma like that."

"No," Regina said. "No, someone *did* pull me out."

She looked at me — trembling, wide-eyed, remembering in pieces.

"A boy on the shore. A little boy. He reached for me."

My heart stopped.

Lila stared at both of us, horror gradually overtaking recognition.

"Garth," she whispered. "You weren't nine when you first encountered it."

The cavern dimmed to a soft glow.

I went still.

Regina went silent.

Lila's voice broke to a trembling whisper.

"You were seven."

I sat back as the truth hit me with a force that felt like drowning all over again.

Seven.

Not nine.

But I only remembered drowning at nine.

I only remembered **once**.

What if I was wrong?

What if my memories were replaced?

Or overwritten?

Or merged with someone else's?

Regina said, "Garth... we were there at the same time."

Something inside my mind cracked open.

A memory I had never accessed — not in sobriety, not in nightmares, not in relapse, not in sleepless nights beside the lake — began to flicker.

Two children on a shoreline.

A girl reaching for a toy.

A boy skipping a stone.

Laughter.

Water lapping.

Ripples.

A pale shape beneath the surface.

A cold hand rising.

Two children screaming underwater.

Not one.

Two.

Regina whispered, "We were together."

Lila drew a shaky breath. "The lake didn't just mark one of you. It marked you both."

Sheila's voice was low, reverent, horrified. "A bonded pair."

Regina collapsed into me fully, shaking. I held her, my arms around her, trying to breathe through the weight crashing down on us.

Lila watched us with a mixture of awe and grief.

"It never let both of you go," she whispered. "Not really. It just waited for the moment you came back together."

Her voice shook.

"And that moment was now."

The dome chamber responded.

The glowing water vibrated, sending ripples across the pooled surface in perfect concentric rings. The air thickened, heavy with an electric charge. A deep hum rolled through the stone — not from the tunnels behind us, but from below.

Regina clutched me tighter. "Garth, it's coming closer."

Sheila shined her flashlight toward the far wall. "There's an opening. There—there's a passage through!"

Lila didn't move.

She stared at the center of the chamber.

Something was rising.

Not from water this time.

From stone.

A single glowing filament began pushing upward through a crack. Another. Then three. Then ten. They twisted like vines, glowing hotter, brighter, pulsing with a rhythm that matched my heartbeat.

The chamber floor began to lift — subtly, but enough to shift dust and water outward.

I pulled Regina to her feet.

"Move," I whispered. "Now."

But Lila didn't move.

She took one step forward, hands trembling.

"I've seen this place," she breathed. "In my dreams. After the lake touched me. This is the first chamber. The earliest one. Before the federal projects. Before the UW labs."

Regina shook. "Lila—please—stop—"

Lila's eyes glistened with tears.

"This isn't a lab."

She turned in a slow circle.

"It's a birthplace."

A violent pulse surged upward through the stone. The lights in our flashlights flickered wildly.

Regina collapsed against me again, whispering into my jacket, "Garth—please get me out of here—please—"

Sheila grabbed Lila's arm. "We're leaving. NOW."

But Lila tore herself free.

"No!"

She pointed to the rising tangle of glowing filaments.

"It's calling us here for a reason."

Regina sobbed, "Why—why this place—why us—"

Lila whispered:

"Because this is where the first host was conceived."

Sheila froze.

Regina went slack in my arms.

And I felt the chamber shift beneath my feet — a slow tilting, like the earth itself was breathing.

A low, ancient voice filled the chamber:

"SEEN."

The walls vibrated. Dust fell like snow.

The glow intensified.

Lila's eyes widened.

She whispered, "It knows you remember. It knows you both do."

Regina cried, "Garth, RUN!"

I dragged her toward the exit passage Sheila had found.

Lila stared at us, torn — wanting to follow, afraid to leave the chamber, unable to resist its psychic gravity.

But then—

A massive crack tore through the chamber floor.

Blue-white filaments erupted upward.

The entire dome lurched.

Sheila screamed, "MOVE, GODDAMN IT!"

I grabbed Lila's wrist. Hard.

"RUN!"

The chamber floor gave way behind us as the three of us sprinted into the passage, dragging Regina between us.

The chamber collapsed in a roar of stone, water, and ancient breath—

And the last thing I heard before the tunnel narrowed behind us was the lake speaking again:

Not *Return.*

Not *Merge.*

Not *Home.*

But something older:

"REMEMBER."

The tunnel we fled into narrowed quickly, forcing us into a crouched, almost crawling gait. The collapse behind us sealed the chamber completely; the sound of it was a tidal crush, stone pulverizing stone, echoing through the passage like distant thunder.

Regina gripped my hand so tightly my fingers went numb. Sheila limped behind us, jaw clenched against the pain in her ankle. Lila moved ahead, not confidently, but with the terrifying surety of someone who had already *seen* the route in visions she hadn't asked for.

The only light came from our failing flashlights and the faint blue-green shimmer seeping through mineral cracks in the stone.

As the passage widened, Regina's legs buckled.

I caught her.

"Garth," she whispered, "I can hear it."

Her voice was barely audible.

"Not the lake... the memory."

Lila turned, eyes reflective in the low light.

"It's unraveling," she said softly. "Your mind tried to hide it. But now the place is too close. The connection is too strong."

Regina shook violently. "I don't want it. I don't want to remember."

Sheila knelt next to her. "You don't have to want it. Just breathe. You're not alone."

But Regina wasn't hearing us.

She was somewhere else.

Her gaze unfocused—lost downward, into herself.

"I remember... water," she whispered. "Not like now. Warm. Summer. Sun above me."

My breath caught.

I remembered that too—

or had thought I did out of imagination and wishful reconstruction.

Lila knelt in front of Regina. "Let it come slowly. Don't fight it."

Regina closed her eyes.

And the past opened.

"I was seven," she whispered.

"A friend's birthday. There was a picnic by the lake. Everyone was distracted. I wandered toward the water with a little plastic boat..."

Her voice wavered.

"And then... something shimmered underneath."

She touched her sternum unconsciously.

"A shape. I thought it was a fish. I leaned closer. And then..."

Regina's entire body tensed.

"It grabbed me."

Sheila inhaled sharply. "Jesus."

Regina shook her head violently. "Not grabbed. Not... not exactly. It was... cold. Like a hand. Around my ankle."

Her fingers tightened on mine.

"I went under before I could scream."

Tears slid down her face.

"I remember the murk. The weeds. The sunlight fading. And I tried to kick free, but I couldn't. And then... another hand. Small. Warm. Human."

Her breathing grew ragged.

"I remember a boy underwater. A boy who grabbed my arm."

My throat closed.

Regina looked at me.

"You."

It wasn't a question.

"You pulled me toward the surface."

I stared, unable to speak.

Lila's eyes glistened. "And the lake touched you both."

Regina nodded.

"And then... something touched *him*."

She choked on the word.

"A pale shape. Behind him. Watching."

She shook harder.

"And then it let us go."

My chest tightened until I felt I might tear in half.

Fragments I'd never allowed myself to consider flickered behind my eyes.

Warm water.

A girl's fingers slipping from mine.

A pale limb brushing my cheek.

A massive eye studying me.

A cold touch to my brow.

A blue-green pulse spreading through the water.

A voice—not words, but meaning—coiling around my bones:

Not yet.

I flinched so hard the flashlight slipped from my hand and clattered onto the stone.

Regina grabbed my wrist.

"Garth—what did you see?"

I swallowed.

"A moment. A feeling."

Lila whispered, "It wasn't drowning. It was choosing."

My hands trembled.

"It marked me," I said. "It touched me first. I felt it. I... I didn't know what it was. I didn't know how to understand it."

Regina nodded slowly. "And it touched me through you."

Sheila stared at the two of us like she was witnessing a ghost story come alive.

"So you're not just marked," she whispered. "You're linked."

Lila nodded, her face pale.

"The lake bonded the two of you with each other. Not just with itself."

Regina's breath steadied for a moment.

"That's why it wants us both."

My stomach dropped.

Because she was right.

Lila added, "And why it can't complete what it started unless you're together."

Regina looked at me with a mix of fear, grief, and something more raw.

"We survived because we were together."

I took her hand.

"And we'll survive this because we're still together."

Sheila sighed, exhausted and terrified. "This is beautiful and deeply upsetting, but we need to move before something else bursts through a wall."

Lila nodded, then pointed to another tunnel leading deeper.

"It's this way. There's another chamber."

The tunnel widened gradually and the air grew dryer — unnaturally so.

When we stepped into the next space, I realized why.

It wasn't a natural chamber.

It was a hallway.

Long. Straight. Reinforced concrete.

Like the abandoned sub-basin route... but older.

Much older.

A tarnished sign hung crooked:

MIDWEST HYDROLOGICAL RESEARCH FACILITY

EST. 1962

AUTHORIZED: AEC, NIH, DTRA

Sheila inhaled sharply. "This was built before the university projects."

Lila nodded. "This is where it all started."

Regina squeezed my hand. "This is where they found the first samples."

I felt a chill.

"No," Lila whispered. "This is where they lost control of them."

We walked forward slowly.

The hallway's tiles were chipped and broken, but not dead.

Filaments glowed beneath them like roots spreading.

Regina trembled beside me. "What were they doing down here?"

Sheila stepped over a collapsed section. "Research. Secret research. Something to do with water quality, ecosystem restoration, maybe biological warfare—"

Lila shook her head.

311

"This wasn't about war. It wasn't about infection. It wasn't about remediation."

She turned slowly.

"This was about communication."

A chill played down my spine.

"What do you mean?" I asked quietly.

She pointed to the glowing filaments crawling up the concrete.

"They thought they found a new lifeform. A new type of enzyme. Something unique to the lake."

Regina nodded. "The enzyme component the university worked on—"

"No," Lila said softly. "Not the enzyme. Not the host. Not the mutation."

She touched the concrete wall.

"This."

The glowing filaments pulsed under her palm.

Regina stared. "The water?"

"No," Lila whispered.

Her voice cracked.

"The network."

My breath caught.

Sheila muttered, "Oh hell—"

But Lila wasn't finished.

"The lake isn't alive. Not like we think."

She looked at each of us with a mixture of dread and clarity.

"It's a **brain**."

Silence filled the hall.

A silence that felt like it was listening.

Regina whispered, "Oh my God."

Lila swallowed. "The water carries electrical pulses. The filaments are neurons. The hosts are bodies. And the caves are the skull. This whole system... it isn't a monster."

She closed her eyes.

"It's an intelligence."

A soft vibration traveled through the floor.

A hum.

Low.

Melodic.

Older than any language spoken on land.

Regina clutched my sleeve. "Garth... Garth, it's singing."

She was right.

The lake wasn't roaring.

It was calling.

And I felt that call deep inside my chest, pulling on something I didn't know was there.

Something that had been dormant since I was seven.

Lila stepped back.

"It remembers the two of you."

Regina whispered, "Why?"

Lila's eyes glistened.

"Because you are its first successful bond."

My heart stopped.

Regina gasped, covering her mouth.

Sheila whispered, "This is bigger than we thought."

Lila nodded. "Which is why we need to see Druitt's vault."

Regina sobbed, "What vault?"

Lila pointed ahead.

"To the place where he learned what the lake really wanted."

The hallway trembled.

And a door at the end — steel, reinforced — slowly began to open.

On its own.

The door at the end of the hydrological research hallway didn't swing open so much as *exhale*. A gust of stale, preserved air drifted out—cold, metallic, tinged faintly with the scent of wet stone. It felt like breath from something that had been waiting decades to inhale again.

Regina tightened her grip on my arm. Sheila instinctively stepped in front of us despite her limp, flashlight raised like a weapon. Lila moved last, hesitation flickering across her face for the first time since we'd entered this part of the tunnel network.

The steel door parted fully.

A vault waited beyond.

Not large.

Not industrial.

Not like the abandoned labs we'd passed through earlier.

This space was **deliberate**.

Circular.

Reinforced.

Lined with panels of cracked glass and rust-flecked instrumentation.

A command center from a forgotten project.

A single chair sat before a bank of machines, half-fused by time. And on the central console—

A reel-to-reel tape deck.

Still intact.

Still powered by a flickering emergency light.

A label, half-peeling, read:

DRUITT AUDIO LOG 3 — DO NOT ERASE

DATE: 10/04/1972

Regina exhaled shakily. "He was here. He recorded something... right before—before everything stopped."

Sheila glanced around. "This room shouldn't have power."

Lila corrected her softly. "It shouldn't have been reachable."

The door clicked behind us—on its own—and sealed.

A soft hum filled the vault, low and resonant.

Regina swallowed. "Garth... please tell me that was the hinges."

"It wasn't," Sheila said flatly.

Lila walked to the console as though approaching an altar. Her hands trembled when she touched the play button.

The tape deck whirred.

A hiss of static filled the vault.

Then—

DRUITT (recorded):

"...test twelve. Audible response pattern confirmed. The subject... responds to rhythmic cues... God help us... it's mapping me."

His voice shook.

A scientist unraveling.

DRUITT:

"This isn't enzyme behavior. This isn't symbiosis. This is... cognition."

The vault hummed in response—

as though the walls remembered the conversation.

Sheila muttered, "Christ..."

DRUITT:

"The filaments aren't a byproduct. They're the mechanism. They share signals across full sub-basin networks. The water is only the medium."

Regina whispered, "He figured it out."

Lila nodded, eyes wide with dread. "He understood it was a distributed intelligence long before the federal team did."

The tape crackled.

DRUITT:

"Subject 01 is... cooperative. Curious. It... it mimics me. It tries to... understand me. But it isn't malicious. It's searching."

A long stretch of static.

DRUITT:

"It's searching for something it lost."

The vault's hum deepened.

Regina tensed.

Sheila drew nearer to us.

Lila stiffened. "It's listening."

She meant the lake.

DRUITT (lower):

"...I believe it made the lake. Or changed it. Or became it. I can't be certain. But the water... reacts to its emotions."

Another static burst.

Then Druitt's voice hardened.

DRUITT:

"If it connects with a human who survives the merging process... the conduit becomes permanent."

The air left my lungs.

Regina whispered, "Oh God—"

I squeezed her hand.

DRUITT:

"The host it chooses... will never belong fully to themselves again."

The vault lights flickered.

Sheila whispered, "We need to know what went wrong. Fast."

The tape continued.

A tremble in Druitt's voice now—fear mixed with awe.

DRUITT:

"I made a mistake. I brought a child to the water's edge. I wanted to see how it responded to innocence. Unmarked consciousness. But it... it reached for the child."

Regina's breath hitched.

Sheila straightened.

Lila froze.

I felt my pulse spike.

DRUITT:

"The child survived. Was returned. But altered. Marked. Not physically... but neurologically. The lake touched him."

317

The walls shimmered faintly.

Regina whispered, horrified, "It was you."

A lump formed in my throat.

Before I could speak, the next line played:

DRUITT:

"..and the child reached for another."

Regina's knees buckled.

"I..." she stammered, "I reached for you. Underwater. When I fell."

DRUITT:

"The lake marked them both. Not separately. Together."

Lila covered her mouth, tears forming.

DRUITT:

"A bonded pair. In symbiosis. This—this was not an accident."

The vault trembled.

Regina's nails dug into my sleeve.

"Garth," she whispered, "we were children. We didn't choose this."

My voice was quiet, raw. "No. It chose us."

Sheila backed toward the sealed door. "We need to leave. Now."

But the tape wasn't over.

Druitt's voice returned—broken, desperate.

DRUITT:

"Subject 01 is becoming aware of the bond. It feels it. It hears them. It..."

A sharp inhale from Druitt.

DRUITT:

"...it loves them."

Regina jolted.

"NO—NO—NO—"

She pressed her hands to her ears.

But TAPE DRUITT kept going, unraveling:

DRUITT:

"It wants them returned. It will not be complete without them. It seeks them. It calls for them."

A chorus of hums rippled through the vault walls—like a tuning fork vibrating the air.

Lila cried softly. "It's getting closer."

DRUITT:

"I can't let it take them. It cannot be allowed to reach the children again. I must destroy the connection."

The vault went still.

Silent.

Waiting.

DRUITT:

"...but I can't kill something that doesn't die."

Regina squeezed my hand so hard it hurt.

"Garth... I'm scared."

"I know," I whispered. "I am too."

DRUITT:

"So I will kill myself instead. Break the conduit. If it thinks I am dead, it will bury the memory of the children. Hide it within the lake. Forget."

Silence.

A final line:

DRUITT:

"If you hear this... I failed."

The reel-to-reel snapped off.

The vault lights died.

Only the faint glow of the filaments beneath the floor remained.

Regina collapsed against me and sobbed uncontrollably.

Sheila stared numbly at the machine. "He killed himself to protect you. And it still remembered."

Lila whispered, voice hollow:

"It remembered because you remembered each other."

The vault began to hum again.

Louder.

Stronger.

Like a heartbeat gaining strength.

The lake was responding.

To the memory.

To the tape.

To us.

Regina shook violently.

"Garth... it's calling."

I pulled her close. "I've got you."

But in truth, the lake wasn't calling her.

Not this time.

Lila's eyes widened.

"It's calling *you both*."

The vault door shook.

Dust fell.

Filaments brightened.

Sheila grabbed her flashlight like a weapon. "We need a way OUT."

Lila pointed to a secondary hatch at the back of the room.

"Through there. The old engineering shafts. Druitt built escape routes."

Sheila limped toward it, shoving her shoulder into the rusted wheel. It groaned but didn't budge.

"Help me!"

I set Regina down gently. "Stay with me," I whispered. "Don't let go."

Then I rushed to help Sheila.

Lila knelt in front of Regina, cupping her face.

"You're not what it wants," Lila whispered. "Not alone. Not without him."

Regina sobbed harder.

"I don't WANT any of this—"

A violent shudder shook the vault.

Something slammed against the sealed steel door.

Sheila's flashlight flickered.

A second slam.

Louder.

Closer.

The lake wasn't outside.

The first host was.

Lila stood.

Her voice broke.

"It found us."

The vault door buckled inward.

Not bent.

Not dented.

Buckled.

Steel groaned like a living animal. Dust rained from the ceiling. The hinges screamed under a force no human—or any terrestrial creature—should've been able to exert.

Regina clutched my jacket, trembling violently.

"Garth... Garth, it's right outside—"

Sheila aimed her flickering flashlight at the door, jaw clenched even through the pain in her ankle.

"What the hell is it hitting us with, a truck?!"

Lila stood absolutely still.

"It's using resonance," she whispered. "It found the frequency the vault was built with. It's trying to break it apart from within."

Another strike.

The door warped further.

A thin line of light—not flashlight, not natural—broke through the seam.

Blue-green.

Pulsing.

Alive.

Regina sobbed, "Garth—please—please—"

I wrapped an arm around her and pulled her tight against my chest.

"I've got you," I whispered. "I won't let it take you."

But my voice trembled.

Because the lake wasn't just calling anymore.

It was **remembering.**

Remembering me.

Remembering her.

Remembering the day we touched its water together.

And it was calling us home.

Sheila slammed her shoulder into the secondary hatch again.

"Garth! Lila! Help me!"

We rushed to her side.

The wheel wouldn't turn.

Lila pressed her palm to the corroded metal—then froze.

"There's something under here."

"What?" Sheila barked.

"Another mechanism. Druitt built a backup lock. A manual override."

She pressed harder, eyes unfocused.

"I can hear it."

Sheila blinked. "You can *hear* a mechanism?"

"No," Lila whispered. "I can hear... how he opened it."

Regina sobbed again.

"Please—just open it—please—"

Lila stepped back suddenly. "Garth. Your flashlight."

I handed it to her with shaking hands. She tilted it toward the hatch frame and inhaled sharply.

A symbol had been etched into the metal years ago:

A circle.

A wave.

A vertical line.

The old AEC sigil for sub-basin access.

But beneath it—nearly invisible—was another mark:

A child's handprint.

Small.

Blurred.

Pressed into soft metal long before it hardened.

Regina gasped. "Oh my God..."

Lila touched the print gently.

"This was you."

Regina collapsed against the wall.

"No—no—no, I've never been here—how—how—?"

Lila shook her head. "Not you."

She turned to me.

"You."

My chest constricted.

A flash—

A memory—

Stone walls—

Druitt pulling me through a narrow corridor—

Me sobbing uncontrollably—

Regina unconscious beside me—

A hastily smudged handprint pressed into soft metal during a panic—

I had been here.

At seven.

And I had forgotten.

Just like the lake wanted me to.

"Garth," Regina whispered, voice cracking, "you were here with him. With Druitt. He saved us."

Another slam hit the vault door.

A crack formed.

Blue-green light spilled through like blood.

Sheila screamed, "NOW, GODDAMN IT!"

Lila touched the handprint—

and the hatch wheel clicked.

Once.

Twice.

Then turned freely.

We spun it as fast as we could.

The hatch groaned.

Opened an inch.

Two inches.

Enough.

I yanked Regina through first.

Then Sheila.

Then Lila.

Then I crawled in last as—

The vault door split.

A massive pale arm forced its way through the steel, tearing the panel like cardboard. The air was sucked out of the room as the pressure shifted.

Lila screamed, "GO!"

The hatch opened onto a vertical maintenance shaft lined with rusted ladders and abandoned conduit.

A draft of cold air rose from below.

Regina clung to me as we descended, step by careful step. Sheila moved slower due to her ankle, every rung a grunt of pain. Lila climbed beneath her to catch her if she slipped.

Above us, the vault behind the hatch erupted.

Stone.

Metal.

A roar like a collapsing cathedral.

Then—

A sound I will remember for the rest of my life:

The host's breath

entering

the vault.

Long.

Slow.

Searching.

Lila froze mid-rung.

"It's smelling us."

Sheila muttered, "I am going to die smelling like Milwaukee sewer water, but THIS is too much."

We kept descending.

Twenty feet.

Forty.

Sixty.

Regina whispered shakily, "Garth... where does this lead?"

Lila answered, "To the first observation gallery."

Sheila winced. "Sounds cozy."

"It's the only place it can't reach directly," Lila said. "It's too small for the host."

I exhaled a trembling breath. "Then we move."

But then—

A memory hit me so hard I nearly slipped.

A corridor.

A door.

Druitt dragging me by my arm.

Regina unconscious over his shoulder.

His voice frantic:

"Don't look at it! Don't look at it—Garth, KEEP YOUR EYES SHUT—"

Me sobbing, lungs burning.

A pale hand pressing against the vault window.

Its enormous eye watching us leave.

A whisper in my head:

Not yet.

Not yet.

The memory surged.

Me reaching for Regina's hand even unconscious.

Her fingers twitching back toward mine.

Druitt seeing it.

His horrified whisper:

"God forgive me. You two are the key. Not the enzyme. Not the host. You."

Me screaming:

"Let her go! LET HER GO!"

And the lake responding:

Soon.

My foot slipped on a rung.

Regina screamed. "Garth!"

I caught myself. Barely.

Sheila shouted from below, "Hey—none of that! We need you alive!"

My breaths came ragged, fast.

Regina pressed her forehead to mine.

"Garth," she whispered, "don't disappear on me."

I held her face with both hands.

"I'm here," I whispered. "I'm here. I remember now."

She trembled.

"What did you remember?"

"That it's not just bonded to us," I said softly. "It's been *waiting* for us to remember each other."

Lila's voice floated up the shaft.

"And now that you do..."

She looked up, eyes haunted, resigned.

"...it will never stop."

When we reached the bottom, the ladder ended abruptly onto a narrow catwalk. The air was freezing, almost sterile.

We stepped into a large domed room with a long, cracked observation window. Beyond it was a massive subterranean reservoir—still water, lit by bioluminescent filaments drifting like constellations.

Regina's breath hitched. "Is that..."

Lila nodded.

"This is where Druitt first communicated with the host."

Sheila limped toward the glass, awe overtaking fear.

"Oh my God..."

The water pulsed.

Softly.

Gently.

Like it was breathing.

A subtle blue-green glow spiraled upward, dancing along the reservoir.

Regina whispered, "It's beautiful."

I swallowed.

"Yes," I said quietly. "And that's the danger."

We stood in silence, listening to the distant hum moving through the rock.

Then—

The water rippled.

Just once.

A single, small wave.

Not violent.

Not threatening.

Soft.

Familiar.

It moved directly to the window.

Stopped in front of Regina.

She stepped backward, trembling.

"Garth..."

I grabbed her hand.

"I see it."

The glow intensified.

The hum rose.

And through the window—not with eyes, not with shape, but with raw presence—we felt the lake speak:

"FOUND."

Regina clutched my arm.

Sheila whispered, "It knows exactly where we are."

Lila nodded, tears forming again.

"And it won't let you go this time."

The glow in the water coiled upward into the shape of a rising column—slowly, like a sentinel awakening.

Sheila backed away.

"Oh HELL no—"

But Lila wasn't looking at the water.

She was looking behind us.

Her voice cracked.

"It found another way."

We turned.

The host's silhouette darkened the hallway behind the gallery door.

It couldn't enter the reservoir chamber.

But it didn't need to.

It had found an adjacent access corridor.

It stood impossibly still, watching us.

And in our minds, softly, unmistakably, we heard:

"COME BACK."

CHAPTER 17

Martinson Arrives

Some footsteps quiet a room long before the man enters it.

Detective Harold Martinson hated lakes.

Always had.

Maybe it was the stillness — the way water pretended to be calm while hiding everything that mattered. Maybe it was the Wisconsin humidity. Maybe it was the way sound traveled across the surface in strange, elastic ways, as if the lake was listening, not echoing.

Today, the lake wasn't pretending.

He could feel it breathing.

Martinson tightened his coat against the cold and stepped off the gravel path toward the Monona shoreline. The sun was gone, swallowed by a flat sheet of storm clouds that pressed low, heavy, and tense. Wind whipped along the water like an animal pacing a cage.

Behind him, the city was muted.

In front of him, the lake waited.

A ripple broke the surface twenty feet offshore.

Small.

Too deliberate for wind.

Martinson froze.

Something was wrong.

More wrong than usual.

The first sign had been the black Suburbans.

Three of them. Parked illegally along the bike path near the Yahara River outlet, two hours before dawn, with no plates and no explanation. Men in dark jackets stood beside them, staring at the lake like they expected it to answer a question they'd been avoiding.

The second sign was the radios.

The feds' radios weren't quiet.

They were *too quiet.*

Like no one wanted to speak the truth aloud.

The third sign was the tape.

A long strip of yellow "DO NOT CROSS" stretched between lampposts, fluttering in the wind. It wasn't Madison PD tape. It wasn't state tape. It wasn't even the FBI.

It was stamped:

FEDERAL RESPONSE DIVISION — CLASSIFIED SITE

Martinson had flashed his badge.

Showed his credentials.

Politely asked what the hell they thought they were doing blocking off a public shoreline.

Agent Bainbridge — dark suit, too-tight jaw, eyes like polished obsidian — had given him the kind of smile that was meant to move people off sidewalks.

"Detective. Best turn around."

Martinson didn't.

"This is city jurisdiction," he said. "Your people can't close municipal land without—"

"Without what?" Bainbridge asked calmly. "Your permission?"

Martinson didn't blink.

"Without cause."

Bainbridge's smile sharpened.

"We have cause."

"What cause?"

The agent's eyes flicked to the lake.

Then to the storm clouds.

Then back to Martinson.

"None of your concern."

And that was that.

Except it wasn't.

Because Martinson had spent twenty-four years in law enforcement, and while he had little talent for bureaucratic bullshit, he had a damn good sense for lies.

And Bainbridge was lying.

Worse, he was scared.

Which meant something was in play that no one wanted to talk about.

So Martinson had come back after dusk.

Alone.

And that's when he saw the ripple.

The lake rippled again.

This time closer.

A slow, widening circle spreading outward.

Martinson stepped onto the pier.

Boards creaked beneath his boots.

"Anyone out there?" he called.

Silence.

Wind.

Then—

A low hum.

Not from the air.

Not from the pier.

Not from the boats rocking gently against their moorings.

From the **lake.**

It vibrated through the water like a cello string plucked by a giant hand.

Martinson's skin prickled.

"What in the hell..."

He leaned forward, squinting at the dark surface.

A faint glow pulsed beneath it.

Blue-green.

Soft.

Like something bioluminescent drifting upward.

Martinson took a step back.

"Okay. Not normal."

He reached instinctively for his phone.

Then froze.

Because the glow was coalescing into a shape.

Not random.

Not chaotic.

Deliberate.

A **word.**

Letters forming in shimmering light beneath the water:

L I L A

Martinson's breath left him.

"Lila...?"

The missing girl.

Regina's assistant.

Disappeared from the UW campus two nights ago.

The case Martinson had been quietly looking into.

The case he had been told to stay away from.

But now—

The lake itself was showing her name?

"You've gotta be kidding me," he muttered.

The letters dissolved.

Ripples scattered.

The glow sank.

Then—

Something whispered.

Right behind him.

A child's voice.

Soft.

Wet.

Barely audible above the wind.

"Mr. Martin..."

He spun around.

No one was there.

Just the empty shoreline.

The taped-off path.

The distant silhouettes of the federal agents guarding nothing.

The pier groaned.

Another whisper.

Closer.

"Detective..."

Martinson's heart thudded hard.

He swallowed.

"All right," he muttered. "Not losing my mind today."

But the whisper came a third time.

And this time it sounded like it came from directly below his feet:

"Help them."

Martinson stepped backward so fast he nearly fell off the pier.

"Jesus Christ—"

The lake stilled.

The glow disappeared.

Silence reclaimed the shoreline.

Martinson regained his breath.

"Okay," he whispered. "Okay... that didn't happen."

Except it did.

He felt it.

He heard it.

He *knew* it.

He stepped carefully onto the lower dock, crouched, and shined his small flashlight into the lake.

Nothing.

Just darkness.

But then—

A shape moved in the water.

Not a fish.

Not a log.

Something large.

Humanoid.

Slowly drifting beneath the pier, just out of reach of the light.

Martinson froze.

His instincts screamed **Run.**

His curiosity whispered **Stay.**

He stayed.

The shape drifted closer.

He tightened his grip on the flashlight.

"Come on," he whispered. "Show yourself."

The shape rose.

Higher.

Higher.

BREAKING—

...

No.

It sank again.

As if it had changed its mind.

Martinson exhaled the breath he'd been holding.

"What the hell are you?"

Lightning flashed across the lake.

Thunder rolled seconds later.

Behind him, the federal perimeter radio crackled.

Agent Bainbridge's voice barked:

"All teams—prepare for the surge event. Repeat: surge event incoming. Keep civilians AWAY from shoreline."

Martinson's blood chilled.

Surge event?

He checked his watch.

The lake rhythmically pulsed three times, matching the thunder.

Then—

He heard screaming in the distance.

Not on the surface.

Not from the shore.

From beneath the dock.

A voice he recognized:

"GARTH—RUN!"

Martinson staggered.

Regina's voice.

Muffled.

Distant.

Echoing through the wood.

Through the water.

Through the **earth.**

He grabbed the edge of the pier and shouted:

"GARTH! REGINA! CAN YOU HEAR ME?"

No answer.

Only the echo.

Only the lake.

Only the storm growing stronger.

Martinson stood, shaking.

"Hold on," he whispered. "I'm coming back. I'm gonna find a way down. Just—hold on."

He walked quickly off the pier, heart pounding, eyes fixed on the forested edge of campus where the storm clouds clustered unnaturally low.

He passed the federal perimeter without a word.

But not without being seen.

Bainbridge watched him go, expression tightening.

And Martinson didn't notice the faint blue-green glow following his steps along the shoreline—

like the lake was marking him, too.

Martinson didn't get ten steps toward the tree line before a black Suburban's headlights snapped on behind him, flooding the path with blinding white. Tires crunched over the gravel. A door opened.

Bainbridge.

Of course.

"Detective Martinson!"

Martinson stopped.

He did **not** turn around.

"Not now," he muttered, hoping the agent would misinterpret his voice shaking from what he'd just witnessed.

Bainbridge stepped into his periphery, immaculate suit cutting through the darkness like a blade. "You're trespassing in a restricted zone."

Martinson exhaled slowly. "You made it a restricted zone." He met Bainbridge's gaze. "You gonna tell me why?"

The agent's eyes were dead.

Professional.

Almost bored.

But beneath the stillness, Martinson sensed something else—

Fear.

"Environmental hazard," Bainbridge said flatly.

"Bullshit."

"A contamination event."

"Try harder."

"Unauthorized research theft."

"Strike three," Martinson said. "You're a terrible liar."

Bainbridge's jaw tightened. "Detective—walk away."

"Can't."

"Why?"

Martinson stared him down.

"Because I heard someone screaming under the goddamn pier."

Bainbridge blinked.

Just once.

Then his voice softened—dangerously.

"You didn't hear anything."

"The hell I didn't."

"You heard *water*. Storm distortion. Nothing else."

Martinson stepped closer, lowering his voice. "Don't gaslight me. I know Regina Evert's voice. And I know what a drowning sounds like. Someone is down there."

"Detective," Bainbridge said quietly, "whatever you think you heard—leave it alone."

"No."

Bainbridge stepped closer.

They were inches apart.

"You're in over your head."

Martinson leaned in.

"So are you."

A flash of surprise crossed the agent's face before disappearing beneath a mask of bureaucratic calm.

"All right," Bainbridge said, almost sighing. "Let me be clear."

He gestured to the storm gathering over Lake Monona.

"Something is happening out there. Something that was buried for decades. Something that doesn't care about badges or jurisdiction or who you think you're trying to save."

"You talk like it's alive," Martinson said.

Bainbridge didn't answer.

Instead he whispered:

"I talk like it's awake."

A chill crawled through Martinson's spine.

Bainbridge straightened his jacket. "Go home, Detective."

Then he walked back to his Suburban, leaving Martinson standing alone on the shoreline, heart thudding in a body that suddenly didn't feel like it belonged to him.

Martinson didn't go home.

He moved along the shoreline, avoiding the floodlights of the patrols, slipping into the tree line where the property dipped into campus grounds. The wind carried strange sounds—like the lake exhaling. Like something brushing the underside of the earth.

He needed an entry point.

Regina and Garth weren't on the surface.

They were under it.

And the tunnels *had* to connect somewhere.

He reached the base of an old utility building, one of those squat concrete rectangles UW never bothered repainting. A rusted sign warned:

UTILITY ACCESS — RESTRICTED

WATER CONTROL & STEAM SHAFTS

Jackpot.

Martinson pulled a crowbar from the trunk of his car. (He kept one for emergencies. This counted.)

The lock snapped.

The door groaned open.

A blast of stale, wet air hit him.

Concrete steps spiraled downward.

Martinson aimed his flashlight.

"Garth," he whispered, "you better be alive down there."

He descended.

The narrow walkway spilled into a system of old steam runs and drainage shafts—low ceilings, sweating pipes, and the smell of mildew and rust.

Water dripped steadily from above.

A rhythmic pattern.

Like fingers tapping.

344

Martinson followed the main steam line until he reached a section where the metal plating had been pried open. Not recently. Years ago. The makeshift opening led to a horizontal shaft carved crudely into limestone.

Not UW infrastructure.

Not maintenance.

Someone had dug through here.

Martinson crouched and shined his light inside.

Scratches marred the limestone.

Deep.

Uneven.

Frantic.

Human.

He swallowed.

"Jesus."

He moved in.

The shaft opened into a larger corridor—one that looked disturbingly like the descriptions Garth had given him years earlier when he mentioned the "old urban legends" about subterranean research projects beneath Madison.

Martinson never believed them.

Now he was walking inside one.

He kept moving, the flashlight shaking slightly in his hand despite his best effort to appear steady.

The tunnel curved.

Wind swept past him.

Cold.

Wet.

Carrying a faint hum.

Martinson swallowed.

"Not wind," he muttered. "Air pressure change."

From deeper underground.

He moved on, rounding another bend.

Then—

He saw it.

Blue-green light.

Faint.

Pulsing.

Reflecting off the damp stone walls.

He froze.

"What in the hell..."

He stepped forward.

His boot hit something soft.

A bootprint.

Fresh.

Small.

Regina's size.

"Jesus Christ—they're down here."

The hum grew louder.

Something moved in the darkness ahead.

Martinson steadied himself, drawing his sidearm.

"Show yourself," he ordered.

Silence.

Drip.

Drip.

Then—

A whisper:

"..Detective..."

Martinson aimed his gun into the dark. "WHO'S THERE?"

Another whisper.

Closer.

"..Harold..."

Martinson's heart slammed against his ribs.

"Come out," he warned. "I'm not playing."

The whisper came again, right behind him this time:

"Detective Martinson..."

He spun—gun raised—

But no one was there.

Just the tunnel.

Just dripping water.

Just darkness shifting like an animal breathing.

His flashlight flickered.

"Don't do this," he whispered to no one.

His radio crackled.

Static.

Then a voice emerged from the static, warped and wet:

"Help... them..."

Martinson staggered backward.

"Regina? Regina—is that—?"

The static deepened.

"Under... here..."

The flashlight flickered again.

Went out.

The darkness became total.

Then—

In the absence of light—

He saw the glow.

A faint blue-green shimmer.

Moving.

Shifting.

Approaching.

Slowly.

Deliberately.

Martinson stepped back until his spine hit the stone.

His throat tightened.

"Who are you?" he whispered.

The glow came closer.

Closer.

He could hear water trickling.

Not water.

Breath.

Then a shape coalesced in the glow.

A human silhouette.

Female.

Young.

Pale in the dim light.

Martinson's voice cracked.

"Lila?"

The silhouette tilted its head.

Then whispered—

"Find... the... door..."

And vanished.

The glow receded.

The darkness collapsed around him.

Martinson fumbled with his flashlight, smashing it against his palm until it flickered back on.

Nothing.

No silhouette.

No glow.

Just tunnel.

But now—something gleamed on the floor.

A metal tag. Half-buried in mud.

Martinson picked it up.

A UW keycard.

Name:

REGINA EVERT

His breath left him.

He pocketed the card.

Then he said it aloud, because someone had to:

"I'm coming for you."

And he ran deeper into the tunnel.

Martinson ran deeper into the tunnel network, boots slapping against the uneven stone. His flashlight beam swung wildly across the walls—limestone streaked with mineral deposits, rusted pipes, abandoned wiring—all of it converging into a labyrinth no sane person would enter voluntarily.

But the keycard in his pocket burned like a warning flare.

REGINA EVERT — ACCESS LEVEL 3

She was alive.

Somewhere down here.

Maybe moments from not being.

The air thickened as he pressed forward—humid, metallic, vibrating faintly with the same low hum he'd heard on the pier. At first he thought it was machinery; then he realized machinery had rhythm.

This hum didn't.

This was **breathing**.

He slowed.

The tunnel curved left, then right, then dipped sharply before splitting into two branches.

A left path, narrow and irregular, carved through stone.

A right path, smoother, reinforced with old steel beams and slabs. Human engineering.

Martinson shined his light between them.

"Which way..." he muttered.

A drip fell onto his wrist.

He flinched.

It wasn't water.

Blue-green.

Viscous.

Warm.

It glowed faintly against his skin before dissipating.

Martinson wiped his hand on his coat.

"Okay. That's enough of that."

He chose **right**.

Toward the human-made path.

Toward the part of this nightmare he might actually understand.

The reinforced tunnel branched again—this time into an alcove where the wall bent inward around a massive slab of steel. A hatch. Industrial. Government issue. A relic from the Cold War era.

A faint rusted sign above it read:

SECTOR G — EMERGENCY ACCESS

Martinson approached slowly, scanning the seams. It looked sealed by time and disuse, but then his light caught something—

Scratches.

Dozens of them.

Not claw marks.

Tool marks.

Someone had tried to pry this door open recently.

He crouched, studying the base.

Footprints in the mud.

Small.

Narrow.

Feminine.

Regina's size.

He exhaled shakily.

"You got this far, at least…"

But the most chilling detail hadn't revealed itself yet.

Not until he looked up.

At eye level, carved into the steel, barely visible under rust—

B.T.

Martinson froze.

"Bob Thomas…?" he whispered.

Garth's AA sponsor.

The janitor.

The missing man from the footage.

The one who kept showing up at the lake at strange hours.

The one Garth trusted more than anyone.

Why was his mark down here?

Martinson brushed away dust.

B.T. again, scratched to the right.

And again below that.

Each mark slightly more frantic than the last.

He tested the door handle.

Frozen.

He braced his legs and pulled harder.

Nothing.

He pressed his ear to the metal.

A cold pulse vibrated through it—like a heartbeat muffled by hundreds of feet of stone.

Martinson staggered back.

"Jesus..."

He didn't know where this door led.

But he knew Regina had to be beyond it.

And he wasn't leaving without her.

He took a step backward, preparing to ram the hinge.

His radio crackled.

Martinson stiffened.

"—Detective Martinson, respond—"

It was Dispatch.

Thank God.

He lifted the radio. "Martinson here."

Static spit, coughed.

"—ton... perimeter... breach—"

"What breach?" he demanded.

The static sharpened:

"—Federal agents converging on your location—"

Martinson's blood chilled.

"Dammit."

He turned instinctively toward the direction he'd come—but that's when he saw them.

Shadows.

Moving down the tunnel toward him.

Flashlights.

Boots.

Voices.

Federal.

They had followed him in.

Or worse—

They had **been instructed** to follow him in.

Martinson clicked off his flashlight and ducked behind the corner of the alcove.

Agents' voices echoed down the tunnel.

"...down this way..."

"...he can't be far..."

"...Bainbridge said bring him back immediately—alive."

Alive.

Not "alive or dead."

Not "detain if necessary."

The specificity was chilling.

Martinson gripped his sidearm and breathed slowly through his nose.

"Okay. Think."

He couldn't go back.

He couldn't wait here.

He couldn't outrun them in a straight corridor.

He needed another way in.

Another path.

He aimed his light at the ceiling.

Pipes.

Bolts.

A maintenance panel two feet above the left edge of the hatch.

Old.

Rusty.

Probably forgotten.

Martinson holstered his weapon.

Pulled himself up onto the adjoining pipe.

The metal groaned under his weight.

He punched the maintenance panel with the butt of his flashlight.

The plate loosened.

Again.

And again.

Until it fell inward with a clang.

He heard the agents stop speaking.

"Did you hear that?"

Martinson climbed into the dark space above the hatch—

a narrow crawlway that smelled like mildew and something sharper.

Chemical.

He pulled himself fully into the shaft and slid the metal panel back into place behind him as quietly as he could.

Light beams sliced across the tunnel beneath him.

He held his breath.

Bainbridge's voice cut the dark:

"No mistakes. He's in here."

Footsteps approached the hatch.

Martinson flattened himself.

Even his heartbeat felt too loud.

A flashlight beam swept across the door.

Someone tried the handle.

"Sealed," an agent said.

"No," Bainbridge replied. "Not sealed. Blocked."

Martinson felt the steel vibrate as they tested the hinges.

Then Bainbridge said something that made Martinson's blood freeze:

"Open it."

"But sir—"

"Open it."

Metal scraped.

Machinery groaned.

They were going to force the hatch.

Martinson stiffened.

If they opened it—

He'd lose his chance.

He crawled forward along the shaft, heart hammering.

The narrow space twisted left, then slanted downward.

He kept going until—

His flashlight illuminated a symbol etched faintly into the metal surface of the crawlway:

A circle.

A wave.

A vertical line.

The same symbol Lila had recognized earlier.

AEC.

Advanced Enzyme Collaboration.

The precursor to the federal division.

And beneath it—

Another mark:

B.T.

Bob had been here.

And not once.

Again and again.

Leading the same path.

Finding the same way.

Martinson swallowed.

"Bob... what the hell were you doing down here?"

The crawlway widened into a merging chamber—small, rounded, carved partially by human hands and partially by something else.

A rusted ladder descended into darkness.

A plaque beside it read:

SUB-BASIN FEED SHAFT C

AUTHORIZED USE ONLY

N.I.H. PROJECT 1970

Martinson exhaled.

This was it.

A real entrance into the deeper system.

Into whatever nightmare Garth and Regina had entered.

He took one last look at the hatch behind him and listened.

The feds were cutting into it.

He didn't have time.

He gripped the ladder—

—and descended.

Halfway down the ladder, the hum grew louder.

The stone walls trembled.

A pulse rolled up through the shaft like a wave through flesh.

Martinson froze.

The hum deepened.

Then—

very softly—

a voice brushed the edge of his consciousness.

Not spoken.

Not echoed.

"Harold..."

He closed his eyes.

"No," he whispered. "No, no, no—"

The voice came again.

Closer.

"Detective..."

His breath caught.

"What do you want?" he whispered to the dark.

Silence.

Then a single, soft answer:

"Help them."

He opened his eyes.

The ladder shook.

Water dripped from above.

The feds were almost through the hatch.

Martinson tightened his grip—

—and climbed down into the darkness as the voice whispered:

"Hurry."

The ladder descended far deeper than Martinson expected. He climbed past layers of crumbled concrete, exposed rebar, stone fractured by time and water. His flashlight cut thin beams across the slick walls, revealing streaks of mineral runoff glowing faintly blue-green.

He tried not to think about why they glowed.

Halfway down, the ladder shook.

Martinson froze, gripping the rungs tightly.

Above him, boots pounded. Voices echoed down the shaft—muffled but urgent.

Bainbridge.

"Spread out! He went into the upper conduits. Find him—NOW!"

Metal rang sharply. Someone kicked the maintenance panel he had crawled through.

"Sir, this one's loose—"

"Pry it open."

Martinson's heartbeat thudded so hard he thought the ladder would vibrate with it.

"Move," he whispered to himself. "Keep moving."

He descended faster.

Twenty more feet.

Forty.

The hum in the walls intensified—as if the stone itself were vibrating.

Then—

BOOOOOOM

The entire shaft shuddered violently.

Martinson pressed himself against the ladder, bracing. Dust and pebbles shook loose from the walls.

Another boom.

Then another.

A voice—unmistakably Bainbridge—shouted:

"Surface breach! The shoreline is destabilizing—EVERYONE OUT!"

Martinson's blood ran cold.

Surface breach?

Shoreline destabilizing?

"Shit," he muttered. "What the hell is happening up there?"

He descended the last twenty feet in a controlled slide.

His boots hit the bottom.

A small utility flooring—metal grate, rusted, warped by water pressure—stretched into a tunnel barely tall enough to stand in.

He flicked his flashlight down the corridor.

The space was half-flooded.

But it wasn't water.

A thin layer of blue-green liquid crawled across the surface—like something alive traversing the metal.

He stepped back.

"No. Nope. We're not doing that."

The hum deepened, rumbling beneath his feet. Waves—actual waves—pressed against the metal grating as though the water on the other side of the wall were rising.

Martinson inhaled sharply.

"This tunnel's gonna flood."

He had to move.

He followed the grated hallway carefully, stepping only where the metal looked stable. The glow beneath the grate brightened the deeper he went.

Martinson whispered, "Garth... if you survived this, I'm buying you a beer so big you'll need a fork."

He rounded a bend—

—and froze.

A framed metal door stood ahead.

Someone had slashed through the corrosion on the middle panel, exposing bare steel underneath. A symbol had been carved into it with almost reverent precision:

Circle. Wave. Vertical line.

AEC.

And beneath it—

B.T.

Fresh.

Clean.

Recent.

"Bob..." Martinson whispered. "You made it this far too."

He pressed his palm to the initials.

Still warm.

He wasn't alone down here.

Bob had been moving through these tunnels minutes—maybe seconds—before him.

But where was he now?

Martinson tested the door.

It opened.

Not locked.

Not sealed.

Almost inviting.

He entered slowly.

The room was small—round—built of thick concrete walls reinforced with steel ribbing. A control panel sat destroyed in the corner, wires ripped from the sockets. A massive drainage pipe—four feet in diameter—ran along one wall, half-submerged in sludge.

Something glinted beside the pipe.

Martinson crouched, brushing away grit.

It was a coin.

A bronze medallion.

Engraved:

44 YEARS SOBER — ONE DAY AT A TIME

Martinson's throat tightened.

"Bob..."

He picked up the medallion, thumb tracing the words.

Bob Thomas.

Garth's sponsor.

Recovering alcoholic.

Forty-four years clean.

And he had been here.

Deep underground.

In the tunnels no one was supposed to know existed.

Martinson pocketed the medallion.

A soft sound echoed from the drainage pipe.

A wet shuffle.

A shift.

A human groan.

Martinson aimed his flashlight at the pipe's opening.

"Bob? Bob—can you hear me?"

The sound came again.

Closer.

Martinson knelt at the pipe entrance, bracing one hand against the slimy metal. "Bob? It's Martinson. I'm here to help you. Just—just tell me if you can hear me."

Silence.

Then—

A whisper.

Faint.

Broken.

"Detective..."

Martinson froze.

That was Bob's voice.

Weak.

Wavering.

Farther inside the pipe.

Martinson shined his light deeper.

Something moved.

Not the host.

Not an organism.

A person.

A human silhouette crumpled inside the pipe, half-submerged.

"Bob!"

He crawled closer, not caring about the slime soaking his sleeves.

"Bob, I'm here. I've got you."

He reached out—

A hand grasped his wrist.

Cold.

Human.

Trembling.

Bob Thomas's voice cracked like shattered glass:

"It's coming."

Martinson swallowed hard. "What is?"

Bob coughed violently, breath rattling in his chest. "The... lake... Harold. It's... moving. It's all... moving. Not—water—"

His eyes rolled weakly toward the ceiling.

Behind him—the glow intensified.

The water in the pipe vibrated.

Shuddered.

Moved upward.

Like something massive was displacing it.

Martinson tightened his grip. "Bob, stay with me. Stay with me!"

Bob whispered, barely audible:

"You can't stop a lake... Detective..."

Martinson gritted his teeth. "I can sure as hell try."

Bob shook his head weakly.

"No... listen. You... redirect. Don't fight... redirect..."

The same phrase he'd written in his notebook.

Martinson leaned closer. "Bob—we have to get you out. We're leaving. Now."

Bob's trembling gaze met his.

And Martinson saw it.

Terror.

Regret.

Resolve.

Bob whispered something else:

"Garth... Regina... below... too deep..."

Lightning cracked overhead—loud enough that the tunnels trembled.

The surface storm was directly above the lake now.

Martinson said, "I'll find them. I swear to God—"

Bob squeezed his wrist once—hard—then let go.

Martinson reached deeper—

But the water surged suddenly, knocking him backward.

He hit the concrete hard, flashlight rolling across the floor.

"BOB!"

The water inside the pipe glowed bright blue-green.

Then—

The shape in the pipe was pulled violently deeper and vanished.

Martinson scrambled forward, throat raw.

"NO! BOB!"

Silence.

Then—

A hum.

Long.

Low.

Deep.

The feed-shunt walls vibrated.

Martinson backed away.

"What..."

A faint distortion spread across the glow.

Then—

A **voice** formed inside the hum.

Not Bob.

Something older.

Terrifyingly calm:

"He cannot return."

Martinson stumbled backward.

"What does that mean?! What do you want?!"

Silence.

Then:

"Help.

Them."

The lights flickered.

The hum intensified.

Martinson's eyes widened.

The storm above—

—was affecting the pressure in the tunnels.

He had seconds to move.

He grabbed his flashlight and sprinted toward the far exit, where another narrow corridor slanted deeper underground.

As he ran, the room behind him began to **flood upward**, water pouring in from cracks in the walls as if the lake were being poured into the tunnels like liquid muscle.

Martinson didn't look back.

He ran.

Hard.

Toward the deeper chambers.

Toward Garth and Regina.

Toward whatever hell awaited all of them.

Above him—

Lake Monona roared.

CHAPTER 18

The Perimeter Tightens

A closing circle doesn't need speed—only certainty.

The cavern shook again—this time harder, like the entire underground system had inhaled sharply and wasn't sure how to exhale. Dust rained from the ceiling in soft little avalanches. The observation glass behind them—already webbed with age fractures—creaked like an old bone threatening to snap.

Regina pressed herself against the stone wall, breathing fast, eyes rimmed red. Her hand clutched my sleeve with the fear of someone who had just seen her past, present, and future collapse inward.

Lila crouched near the shattered console, staring at the glowing reservoir. Sheila leaned heavily on the metal railing, knuckles white, ankle trembling from pain.

I kept my arm around Regina, steadying her.

"We need to move," I said. "Now."

The glow in the water pulsed again—three beats.

Not random.

Not chaotic.

A **pattern**.

Lila swallowed. "It knows we're still here."

"And it's calling?" I asked.

She shook her head.

"It's... counting."

Regina stiffened. "Counting down to what?"

Lila turned toward us slowly, her voice trembling.

"To when the tunnels realign."

Sheila blinked. "Realign? Like... doors closing?"

"No," Lila said softly. "Like arteries redirecting blood. The water routes are shifting. The paths we used to get here won't exist in a few minutes."

The cavern throbbed once more—an echo rolling through the rock.

"How do you know?" I asked.

"Because I can hear them." Lila touched her temple. "The paths. The currents. The—signals. It's rearranging the system to funnel us somewhere."

Regina whispered, "Where?"

Lila looked at me.

"The center."

I swallowed hard.

"The Primordial Chamber."

She nodded slowly.

"It wants you there... both of you."

Another tremor shook the cavern.

Sheila muttered, "Great. So we've got a biblical lake intelligence playing interior decorator with limestone tunnels."

"Not funny," Regina whispered.

"I wasn't trying to be."

The reservoir rippled.

A pale shape drifted just beneath the surface.

Watching.

Waiting.

Lila's voice broke.

"We don't have long."

I grabbed Regina's hand. "We move."

Martinson slipped through the narrowing corridor as the feed-shunt chamber behind him flooded fast—water exploding outward in a pressurized blast that rattled the metal grating under his boots.

He didn't dare look back.

The tunnels were coming alive.

Breathing.

Shifting.

A low rumble shook the shaft, followed by a distant groan of steel under strain. He steadied himself against the wall.

Then his radio crackled violently.

"—Tactical—this is Sector Delta—shoreline collapse underway—repeat—collapse—"

Static.

A second voice cut in:

"Multiple surge points—Monona breach expanding—something's moving under the ice—"

Martinson swore. "Ice? It's fall. What ice?"

The comm sputtered again.

"Not ice—just looks like—oh God—pull back pull ba—"

Screech.

Silence.

Martinson slowed, breath fogging in the cold air funneling through the tunnel. A tremor rolled through the stone under his feet, almost knocking him sideways.

"This is bad," he muttered. "This is real bad."

He reached the intersection where the tunnel split into three directions—left toward collapsed utility lines, right toward a deeper corridor, forward into a narrowing crawlspace marked with faded stenciling:

RESEARCH ACCESS — SUB-BASIN E

He checked the ground.

Footprints.

Three sets.

One heavier.

Two lighter.

All heading forward.

"Regina…"

He crouched, testing the freshness by the softness of the mud.

Minutes old.

Martinson took a calming breath, steadied his flashlight, and pressed forward.

"You're close," he whispered. "Hold on."

We moved fast—Lila leading, Sheila limping, Regina gripping my hand in a way that told me she wasn't sure if she was holding onto me or if she needed me to hold onto her.

The tunnel ahead pulsed with faint blue light seeping through cracks in the limestone.

Regina flinched at every pulse.

"It feels like it's inside my head," she whispered.

"It's not trying to hurt you," Lila said gently. "It's… remembering you."

"That doesn't help," Regina snapped.

Lila stopped walking—suddenly, sharply.

"Shh."

She froze.

We all froze.

A sound drifted from far behind us.

Soft.

Wet.

Dragging.

Then—

A low hum.

Deeper than before.

Closer.

Sheila whispered, "It followed us?"

"No," Lila said. "It didn't follow."

She looked back down the tunnel.

"It's been waiting."

Regina whimpered and pressed into me.

"Garth, I can't—"

"You can," I said. "You already have."

I squeezed her hand.

"We're not giving it what it wants."

But the truth was bitter in my mouth:

What it wanted

was **us.**

The crawlspace narrowed to the point he had to move on his forearms. His flashlight beam jittered across the rough stone walls.

Then he saw it.

A streak of fresh blood smeared across a panel of limestone.

Just a small swipe.

Not a wound pattern.

More like someone caught themselves on a jagged edge.

Martinson's jaw clenched.

"Sheila... that you?"

He pushed forward.

Another tremor shook the tunnel.

And then—

from the darkness ahead—

A voice.

Not whispered.

Not telepathic.

Human.

Weak.

Hoarse.

"Help."

Martinson nearly dropped his flashlight.

"REGINA!"

He crawled faster, heart hammering.

But when he reached the end of the crawlspace, the voice was gone.

Only the echo remained.

He shined his light downward.

Below him:

A chamber.

Large.

Half-collapsed.

A rusted service ladder ran down the wall.

He lowered himself and began climbing.

Halfway down—the hum hit him like a physical force.

A resonance that vibrated his ribs.

Martinson gritted his teeth.

"What the hell *are* you...?"

The hum pulsed twice.

The stone walls glowed faintly.

He felt—

for the first time—

something like fingers brushing the edges of his thoughts.

Not entering.

Not speaking.

Just checking.

"NO," Martinson barked. "Not in my head."

The pulse withdrew instantly.

Like a startled animal.

He exhaled shakily.

"Good. We understand each other."

He climbed the last few rungs.

And when his boots hit the chamber floor—

he saw the footprints again.

Fresh.

Heading toward a narrow passage.

Martinson raised his weapon.

"I'm coming," he whispered.

We reached a stone platform overlooking a dark drop. A metal catwalk spanned across the void, swaying gently with the tunnel tremors.

Regina gasped. "Oh my God.."

Blue-green filaments crawled like veins across the stone surface, illuminating the cavern below.

The catwalk groaned.

Sheila stepped back. "Oh hell no. Nope. I'm not dying on a bridge that looks like it was built by interns."

"It's the only way," Lila said quietly.

Regina clutched my arm.

"Garth," she whispered, "I see something down there."

I followed her gaze.

The filaments in the cavern below were moving.

Not in currents.

Not random.

Spelling something.

A shape.

A letter.

G

Then—

A

Then—

R

Regina began to cry.

"It's calling you."

I swallowed.

"No," I whispered. "It's calling us."

The cavern shook violently.

The catwalk lurched sideways.

Sheila grabbed the railing. "MOVE NOW!"

Lila sprinted across first.

I pulled Regina close and ran.

Behind us—

from the darkness of the tunnel—

the host stepped into view.

Tall.

Pale.

Glowing.

It hummed once.

Long.

Low.

Reverent.

Regina screamed.

I grabbed her and kept running.

We reached the far side of the catwalk just as the host placed one massive hand on the metal platform behind us.

The entire structure trembled.

Lila shouted, "GO—GO—DON'T LOOK BACK!"

We ran into the narrow stone throat of the next tunnel.

Behind us—

with slow, terrible certainty—

the host climbed onto the bridge.

The metal howled beneath its weight.

And then—

it began to follow.

Martinson reached a fork in the corridor.

The footprints split:

- Two sets went left

- One went right

- A long, dragging line curved toward the left passage

He crouched.

The dragging line was a handprint. Sheila's size.

"This way," he whispered.

He followed left.

The hum grew louder.

A distant metallic groan echoed through the stone.

He froze.

That sound—

He knew it.

A metal walkway.

Under stress.

Underweight.

Martinson raised his flashlight.

Far ahead—

a faint light flickered.

Not artificial.

Bioluminescent.

He ran toward it.

And as he did—

he heard something else.

A whisper.

Faint but clear.

"Detective..."

He didn't flinch this time.

He answered:

"Not now. I'm busy."

We sprinted down the tight stone passage until the tremors behind us softened.

The catwalk groans faded.

The hum dimmed.

Only then did Regina collapse against the wall, gasping.

I crouched beside her.

Her hand trembled in mine.

"Garth," she whispered, "I think it's... her."

My pulse spiked. "Who?"

Regina swallowed.

"The host. The one following us."

Her voice broke.

"I think it's... Lila from before. From when she drowned."

Lila turned sharply.

Her face went white.

"She's not me," Lila whispered. "She's... something else."

The tunnel pulsed once more.

A deep, low resonance rolled through the stone.

Lila shuddered.

"It's close."

Regina buried her face against my shoulder.

And as I held her—

—another hum rippled through the tunnel, making the stone vibrate under our hands:

"FOUND."

The tunnel narrowed again before widening abruptly into a cavern that stank of cold stone, rust, and something faintly biological. Martinson's boots skidded to a halt at the edge of the drop.

The catwalk below was destroyed.

Half of it hung twisted over the chasm. Metal slats were bent upward like peeled skin. Bolts lay scattered across the stone floor. A faint blue-green smear glistened where something had stepped—*hard*—on the platform.

Martinson crouched, examining the wreckage.

The footprints were strange:

- **Broad**

- **Too long**

- **Flat, webbed spreads**

- **Almost human, almost not**

He muttered, "Okay. That's new."

But it wasn't the footprints that made his stomach tighten.

It was what he found on the far side.

A thin strip of fabric.

Torn.

Caught on a jagged corner of the metal rail.

He picked it up.

Navy-blue cotton, soft—shirt material. Women's size small.

Regina's.

Martinson pocketed it, breath catching.

"They made it across," he murmured. "Still moving. Still alive."

He scanned the far tunnel.

The hum vibrated through the stone again—low and slow, the same pulse rhythm he'd felt since entering the sub-basin shafts.

He raised his flashlight.

"Don't worry," he said to the dark. "I'm coming."

Then he spotted something else.

Scratched into the stone, shallow but fresh:

← 3

Martinson brushed it with his thumb.

A direction.

And a number.

A countdown?

No.

A signal.

Someone had left it intentionally.

He ran on.

The tunnel ahead of us forked like a trident—three narrow passages, each sloping downward into deeper darkness.

The hum was changing.

It had been a pulse.

Stable.

Predictable.

Now it was shifting—

syncopating, almost like breathing irregularly.

Lila stopped dead.

Her eyes fluttered.

"Oh God."

Regina clutched my sleeve. "What?"

Lila pressed her hand against the wall.

"It's... re-routing. The tunnels. The currents. Everything. It's—it's closing off all but one path."

Sheila limped past us, wincing. "You're saying the cave system is rearranging itself like a—like a Rubik's Cube?"

"Not the rock," Lila whispered. "The passages. The water routes. The membranes between chambers. They're thinning, shifting, sealing."

I swallowed.

"So which one do we take?"

Lila shook her head violently.

"I'm trying—I'm trying—give me a second—"

She pressed her palms to her temples, teeth gritted.

Regina stepped forward and grabbed her wrist.

"Lila—look at me."

Lila looked up, eyes red and frightened.

"You don't have to tell it," Regina whispered softly. "You don't have to obey it. Just listen for the part that sounds like you."

Lila froze.

Her breath steadied.

Then her eyes widened slowly.

"The right passage," she said. "That's the artery that stays open."

I nodded. "All right. We go right—"

Sheila grabbed my arm. "Garth."

Her hand trembled as she pointed to the wall beside the right-hand passage.

A symbol marked in mud.

Fresh.

← 3

My pulse spiked.

"That's... I know that."

Regina stared. "It's the mark from Druitt's logs. The directional code."

"No," I whispered. "It's not Druitt's handwriting."

Sheila blinked. "Then whose—"

A deep rumble shook the passage.

The rocks above us cracked.

Dust rained down.

"MOVE!" Lila screamed. "THE OTHER PATHS ARE CLOSING!"

We sprinted into the right-hand tunnel just as the left and center passages collapsed behind us like closing throat valves.

Martinson followed the ← 3 marks through a series of tight squeezes, low arches, narrow maintenance runs, and one terrifying crawlspace that felt like the inside of a coffin.

He kept going.

Always forward.

Always following the marks.

He didn't notice at first when they started appearing more frequently.

On the stone.

On dislodged metal.

Even scratched into the silt on the floor.

Each one pointing deeper.

Each one marked with the same hand.

"Bob Thomas," he whispered.

That old bastard had mapped these tunnels with more clarity than the FRD had ever admitted.

He reached a chamber where the floor dipped into an ankle-deep pool of cold water. The footprints ahead of him were clear:

- One limping (Sheila)

- One dragging slightly (Regina—fear, exhaustion)

- One lighter (Lila)

- One heavier (me)

He followed them.

As he moved deeper, the hum in the walls grew louder.

It wasn't mechanical.

It wasn't water pressure.

It wasn't the host.

It was the intelligence.

And it was concentrating.

He muttered, "If I end up in a horror sequence because of you people..."

Then something changed.

The hum shifted.

A single pulse rolled down the corridor.

A word formed inside it—

"**FOUND.**"

Martinson whispered, "Oh no."

He broke into a run.

We descended into a narrow, sloping tunnel that felt carved by rushing water centuries ago. The walls were smooth, almost polished. Filaments glowed faintly beneath the stone like veins tracing a living thing.

The hum deepened.

Regina's fingers dug into my hand.

"Garth... something's wrong."

Lila nodded, breath trembling. "The hum—it's not searching anymore. It's locating."

"Us?" Regina whispered.

"No," Lila said. "Him."

She pointed toward me.

My stomach dropped.

"Why me?"

Sheila answered before Lila could.

"Because you were the first to be marked."

The tunnel ceiling groaned.

A crack split along the spine of the chamber.

A stray pebble fell from above.

Regina flinched. "It's collapsing!"

"No," Lila said. "Not collapsing. Directing."

"Toward what?" Sheila snapped.

Lila didn't answer.

She didn't need to.

We heard it.

Behind us—

from somewhere impossibly far and impossibly close—

A sound like breath moving through bone.

Then a hum.

Slow.

Low.

Vibrating the soles of our feet.

The host.

Sheila shined her flashlight back into the darkness. Her voice cracked.

"Oh holy hell—"

There it was.

Its pale outline filling the passageway behind us.

Arched back.

Elongated limbs.

Luminous eyes like two reflected moons.

And it was moving toward us—

Quietly.

Deliberately.

Purposefully.

"RUN," Lila snapped.

We ran.

Martinson reached a drop-off where the tunnel plunged into a deeper shaft. A metal ladder descended along the right side, half-rusted, half-melted from some past event.

He shined his flashlight downward.

Nothing.

Then—

A faint echo.

Running.

Voices.

Human.

Far below.

Martinson exhaled shakily.

"I see you."

He slung his weapon, grabbed the ladder, and descended fast.

A tremor shook the shaft.

Then another.

Dust poured down like rain.

Martinson pressed his boots harder into the rungs and slid the last twenty feet. His knees hit stone hard but he didn't stop.

The tunnel ahead glowed faintly.

A fresh set of footprints led right.

Regina.

Garth.

Sheila.

Lila.

He ran.

The hum intensified.

The stone under his boots vibrated.

Something ahead was moving them deeper—fast.

He picked up speed.

We burst into a widening chamber—thin pillars of eroded limestone rising like ribs around us.

The hum warned.

The ground underfoot trembled.

The walls pulsed with blue-green filaments.

The host's hum grew louder behind us.

Lila grabbed my shoulder.

"It's turning the tunnels," she said breathlessly. "We won't get back to the surface. Not through any way we came."

Regina clung to me. "Then where is it taking us?"

Lila swallowed hard.

"It wants to bring you to the center."

"The Primordial Chamber?" I asked.

"No," she whispered. "Deeper. The chamber beneath that."

Sheila blinked. "There's something *beneath* the primordial chamber?"

Lila nodded.

"Druitt called it the Heart Basin."

A crack tore through the stone behind us.

The host's silhouette filled the entrance.

Regina grabbed my face with both hands, terrified.

"Garth—Garth it's not walking—"

I swallowed.

Because she was right.

It wasn't.

It was gliding.

The hum deepened—

—and the intelligence spoke:

"COME BACK."

Regina screamed.

I pulled her behind me.

Lila pointed down a narrow chute of stone winding into darkness.

"DOWN!" she shouted. "We go down!"

We ran toward the chute—

And as we dove into it—

A voice echoed in the tunnel behind us.

Human.

Desperate.

Loud.

"GARTH! REGINA!"

Regina gasped.

"That's—"

"Martinson," I whispered.

The host turned its head.

The entire cavern seemed to tighten.

And then—

Martinson's voice again, closer, furious:

"DON'T STOP—GO! I'M RIGHT BEHIND YOU!"

The host roared.

The stone chute dropped at a steep angle—too steep for running, not quite vertical, but close enough that we were half-sliding, half-falling. The walls were smooth, polished by centuries of waterflow. Blue-green veins of bioluminescent filament shimmered along the stone like constellations.

Regina screamed as she slid ahead of me—her hands scraped against the walls, trying to slow herself. I lunged, catching her wrist.

"Got you!"

A tremor rolled beneath us, vibrating the chute like a throat clearing itself. The hum resonated inside my ribcage. The lake was sending pulses through the stone—signals, not warnings.

Guiding us.

Pushing us.

Sheila slid past, cursing like a sailor with a broken rudder. "This is *not* the scenic route you promised!"

Lila descended last, her palms pressed to the walls, eyes closed, riding the vibrations like she was listening to them.

"It's directing the flow," she called. "The paths are redirecting!"

"You keep saying that!" Sheila shouted. "What does that actually *mean*?"

"It means we're going exactly where it wants us," Regina said hoarsely.

She wasn't wrong.

The chute suddenly widened near the bottom—too late for braking. We spilled onto a narrow ledge overlooking a vast, dimly glowing chamber.

Regina and I landed hard, tangled. Sheila skidded beside us. Lila slipped last, landing gracefully because of course she did.

I pushed myself up, wincing.

"What... is this place?"

Below us—

A sea.

An underground lake.

Silent, still, glowing faintly from beneath.

Like a starless sky flipped upside down.

Regina squeezed my arm.

"Oh God... it's beautiful—"

"No," Lila whispered.

"It's waiting."

Sheila limped forward, shining her flashlight across the water.

"Where's the host? Did we lose it?"

A deep hum rolled through the chamber like a breath.

Regina shuddered.

"No. We didn't lose it."

The sound was coming from above—

Martinson sprinted into the cavern just as the host dropped into view from the upper tunnel like a pale nightmare descending a staircase.

He froze.

"What the—"

The creature—

No.

The *host*—

turned toward him with slow, eerie precision.

Its limbs unfolded like something recalling old muscle memory. Its skin shimmered faintly with filaments beneath the surface. Its eyes—

Its eyes were human-shaped but not human.

Reflective.

Depthless.

Alive with pale luminescence.

Martinson raised his sidearm with both hands.

"STOP!"

The host tilted its head, studying him with clinical interest.

Martinson's voice cracked with involuntary fear.

"I said STOP, damn it!"

The host took one slow step forward.

Martinson fired.

The gunshot cracked through the cavern like thunder.

The bullet hit the host's shoulder—

—and passed through as if punching into gelatin.

A light spray of luminescent fluid arced out—blue-green, shimmering—

Then the wound closed.

Instantly.

Martinson staggered backward.

"Oh... oh no. Nope. That's not—

The host moved.

Not fast.

Not slow.

Just... *inevitable.*

Martinson fired again, aiming for the leg this time.

The bullet hit—

And dissolved.

The host blinked.

Not startled.

Not hurt.

Just... aware.

It hummed.

A low, resonant tone that vibrated Martinson's bones.

He gasped as a pressure wrapped around his skull—a sensation like someone trying to remember *him.*

"Get—out of my head—"

The pressure withdrew immediately.

Like the host was startled.

Martinson lowered his weapon, chest heaving.

"You... you can hear me?"

The host straightened to full height.

Seven feet of pale, resonant silence.

Slowly, impossibly gently—

It raised one elongated arm

and pointed

down the chute where Garth and the others had gone.

Martinson felt ice in his veins.

"You want me to go down there?"

The host stared at him.

No aggression.

No hostility.

No malice.

Only purpose.

Martinson swallowed hard.

"You're not trying to stop me."

Silence.

"You're... letting me through."

A hum of confirmation tremored through the room.

Martinson's voice cracked.

"...why?"

The host's gaze didn't waver.

And then—

Softly, impossibly—

A whisper inside Martinson's mind:

"Help... them."

Martinson's eyes widened.

He holstered his weapon.

"Okay," he whispered. "Okay then."

He approached the chute.

The host stepped aside.

Martinson took one last look at it.

"You're not the monster here, are you?"

The host tilted its head.

Almost sadly.

Martinson descended the chute.

Behind him—

The host glowed brighter.

Then followed.

Regina sat against the wall, trembling. I crouched beside her, smoothing her hair, grounding her. The chamber hummed quietly, the underground lake glowing below us like a cosmic pool.

"It's happening again," she whispered.

"What is?"

"My head. The memories. They're—bleeding."

"Bleeding?"

She nodded.

"Between us."

I felt something tighten in my chest.

"Tell me."

She swallowed.

"When we were kids... when you pulled me from the water... I don't just remember what *I* felt anymore." Her eyes glistened. "I remember what *you* felt."

I froze.

Regina's breathing trembled.

"You were so scared," she whispered. "Not of drowning. Of losing me."

The hum deepened.

A memory forced itself forward in my mind—

Water.

Warm.

Sunlight scattering.

Regina slipping from my grasp.

A pale shape behind me.

A cold touch to my temple.

Not yet.

The memory wasn't mine.

It was hers.

Bleeding into me.

Regina sobbed softly.

"It's merging us, Garth. The intelligence is... linking our minds."

Sheila exhaled shakily. "That's—real bad, right?"

Lila answered.

"It's what it wanted all along."

Regina choked. "Why us? Why—why—"

But her words cut off as another memory hit her.

She gasped.

Lila gripped her shoulders. "Regina—focus—what do you see?"

Regina stared into nothing.

"Him," she whispered.

"Who?"

Regina's voice turned hollow.

"Druitt."

My spine stiffened.

"What about Druitt?"

Regina blinked slowly, trembling harder.

"He wasn't alone."

The chamber trembled.

Sheila cursed. "What the hell is THAT supposed to mean?"

Regina looked at me.

Tears formed.

"Garth… there were two children."

I shook my head.

"No. Regina, I—"

She whispered:

"Two boys."

Time stopped.

My throat closed.

"What?"

"I saw two boys with Druitt. Not one. Two. One was you. The other—"

She clutched the stone wall, gasping.

"The other was... crying. Calling for you."

My breathing slowed.

Regina grabbed my wrist.

"Garth—there was another child with you. Another boy. You weren't alone."

I froze.

Completely.

The hum surged.

The chamber vibrated.

Lila staggered. "It's accelerating—Garth, your memory's unlocking faster than—"

Regina whispered:

"Garth... you had a brother."

My pulse stopped.

Regina sobbed.

"You had a brother. You had a brother. And Druitt took him."

Martinson slid down the chute, landing hard on his shoulder. His flashlight clattered across the stone.

He groaned, stood, grabbed it—

And froze.

The host was descending behind him.

Slowly.

Gracefully.

Unstoppable.

Martinson raised a hand.

"Wait..."

The host paused.

Martinson pointed down the tunnel.

"They're close."

The host hummed once.

A low, confirming tone.

Martinson exhaled shakily.

And then—

The ground trembled beneath them.

The hum surged.

The air thickened.

Something was coming.

The host arched its back slightly—like an animal picking up a scent.

Martinson swallowed.

"What is it?"

The host turned its pale, luminous eyes toward Martinson.

And in his mind, he heard:

"Brother."

Martinson's blood froze.

"What?"

The host pointed deeper into the tunnels.

"His... brother."

Martinson's voice cracked.

"Garth's brother?"

A hum.

"Yes."

Martinson whispered:

"Oh... God."

Regina sobbed as the memory overwhelmed her.

Lila steadied her. Sheila crouched beside me, stunned.

Regina's voice trembled:

"He was little. Maybe six. Maybe seven. He called your name."

My heart hammered.

What name?

Regina swallowed.

"He called you—'Garry.'"

The name hit me like a brick.

I almost fell backward.

Garry.

Nobody had called me that since I was a child.

Since before—

Before what?

Regina wiped her tears.

"Garth... Druitt didn't just save us."

She looked down into the glowing water.

"He took someone else."

The chamber pulse intensified—

BOOOOM

Dust rained from above.

Lila looked up, terrified.

"It's collapsing! MOVE!"

Behind us—

from the chute—

Martinson shouted:

"GARTH! REGINA! DON'T MOVE—"

Regina clutched me.

I pulled her close.

And the host stepped into the chamber behind Martinson.

Its hum shook the walls.

Not threatening.

Not calling.

Not summoning.

But recognizing.

It looked at me.

And I understood.

For the first time.

The host wasn't coming for me.

It wasn't coming for Regina.

It was coming for—

"**Garry...**"

My knees buckled.

Regina gasped.

Lila froze.

Sheila whispered, "Oh my God..."

Martinson stared at me, horrified.

The host hummed one final time.

Deep.

Soft.

Sad.

"**Return... brother.**"

The chamber cracked open beneath us.

And the floor dropped.

The stone gave way beneath our feet like wet cardboard.

One moment we were standing on the ledge.

The next—

CRACK—BOOOOM—

The entire shelf dropped, plunging us downward in a cascade of rock, dust, and screaming.

Regina's fingers tore from my grip.

"GARTH!"

I reached for her—caught air.

Sheila tumbled sideways, hitting a jut of stone before vanishing into the dark.

Lila curled into herself as she fell, trying to ride the collapse.

Martinson grabbed a projecting pipe with one hand—

slipped—

and plunged after us.

I fell last.

Or maybe first. The sensation was impossible to track. My body tumbled, bounced, slammed against cold stone. Dust blinded me. The world spun into a blur of blue-green luminescence and violent descent.

Then—

We broke through a membrane of thin stone.

Air rushed up past me.

A vast chamber opened below—

lit from underneath by a swirling, bioluminescent expanse.

The **Heart Basin.**

I hit the ground hard—hard enough to knock the breath out of me, but not hard enough to break anything major. I gasped, coughing dust.

Somewhere to my right, Sheila groaned.

To my left, Lila's flashlight flickered.

Regina—

"Regina!"

My voice echoed against the cavern walls, swallowed by their size.

"REGINA!"

Then a faint reply:

"Garth—h-here—"

I scrambled toward the sound, slipping on loose stone and bioluminescent dust. The ground here was different—not solid rock but a thin crust over deeper water channels, like the dense surface of an alien swamp.

I found Regina half-buried in a mound of rubble, coughing.

I knelt, desperate.

"Regina! Are you hurt?"

She shook her head weakly. "Bruised... winded... but okay."

Relief hit me with the force of a punch.

I pulled her into my arms.

She clung to me, trembling from adrenaline and fear.

Lila crawled toward us, eyes unfocused. "The basin... we're in the basin..."

Sheila limped up behind her, leaning heavily on her good leg. "Holy... hell... I think I broke my favorite swear word on the way down."

"Where's Martinson?" Regina gasped.

I scanned the chamber.

He lay sprawled twenty feet away—unmoving.

My stomach dropped.

"Martinson!"

I sprinted to him.

He groaned just as I reached him.

"Oh, thank God..."

He pushed up on his elbows. Dust streaked his hair. His coat was torn at the shoulder.

"Did... we win?" he croaked.

"Far from it."

He blinked blearily at me. "Thought so."

Now that my eyes adjusted, I finally saw it:

The Heart Basin wasn't a chamber.

It was an **organ.**

A massive, hollowed sphere of limestone, ribs of stone arching overhead like the underside of a colossal skull dome. Beneath the cracked floor lay an entire subterranean lake glowing softly—blue-green filaments drifting through it like neural pulses.

The hum here was constant.

Steady.

Low.

Ancient.

The space breathed.

Slowly.

Massively.

Regina whispered, "Garth… it's not just alive…"

I finished the thought for her.

"It's thinking."

Lila nodded. "This chamber… is the core of the network. The oldest part. The original site where the intelligence first rooted itself."

She knelt, touching the glowing stone.

"It's remembering us. All at once."

Sheila murmured, "That's comforting."

A tremor rolled through the basin.

A slow, shifting pulse beneath the glowing water.

Martinson struggled into a kneel. "Why does it feel like there's something big under this floor?"

Lila didn't answer.

Because she didn't need to.

We all felt it.

Like something massive—impossibly massive—moving beneath us.

The hum deepened.

The ground vibrated.

Martinson whispered, "That's not water movement."

Lila nodded.

"That's a heartbeat."

The ceiling above us split with a jagged crack.

Regina clutched my arm.

Lila backed away, eyes widening.

Something pale and immense slid through the break in the stone—

Descending.

Quietly.

Gracefully.

The host.

It dropped the last few meters in a controlled fall, landing lightly on the cracked basin floor. Dust swirled around its elongated feet.

Martinson raised his sidearm on instinct.

"Don't," I said, grabbing his wrist.

"It won't hurt us."

The host turned its luminous eyes toward me.

Recognition.

Not hunger.

Not predation.

Not possession.

Recognition.

Then it turned to Regina.

And the hum deepened into something like sorrow.

She clung to me.

"Garth..."

The host lowered itself into a kneeling posture—

hands outstretched, not in attack

but in supplication.

Lila whispered, "It's not here as a hunter."

Martinson scowled. "Then what the hell is it?"

Regina's tears welled.

"It's here... as family."

The host hummed gently.

Regina stepped backward.

Sheila muttered, "What in the name of cryptozoological fuckery does *that* mean?"

Regina looked at me.

"It's him."

My pulse stopped.

"Him... who?"

Regina swallowed hard.

"Your brother."

The host's hum intensified.

Warm.

Soft.

Painful.

Martinson whispered, "Oh Jesus..."

I stared at the creature. Its posture. Its face. Its eyes.

No memory.

No sudden flashback.

But something deeper.

Recognition.

Without remembering.

My throat tightened.

"How..." I whispered. "How could—he drowned. We drowned together. I pulled you out but I—"

A flicker of memory.

A pale arm pulling me upward

as another set of fingers slipped from mine

small fingers

warm

human

Regina sobbed.

"He drowned, Garth. But he didn't die."

The host tilted its head ever so slightly.

The hum vibrated the stone.

Not demanding.

Inviting.

Calling.

Lila whispered:

"He was the first bond."

Martinson stepped forward, shaken.

"Druitt didn't save just you two."

Regina nodded.

"He saved your brother too. He hid him. Garth... the lake took him. But it didn't kill him. It kept him."

"Why?" I whispered.

Lila answered, voice trembling.

"Because he was the first compatible host. The first child whose mind didn't fracture under the merge."

I shook.

Regina held me.

"It used him to try again," she said. "And then it found us."

My knees gave out.

I hit the stone floor hard, hands shaking.

Lila crouched beside me.

"Garth, the lake didn't take your childhood from you. Druitt did. He erased the memory to protect you."

"But he left my brother—"

Regina touched my face gently.

"You never would have left him. Druitt knew that."

I whispered:

"I would've died for him."

Regina whispered:

"You still might."

The host reached out again.

Its fingers were long, glowing faintly at the joints.

Waiting.

Not attacking.

Not demanding.

Waiting for me to touch its hand.

To complete something broken for thirty years.

The moment I looked into the host's eyes, the memory hit me—

Full force.

Not fragmented.

Not partial.

Complete.

A summer day.

Warm water.

Two boys laughing.

A plastic boat drifting.

Regina slipping.

My brother diving after her—

brave

fearless

just like always

Druitt screaming from the shore—

"BOYS! STAY BACK—!"

A pale shape rising from the dark.

A cold pulse through the water.

A whisper inside my skull:

"Not you.

Him."

The pale shape reached for my brother.

He turned too late.

And the lake opened—

like a mouth.

The last thing I saw was his fingers reaching for me as he was pulled below.

Not violently.

Gently.

Like he was being collected.

I screamed his name:

"GARRETT!"

The host's hum echoed the name inside the chamber—

"Garrett..."

Regina collapsed into sobs.

Martinson looked stricken.

Sheila muttered, "Holy... mother of God..."

My brother.

My little brother.

Alive.

Alive in the only way the lake could keep him.

Merged.

Altered.

Changed.

But alive.

The host touched its chest.

Then touched mine.

Then pointed to the glowing water beneath the cracked floor.

Lila swallowed.

"It wants you to see the rest."

A violent tremor slammed through the Heart Basin.

Cracks spread across the floor.

The underground lake surged upward, pressure building beneath the crust.

Regina grabbed my arm.

"Garth—we have to move!"

But the host didn't move.

It knelt—

hands on the stone—

humming a steady resonance.

Like it was holding something back.

Lila gasped.

"The lake is rising. The storm above—combined with the desalination overflow—the tunnels are going to flood."

Sheila shook her head violently. "We need a goddamn exit!"

"There is no exit," Lila said.

"Not yet."

Martinson stepped forward.

"Then what's the plan?!"

Lila turned to him slowly.

"The lake doesn't want to drown you."

"Oh, that's reassuring."

"It wants to *redirect* you."

Martinson froze.

Bob's words.

"Redirect..."

Lila nodded.

"Sheila. Regina. Martinson. Move to the upper ledge."

"What about Garth?" Regina cried.

Lila looked at me.

"He stays."

Regina lunged toward me. "NO!"

I caught her, holding her tight.

"I have to," I whispered.

"Garth—don't—you can't—"

"I have to know. I have to finish it."

She sobbed against me.

The host hummed, and the chamber vibrated again.

The water beneath the floor bulged upward—

cracks radiating outward—

blue-green luminescence flooding through them.

Lila screamed:

"GO NOW—THE FLOOR IS BREAKING!"

Sheila grabbed Regina and Martinson, dragging them toward the upper ledge. Regina clawed for me, screaming my name, but Sheila was stronger than she looked.

The host reached out again.

Not to take me.

To steady me.

To guide me.

I took its hand.

The moment our palms touched—

The floor beneath us shattered.

The water erupted upward—

And everything went white.

CHAPTER 19

What the Lake Remembers

Water forgets nothing—it only waits for the surface to still.

In the moments before consciousness returned, I felt only warmth.

Not surface warmth.

Not sunlight.

Not memory.

Something older.

Like being remembered by something that had always been there, waiting beneath the floor of my mind.

Then the warmth shifted.

It pressed.

It asked.

Are you here?

My first breath came like an explosion.

Cold air.

Salt-metal taste.

My body shuddered.

I opened my eyes.

Darkness.

But not empty darkness.

A dim, rippling teal glow pulsed beneath me, illuminating the cracked basin floor in intervals—

light

dark

light

dark—

as though something below the surface were breathing.

I was lying half-submerged in shallow water pooling over slick stone. The basin had collapsed into levels—terraced fractures leading down into a massive pit of bioluminescent fluid.

Regina's voice echoed faintly above.

"GARTH! Garth, answer me!"

I tried to respond. My throat felt packed with cold sand.

"Regina..." My voice cracked into a whisper.

Her silhouette appeared high above—maybe thirty feet up—standing on a narrow ledge with Sheila and Martinson. All three leaned dangerously over the edge, their faces lit bluish by the light rising from below.

Regina cried out, "He's awake!"

Martinson shouted something, but the cavern swallowed the sound before I could make it out.

I tried to push myself upright, but my palms slipped in the water. Thin tendrils of blue-green light swirled beneath the surface—moving with purpose, like intelligent currents rearranging around me.

It pulsed again.

light

dark

light

My chest tightened.

It wasn't breathing.

It was remembering.

Something stirred at the far edge of the basin.

The host.

Garrett.

He—*it*—stood in the shallows, half-lit, half-shadow. The long limbs, the strange geometry of the body, the faint bioluminescent pathways beneath the translucent skin—

—but the face—

The face was younger than the rest of the form.

Still stretched, still altered, but *familiar* now that the memory had been partially restored.

A child's face grown into something else.

A brother's face.

Garrett took a slow step toward me.

Regina screamed his name behind me—but it wasn't my name she screamed.

"GARRETT!"

The host flinched.

Not from fear.

From recognition.

He tilted his head toward the sound, almost human, almost boy-like.

His luminous eyes returned to me.

And then I heard it—not in my ears, but behind them:

"Garry."

My knees buckled.

I nearly fell again.

Nobody called me that except—

Except him.

Thirty years collapsed into a single instant.

A flash:

Warm water.

Garrett laughing.

Plastic boat drifting.

Regina's scream.

The lake opening.

Hands—his—slipping from mine.

The memory struck hard enough to buckle my spine.

I gasped.

Garrett reached out.

Slowly.

Delicately.

Like he was afraid I might break.

Behind him, the basin pulsed—

deep, slow, vast—

like the neural firing of a submerged brain older than anything human.

Light

dark

light

dark

Then a wave of images surged into my mind—

Not memories.

Not dreams.

Something else.

Threads of thought braided through time.

A storm over the lake in 1971.

Ice cracking in 1980.

Druitt kneeling beside a caged aquatic sample in 1989.

A child's footstep on a pier—mine.

Another child's hand—Garrett's—reaching for a dragonfly.

A flood of consciousness spiraled through the basin, and for a moment, the boundary between me and the lake thinned:

- **Currents carried regret**

- **Water held memory**

- **Stone stored sorrow**

- **Light remembered us both**

I heard Regina shout again, her voice high with fear.

"Garth—don't touch him! Not yet! Garth!"

But Garrett kept coming.

He extended one long, glowing hand.

And I knew—deep in my bones—that if I touched him here, in the basin, the memory link would flood completely.

The lake would show me everything.

Why did Druitt save me?

Why did he erase my memory?

How did Garrett survive?

Why did intelligence take him?

And worst of all—

What does it want now?

Garrett's massive frame lowered. He crouched like a child trying to make himself smaller. His head tilted as though listening to something inside me.

He whispered inside my skull again:

"Come back."

Not to him.

To the memory.

To the moment.

To the fracture.

To the thing I'd spent my whole life forgetting.

I stepped back, trembling.

"Garrett... please..." My voice broke. "I don't—I don't know if I can..."

The host's glow pulsed once.

Not a demand.

A plea.

Behind me, stone buckled as a huge crack split the basin floor further. Water surged upward, spraying cold droplets across my face.

Martinson shouted from above:

"Garth! THE FLOOD IS COMING—MOVE!"

But I couldn't move.

Not yet.

The water pulsed again—

light

dark

light—

and I felt something rising through my nerves like electric memory:

We were here before.

All of us.

Three children.

Two saved.

One kept.

Garrett extended his hand again.

Not monstrous.

Not alien.

Just...

a brother.

I took one step toward him—

And the basin swallowed the world.

For a moment, I thought I had fallen into water.

Not real water.

Not lake water.

Not physical depth.

This was something else—

a medium made of memory,

light,

and long-held grief.

I wasn't drowning.

I was sinking

into someone else's recollection of drowning.

Garrett's.

The world dissolved into a slow green glow.

Not water—

not air—

a viscous, living interface.

A membrane.

A conscious boundary.

I felt it close around me like cool silk, absorbing sensation the way skin absorbs temperature. Every pulse, every flicker of luminescence in the basin carried a memory fragment, suspended like silt in a current.

A voice drifted through the medium—soft, childlike, familiar:

"Garry…"

I tried to speak but my voice emerged as ripples, not sound. The lake translated thought into motion.

Garrett? Garrett, is that you?

A pulse answered.

And the world of the basin shifted.

I was standing—except I wasn't—on the water's surface. The basin around me warped into a tableau:

A Wisconsin summer.

Sunlight fracturing on lake waves.

Two boys and a girl playing near a half-rotten pier.

Me.

Regina.

Garrett.

I watched the scene like an outsider and participant simultaneously.

Garrett pointed at something in the water—a dragonfly skimming the surface. He laughed and leaned over too far. Regina grabbed his shirt to steady him.

I remembered this day.

But only the first few seconds.

The rest had been scrubbed, cauterized out of me by someone who thought he was saving me.

The memory shifted, aligning itself with sensation.

Warm sun.

Cool water lapping at the shore.

The smell of wet wood and algae.

Then the tone changed.

A hum began—faint, like water vibrating with low frequency.

The lake was remembering too.

Garrett called something out, but the sound warped under the basin's filter, twisting syllables into luminous waves. The memory shifted into slow motion the moment tragedy struck.

Regina slipped.

Garrett lunged to grab her.

I reached for him.

And in the original memory—the one I grew up believing—this is where everything vanished. Just a white flash, screams, and waking up on the shore with Druitt beside me.

But the basin restored what Druitt erased.

The water did not simply close over us.

It opened.

Like a mouth.

A soft, gentle mouth, taking in a lost child.

Tentacles of light—filaments—rose from the depths like the fingers of a giant hand, wrapping around Garrett's ankles. He didn't scream. He didn't thrash.

He looked up at me.

Confused.

Then he said, softly:

"Garry? Don't let go."

My chest tightened until I couldn't breathe. I reached again—my hand inches from his—

but the filaments wrapped tighter.

Not pulling him down violently.

Inviting.

Accepting.

Absorbing him into the light.

The filaments pulsed once more, enveloping Garrett completely.

And then—

the memory paused.

A new layer appeared.

Something I had not seen before.

The water erupted around me—not the real water, not the basin water, but the **memory of the water's surface** splitting open.

Druitt burst through, gasping for air.

Younger than I remembered him.

Stronger.

Hair dark, face desperate, eyes scanning the water like a man hunting ghosts.

He dove once.

Twice.

Three times.

He surfaced with an arm wrapped around a child.

Me.

I wasn't breathing.

Regina clung to him, hyperventilating.

Garrett was gone.

But Druitt didn't give up.

He dove again.

The memory tilted sideways, shifting perspective—now I saw it through Druitt's eyes, through his emotions.

Cold.

Pressure.

Terror.

Resolve.

He followed the glowing filaments downward.

He saw them curling around Garrett, cocooning him gently like a jellyfish nest cradling a pearl.

He tried to pull him free.

The filaments tightened.

Druitt screamed underwater, bubbles exploding from his mouth.

He reached again—

And this time something touched his mind.

Not a hand.

Not a voice.

A **memory** that wasn't his.

Young Garth's voice.

Young Regina's fear.

Young Garrett's heartbeat.

A headache so violent Druitt nearly fainted.

The lake was **communicating**, transmitting information in raw, painful pulses.

Druitt, panicking, surfaced again and collapsed onto the pier, clutching me—the only child he could pull free.

I watched him breathe hard, chest heaving, as he looked back into the water.

He whispered:

"Please... let him go. He's just a boy."

Silence.

Then:

light.

The lake glowed once, pulsing like a yes,

but not the yes Druitt wanted.

Regina screamed behind him.

He gathered me in his arms—stunned, shivering, barely conscious—and made a choice that shattered all of us:

He left Garrett with the lake.

He pressed a kiss to my forehead.

"I'm sorry, son. I'm so damned sorry. But if I tell you... you'll come back. And if you come back... the lake will take you too."

I saw him run to shore.

He carried me to the nearest house.

Regina ran beside him crying.

Garrett's name hung in the air between them.

Then Druitt whispered the words that rewrote my entire childhood:

"You have one son now."

The basin around me pulsed, affirming the memory.

Light.

Dark.

Light.

The vision fractured—light splitting like a prism through water.

I found myself back in the basin, half-submerged, shaking so hard I could barely stand.

The host—Garrett—stood before me, chest rising and falling with slow, tidal motion. He wasn't threatening. He wasn't lost.

He was waiting.

Regina shouted from the ledge overhead:

"Garth! What is it showing you?!"

I tried to answer, but my voice failed.

Garrett reached out again.

The water around us vibrated gently.

"You remember," he whispered inside my head.

Regret hit me like a riptide.

"I let go," I whispered to him. "I let you go."

The host shook its head with strange, childlike softness.

"No. I slipped."

The simple line broke me.

Garrett stepped closer.

"I wasn't scared. Not until Druitt pulled you away. Then I was alone. The lake kept me warm. Kept me alive. Kept me growing."

He placed one massive palm against my chest.

"But it didn't know how to give me back."

Behind him the basin pulsed again, brighter.

Images flickered at the edges:

- Lake Monona during storms

- Subterranean arteries

- Filament networks

- UW hydrology labs

- Lila falling through memories of her own

- Sheila searching for stability

- Martinson holding the others together

- Regina crying on the ledge

The intelligence was showing me everything.

All at once.

Because I was marked.

Because I had been inside this water before.

Because this place was part of me as much as it was part of Garrett.

Garrett withdrew his hand.

And in my mind, a final sentence formed:

"You can take me with you…

or you can let me stay."

The basin trembled.

A flood tremor.

A warning.

Martinson's voice echoed from above:

"GARTH—THE TUNNELS ARE STARTING TO COLLAPSE—NOW OR NEVER!"

The host—Garrett—looked at me with the last fragment of boyish humanity lingering in the glow under his eyelids.

I had never made a harder choice in my life.

For a brief and terrible moment, I could not breathe.

Not because I lacked air, but because some part of me—the part that spent thirty years forgetting my brother existed—was trying to recoil from the truth now flooding in.

But there is a point beyond which a mind can't retreat—

and I had crossed it.

The basin's slow teal glow throbbed in time with my pulse.

The host—Garrett—stood only a foot from me, water swirling around him in bioluminescent rings.

His towering form was alien, but the tilt of his head, the shape of his eyes—

That was my brother.

The brother I'd failed.

The brother I'd forgotten.

The brother who had been taken not by death, but by the intelligence beneath Lake Monona.

And the worst realization:

He wasn't angry.

He wasn't vengeful.

He was lonely.

Garrett extended his hand again, palm open, fingers glowing faintly from within—translucent, vascular, patterned like algae-fed coral.

"Come with me."

The words weren't spoken aloud.

They vibrated through the cracked basin floor, through the pooled water, through me.

A long-dormant memory surfaced—Garrett tugging my sleeve on that pier years ago, his voice softer than mine:

"Come see. It's pretty."

Back then it was just a dragonfly.

Now it was an entire consciousness.

Behind us, stone trembled as another crack split open, sending up a spray of silver droplets that glittered like mercury before falling back into the glowing pool.

From the ledge above, Regina screamed my name again.

"Garth! Don't touch him—please, don't!"

Her voice trembled—not with fear of the host, but with the terror of losing me again.

The way she nearly did the day of the drowning.

I looked up at her.

Her face was streaked with tears, illuminated by the basin's blue light. Sheila clung to her shoulder. Martinson had one arm braced against the wall, gauging the floodwater inching upward behind them.

Regina's expression was a mixture of anguish and something deeper—something like recognition.

She whispered again, this time barely audible:

"Don't leave me."

The words hit me harder than the memories.

But Garrett wasn't malicious.

In fact, his mind pressed into mine with something like sorrow.

"You don't have to stay," he whispered in the inner voice. "Not like me."

I swallowed hard.

"I don't have a choice."

Garrett blinked—his eyes glowing with shifting teal circuitry beneath their surface.

"You always had a choice," he said. "Druitt made it for you."

My voice cracked.

"I never would have left you."

His gaze softened, and for a moment he wasn't host, or hybrid, or emissary—

—he was just a boy again.

"I know."

The basin pulsed once, deeply, like a sigh from something ancient beneath us.

light

dark

light

Floodwater surged behind Martinson, splashing over the edge of the ledge where Regina and Sheila clung.

Time was nearly up.

The lake wanted me to choose.

To leave.

Or to stay.

And Garrett was the interface through which that choice would be made.

He stepped closer.

433

I didn't step back this time.

Not when I saw what glimmered in his glowing palm—a small object, embedded in his skin. No, not embedded. Carried.

A dragonfly.

Not a real one—

a memory-fragment, shimmering, semi-formed, composed of prismatic light.

My breath caught.

I remembered the day by the pier.

Garrett had leaned over to watch a dragonfly dancing on the water.

Now the lake held that moment—

the last moment we had shared as brothers—

and offered it back to me.

Garrett pressed the memory into my chest.

Heat pulsed outward.

Images flashed:

Garrett's giggle.

The dragonfly landing on his wrist.

My hand steadying him.

Regina's braids whipping in the wind.

Druitt laughing softly from the shore.

The memory wasn't painful.

It was beautiful.

And the basin wanted me to have it again.

But behind that beauty lurked something darker—another memory rushing forward violently:

The lake's intelligence reaching for Garrett.

Wrapping him in filaments of light.

Preserving him.

Changing him.

And then—

Druitt pulling me back, my hand slipping from Garrett's.

The basin struck me with this memory like a blow.

I staggered.

Garrett steadied me gently with one enormous hand.

"Now you see," he whispered.

My knees weakened.

"Why didn't the lake give you back?"

Garrett shook his head slowly.

"It tried. But you were gone. And I was already changing."

"Because of the filaments?"

He shook his head again.

"Because I was alone."

A piercing ache stabbed behind my ribs.

Garrett lifted his other hand.

"For thirty years, Garry... I remembered you."

The tears came then—hot and unstoppable.

"I didn't," I whispered.

He didn't flinch.

"I know. Druitt made you forget."

"But I should have found you."

He smiled—the only fully human expression he had left.

"You did."

Behind us, the basin lurched, sending a shockwave through the water.

Stone groaned.

The chamber roof shed debris.

A roaring noise—like something collapsing at a great distance—echoed through the tunnels.

Martinson shouted:

"GARTH! NOW! MOVE!"

Regina sobbed:

"Please! Please just come here!"

Garrett slowly lowered his hand.

"You have to go," he whispered, voice trembling.

I stepped closer.

"No. Not without you."

Garrett's expression shifted—something between grief and resolve.

"You can't take me with you. I'm not meant for the surface. I haven't been... for a long time."

His glow dimmed.

The basin's pulse slowed.

The intelligence below was preparing for collapse or retreat—it was unclear which.

Garrett touched my shoulder lightly, and the touch burned with memory.

"But you can let me go," he said.

My lip quivered.

"I don't know how."

"You do."

His voice faded into the water.

"You already did once."

The basin lifted me—

not physically,

but psychically.

I saw a final surge of memory:

- Garrett's first night inside the intelligence

- The filaments wrapping him in warmth

- His fear turning to wonder

- His wonder turning to dependence

- His dependence turning into transformation

- His transformation turning into purpose

- His purpose turning into waiting

Waiting for me.

Waiting for someone to remember him.

Waiting for someone to choose.

The memory hit with surgical precision—

not cruelty,

but clarity.

The basin withdrew the vision.

Garrett looked at me one last time.

Soft.

Sad.

Resigned.

"It's okay," he said quietly. "I'll stay."

Another crack split the floor—

water surged violently—

Regina screamed again—

Sheila clung to the ledge—

Martinson cursed loudly behind them.

I grabbed Garrett's wrist.

"No. No—Garrett—please."

He placed his other hand over mine.

Our fingers didn't match size or shape or species.

But the gesture was human.

He leaned in and pressed his forehead to mine—

luminous skin to mortal skin—

glow to pulse—

memory to memory.

"You didn't let me go," he whispered.

"You survived."

And then—

he pushed me gently backward.

I stumbled.

The basin's current caught me.

And Garrett—

my brother—

the host—

the lost child—

the returned memory—

walked backward into the light.

His final words echoed inside me as the basin's pulse escalated:

"Live, Garry."

Then he sank beneath the water,

light swallowed by deeper light,

fading

slowly

into the depths.

The basin surged upward, throwing me toward the escape ledge.

Voices screamed my name.

The flood began.

CHAPTER 20

The Heart Basin

Every secret has a pulse, some chambers are carved to hold it.

I hit the water hard—

not the glowing basin pool where Garrett had vanished,

but a colder, heavier current surging upward through the newly opened fractures.

The chamber roared like a living throat exhaling.

Stone trembled.

Bioluminescent filaments snapped free from their moorings, swirling in the flood like drifting synapses.

Through the rush of water, the echo of Garrett's final words still reverberated inside my skull:

Live.

A hand grabbed my jacket collar—rough, urgent, human.

"Garth! I've got you! Hold on—dammit, hold on!"

Martinson hauled me upward toward the ledge.

His face was streaked with dust and phosphorescent droplets.

Regina cried out when she saw me.

"Pull!" she screamed. "Bob Thomas's sake—just pull!"

Sheila pressed herself against the stone, bracing her feet to keep Martinson from slipping as he dragged me up. Water surged violently below; each pulse threatened to rip me out of his grip.

The basin was collapsing—

not simply flooding—

contracting,

as if the intelligence were withdrawing into its deeper neural layers.

With a grunt, Martinson pulled me over the edge.

I collapsed beside Regina, chest heaving, fingers numb. She grabbed my face between her hands, staring into me with a mixture of terror and heartbreak.

"You're alive."

Her voice cracked.

"You came back."

I couldn't speak yet.

Not about Garrett.

Not about what I saw.

Not about what I had to leave behind.

The rocks behind us groaned again, then cracked open as another wave of dark water surged upward, flooding the lower basin.

Martinson looked over the edge and swore.

"Sheila! Move! Garth, Regina—on your feet! NOW!"

We staggered down a narrow secondary tunnel—a maintenance conduit running parallel to the main basin chamber. The walls were lined with decayed piping, rusted clamps, and strips of old hydrology insulation that peeled away like wet paper.

Behind us, the Heart Basin roared.

Ahead of us, the tunnel curved upward.

The ground shook violently, and Sheila screamed, clinging to a rusted pipe as a torrent of water smashed through the floor behind her.

Martinson grabbed her wrist and yanked her forward.

"Go!" he shouted, his voice breaking on the final syllable.

We scrambled into the rising tunnel until the roar of water receded slightly.

Just enough to hear the heartbeat.

Not ours.

Not mine.

Not any human's.

A deep, slow resonance pulsed through the stone.

thum—p

thum—p

thum—p

The lake's intelligence had not collapsed.

It was waking.

As we climbed, the tunnel widened into a circular stone chamber. A former hydrology junction—metal scaffolding around the edges, dark water dripping rhythmically from above, the sweet metallic scent of wet limestone.

Except the walls...

moved.

Slowly.

Gently.

Like a creature breathing through a membrane.

Regina froze.

"Garth... do you hear that?"

I nodded.

It wasn't just sound.

The heartbeat vibrated through the walls, through the floor, through the very air.

Sheila shook her head in disbelief. "What in God's name is this?"

Martinson looked at me.

"I'm assuming you have an answer."

I wiped water from my eyes.

"I have... part of one."

The chamber pulsed faintly.

A filigree of bioluminescent veins ran through the walls, glowing gently, shifting like neural pathways firing beneath translucent skin.

Regina stepped closer to the wall.

"No," I said instinctively, grabbing her wrist. "Don't touch—"

But she didn't touch it.

The wall touched her.

A thin line of light branched outward, illuminating under her palm as though recognizing her.

She gasped and staggered back, but the glow remained, following the outline of her hand before retracting like a withdrawing tendril.

Martinson steadied her.

"What was that? Did it hurt you?"

Regina shook her head emphatically.

"No. It was... curious."

She looked at me.

"Garth... I think it recognizes us."

Sheila shook her head, horrified.

"Recognizes you? The hell does that mean, Regina? It's a wall—"

"No," Regina whispered. "It's not."

The heartbeat intensified.

And I finally spoke the truth:

"This chamber is part of the intelligence. Part of the lake network. These are neural pathways. The whole underground system—the arteries, the basin—it's all alive."

Martinson's jaw tightened.

"What's controlling it?"

I swallowed.

"Not what..."

I looked back toward the flooded basin.

"...who."

Regina inhaled sharply.

"Garrett."

I couldn't answer.

Because the truth was more devastating:

Garrett wasn't *controlling* it.

He was a **conduit**.

A bridge between human memory and the intelligence.

And I had just left him behind.

We reached another chamber—smaller, with metallic grating across the floor. Old UW maintenance signage flaked off the rusted door frames.

Lila was there.

Half-slumped against the wall, trembling, her eyes glowing with faint teal filaments threading through the whites. Her irises pulsed like the basin.

Regina gasped. Sheila cried out her name.

Lila looked up.

Her voice came out layered—

her own,

and something beneath it.

"You left him."

I froze.

"Lila—what are you talking ab—"

She leaned forward, shaking violently.

"You left your brother."

The words struck like a blow.

I staggered, losing my breath.

Lila crawled toward me, her fingers trembling, veins glowing under her skin like faint circuitry.

Her voice—both voices—whispered:

"The lake is in pain."

A tremor rolled through the ground.

Stone dust rained from the ceiling.

"The host is receding. The intelligence is collapsing. The basin is contracting inward."

Regina grabbed Lila by the shoulders.

"Lila! Focus—what do we do?"

Lila turned her head toward Regina.

Her eyes softened.

"He loves you too."

Regina's breath caught in her throat.

Another tremor rippled through the chamber. Filaments ran along the walls rapidly, like signals racing through a living neural network.

Lila clutched her head, screaming.

Martinson crouched beside her. "Lila! Talk to us. What's happening?"

She gasped, shuddering violently.

"The intelligence is pulling the tunnels back—closing them. Retreating. It's afraid."

I felt the truth of it.

I felt Garrett's fear inside the pulse.

The intelligence wasn't trying to kill us.

It wasn't attacking.

It was **defending itself** from collapse.

Lila looked up at me, eyes wide and glowing.

"You have to choose again."

My heart stopped.

"What?"

The light behind her eyes flickered.

"Garrett is fading."

Regina grabbed my arm.

"Garth—no—no, you are NOT going back—"

Lila interrupted.

"If you don't choose... the intelligence dies. And Garrett dies with it."

The chamber shook violently.

Stone cracked.

Water surged upward in the tunnel behind us.

Martinson grabbed the rail. "We need to MOVE!"

But Lila raised her hand, steadying us with a force far beyond human strength.

Her voice deepened again—lake layered over girl:

"The heart basin will collapse.

The tunnels will fill.

The lake will go silent.

Unless one of you returns."

Regina's nails dug into my arm.

"No. Garth—no. You left him once. You're not leaving *me*. Not again."

I looked at her.

Then at Lila.

Then at the moving walls.

Then at the shaking chamber.

Then back toward the basin's glow.

And the truth hit me:

This wasn't a choice between my life and my brother's.

It was a choice between:

Memory

and

Loss.

The two forces that had shaped my entire life.

And now—

the lake wanted its answer.

For a long moment, no one moved.

Not Regina, whose nails cut crescents into my arm.

Not Sheila, whose breath came in panicked bursts.

Not Martinson, who stood braced against the shaking wall with the grim face of a man preparing for the second collapse.

Not Lila, who knelt trembling on the metal grate, eyes lit like submerged stars.

Only the chamber moved—

breathing, tightening, pulsing—

the living stone flexing as though the lake itself were trying to decide whether we were threat or memory.

Lila gasped again.

"The heart basin... it's rupturing.

It can't hold its shape without him."

Her voice layered and strained—her own and something deeper, resonating through the walls like a tuning fork struck underwater.

Regina turned on me, tears streaking down her face.

"You are not going back down there."

Her voice broke.

"Not again. Not after what I just saw. Not after what you told me. Not after losing you once."

I could barely meet her eyes.

Because the last time, I hadn't chosen.

Druitt had dragged me out.

Garrett had slipped away.

Regina had watched me pulled from the lake while Garrett sank into light.

Now the choice was mine alone.

A deafening crack tore through the chamber.

The ceiling split, sending a waterfall of debris and cold water into the room.

Martinson shoved Sheila aside as a heavy beam crashed down where she'd been standing.

"MOVE!" he shouted. "The whole structure's failing!"

Water surged from the tunnel we'd come through—violent, dark, growing fast.

The intelligence was pulling back the arterial pathways, collapsing everything that wasn't essential.

Retreating.

Protecting itself.

Or dying.

I grabbed Lila by the shoulders.

"Is there time to reach Garrett?"

Her dilated pupils flickered between human and something otherworldly.

"If you go now," she whispered.

"If you don't hesitate."

She reached toward me with trembling fingers.

"But the deeper you go... the more you'll change."

Regina yanked me back.

"No. Garth, look at me. LOOK at me."

I did.

She held my face in both hands, her forehead against mine, her whole body pressed against me to anchor me to the physical world.

"You come back to me," she whispered.

"You survive. You always survive."

My breath caught.

Her voice was shaking, but her grip was unbreakable.

"I won't lose another person to that lake. I won't lose you. Not now. Not ever."

A memory rose inside me unbidden—

the lake pulling Garrett,

Regina screaming,

Druitt hauling me up the shore,

the world going silent.

I had been rescued by accident.

Garrett had been kept by intention.

Regina saw the decision forming in my eyes.

"No," she whispered. "No, Garth. Don't—"

A second crack split the floor.

The chamber tilted.

Water began pouring in from three directions.

Sheila screamed, clinging to the wall.

Martinson dragged her toward the high point.

"WE HAVE TO MOVE!" he roared.

"We have maybe thirty seconds before this whole chamber floods!"

But Lila reached out and grabbed my hand with surprising strength.

It wasn't just her strength.

It was the lake's.

"You asked what the lake wants," she whispered.

Her voice doubled again—hers and something vast beneath her.

"It wants to survive. And it wants him."

Her glowing eyes locked onto mine.

"And it wants you to understand."

The wall behind Lila buckled inward suddenly, and she cried out as she was thrown forward onto me.

Regina tried to pull me away again, sobbing now, frantic.

"Garth, PLEASE—"

But it was Lila's final words that froze me still:

"He's dying."

Water roared into the chamber like a living beast.

The floor vibrated with the tremors of deeper collapses.

Filaments of light raced along the walls—signals firing too fast to interpret.

Sheila and Martinson were nearly at the exit tunnel.

Regina clung to me desperately, arms wrapped around me, refusing to let go.

"Don't leave me," she begged.

"Please. Please, Garth. Don't leave me again."

Time fractured.

Regina's tears on my cheek.

Garrett's glowing hand reaching out in the basin.

Lila shaking violently, veins pulsing with lake light.

The intelligence pressing memory into my skull.

Druitt's voice whispering in memory:

"If he comes back, the lake will take him too."

But Druitt was wrong.

I wasn't a child now.

And I wasn't helpless.

Garrett was dying—

fading—

returning to nothingness in a collapse the lake could no longer hold back.

He wasn't just a host.

He was family.

My brother.

My responsibility.

I had failed him once.

I would not fail him again.

I cupped Regina's face gently with one hand.

"I love you," I whispered.

Her breath caught.

"But I have to go."

She broke.

Her knees buckled.

A sharp, keening sound escaped her throat—raw, primal, like the scream she'd released as a child when Garrett was taken.

"NO—no no NO—Garth please, PLEASE—don't—"

I kissed her—quick, desperate, the taste of lake water and tears and endings.

Then I turned.

And jumped.

The chamber floor fell away beneath me as I leaped into the collapsing lower tunnel.

Cold water hit me with the force of a punch.

The current grabbed me immediately, pulling me downward into the arterial chute feeding the Heart Basin.

The world narrowed.

Sound condensed into a rush.

Light dissolved into streaks of blue and green.

My lungs seized.

But there was no going back.

Garrett needed me.

And the intelligence was guiding me—

the tunnel walls glowing faintly where I should swim,

the currents shifting just enough to keep me from smashing into stone.

The lake wasn't trying to kill me.

It was trying to bring me home.

A bright pulse flashed up the tunnel ahead—

a signal.

A beacon.

Garrett.

I kicked harder, following the glow.

Pain spread through my limbs as my body screamed for oxygen, but I pushed deeper, pulling myself along jagged stone ridges, letting the current do most of the work.

Another pulse:

light

dark

light

I felt a voice—not a sound, not a word—

Garreth

Garreth

Garreth

My childhood nickname twisted through water.

Garry. Garry. Garry.

The tunnel widened.

Then dropped.

I plunged into open water.

The Heart Basin was collapsing.

Filaments snapped and spiraled downward like jellyfish tentacles ripped free.

Stone slabs cascaded into the core.

The water churned with violent undertow.

And there—

on the far side—

partially submerged—

glowing faintly—

was Garrett.

He was staggering, barely upright,

the bioluminescent patterns under his skin flickering irregularly.

Weak.

Dying.

He raised his head as I swam toward him, and his eyes—

still luminous, still alien—

widened with something painfully human:

Relief.

Fear.

Love.

He reached out with one trembling arm.

His voice echoed faintly inside me:

"You came back."

The basin roared around us like the inside of a collapsing lung.

A hundred spider-webbed fractures across the stone walls.

Every few seconds, another slab tore loose and vanished into the churning water below.

But all I could see was him.

Garrett.

Standing—barely—on a narrow stone shelf that shook beneath his weight as though rejecting the impossible biology lodged inside him. His skin flickered, light patterns firing irregularly beneath the surface—like a dying signal trying to reboot.

His silhouette swayed.

His breathing stuttered.

The lake was losing him.

He was losing himself.

I swam hard, fighting the current pulling me sideways toward the basin center, until at last I reached the shallows near his ledge.

My hand shot out, grabbing hold of a jagged rock to anchor myself.

"Garrett!"

His head flicked up in quick, broken motions, as if his mind lagged half a second behind the movement.

When he whispered, the voice inside my skull sounded weaker than I'd ever heard it:

"Garry... I can't hold it."

He took one faltering step toward me.

The entire ledge shifted, groaning under his weight.

I tried climbing up, fingers slipping against the slick stone. I managed to swing one leg over the edge, pulling myself onto the trembling ledge beside him.

Up close, he looked worse.

Much worse.

The glow beneath his translucent skin blinked wildly—sometimes bright, sometimes fading so fast he almost appeared human again.

The patterns—once rhythmic, like the calm pulse of a large organism—were now chaotic, glitching like a corrupted neural feed.

He staggered.

I grabbed him instinctively.

The moment my hand touched his skin, light shot up my arm like a shock. Memory pulsed through me—Garrett at age five, hiding behind a tree; Garrett at eight, showing me a rock he found near the lake; Garrett holding my hand on the pier—

Then the light flickered out again.

His body convulsed.

He nearly collapsed.

I caught him, my arms around his chest. He was impossibly heavy now, far denser than a human body. But he leaned into me like a desperate child.

His voice broke through the noise:

"The lake can't keep me... together."

My throat tightened.

"It's because you're alone."

He trembled violently; the glow beneath his skin dimmed almost to darkness.

"I don't want to... disappear."

"You won't," I said; my voice cracked.

"I will," he whispered. "I can feel it."

A sharp tremor reverberated through the stone beneath us.

The basin was collapsing faster now—experiencing a catastrophic core failure. The intelligence was pulling back all its filaments, withdrawing into some deeper reservoir to protect itself.

But Garrett—

Garrett was stuck halfway between two worlds.

Too human to collapse inward with the lake.

Too altered to survive without it.

He was in pain.

Terrible pain.

I held him tighter.

"You're not alone anymore," I whispered.

"I'm here."

His head dropped against my shoulder.

And for the first time, I felt him cry.

Not with tears.

With trembling.

With flickers in the light.

With little spasms of memory discharging through his skin.

The memories wrapped around us like soft bioluminescent ribbons—

me teaching him to skip stones,

him tracing shapes in the sand,

us whispering to each other under blankets during storms.

Moments I hadn't known were missing.

Moments he'd carried for decades without me.

He had kept my childhood safe inside himself even after I abandoned him—not by choice, but by ignorance.

And now he was dying.

The ledge beneath us buckled.

The basin heaved.

A roar tore upward as a new fissure opened along the far wall.

Water surged up in violent plumes.

Garrett flinched in my arms.

"Garry... it hurts..."

I pressed my forehead to his.

"What do I do? Tell me. Please—tell me how to help."

His breath warbled, the glow under his skin flickering again.

"The lake is trying to pull everything back. It doesn't... want to lose what it learned. It's taking all its memories with it. But I'm stuck."

He lifted one twitching hand, reaching weakly toward my head.

"I can't hold together unless someone bridges the signal."

"Signal?"

He nodded weakly.

"Like... like enzyme kinetics."

His voice cracked.

"A substrate... that needs a catalyst."

My heart lurched.

The lake didn't need me physically.

It needed my **memory** as a conduit.

A stabilizing agent.

A buffer.

A bridge.

Garrett looked at me, eyes dimming.

"You have my memories now. And I have yours. If you link with me... the lake can finish the transfer."

"And if I don't?"

The ledge shuddered beneath us.

Garrett's body flickered again—

skin going dim,

patterns breaking apart,

light sputtering like candle flame in a storm.

"I'll fall apart," he whispered.

"No." My voice cracked. "No, no—Garrett—"

"It's okay."

He placed a trembling hand over my heart.

"You came back. That's all I ever wanted."

Another tremor tore through the basin.

Chunks of ceiling crashed into the water.

A massive plume erupted skyward.

Time was nearly gone.

I clenched his hand.

"What happens if I *do* link with you?"

Garrett leaned into me, his forehead pressing to mine again.

"You'll see everything."

The chamber shuddered.

"Everything," he repeated softly.

"The lake won't hide anything from you. Not its origins. Not its failures. Not its purpose."

"And you?"

He swallowed hard.

"I'll... stay. But I won't be the same."

Meaning:

He'd survive,

but he would not return to the surface.

He wouldn't walk out of here with me.

He couldn't.

He'd be—

something new.

Something stable.

Something eternal.

Garrett, the lost boy, would remain.

Garrett, the human, would fade.

I felt the answer forming inside him before he spoke it:

"You'll leave. I'll stay."

A jagged crack split the ledge behind us.

There was no time left.

And the decision was mine.

I cupped his face.

Garrett's glowing tears—if that's what they were—spilled down his cheeks, flickering as they fell into the water.

He whispered:

"I'm scared."

"I know. Me too."

His eyes dimmed further.

"You were never... supposed to come back, Garry."

I laughed softly through tears.

"But you knew I would."

A faint smile.

"You were always the brave one."

"No," I whispered.

I pressed my forehead to his again.

"I'm brave *because of you.*"

A deep tremor rocked the basin.

The water swelled upward, swirling into a vortex.

Garrett exhaled sharply.

"It's happening," he whispered. "If you're going to link… you have to do it now."

I closed my eyes.

I thought about Regina—

her voice,

her hands on my face,

her plea not to lose me.

I thought about Sheila—

steady, loyal, pragmatic.

I thought about Martinson—

fighting back fear with grit.

I thought of Bob Thomas—

his warning,

his love,

his sacrifice.

I thought of Druitt—

broken man,

doing the best he could.

And then—

I thought of the boy I once had,

and the boy I had just found again.

I opened my eyes.

And whispered:

"I won't leave you alone."

Garrett inhaled sharply.

I placed both hands on his chest.

Light flared—

brilliant, blinding—

not from the basin,

but from him.

His thoughts poured into me—

all at once—

like a tidal wave of memory.

My body shook violently.

Garrett's voice—

the lake's voice—

the intelligence's voice—

overlapped in a symphony of layered consciousness.

"You are the bridge."

Heat surged up my arms.

Water roared around us.

Stone cracked in a deafening chorus.

I felt myself dissolving—

Not dying.

Expanding.

Becoming part of memory itself.

Garrett convulsed against me, gripping my shoulders.

Not in pain.

In transfer.

In connection.

We were two halves of one memory completing each other for the first time since childhood.

The basin pulsed with unbearable brilliance.

And then—

Everything went white.

CHAPTER 21

Druitt's Burden

Some weights aren't carried in the hands, but in the quiet
corners of the mind.

There was no light at first.

No water.

No sound.

Only pressure.

Not crushing, not painful — more like being pressed between two warm palms. The basin's white flash faded, and I realized I wasn't floating or sinking anymore.

I was **inside** something.

Inside memory.

Inside someone else's mind.

No — inside **three minds** braided together:

Mine.

Garrett's.

And the lake's.

The boundary between the three began to blur, then dissolve entirely.

A flicker sparked at the edges of vision. A reel of images unfurled slowly:

- Lake Monona on a winter morning, ice shifting like old bone
- A boy in a red jacket leaning over the pier
- A gloved hand grabbing him too late
- A storm rolling in across rooftops
- A man sprinting, diving, screaming underwater

Druitt.

The memory sharpened until it became whole.

I saw Druitt standing on the pier in 1971 — younger, leaner, hair black, coat soaked through from sleet. He was shouting my name.

"Garth! Garrett!"

The sound warped around the edges, muffled by the memory-filter, but the raw panic was undeniable. His breath came out in white bursts as he sprinted toward the lake.

I watched myself — six years old — thrashing at the water's surface.

Garrett was already below.

Regina screamed from behind Druitt, stumbling on the icy planks. Her braids swung wildly as she shouted for us.

Druitt dove.

I felt his cold shock, the biting pain when he hit the water, the frantic stroke downward toward the faint silhouette of two boys slipping into the lake's mouth.

He grabbed me first.

Not out of preference.

Not out of choice.

Because I was higher in the water column by inches — only by inches — and he was a human man trying to save two children with only two arms.

He kicked upward, pulling me with him.

Garrett drifted deeper, enveloped by filaments of luminescent algae that pulsed with strange rhythms.

Druitt surfaced, gasping.

"You stay!" he choked, thrusting me into Regina's arms. "Hold him! Don't let him back in!"

Regina sobbed and collapsed onto the pier with me.

Druitt dove again instantly.

The memory flickered, shifted —

showing the world through Druitt's eyes now.

Dark water.

Bioluminescent spirals.

Filaments wrapping gently around Garrett.

His small face peaceful, almost curious.

The light cocoon welcoming him like an anemone embracing prey it doesn't intend to kill.

"Garrett!"

Druitt's scream vibrated through the water as he lunged toward the light.

The lake remembered this moment.

Garrett remembered this moment.

Now *I* remembered this moment.

The filaments tightened, not in violence but in protection, as if sensing Druitt's intrusive panic. The intelligence did not understand fear yet. It only understood **absorption**.

Druitt reached for my brother — fingers inches away —

when the first psychic pulse hit him.

A blast of sensation —

like memory being poured into his skull,

like thousands of whispered voices pressed into a single thought.

Druitt convulsed underwater, clutching his head.

The lake was communicating.

Not with language,

but with **remembering**.

Images flooded him:

- The history of the lake

- Past drownings

- Old hydrology currents

- The skeleton of pre-industrial channels

- The neural pattern it had become over centuries

He tried to scream but only bubbles escaped.

He forced himself deeper.

He reached Garrett —

grabbed his arm —

pulled —

But the filaments tightened around Garrett's chest and legs, glowing brighter, responding to the lake's instinct to preserve the fragile thing it had tasted.

The lake wasn't trying to kill Garrett.

It was trying to **keep him alive**.

Druitt yanked harder, screaming underwater.

Garrett's tiny hand reached for him —

then slipped,

slipped like memory,

slipped like breath,

slipped back into the luminous folds.

Druitt's lungs gave out.

He was forced to surface.

He crawled onto the pier, shaking violently.

Regina was crying into her hands.

I was unconscious.

I watched the entire scene from the outside and the inside — my small body limp in Regina's arms, and Druitt's horror as he forced air into my lungs, begging me to live.

Not because he loved me more.

Because he knew — even then — that the lake had chosen Garrett.

And it would choose him again and again.

Unless I was hidden.

The vision shifted abruptly.

Same man.

Same lake.

Different season.

Druitt in a lab coat now, older by twenty years, face lined by grief. The Enzyme Institute lab glowed with fluorescent light. Papers littered his desk. Coffee cups piled in corners.

He replayed the drowning in his mind —

again,

again,

again —

each time writing a different hypothesis:

"Memory distribution?"

"Sub-neural photonic encoding?"

"Fluid intelligence transfer?"

"Self-preserving matrix?"

His notes were filled with sketches of underwater filaments, brain stem structures, enzyme catalytic pathways overlaid on hydrological channels.

And always, always,

471

the same conclusion circled:

"The lake remembers."

He tested samples pulled from the shallows —

found photonic activity that shouldn't exist.

Ran assays that glowed faintly in the dark, like tiny versions of the basin.

He stabilized some filaments.

Lost others.

Failed often.

Never stopped trying.

And beside every scribbled theory:

"Garrett?"

Then came the page I felt before I saw:

"The older boy — residual bond — possible recall?"

Me.

He had realized the lake held my memory too.

That what it kept of Garrett, it kept of me.

That I was... marked.

And his next page contained only one line:

"If he remembers, he will return."

I felt the moment he made the decision.

A man breaking in two.

He looked at a photo of the two of us —

me and Garrett on that pier,

clouds behind us,

smiling as though the world was simple.

He pressed the photo to his forehead.

And whispered:

"I can't lose him twice."

The scene shifted again.

Snow.

A small farmhouse.

Regina pacing nervously in the living room.

Me asleep on a couch, pale, recovering.

Druitt sat beside me and placed two fingers on my temple.

He didn't drug me.

He didn't hypnotize me.

He didn't coerce me.

He did something far more desperate.

He used the lake.

He had taken a small filament sample —

a living photonic strand —

rigged to a battery-controlled light interface.

And gently, tremblingly,

he held it near my forehead.

The filament glowed, activated by proximity to a damaged neural circuit.

And it erased the memory.

The filament did not remove the trauma.

It removed the **context**.

The lake's memory overwrote mine.

His breath hitched as he watched me sink into peaceful unconsciousness.

He wept quietly and whispered:

"Forgive me."

"I'm saving you."

"I'm so sorry."

The memory shifted back into white light.

I gasped as the vision dissolved.

The basin's glow returned around me in fragments.

The trembling ledge beneath me.

The cold water.

Garrett's glowing body next to mine.

I staggered.

Garrett held my arm, steadying me.

"You see?" he whispered.

I swallowed, my throat burning.

"He didn't betray you."

Garrett nodded slowly.

"He saved you."

"And he tried to save you," I whispered.

Garrett looked down, expression flickering between child and host.

"I know. I remember him trying."

The basin trembled; stone cracked loudly.

Time was running out.

I looked at Garrett —

the glowing eyes,

the trembling hands,

the fracturing patterns under his skin.

"You've been carrying his guilt your whole life," I whispered.

Garrett looked up.

"You've been carrying his grief."

His voice softened:

"And now you carry his truth."

A pulse moved through the basin —

strong, steady, like a heartbeat finding rhythm.

Garrett inhaled sharply.

"Garry... the lake is stabilizing."

I blinked.

"What?"

He lifted his glowing hand —

and I finally realized:

It wasn't his hand glowing.

It was mine.

Because I was linked.

Because I was the bridge.

Because the lake could settle its memory only through **us.**

The final pulse shook the chamber.

Garrett looked at me with a sadness beyond words.

"Now you know why he did it," he whispered.

"Druitt didn't erase your memory to protect himself."

He swallowed.

"He erased it to protect me."

The weight of that truth hit like a tidal wave.

I pulled Garrett toward me, gripping him tightly.

And he whispered the line that shattered what was left of my heart:

"He didn't want you to drown twice."

For several seconds, there was no sound except the distant groan of collapsing chambers and the wet suck of the basin pulling itself inward, contracting like a living heart in distress. Garrett's last sentence—**"He didn't want you to drown twice"**—hung in the air between us like a truth too heavy to hold.

The lake pulsed once beneath the stone, slow and low, a reminder of both its presence and its pain.

Memory is not gentle.

Memory is not merciful.

Memory is a truth-tide, and when it comes, it comes for everything.

I sank to my knees on the trembling ledge, water sloshing over my legs as the basin continued to collapse around its core. Garrett crouched beside me—his large, strange hands resting gently on my shoulders.

His touch grounded me, even as every part of me felt like I was falling through time.

The basin pulsed again—

light

dark

light

—and I felt the memory continue unspooling inside me like a reel that had been waiting decades to resume.

Druitt's hands on my six-year-old forehead.

Regina crying in the stairwell.

A filament pulsing with faint, borrowed light.

A memory dissolving like sugar in hot tea.

The lake's voice echoed through the chamber—not words, not sound, but an emotional resonance:

We remember.

We keep.

We protect.

Garrett squeezed my shoulder gently.

"You see it now," he whispered. "Why he did what he did."

I swallowed hard.

"He took my childhood."

Garrett shook his head slowly.

"He gave you your life."

"No," I whispered. "He stole you from me."

Garrett's face twisted with something like grief and forgiveness fused.

"You think I don't know that?"

The ledge beneath us groaned. A deep chasm split the basin wall across from us, sending a torrent of glowing water exploding outward.

Garrett steadied me again.

"Garry... you didn't lose me because Druitt rewrote your memory. You lost me because the lake chose me. And he couldn't pull us both out."

My chest clenched.

"He had a choice."

Garrett's voice softened.

"And he chose you."

The words struck like a physical blow.

I pressed my palms to my eyes, trying to hold in the heat behind them.

Garrett continued:

"He was terrified you'd go back for me. He was terrified you'd drown in the same light that kept me alive."

My breath hitched.

"But he could have told me. Later. When I was older. When I could understand."

Garrett shook his head again.

"You think you could have carried this at twelve? At eighteen? At thirty?"

"I'm carrying it now."

"And it's breaking you."

He was right.

It was.

But it was also rebuilding me into the version of myself I should have been.

The bridge between memory and forgetting.

Between two brothers who had been severed by water.

A low thrumming sound filled the basin—like an underwater turbine reversing direction. The intelligence was shifting patterns, pulling back into some deeper, protected space.

Garrett's glow flickered with the same rhythm.

I stared at him, the shape of the boy he once was flickering beneath the host's impossible frame.

"That day on the pier," I whispered. "Before we fell... I wasn't afraid."

"You were brave," Garrett murmured. "You always were."

"I should have held onto you."

"You did."

He lifted my hand, placing it against his chest.

"You held on the whole time."

"I let go."

"No," he said. "The lake took me. You didn't let go."

The memory rose again—Garrett slipping into the filaments like a child stepping into warm light.

"You weren't scared," I whispered.

He smiled faintly, eyes dim and bright all at once.

"I wasn't. Not until I saw you getting pulled away."

I closed my eyes.

"And you were alone."

Garrett's voice cracked.

"Yes."

The loneliness in that word—the decades of silent wanting, waiting, remembering—hit harder than the memory of the drowning.

It was the price Druitt had tried to spare me.

But in sparing me, he placed the burden entirely on Garrett.

The light beneath Garrett's skin flickered again.

He staggered.

I caught him before he fell.

The basin trembled violently now—too many neural pathways collapsing at once.

The intelligence's architecture was failing.

"Garrett," I whispered, "if we finish the bridge... if I follow the link through... will it save you?"

He shook his head.

"No. It will change me. But it won't bring me back."

"What does 'change' mean?"

"I won't be this," he said, gesturing to the collapsing form that housed decades of twisted biology. "I'll... stabilize. Become part of the network. Not the lake, not the host—something in between."

"And if we don't finish it?"

He swallowed hard.

"I'll die."

Another fissure opened in the chamber ceiling, sending debris falling into the water. A massive slab crashed into the basin center, sending shockwaves echoing through the collapsing cavern.

"We don't have time," Garrett whispered urgently.

The patterns in his chest sputtered.

His fingers twitched.

He was fading.

Fast.

"Look at me," he said, gripping my forearm.

"Live or die — you have to see this through."

"And what about Regina? What about my life? My work? My sobriety? My students? My future?"

Garrett's face softened.

"They'll still be there.

But this moment won't."

I felt a tear slip down my face, hot against the cold basin air.

He touched my cheek gently.

"You came back. That's enough."

My voice broke.

"I'm not leaving you again."

Garrett smiled sadly.

"You are. But this time, it's the right direction."

The basin glowed suddenly—

bright, blinding—

and a new memory surged into me.

Druitt again, years after the drowning, sitting in his empty office late at night. A single lamp lit his desk. A folder lay open in front of him, filled with sketches of the host structure, enzyme pathways, hydrology channels twisted into neural diagrams.

And an unsent letter.

Addressed to me.

I leaned closer in the memory.

"To Garth—

There is something I have not told you.

I pray you never need to know it..."

My pulse quickened.

Garrett's hand squeezed mine as the memory continued:

"...If you ever return below, it will be because the lake called you.

And if it called you, it is because your connection to Garrett has not faded.

The lake remembers what we forget.

It keeps what we lose.

It holds what we abandon.

And it calls us home to finish what was left undone."

I swallowed, my throat burning.

"If you are reading this, you must decide whether to finish the bridge I interrupted all those years ago.

You will know what to do.

And I will accept whatever choice you make."

The last line hit with impossible weight:

"I broke one son to save the other.

I know that now.

Forgive me."

The memory dissolved.

I was back on the ledge.

Garrett's hand was in mine.

The basin trembled, edges fracturing.

"We're out of time," he whispered.

And I knew the truth:

It wasn't about the lake.

It wasn't even about memory.

It was about **the price of remembering**

and whether I was willing to pay it.

There are drownings that happen in water,

and drownings that happen in memory.

The first steals breath.

The second steals certainty.

The worst steals both.

Standing on that collapsing ledge in the Heart Basin — holding the trembling form of the brother I had lost, found, and was about to lose again — I realized something terrifying:

I wasn't afraid of the water anymore.

I was afraid of the choice.

The basin shuddered violently.

A deep boom echoed from somewhere below, followed by the screech of stone tearing away from ancient seams. Water surged upward, foaming against the ledge, spraying us both in freezing arcs.

Garrett staggered as the ledge shifted again.

His breath stuttered, the glow under his skin flickering like a dying star.

"Garth..."

His voice wasn't layered anymore — not host and human — just boy.

Just Garrett.

Just the little brother who followed me down the pier that afternoon.

I tightened my hold on him.

"I'm here."

He rested his forehead against mine.

"Are you ready?"

My breath caught.

"Ready for what?"

Another tremor fractured the basin floor.

Cracks raced outward from the center like lightning through stone.

A whirlpool began forming where the fractures converged — slow at first, then gaining speed.

"The transfer," Garrett whispered.

"The bridge. The second drowning."

My chest tightened.

"Tell me what happens."

Garrett's glow dimmed further.

"If you open the link… you'll carry my memories.

All of them.

The lake's too.

Everything it gave me.

Everything it took."

He swallowed, flickering weakly.

"You'll go under.

Not physically.

Not like the first time.

But your mind — it will drown in mine.

And then come back up different."

The whirlpool deepened below us, pulling debris and filaments into its spinning core.

A sharp, electric hum radiated from the water.

"Will I survive it?"

Garrett hesitated — the first hesitation I had seen since our reunion.

"I don't know."

The honesty broke me.

"And you?" I whispered. "What happens to you?"

"I stabilize," he said softly.

"But only if you... finish what Druitt interrupted."

"And if I don't?"

His hands trembled.

He pressed one glowing palm to his chest.

"Then I fall apart."

The ledge cracked under us.

I instinctively pulled him closer.

"You're asking me to risk my life."

Garrett shook his head and touched my cheek gently.

"No, Garry. I'm asking you not to let me die alone."

The surviving part of me — the rational, sober, academic part — screamed that this was madness.

But another part — the part that remembered the dragonfly, the warm summers, the laughter we shared — whispered a truth I could no longer deny:

I could not let history repeat itself.

Not again.

Not like this.

Not at the threshold of the only moment that mattered.

The whirlpool widened, the water glowing from within like a bioluminescent vortex. The sound was deafening now — a deep resonant thrum that reverberated through bone instead of air.

485

I gripped Garrett's shoulders.

"Tell me what to do."

He placed one trembling hand against my sternum.

"The link has to start with you. The human mind can't take memory of this magnitude unless it enters willingly."

"And then?"

"I... follow."

"Then the lake?"

"It merges."

"Then what?"

He looked at me with shimmering eyes.

"Then we stop being alone."

The ledge beneath us cracked again, opening a fissure at our feet. Water surged upward, nearly knocking us both off balance.

Garrett winced in pain — the glow beneath his skin collapsing into spasms of flickering light.

"I can't hold it together much longer."

I cupped his face.

"You held on for decades."

His eyes filled with luminescent tears.

"For you."

A deeper tremor ripped through the basin.

This one didn't feel structural.

It felt emotional.

The intelligence — the lake's mind — was bracing itself.

Preparing.

The whirlpool slowed suddenly, shifting from violent collapse to a smooth, beckoning spiral. The shape of it changed — narrowing to a precise geometry. A perfect circle.

An invitation.

A ritual.

A place of memory.

Garrett exhaled, trembling.

"It's ready."

My heart hammered.

"What do I do?"

"Hands," he whispered.

"Press your palms to my chest. Where the light is brightest."

I hesitated — not because I doubted him, but because I feared the answer to the next question:

"And then?"

He took my hands gently and placed them over the glowing points on his chest — two faint luminescent spirals pulsing in soft rhythm, the closest thing he had left to a heartbeat.

"Then," he whispered,

"You drown."

My mouth went dry.

"Garrett—"

"Not in water," he said quickly. "In memory."

"And I come back?"

He swallowed again — glow stuttering.

"If you hold on."

"If I don't?"

He looked down.

"Then I carry both of us."

I took a shaking breath.

I thought of Regina's tears.

Of Sheila's steadiness.

Of Martinson's grit.

Of Bob Thomas's quiet wisdom.

Of Druitt's guilt.

Of the years I spent building a life that felt borrowed, empty, incomplete — because it was missing him.

I thought of the truth we finally found.

I placed both palms firmly against his chest.

Garrett inhaled sharply, light bursting under my hands.

"Ready?" he whispered.

"No," I said honestly.

He smiled.

"Me neither."

We pressed our foreheads together.

And the world dissolved.

There was no cold.

No panic.

No lungs screaming for air.

There was only **pressure**,

light,

and an impossible flood of memory.

The basin faded.

The ledge vanished.

The water receded.

I fell through Garrett's life in an instant:

- His first night inside the glowing cocoon

- His fear turning to wonder

- His wonder turning to loneliness

- His loneliness turning to acceptance

- His acceptance turning to longing

- His longing turning to me

I drowned in his memories

and resurfaced in mine.

We were six again.

Laughing.

Running.

Skipping stones.

Holding hands on the pier.

We were twenty.

Regina was between us, reading notes aloud.

We were thirty.

I was alone.

He was beneath the lake.

Both of us incomplete.

The memories surged faster, collapsing into a vortex of shared consciousness.

Garrett screamed.

Or maybe I did.

Or maybe the lake did.

The light intensified —

brilliant, unbearable —

a thousand memories crossing wires in the same instant.

And then —

a final pulse.

A heartbeat.

Not his.

Not mine.

Both.

The bridge was formed.

I gasped —

the kind of gasp that comes after deep drowning —

and fell backward onto solid stone.

Cold.

Real.

Immediate.

The basin was still collapsing — the whirlpool now a narrow drain of glowing water spiraling into darkness. The ledge shuddered under me, threatening to break off entirely.

I tried to stand.

My body trembled violently.

My vision blurred.

Memories layered over each other —

his first breath,

my first dive,

his loneliness,

my guilt,

his light,

my darkness —

braiding into something new.

"Garth..."

The voice was different.

Gentler.

More human.

More him.

I blinked, forcing my vision to stabilize.

Garrett stood before me.

Same height.

Same glow.

But his form was stabilizing — no longer flickering erratically.

The light beneath his skin pulsed in slow, consistent waves.

He exhaled, and the chamber responded —

a soft ripple of light echoing through the basin.

He wasn't collapsing.

He was becoming.

He knelt beside me.

"You made it," he whispered.

I reached out, touching his face with trembling fingers.

"So did you."

He smiled — a real smile, fragile and luminous.

"Thank you."

The basin groaned — louder now.

Everything was about to fall.

Garrett looked up, then back to me.

"You have to go."

"No."

"You must."

"Garrett—"

He shook his head gently.

"I'm part of it now. I can hold the basin together long enough for you to escape, but I can't leave."

"Garrett—"

He leaned close and pressed his forehead to mine.

"You survived the second drowning," he whispered.

"I'll survive the rest."

The ledge cracked violently behind me.

I staggered to my feet.

Garrett stepped back toward the center of the basin as the lake's glow flowed into him, stabilizing his new form entirely.

"Go," he whispered.

"I'll find you," I said.

His eyes softened.

"You already did."

And then the basin exploded into light.

CHAPTER 22

The Collapse

Some endings don't fall apart—they fall through.

There is a silence that comes after revelation.

Not peaceful.

Not gentle.

A stunned, ringing quiet — the kind that makes the world feel too sharp, too bright, too real after everything that came before.

That was the silence I heard as the basin exploded into light behind me.

Then all hell broke loose.

The ledge beneath my feet recoiled like something alive, snapping upward and tossing me toward the exit tunnel. I slammed into the wall, slid down hard, gasping as pain shot through my ribs.

Behind me, the basin's core collapsed in a roar of cascading stone.

Light surged upward — not warm, not gentle, but blinding and electric, like lightning erupting from a wound.

"GARTH!"

Regina's voice, faint but rising, echoed somewhere above.

"GARTH, ANSWER ME!"

I pushed myself up — dizzy, shaking, barely able to feel my fingers.

The tunnel that once led back toward the living chambers was now a funnel of rushing water. The intelligence was pulling back its arteries — every tunnel retracting, rerouting, sealing, collapsing.

It was sealing itself off.

Protecting its new heart.

Protecting **Garrett**.

I staggered toward the incline, coughing as water surged around my knees.

"Regina!" I shouted, voice cracking. "I'm here!"

A slab of stone the size of a refrigerator smashed into the basin behind me, sending a massive shockwave of freezing water rushing up the tunnel.

The flood hit me before I could brace.

It ripped my legs out from under me.

Slammed me against the wall.

Dragged me backward toward the collapsing void.

A hand caught my wrist.

Strong.

Human.

"Garth!"

Martinson.

He lay flat on his stomach atop a narrow ledge jutting from the tunnel wall, his boots braced, his teeth gritted.

"Don't—let—go!" he shouted through clenched jaws.

I almost laughed at the bitter symmetry.

I had told myself I would never let go again.

And here I was, being dragged into darkness by the same choice, the same water, the same gravity.

"I've got you!" Martinson yelled.

And he did.

He hauled me upward inch by inch until I could plant my other arm onto the ledge and pull myself up beside him, soaked and shivering.

He gave me a heavy pat on the back — harder than necessary, but more relieved than angry.

"You look like shit," he muttered.

"You should see the other guy," I wheezed.

He snorted — a tense, exhausted sound.

Then shouted up the incline:

"SHEILA!

HE'S WITH ME!"

Above us, I heard Sheila scream in relief.

Then I heard Regina.

"Garth — Garth, PLEASE — climb!"

We crawled upward on hands and knees as the flood rose behind us.

The tunnel twisted sharply right, and we rounded into a small chamber — the same neural-breathing room we had passed earlier.

But now it was dying.

The walls that once pulsed softly now trembled violently.

The bioluminescent veins flickered.

Some tore free from the stone, snapping like tendons stretched past their limit.

I staggered to my feet, grabbing the rail.

"Where's Lila?" I asked.

Martinson's jaw tightened.

"She made it through. She's with Sheila. We've got to move."

A deeper boom thundered behind us.

The tunnel we had just crawled through imploded in a torrent of stone and water.

Regina screamed.

"Garth—RUN!"

Martinson grabbed my arm.

We sprinted.

The room lurched sideways, one wall buckling inward like a diaphragm collapsing after a final breath.

The intelligence was withdrawing.

Collapsing the paths that no longer mattered.

Sealing the chambers that no longer served purpose.

Only the core remained — the heart — the place where Garrett now stood.

He was safe.

We were not.

We reached the vertical maintenance shaft — narrow, rusted, claustrophobic.

Sheila waved desperately from above.

"Hurry! Hurry!"

Regina was already at the top, gripping the edge with white knuckles, eyes wild with terror as she searched for me.

Her voice broke.

"Garth — MOVE!"

Martinson cupped his hands and shouted upward:

"VENTILATION SHAFT COLLAPSING — GET CLEAR!"

I heard a distant rumble.

Then the scream of metal tearing.

A grate somewhere above sheared loose, crashing down the shaft. It smashed against the wall inches from us, ricocheted, and plunged past into the flooded darkness below.

We didn't have time to think.

Martinson grabbed my belt and shoved me upward.

"Climb, Professor! CLIMB!"

I scrambled up the narrow rungs — they shook beneath my hands, weakened by years of rust and the recent quake.

Halfway up, the shaft shuddered violently.

Regina screamed my name again.

"GARTH!"

I didn't look down.

I didn't look up.

I just climbed.

Water exploded into the shaft behind us — a geyser shot upward by the collapsing basin below.

The surge hit Martinson full-force.

He lost his grip on the rung.

He slammed hard into the wall.

"Martinson!" I shouted.

He coughed, grabbed the rung again.

"GO!"

Another surge.

This one stronger.

The shaft tilted.

A wrenching metal groan echoed down its length.

This wasn't just a collapse.

It was a burial.

Martinson shouted one last time:

"MOVE, GODDAMN YOU!"

And then the next surge hit him, ripping his feet off the rung, throwing him backward into the flood.

I reached down instinctively.

Our fingers brushed.

He shoved me up with his last strength.

"Get to her!" he roared.

Then he disappeared into the darkness below.

Regina screamed.

Sheila sobbed.

I climbed with everything I had left.

A hand reached down — Regina's — shaking, desperate.

I grabbed it.

She hauled me up through the final opening as the shaft behind me collapsed entirely. The floor vibrated. Dust poured down like rain.

Sheila grabbed my other arm and dragged me the last foot.

Then the grate caved in behind us — the entire wall folding under the surge of water.

Regina threw her arms around me and sobbed into my neck.

"Don't you ever — EVER — do that to me again."

I pressed my forehead to hers, breath heaving.

"I won't," I whispered.

"I promise."

She pulled back, hands shaking.

"Where is he? Where's Martinson?"

I opened my mouth.

Nothing came out.

Sheila's face folded into horror.

Regina covered her mouth with both hands, eyes wide and wet.

The ground shook beneath us again.

We had to run.

But I stood for one final moment —

breathing in air,

soaking in gravity,

feeling the weight of the promise I had made seconds before spilling out of my shaking lips.

Garrett was alive.

Martinson might not be.

The lake was collapsing.

And the final escape path — the one leading to the surface — was ahead.

The surface tunnels of the University's forgotten underbelly were never meant to carry this much water.

They groaned like ribs under crushing weight.

Rust flaked off in sheets.

Pipes screamed as pressure slammed through their hollow guts.

Concrete cracked in sharp, echoing snaps.

And through it all, the ground shook with the same dull heartbeat that pulsed through the entire subterranean network — weaker now, irregular, fading.

The intelligence was collapsing inward...

but it hadn't fully died.

Not yet.

Regina clung to my hand like a lifeline as Sheila led us through the first corridor: a low, claustrophobic span of concrete patched with rusted rebar. Every few steps, water burst through seams in the wall, spraying us in freezing jets.

"Keep moving!" Sheila shouted.

Her voice ricocheted off the concrete like a whip crack.

Regina stumbled, and I caught her around the waist.

"I'm fine," she insisted, breath ragged. "Keep going."

The corridor tilted sharply downward as we reached an intersection.

A faded stencil on the wall read:

MAINTENANCE — LEVEL C

NO UNAUTHORIZED ENTRY

Sheila hesitated.

"Left or right?" she muttered.

I closed my eyes for half a second, feeling the faint pulsing beneath the concrete.

Left was colder.

Heavier.

Sinking.

Right was warmer.

Ascending.

Alive.

"Right," I said.

Sheila didn't argue.

Regina squeezed my hand tighter.

Behind us came the distant groan of collapsing stone — the sound of the basin retracting deeper into the lake. The intelligence was pulling back, sealing its innermost layers.

And along with it—

A faint pulse flickered through the wall, like a heartbeat.

Garrett was alive.

The realization hit me like a physical force.

Sheila glanced back at me, reading something in my expression but saying nothing.

We moved.

The tunnel sloped upward now, but the incline was treacherous. Water poured down the steps in miniature waterfalls, creating slick currents that threatened to sweep our feet out from under us.

Regina wheezed.

"I can't—"

She slipped.

I caught her hard, pulling her against me.

Her hair was plastered to her face.

Her eyes were wide and red.

Her hands shook from adrenaline and cold.

I touched my forehead to hers briefly.

"We're close," I whispered.

"You can do this."

Her breath steadied.

She nodded.

We kept climbing.

A pipe overhead burst with a metallic shriek, showering us with near-boiling steam. Sheila yelped, covering her head.

"Damn it, MOVE!" she shouted.

We sprinted through the cloud, coughing.

By the time the steam cleared, the walls were trembling with a slow, rhythmic pulse — a pulse that steadied even as the tunnels collapsed around it.

Regina looked at me, voice barely audible:

"It's him, isn't it?"

I didn't answer.

I didn't need to.

She knew.

The next turn was unexpected.

A corridor that hadn't been there before.

No — that wasn't right.

It *had* been there, but sealed behind a wall that now lay shattered on the ground.

"Jesus…" Sheila whispered. "This wasn't open before."

Regina's voice trembled.

"It opened… for us."

We stepped into the corridor cautiously.

The air was warmer here.

Still damp — but not as suffocating.

The low hum of the intelligence vibrated through the walls.

This was not collapse.

This was a **choice**.

The lake was giving us an exit.

Not because it needed us.

But because **Garrett** wanted it to.

A weight settled in my chest.

He was stabilizing.

He had some measure of agency again.

Enough to guide us.

The corridor ahead glowed faintly with bioluminescent streaks, like threads of neural fireflies drifting through rock fissures.

Regina pointed upward, breath catching.

"Look."

The ceiling was cracked, but instead of water pouring in, faint beams of natural light shone through.

Daylight.

We were beneath the campus.

Beneath the soil.

Maybe only fifty feet from freedom.

But the tunnel shook again — violently this time — as something heavy collapsed deeper below.

Sheila flinched.

"We have to run."

We did.

Water roared behind us — the sound swelling into a deafening wave. The intelligence was retracting too quickly now; some chambers were collapsing in chain reactions.

Regina stumbled again. I caught her and shoved her forward.

"Go! Go!"

The floor buckled.

A slab of concrete cracked loose above us.

It fell.

I shoved both women aside.

The slab struck my shoulder, knocking me hard to the ground.

"Garth!" Regina shrieked.

Sheila grabbed my arm, trying to haul me up.

But then —

Cutting through the roar of water and stone —

came a voice.

A familiar one.

From far below.

Not human.

Not spoken.

But unmistakable:

"Garry—keep going."

My breath caught.

Regina froze, eyes wide in terror and awe.

She had heard it too.

"Garth... that was—"

"I know."

Another pulse through the floor.

A deeper resonance.

Garrett was holding the intelligence steady —

slowing the collapse —

keeping the tunnels open long enough for us to escape.

He was sacrificing the last remnants of his human body

to protect us.

To protect *me.*

I forced myself up despite the pain shooting through my shoulder.

"We have to move."

Sheila nodded, grim and determined.

Regina hesitated, tears spilling over her lashes.

"Garth, I—"

I squeezed her hand.

"I know."

And we ran.

The tunnel ascended more steeply now.

Water thundered behind us—violent, unstoppable, devouring the tunnel like a living beast.

We skidded into the ascent shaft.

Regina climbed first. I followed. Sheila stayed below, bracing her body against the frame as another surge slammed into her back.

"GO!" she shouted, voice cracking. "Climb!"

"Come with us!" Regina screamed.

"I will—just MOVE!"

Water blasted outward. Sheila screamed—not in pain, but in effort—shoving the flood back with everything she had.

The tunnel floor buckled.

A pipe overhead snapped.

A full torrent hit Sheila sideways, ripping her hands from the frame.

"Sheila!" I yelled.

She lost her footing.

The wave didn't swallow her—it took her sideways, into a dark opening I hadn't noticed.

A broken conduit.

A breach in the tunnel wall.

Her body vanished into it in an instant.

"NO!" Regina screamed.

"Sheila!" I lunged downward, but Regina grabbed me.

"GARTH—CLIMB!"

Another surge hit.

The entire shaft twisted.

I had no choice.

We climbed.

At the top, the hatch burst open to daylight as the shaft collapsed behind us. Regina pulled me into the cold November air as the tunnel below sealed itself with a deep, final groan.

Martinson dragged himself out of another vent minutes later, coughing up lake water and swearing at gravity.

But Sheila didn't surface.

Not here.

Not now.

Regina sobbed.

I stared into the ruined shaft.

Martinson put a hand on my shoulder.

"We'll get search teams in. She might've been pushed into a drainage conduit."

I shook my head, numb.

"I didn't... I didn't see where she went."

"You weren't meant to," Martinson said quietly.

And the world swallowed our grief.

Cold November air hit my face.

I sprawled on the muddy ground behind the UW Chemistry building, coughing, shaking, blinking against the brightness.

Regina collapsed beside me, sobbing uncontrollably.

I rolled onto my back.

The sky above was pale blue.

It didn't look real.

Nothing looked real.

Regina crawled toward me and collapsed into my arms.

"You made it," she whispered, voice broken.

"You're alive. You're alive."

I held her trembling body against mine.

Sheila was gone, perhaps.

The tunnels were gone, definitely.

Garrett...

Still alive.

But no longer mine.

The ground vibrated once beneath us — a final, gentle pulse.

Regina clutched my arm.

"What was that?"

I swallowed hard.

"That," I whispered,

"was goodbye."

CHAPTER 23

The Surface Isn't Safe

Danger doesn't vanish at the surface—it just changes its shape.

The campus should have been noisy.

Even in late November, even at dawn, even during exam season, there should've been footsteps on the sidewalks, bikes rattling over cracks, early risers heading to labs or libraries, buses sighing along University Avenue.

But the world that greeted us was wrong.

Too still.

Too empty.

Too quiet.

Regina helped me sit up, her hands shaking, her hair plastered to her face with mud and tunnel water. She kept touching my cheek like she was afraid I'd vanish if she blinked too long.

I didn't want to tell her that I felt the same.

We both turned as the hatch behind us groaned and slammed shut on its own, sealing the path back underground forever.

A final, faint tremor rippled beneath us—

not violent,

not destructive,

just a **heartbeat**.

A goodbye pulse.

Then silence.

Regina exhaled a sound between a sob and a gasp.

"Garth..."

She couldn't finish the sentence.

I put a hand over hers.

"I know."

But I didn't.

Not really.

Not yet.

The full weight of **losing Sheila** hit the moment I tried to stand and saw there were only **two sets of footprints** in the mud.

Regina looked too.

Her eyes filled instantly, her lips trembling.

"She—she held the tunnel... so we could—"

Her voice broke apart.

I placed a hand on her shoulder, feeling the heaviness in her.

"She saved us."

Regina squeezed her eyes shut.

"She had kids. Garth. She had KIDS."

I nodded slowly.

There is no right answer in moments like this.

Just the truth:

"She was braver than I ever was."

Regina leaned into me, curling her fists into my jacket as though anchoring herself to the earth.

We stayed like that for a long moment.

Long enough for the shock to settle.

Long enough for reality to sharpen.

Long enough for grief to become a living thing between us.

Then footsteps crunched behind us.

A familiar voice rasped:

"Well...

you two... look like shit."

Regina froze.

Her face jerked upward.

My breath stopped cold.

We turned.

Detective Martinson stood twenty feet away, dripping wet from head to toe, covered in silt and grime, his left arm hanging at a strange angle and his right cheek split open.

But alive.

Breathing.

Standing.

Barely.

Regina screamed his name and ran to him.

He staggered into her arms with a grunt.

"You... dropped me," he rasped, glaring at me with one eye barely open. "Next time... try pulling."

I laughed—a short, wild, hysterical sound that didn't feel like laughter.

"How?"

He shrugged painfully.

"Got pinned against a conduit... rode the surge up a different vent... nearly drowned twice." He grimaced. "I wouldn't recommend it."

Regina hugged him tighter; he winced.

"Careful. Still attached... barely."

I walked over and gripped his uninjured shoulder.

"Martinson... I thought you were—"

He cut me off.

"Well, I'm not."

A pause.

"Not yet."

Regina swiped tears from her face.

He looked at her, softened, and said quietly:

"Thank you. For yelling louder than the water."

Then he looked at me.

"You look like you've seen a ghost."

I swallowed hard.

"I have."

He raised an eyebrow.

"Your brother?"

I nodded.

His jaw clenched, but he didn't press further.

He was still a detective.

And he knew when not to ask.

Sirens wailed in the distance—dozens of them.

Ambulances.

Campus police.

City responders.

Martinson winced.

"They're here for the sinkhole."

Regina blinked.

"What sinkhole?"

Martinson gestured toward the lake.

"Half of the east parkway collapsed. Looks like a damn meteor hit it. Some students thought it was an accident in the steam tunnels."

He glanced at me.

"They're wrong, aren't they?"

I didn't answer.

He didn't expect me to.

Regina looked toward Lake Monona's shoreline, where a mass of emergency vehicles circled around a cordoned area. Floodlights cast long beams across churned mud and ruptured pavement.

A massive section of ground had caved inward, leaving a jagged crater that still shivered faintly beneath the surface.

I felt the tremor

in my bones

in my chest

in the place where the link still hummed faintly like an echo.

Garrett was still there.

Holding the collapse steady.

Keeping the rest of the campus from dropping into the lake.

Martinson followed my gaze.

"Something's still... moving down there."

Regina shivered.

I said nothing.

Before we could move, three campus police cruisers pulled up near us. Officers jumped out, hands hovering near weapons as they approached.

The leader, a tall man with a booming voice, shouted:

"YOU THREE—STOP! IDENTIFY YOURSELVES!"

Martinson straightened, wincing as he did.

"Detective Martinson. Madison PD. I need medical, a secure perimeter, and I need—"

The officer cut him off, incredulous.

"...Martinson? Jesus Christ, we thought you were under the collapse!"

He blinked, then gave a weak smirk.

"Turns out... I'm hard to bury."

The officer exhaled a shaky breath.

"What... what the hell happened down there?"

Martinson's eyes shifted briefly toward me.

Then he answered like a man who knew exactly how much truth to give:

"Partial collapse of a sealed research annex. Old infrastructure. Very old. I'll file a full report later."

The officer hesitated.

"You need to see campus security. And... environmental services."

Regina stiffened.

"Why environmental?"

"Because," the officer said, swallowing hard,

"We found something living in the crater."

My blood went cold.

Regina grabbed my hand.

Martinson looked at me sharply.

"What kind of something?"

The officer shook his head.

"We don't know. It's... glowing."

As if responding to the officer's words, the ground beneath us pulsed again — a soft, steady, **reassuring** vibration.

Regina gasped.

Martinson steadied himself.

I closed my eyes.

And I heard it:

"Garry."

Not a plea.

Not a cry.

Not a command.

A whisper.

A thank-you.

A goodbye.

A promise.

The last gift of a brother who had spent thirty years trying not to be forgotten.

I opened my eyes.

The officer stared at me.

"What was that?"

I shook my head.

"Nothing.

Just the ground settling."

He nodded slowly, unconvinced.

Regina stepped closer, her voice barely audible.

"Garth... what now?"

Martinson looked between us.

"Yeah, Professor. What now?"

I stared toward the lake.

The glow at the edge of the crater dimmed slowly, then faded entirely.

The intelligence wasn't dead.

It was retreating.

Consolidating.

Reforming.

And Garrett...

Garrett was part of it now.

A guardian.

A memory keeper.

A bridge.

"I think..." I whispered,

"...this isn't over."

Regina shuddered.

Martinson cursed under his breath.

Wind rippled across the lake like a sigh.

And beneath it all, faint but present, pulsed the memory of a heartbeat.

There's a specific kind of trouble that only comes when too many people with badges, clipboards, and hollow authority show up at the same place at the same time.

That's what we walked into.

A swarm of campus police.

Madison PD.

Environmental Safety.

UW Facilities.

A handful of state emergency officials.

A couple of men in suits — the kind who move like they own your oxygen.

And then there was us:

- Regina, shaking, eyes still red

- Martinson, soaked, injured, and furious

- Me, covered in tunnel silt and secrets

- No Sheila

- No Lila

And behind us — the smoldering crater where the ground had collapsed.

The investigators moved toward us like vultures smelling blood.

Regina tightened her grip on my arm.

Martinson's jaw flexed.

I forced myself to breathe.

We had to play this smart.

Because the worst thing we could do right now was tell the truth.

"Detective Martinson."

The nearest suit — tall, sharp features, black gloves — stepped out of the police perimeter like he owned the crime scene.

Martinson muttered, "Oh for Christ's sake."

"You know him?" I whispered.

"That's Special Agent Arlen Hodge," Martinson replied tightly. "State Special Investigations. And he's a pain in my ass."

Hodge reached us with a humorless smile.

"Well," he said, "you look like someone flushed you through four miles of sewer pipe."

Martinson glared.

"It was only two miles."

Hodge's eyes flicked to me, then to Regina.

"And these are...?"

"My colleagues," Martinson said without hesitation.

I blinked.

Regina blinked.

Hodge raised one eyebrow.

"Colleagues. In an old steam tunnel collapse."

Martinson shrugged, deadpan.

"Lotta colleagues go hiking through utility spaces these days. It's a trend."

Hodge didn't smile.

Instead, he stepped closer to me.

"Professor Myers," he said.

My pulse tightened.

"How do you know my name?" I asked cautiously.

He tapped his clipboard.

"Your ID badge activated a defunct geofence when the collapse happened. The University's system alerted us."

I cursed internally.

521

Martinson muttered under his breath, "Of course it did."

Hodge studied me.

"You want to tell me why a chemical engineer was fifty feet underground, in a sealed and condemned tunnel system from the 1960s?"

My mind ran through a dozen lies.

Martinson cut in first.

"He was helping me investigate missing infrastructure equipment."

Hodge blinked slowly.

"Missing equipment."

"Yep. Copper wiring, gauges, insulation. People strip old tunnels all the time."

Hodge didn't buy it.

But he also couldn't disprove it.

Two paramedics rushed Martinson onto a gurney — he resisted, but Regina stared him down until he gave in.

As they rolled him toward the ambulance, Martinson grabbed my wrist tightly.

"Don't talk," he whispered. "To anyone."

"I won't."

"If they press," he added, barely audible,

"lie."

I nodded.

The paramedics loaded him in.

Regina tugged at my sleeve, voice breaking.

"Garth... what do we tell them about Sheila?"

The pain hit me all at once — the image of her being swept into the side conduit, her scream torn away by the water.

I swallowed.

"We tell them the truth we can afford," I said quietly.

"That she was swept away in the collapse."

Regina's voice quivered.

"And if — if she's alive?"

"Then we tell them she crawled out somewhere else."

Regina nodded but didn't look convinced.

Before she could say anything else, a young environmental technician jogged toward Hodge, pale and trembling.

"Sir—sir! You need to see this."

Hodge turned.

"What is it?"

The tech swallowed hard.

"At the bottom of the crater. We... we found movements."

Martinson froze on the gurney.

Regina's fingers dug painfully into my arm.

Hodge frowned.

"What kind of movements?"

The tech stammered.

"I don't know how to explain it. It's... lights. In the mud. Like—like bioluminescence."

Hodge stiffened.

"Show me."

He and three officers followed the technician toward the crater.

Regina turned sharply.

"Garth..."

"I know."

Her voice dropped to a whisper.

"Do you think it's him?"

I didn't answer, but the answer was already written across my face.

Regina's breath caught.

We followed the investigators at a distance.

Was it safe?

No.

Did I care?

Less than I should have.

The crater was enormous — a 40-foot-wide wound in the earth, the ground caved inward with jagged lines radiating like the cracks of a shattered mirror.

Mud churned at the bottom.

Water bubbled up in thick, viscous spurts.

And beneath the mess—

A faint bluish glow pulsed like a breathing heart.

Hodge stared down.

"What the hell is that?"

A UW hydrology engineer beside him stammered:

"It's — it's impossible. There's no electrical source there. It's not gas luminescence. I don't — I don't know what we're seeing."

Hodge crouched, eyes sharp.

"Could it be chemical runoff?"

"No," the hydrologist said, shaking his head.

"This isn't contamination. This is... this looks like signaling."

"Signaling?" Hodge snapped.

"Like communication," the hydrologist said, voice cracking.

"Like—like it's responding to us."

I exhaled sharply.

Regina clutched my hand.

Hodge's head snapped toward us.

"You two," he barked.

"Back. Now."

But he turned too late.

The glow intensified — a gentle, slow pulse rising through the crater floor.

light

dark

light

dark

Regina gasped.

She squeezed my arm so tightly it hurt.

"Garth... that's him."

The pulse slowed.

Calmed.

Softened.

It wasn't panic.

It wasn't threat.

It was recognition.

A greeting.

A farewell.

And then —

as if sensing the strangers above—

The glow dimmed.

Slowly.

Respectfully.

Like someone lowering their voice in the presence of a grieving family.

Hodge stared, utterly unprepared for what he was seeing.

"What was that?" he whispered.

The hydrologist swallowed.

"I think… it was alive."

Regina's eyes met mine.

She was crying again.

But not from fear.

Hodge turned toward us.

"Professor Myers," he barked. "Come here."

Regina stiffened.

"Don't," she whispered.

But I stepped forward anyway.

Hodge stared me down.

"You know something," he said.

"This started with your badge trip. You were underground during the collapse. And now there are... phenomena in that crater."

He pointed to the faint glow now fading into the mud.

"What exactly were you doing down there?"

Regina stepped forward, defiant.

"He saved my life."

"I'm not asking about your safety," Hodge snapped. "I'm asking what he was doing in a restricted collapse zone."

I met his gaze.

The truth rose in my throat.

Then the memory of Martinson's whisper returned:

If they press... lie.

So I did.

"We were looking for Lila Wilcox."

Hodge froze.

"The missing postdoc?"

"Yes," I said, voice steady.

"She had been paranoid about the steam tunnels for weeks. She thought someone was following her. I was trying to track her movements. We went down to see where she'd been last."

"And the collapse?"

"Suction effect," I said.

"Corroded infrastructure. Decades of neglect. It gave out."

Hodge didn't buy a word of it.

But he couldn't disprove it.

"Where is Lila now?" he asked.

Regina answered this one.

"Missing," she said softly.

"Still."

The truth behind her voice made the lie unassailable.

Hodge turned away, rubbing his temple.

"This is a mess," he muttered.

Regina stared at me.

"We can't tell them, can we?"

"No," I whispered.

"Not yet."

"Because they wouldn't believe it?"

"No."

I looked back at the crater.

"Because they would."

As we stood there, surrounded by investigators and chaos, Martinson shouted from the ambulance door.

"MYERS!"

I turned.

He held a paramedic's radio handset out toward me.

"It's for you!"

"For me?"

He nodded, pale.

"You'll want to take it."

I walked over, heart pounding.

Martinson pressed the radio into my hand.

"It's UW Hospital."

My throat tightened.

"Who—who is it?"

He met my eyes, expression shifting.

"I think... you'll want to hear it yourself."

Regina pressed against my side.

I lifted the radio.

"This is... Dr. Garth Myers."

A woman's voice answered.

Calm.

Professional.

Slightly bewildered.

"Dr. Myers? This is Nurse Blythe at UW ER."

"Yes."

"You're listed as an emergency contact for... Sheila Lammers?"

Regina gasped.

I nearly dropped the radio.

"She's alive?" I breathed.

"Yes," the nurse said.

"She was found unconscious in a storm drainage culvert off Charter Street. Hypothermic, but stable."

Regina's knees buckled.

I caught her before she fell.

The nurse continued:

"She keeps asking for you."

I closed my eyes.

Relief — dizzying, overwhelming — washed through me.

I swallowed hard.

"I'm on my way."

I handed the radio back to Martinson, who gave a weak, crooked smile.

Then Regina and I looked at each other.

And both of us cried.

CHAPTER 24

What Surfaces and What Doesn't

Not everything that rises is ready to be seen—and not everything that sinks is gone.

Hospitals at dawn are liminal places — too clean, too quiet, too full of things just barely held together by fluorescent light and exhausted hope.

UW Hospital was no exception.

As Regina and I walked through the automatic doors, half-frozen, caked in tunnel grime, soaked to the bone, we drew more than a few stares. A nurse at the front desk paused mid–coffee sip, blinked, set her mug down carefully, then wordlessly pointed toward the ER wing, as if to say:

Whatever this is, take it somewhere else.

We didn't stop until we saw her.

Sheila.

Alive.

Bruised, wrapped in heated blankets, hair matted and stiff with sediment, oxygen cannula under her nose — but conscious. Awake. Propped up in a hospital bed like a war veteran after a long night.

She looked up at us.

Her face crumpled.

And then she said the most Sheila thing possible:

"You two look like hell."

Regina burst into tears.

I wasn't far behind.

We rushed to her bedside.

Sheila held up a weak hand.

"Careful! I still have all my bones but they feel like they were put through a stand mixer."

Regina ignored her and wrapped her in a gentle hug.

"Don't you ever—EVER—scare me like that again."

Sheila hugged back, wincing.

"Sweetheart, the *water* scared me more than you ever could."

Her eyes drifted to me.

"You okay, boss?"

Boss.

My throat tightened.

I nodded carefully.

"Better now."

Sheila studied me quietly.

"You saw him, didn't you?" she whispered.

Regina stiffened.

I swallowed hard.

Sheila's eyes softened.

"I heard... something. Down there. Before the water took me sideways. Like someone saying goodbye."

My breath caught.

"Yeah," I whispered.

"You heard him."

She nodded once, tears forming but not falling.

"I figured."

Regina looked between us, voice trembling.

"Should we... should we tell her?"

I shook my head gently.

"She already knows."

Sheila wiped her eyes, trying to act tough.

"You're a terrible liar, Garth Myers. I've known for months something strange was happening under that lake."

She sighed.

"And now I know why."

A knock came at the door.

A doctor.

A nurse.

And behind them—

Special Agent Hodge.

Because of course he was.

He stood in the hallway, arms crossed, jaw clenched like he had bitten down on a lemon filled with anger and suspicion.

He motioned with two fingers.

"Myers. Outside. Now."

Regina bristled instantly.

"She's barely awake, can't this—"

"He's not here for her," I said softly.

Sheila nodded.

"Go. Before he kicks the door off the hinges."

I stepped into the hallway.

Hodge didn't speak at first.

He just stared at me the way a biologist might stare at something that shouldn't be alive.

Then he said:

"You want to explain how a university staff member was washed half a mile through a storm culvert and survived with only bruises?"

I kept my voice flat.

"Luck."

He tilted his head.

"No. Luck is winning a scratch-off ticket. This is... something else."

"We were trying to escape," I said. "The tunnels collapsed. She was carried by the current."

"And the glowing mud in the crater?" he pressed.

"Minerals. Chemicals. Some kind of luminescent algae bloom."

He took a step closer.

"No bloom behaves like *that*. No water collapses in patterns. No tunnel system pulses. No chemical glow responds to human voices."

His voice dropped lower.

"Something happened down there. Something extraordinary."

I met his gaze evenly.

"A barricaded maintenance corridor collapsed after years of neglect. We were lucky to be alive. That's all."

He stared at me for a long, tense moment.

Then he said:

"You're lying."

I didn't blink.

"Prove it."

Hodge's eyes narrowed.

And then something happened I didn't expect.

He smiled.

Not a kind smile.

A hunter's smile.

"Oh, I will," he whispered.

Then he turned and walked away.

The threat hung in the air like smoke from a match.

Regina opened the door behind me.

"Garth? Are you okay?"

I exhaled slowly.

"No."

Back inside the room, Sheila patted the edge of her bed.

"Sit. Both of you. I hate watching Garth's blood pressure spike."

Regina took my hand, and we sat.

Sheila looked at us with a seriousness I didn't know she possessed.

"Lila didn't make it out, did she?"

Regina's breath wavered.

"No."

Sheila nodded, eyes closing.

"I thought so."

"But," Regina added, "I don't think she's gone because she died."

Sheila opened one eye.

"What does that mean?"

I swallowed.

"The lake... took her. Or absorbed her. Or... connected with her. I don't know what to call it."

Sheila exhaled.

"Doesn't surprise me."

Regina blinked.

"It doesn't?"

Sheila shook her head.

"She was drawn to it. Drawn in ways you two never were. Almost like... it picked her before it picked anyone else."

She looked at me pointedly.

"Except maybe Garrett."

I closed my eyes briefly.

She was right.

Lila had been the first one to hear it.

The first one it trusted.

The first one who saw the intelligence not as a threat — but as a living thing.

Her fate was sealed long before any of us entered the tunnels.

Regina whispered, "So what does that mean?"

Sheila looked out the window at Lake Monona.

"That she's not gone.

Just... somewhere else."

A soft knock interrupted us.

A nurse peeked in.

"Ms. Lammers? You have another visitor."

Sheila frowned.

"I do?"

The nurse stepped aside.

Old worn work boots.

A plaid shirt.

A face lined by forty years of hard work and harder wisdom.

Bob Thomas stepped inside.

Sheila gasped.

Regina froze.

I couldn't breathe.

Bob looked at the three of us — his eyes landing on me last — and said in his gravel-soft voice:

"Well. Looks like you finally found the bottom, Garth."

I swallowed.

"Bob..."

He walked to Sheila first, placing a gentle hand on her arm.

"Good to see you made it, kiddo."

Then he looked at Regina, nodding respectfully.

"You kept him alive. That counts."

Finally, he turned back to me.

And for a moment, everything else — the lake, the tunnels, the intelligence, the collapse, the dead, the missing, the impossible — faded.

Bob's eyes softened, but only barely.

"Sit down, son."

I did.

He leaned in.

"Whatever followed you back up... you're not done with it."

Regina shivered.

Sheila straightened.

I met Bob's eyes.

"I know," I whispered.

His voice dropped lower.

"And whatever is waiting above water?

It's already looking for you."

A chill rippled through the room.

Regina exhaled.

Sheila swallowed.

Bob squeezed my shoulder.

"Stay sober. Stay steady. And stay ready."

He stepped back.

"I'll check in tomorrow."

Then he left as quietly as he arrived.

Regina sat down, gripping my hand.

Sheila whispered:

"What. The. Hell. Was that?"

I exhaled.

"Bob being Bob."

But Regina shook her head.

"No," she whispered.

"That was a warning."

Hospitals have their own rhythms — the soft beeping of monitors, the shuffle of nurses' shoes, the distant cough of someone three rooms away. Normally those sounds ground you.

Tonight they only made the silence between them louder.

Sheila had drifted into a fragile, exhausted sleep. Regina sat beside her, fingers laced with mine, squeezing occasionally to reassure herself I was still real.

I wasn't entirely sure that I was.

The link with Garrett — the bridge — hadn't severed when we surfaced. It had retreated, quieted, dimmed, but something in the back of my mind still pulsed faintly.

The way a phantom limb aches.

The way a memory breathes.

Regina looked at me with worried eyes.

"You're somewhere else," she whispered.

I forced myself to shake my head.

"No. I'm here."

She didn't believe me.

She never did when it mattered.

It happened at 7:12 p.m.

Subtle at first.

Almost nothing.

A cup of water on Sheila's bedside table trembled, sending tiny ripples across the surface.

Regina noticed first.

"Garth..."

"I see it," I murmured.

Another ripple.

Stronger.

The bedside lamp flickered — once, twice — then steadied.

A low vibration crept through the floor, barely perceptible, but unmistakable to me.

Regina squeezed my arm.

"Is that—"

"Yes."

"Sheila's here," Regina said. "Is she safe?"

I didn't answer.

Because at that moment, I wasn't looking at Sheila.

I was looking at the wall-mounted digital clock above the door.

Its LED display blinked.

Then distorted.

The numbers rippled like submerged reflections.

Regina gasped.

"Garth—!"

I stood slowly, tightening my jaw.

"It's okay."

"It's NOT okay!" she whispered harshly. "This is the hospital. If something—if IT—"

"It's not attacking," I said quietly. "It's communicating."

A pulse traveled under my skin.

Warm.

Familiar.

Alive.

I closed my eyes.

"Garth?" Regina whispered, terrified.

"It's him."

The lights flickered softly.

The clock steadied.

The ripples in the water stilled.

And for a moment —

just a moment —

the room felt warmer, like someone had placed a gentle hand on my shoulder.

Regina covered her mouth, breath trembling.

Sheila murmured in her sleep.

I exhaled.

"It's a message," I whispered.

"He's telling me he's stable. He's alive."

Regina swallowed hard.

"How do you know that?"

I placed a hand over my chest.

"Because I felt it."

But the lake never speaks without cost.

At 7:17 p.m., the second ripple came.

No flicker.

No warmth.

A cold, sharp jolt of dread.

Like icy fingers tightening around my spine.

I staggered.

Regina grabbed my arm.

"Garth—what is it?"

My pulse raced.

Something darker pressed at the link.

Not Garrett.

Something else.

Someone else.

I pressed a hand to my temple.

"The intelligence," I whispered.

"The lake itself. It's..."

Regina's voice shook.

"It's what?"

"Searching."

"For what?"

My breath caught.

"For me."

Regina's face drained of color.

"But why? Why would it—"

"It needs something," I whispered.

"Something I carried up with me."

Sheila stirred, groggy.

"What... what's happening?"

Regina rushed to her.

"Shh, it's okay—nothing's wrong—"

Sheila blinked at me, sensing everything anyway.

"Bullshit," she rasped.

"What do you mean it's *searching*?"

The fluorescent overhead light buzzed violently — then steadied.

But the message was clear:

The lake hadn't let go.

Not fully.

Not safely.

And the intelligence wasn't finished with me.

Sheila gripped Regina's wrist.

"Get him out of here," she whispered urgently.

"Now."

At 7:20 p.m., the third ripple hit like a strike of electricity.

This one didn't tremble cups.

Or flicker lights.

Or bend clocks.

It struck me directly.

A burst of raw sensation shot through my chest, knocking the air from my lungs. I stumbled backward into the wall, fingers clawing for stability.

"GARTH!" Regina screamed.

Sheila jerked fully awake, eyes wide.

The world blurred.

The hospital room dissolved around me.

And suddenly—

I was underwater again.

Not drowning.

Not sinking.

Just... *present.*

A deep, glowing chamber formed in the darkness around me.

Not physical.

Not real.

A memory.

An echo.

A summoning.

Soft teal light illuminated the space like breath.

And then I felt him.

Garrett.

"Garry."

His voice resonated inside my mind — clearer than before, less distorted, more human.

"I'm here," I whispered.

Regina's voice cried somewhere in the distance.

Sheila's voice shouted.

But the link drowned them out.

"They're coming."

"Who?"

"Not the lake."

My heart pounded.

"Garrett—what's happening?"

His presence flickered, stabilizing with effort.

"There are people. On the surface. They know about me. About the basin. About you."

The image sharpened — faint silhouettes on the shoreline above the crater.

Not campus police.

Not the state investigators.

Different shapes.

Different shadows.

Moving with intent.

"Who are they?"

Garrett's presence trembled.

"I don't know.

But they have machines.

They're scanning the lake."

My blood ran cold.

"Scanners? For what?"

"For me."

The link pulsed again—urgent, strained.

"You have to stay alive.

You have to run.

They cannot find you."

And with that—

The chamber burst apart in a blast of light.

I gasped violently back into consciousness.

My knees buckled.

I collapsed against the wall.

Regina grabbed my face between her trembling hands.

"Garth! Garth—look at me!"

I forced my eyes open.

Her tear-streaked face came into focus.

Sheila leaned forward, oxygen tubes slipping from her nose.

"What did he say?" she demanded.

I swallowed hard.

"He said...

they're coming."

"Who?"

I wiped sweat from my forehead.

"I don't know. But they're not from campus. Not from the county. Not police."

Regina's voice broke.

"What do they want?"

My throat felt like sand.

"Garrett.

The intelligence.

Me.

All of it."

Sheila's face hardened.

"How long do we have?"

I closed my eyes.

"Hours. Maybe less."

Regina grabbed my arm.

"Then we go. NOW."

I shook my head slowly.

"No."

Her voice cracked.

"NO? What do you mean no?"

I stood — weak, shaking, barely holding upright — but with clarity burning through me:

"They're not just looking for me."

Regina blinked.

"What?"

"They're looking for all of us."

Sheila's breath caught.

"Then we leave together."

I shook my head again.

"No."

Regina's voice rose, desperate.

"Garth—"

"If we move together, we're easy to track. Easy to corner. Easy to take."

I steadied myself, meeting both of their eyes.

"We split up."

Regina went white.

Sheila whispered:

"That's suicide."

"No," I said quietly.

"It's strategy."

The floor trembled again — a faint, almost delicate vibration from the direction of Lake Monona.

A final warning.

A final push.

I exhaled.

"They're coming for the lake tonight.

They're coming for me right after.

And if I stay here... all three of us die."

Regina shook her head violently.

"I'm not leaving you!"

Sheila gripped my wrist.

"Neither am I."

I felt something break inside me — something old, something tender.

"I know," I whispered.

"But you have to."

Regina's hands trembled against my chest.

"I almost lost you today. Twice."

"And you didn't," I whispered. "Because Garrett helped me. Because Sheila helped me. Because Martinson helped me. Because you—"

My voice cracked.

"Because you kept me alive when I didn't want to be."

Her tears fell freely now.

"And now you want to walk away?"

"No," I whispered.

"I want to keep you both alive."

The overhead lights trembled lightly.

The windowpane vibrated.

A series of faint, metallic clicks echoed down the hallway.

Not natural.

Not random.

Boots.

Multiple pairs.

Moving with purpose.

Sheila's eyes widened.

"They're here."

CHAPTER 25

When They Come for the Lake

Some invasions begin with silence—and end where the water
can no longer hide.

The clicking of boots in a hospital corridor sounds wrong.

Hospitals aren't meant for hard soles. They're meant for rubber, for quiet, for people who walk like they respect the dying. The boots we heard were none of those things.

Regina stiffened under my arm.

Sheila, weak as she was, swung her legs over the edge of the bed and gripped the railing with a ferocity that belied her bruises.

Three knocks hit the door.

Not timid.

Not curious.

Announcing.

"Dr. Myers," a man said through the crack, voice calm, professional, wrong.

"We'd like a word."

Regina whispered, "Don't answer."

Sheila leaned toward me, eyes blazing through fatigue.

"Garth. That's not campus security."

I nodded.

"I know."

A pause.

Then the doorknob rattled.

"Sir, we know you're in there."

Regina grabbed my hand so tightly her nails dug into my skin.

"Garth—please."

The voice on the other side of the door softened unnaturally.

"Dr. Myers... you're not in trouble.

We're here to help."

I laughed quietly under my breath.

They always say that right before they take you.

Sheila whispered, "Back wall. There's a secondary exit—staff only. You can slip out before they breach."

Of course she knew that.

She ran the department like a mother hawk.

She knew every vent, every closet, every back route.

Regina grabbed her arm.

"No. He's not going alone."

Sheila looked at me.

We were thinking the same thing.

"If we all bolt," I whispered, "they'll chase three moving bodies."

Sheila frowned.

"So?"

"So," I whispered, "they'll catch us."

Regina's voice cracked.

"They'll catch you *first*."

Another knock.

Harder.

"Dr. Myers, please open the door."

I pressed a finger to my lips for silence.

Then I leaned in and kissed Regina's forehead.

She froze.

"Garth—"

"I'm not leaving you," I whispered. "I'm just buying time."

She shook her head, tears rising.

"You don't have time. They're right there."

"I know."

Sheila grabbed my sleeve.

"If you die again—if I have to watch you almost drown *again*—I swear on every file in your office I'll beat you back to life myself."

I smiled.

Then I moved.

Quiet.

Swift.

Sliding behind the curtain and into the staff alcove.

The moment I slipped through the side door—

The main door burst inward.

Regina gasped.

Sheila cursed.

And I heard them enter.

Boots.

Weapons.

Purpose.

"Regina Evert?" a voice asked sharply.

She didn't answer.

"Ms. Lammers?"

Silence.

Then the sound of someone flipping the privacy curtain.

And then—

"Where is he?"

Sheila's voice came through clenched teeth.

"Go to hell."

The hallway was dim and sterile, lit by dying fluorescent bulbs. I moved quickly, every instinct screaming that they were seconds behind me.

I hit the stairwell door, pushed through, and sprinted down two flights toward the east exit.

One thing kept me going:

A ping.

Faint at first.

Then sharper.

Then unmistakable.

Garrett.

He was trying to reach me.

Not to soothe.

Not to warn.

To guide.

A mental pull — like a compass needle turning under my ribs.

Come to the lake.

I pushed through a fire door and burst out into the freezing night. Winter wind tore at my wet shirt and tunnel-stained jacket.

Across the dark parking lot, Lake Monona glimmered faintly beneath the streetlights.

And at the far shoreline—

silhouettes.

Equipment.

Tripods.

Vans.

Men moving like insects around machinery that hummed with an unnatural metallic song.

Regina was right.

Sheila was right.

Bob was right.

This wasn't over.

This was barely beginning.

When I reached the shoreline, I stayed low behind a row of boulders and watched.

There were at least **eight agents**.

Black jackets.

Unmarked.

Faces blank and precise.

They were lowering something into the water.

A cylindrical device, humming with a deep, throbbing resonance.

A pulse emitter.

Subterranean scanner.

Or worse—

A disruptor.

Garrett's presence flickered through me.

Urgent.

Pained.

"Stop them."

I whispered under my breath.

"I can't. I'm one man."

The pulse surged through me again — more desperate — and I stumbled to one knee.

Pain shot through my skull.

Not mine.

His.

He was suffering under the machine's frequency.

They were targeting him.

The agents moved with military precision, tightening the last cables.

One of them spoke into a radio headset.

"Device calibrated. Preparing to initiate sweep."

Another voice crackled through the headset.

"Confirm subject's resonance signature."

The agent looked at a handheld monitor.

"Confirmed."

Resonance.

Signature.

Garrett.

My heart pounded so hard it hurt.

A second voice — colder — answered through the radio:

"Begin extraction protocol."

Extraction.

Not hunting.

Not scanning.

Extracting him.

A tremor rippled through the water — violent, unnatural.

Garrett's presence spasmed inside my skull.

"Stop," I whispered. "I can't—"

"Garry—RUN."

Run?

Run where?

Then it clicked.

They weren't just scanning for him.

They were scanning for **anyone linked** to the intelligence.

Me.

If I stayed here, if the disruptor swept again—

It would tear me apart from the inside out.

I stumbled back.

An agent snapped his head toward me.

"Movement!" he shouted.

Another turned.

"Dr. Garth Myers—visually confirmed!"

Spotlights snapped on, blinding white tearing across the shoreline.

I bolted.

The sprint across the southwestern shoreline felt like running through a nightmare:

- frozen grass crunching beneath my feet

- breath tearing in my chest

- the lake pulsing behind me like a wounded animal

- the echo of Garrett's voice somewhere between my heart and skull

Agents were shouting.

"Cut him off!"

"He's heading west—flank!"

"DO NOT let him near the water!"

Boots pounded pavement.

Engines started.

A drone lifted into the sky with a high-pitched whine.

Regina's voice echoed in my mind:

"I'm not leaving you."

Sheila's voice layered over it:

"Don't die stupid, Garth."

Bob's voice anchored both:

"Stay steady."

I darted between pine trees.

Cut behind a maintenance shed.

Leapt over a split-rail fence.

A spotlight blasted the ground inches from my feet.

The lake's voice pulsed again:

"Garry—LEFT."

I turned left without thinking.

A searchlight swept where I had been a heartbeat earlier.

The link was saving me.

But it was also killing me.

Every pulse sent sharp pain up my spine, like sparks bursting behind my eyes.

I skidded down a muddy slope and slammed into a drainage culvert.

A hand grabbed my ankle.

I jerked backward, ready to fight—

But the grip was gentle.

Human.

Warm.

"Garth!" a voice hissed. "Get *in*!"

It was Martinson.

One arm in a sling.

Covered in bandages.

Bleeding from the temple.

But alive.

And furious.

I crawled into the concrete culvert beside him.

"Jesus Christ," I gasped. "You followed me?"

He glared.

"Followed? I *saved your ass*. Again."

A flash of searchlights swept above the culvert opening.

Martinson whispered:

"You need to get off this shoreline. They're setting a perimeter."

My breath steamed in the cold air.

"They're after Garrett," I whispered.

"They're after *you*," he snapped.

"You're the conduit. You're the goddamn transmitter."

He grabbed my collar.

"Tell me how we survive this."

I swallowed.

"I have to go back to the lake."

He stared at me like I'd grown an extra head.

"Absolutely not."

"It's the only way."

Regina's voice rang in my skull—

not through the link, but through memory:

"I'm not losing you again."

I pressed a hand to the cold concrete.

"I can't outrun them. Not now. Not tonight.

But I can draw them away."

Martinson shook his head angrily.

"You're not a martyr."

"No," I whispered.

"I'm a Myers."

He cursed quietly.

Searchlights swept the grass again.

Martinson breathed out sharply.

"Fine. But you're not doing this alone."

I stared at him.

"You're hurt."

"I've been hurt worse by an ex-wife and a snowblower."

He cracked his neck.

"If you're walking into hell, I'm walking with you."

Another tremor rippled through the lake — deeper this time, desperate.

Garrett's voice fractured:

"Garry—please—"

I exhaled a trembling breath.

"Okay."

We crawled deeper into the culvert.

The agents regrouped.

The lake pulsed.

The night grew sharp and cold.

And the final confrontation began.

The culvert emptied out near the south edge of the campus, a series of concrete mouths facing the lake like a row of silent watchers. The air here was colder, sharper, as if the lake exhaled fear instead of mist.

Martinson crawled out first, scanning the shoreline.

"Two units east. One drone overhead. No visual on the main group."

He turned back to me.

"You ready?"

I wiped tunnel grit from my eyes.

"No."

He smirked.

"Good. Means you'll think before you run."

The moment I stepped out of the culvert, the link pulsed again — sharp, fragmented. Garrett's voice broke through like a radio transmission on the edge of range.

"...hurts... stop them... hurry..."

The pain hammered through my skull.

Martinson steadied me.

"Let's move."

We crouched behind a stand of winter-bare oaks that bordered the lake. Through the branches, we saw the agents clearly now.

Two vehicles.

A portable generator humming.

Cables stretching from the vans to the water.

A tripod-mounted cylindrical device pulsing with rhythmic metallic thumps.

A disruptor.

Designed to destabilize biosignatures.

Designed to interfere with resonance.

Designed to rip Garrett apart.

A man in a black coat — someone higher-ranking — stood at the edge of the lake, headset pressed to his ear.

He spoke calmly, as if discussing weather patterns:

"Begin Phase Two sweep. Increase amplitude by fifteen percent."

A technician hesitated.

"Sir, the frequency spike may destabilize the—"

"I said fifteen."

The technician swallowed.

"Yes, sir."

He turned a dial.

The disruptor hummed louder.

The lake reacted instantly.

A shockwave rippled across the surface, as if something enormous shifted beneath the water.

Martinson grabbed my arm.

"Garth—talk to me. What's happening?"

I pressed a hand against my temple.

"He's in pain. Too much."

"What does that mean?"

"It means they're close," I whispered.

"It means they found the chamber."

The underside of the lake glowed faintly, as if bioluminescent veins pulsed through the sediment.

Martinson cursed under his breath.

"And they're trying to pull him out."

Martinson scanned the shoreline.

"Okay, professor. What's our move?"

I swallowed hard.

"I need to disrupt the disruptor."

"By doing what? Throwing sand in the gears? Garth, that thing looks like it could knock down a building."

"I don't need to knock it down," I said quietly.

"I just need to change its signal."

"How?"

I tapped my chest.

"They're tracking resonance."

Martinson blinked.

"You mean—"

"They're tracking *me*.

And Garrett.

And whatever the intelligence still holds on to."

Martinson paced, thinking.

"So if you get close—"

"I can interfere."

He exhaled.

"Great. So the plan is: walk right into the death machine and hope your brainwave is louder than theirs."

"Essentially."

He rolled his eyes.

"You need a new hobby."

We moved low across the grass, using every shadow, every tree, every boulder to keep ourselves hidden.

But even from here, we could hear the disruptor's pulse — a sickening oscillation that resonated somewhere deep in my spine.

My vision blurred.

My knees trembled.

Martinson grabbed me.

"You good?"

"No. But I'll get closer anyway."

He snorted.

"You're either brave or stupid."

"Both."

"Good. Fits with my night."

The wind picked up suddenly.

Not normal wind.

It carried something with it.

A whisper.

A memory.

A plea.

"Garry... please..."

I clenched my teeth, fighting back a wave of nausea.

Martinson watched me closely.

"He's holding on. Isn't he?"

"Yes."

"And they're killing him."

"Yes."

Martinson straightened.

"Then we're ending this."

We crawled behind a squat service building twenty yards from the agents. From here, we saw the disruptor's control panel clearly.

A technician knelt beside it, adjusting dials.

The senior agent barked:

"We're losing cohesion. Increase to Phase Three."

The tech hesitated.

"Sir, that could—"

"Phase. Three."

The technician's hand shook as he moved the dial.

The disruptor thrummed deeper, louder, the ground shaking with each pulse.

I gasped as agony tore through my skull.

Martinson steadied me again.

"What do you need me to do?" he whispered.

I looked at the panel.

"There's a signal modulator on the left. If you can hit it hard enough—"

"With what? My good arm? My broken arm?"

"A rock might do."

He cracked a thin smile.

"Now you're thinking like a detective."

He scanned the ground, found a fist-sized stone, and nodded.

"On your signal."

I swallowed.

"I need to get closer to confuse the readings."

He gave me a long look.

"Don't die."

I nodded.

"Try not to let me."

I stepped out from behind the building.

Just a foot.

Just enough.

Instantly, the disruptor's pitch changed.

Technicians froze.

"Sir, the resonance is spiking—something's interfering—"

The senior agent stiffened.

"Locate source."

One tech pointed toward the building's side.

"Movement detected."

Martinson's whisper reached me:

"Now or never."

I took a step forward.

The disruptor shrieked — a metallic screech like steel dragged through teeth.

The lake writhed with light.

Garrett's voice shattered through me:

"STOP THEM!

NOW!"

The pain exploded through my chest.

The technician screamed:

"Total resonance breach—what the hell—"

The senior agent snapped:

"Stabilize it!"

"We can't! Something's counter—"

Martinson moved.

Fast.

Hard.

Precise.

He lunged from behind the building and hurled the rock with perfect aim.

It smashed into the disruptor's signal modulator with a crack.

Sparks exploded.

The device convulsed.

Then—

Silence.

Dead.

Dark.

Offline.

The lake exhaled a long, low sigh.

Garrett's presence steadied.

Martinson grinned.

"Hell yes—"

A gunshot tore past his shoulder.

The senior agent spun toward us, weapon drawn.

"DOWN!" Martinson yelled.

I dove behind the building.

Martinson dropped beside me, panting.

"We pissed them off," he said.

"Yeah," I gasped. "I noticed."

Bullets tore through the wooden siding.

"They'll flank left," Martinson whispered.

"Aren't you injured?"

"Yes."

"Do you care?"

"No."

He drew his sidearm with his good hand.

"Stay low."

"I am low."

He smirked despite the circumstances.

"Lower."

The ground trembled — not from machinery this time.

From the lake.

A deep pulse rippled across the water's surface.

The agents froze.

"What the hell—"

The water glowed faintly.

Not bioluminescence.

Not machinery.

Intention.

Presence.

Garrett.

The senior agent shouted:

"Get that machine back online!"

The technician yelped:

"It's fried! The internal coupler—"

"I DON'T CARE! RESTART IT!"

Martinson and I exchanged a glance.

"Your brother's angry," he muttered.

"No," I whispered.

"He's defending himself."

The lake pulsed again—

strong enough to knock the shoreline sediment loose.

The agents stumbled.

The technician fell.

The senior agent steadied himself, staring at the water with fear for the first time.

"What is that?"

Martinson smirked.

"Intelligent life, asshole."

Another ripple surged across the lake — stronger, brighter, more deliberate.

The agents backed up.

"What's happening? What's HAPPENING?"

I stepped forward.

My voice was low.

Steady.

Clear.

"You went looking for something you didn't understand."

The senior agent whipped his gun toward me.

"DON'T MOVE!"

I kept walking.

"You tortured it."

"STOP!"

"You hurt it."

"I SAID—"

"You tried to rip it out of the world."

The last pulse surged.

The lake erupted in teal light, casting long shadows across the campus.

The disruptor cracked open like an egg dropped from a skyscraper.

The technicians screamed.

The senior agent shielded his face.

Even Martinson ducked.

And the light washed over us.

Warm.

Gentle.

Alive.

The pain in my head vanished.

My breath steadied.

My vision cleared.

Only one word remained in the link—

"Live."

Then the light faded.

The lake was still.

And silence reclaimed the shoreline.

When my vision stopped swimming, the agents were gone.

Retreated.

Scrambled into the vans.

Sped off with tails tucked between their legs.

Martinson exhaled.

"I think we scared them."

"No," I murmured.

"He did."

We stood shoulder to shoulder, watching the lake settle.

Martinson rubbed his temple.

"You know this isn't the end, right?"

"Yes."

"You know others will come."

"Yes."

He looked at me — truly looked at me — and nodded.

"Then we'll be ready."

My breath caught.

"'We'?"

He smirked.

"You think I'm letting you do this alone?"

We stood together in the cold.

The lake breathed quietly.

Garrett whispered a final message deep in the marrow of my mind:

"You are not done."

I whispered back:

"I know."

CHAPTER 26

The Weight of the Water

Water carries what we cannot—and returns it when we least expect.

Dawn over Lake Monona is usually soft.

Muted pink.

Wisps of fog drifting lazily off the water.

A kind of gentleness that makes you believe the world can pause long enough for you to breathe.

Not today.

Today the lake looked... different.

Not threatening.

Not angry.

Just **aware**.

Like a creature that had finally opened its eyes after a long, exhausted sleep.

Martinson stood beside me near the shoreline, one arm in a sling, a steaming cup of black hospital coffee in his good hand.

"You know," he said, "when I woke up this morning, I thought the weirdest thing I'd deal with was a burst water pipe on University Avenue."

I stared at the lake.

"Sorry to disappoint."

He snorted.

"You didn't disappoint."

A beat.

"You terrify me, but you didn't disappoint."

We stood in a long silence.

The aftermath of the confrontation still clung to the shore: muddy tracks, shattered equipment, and a faint, metallic smell from the disruptor's melted casing.

But the agents were gone.

And for the first time in weeks...

the lake wasn't pulling me toward it.

It was letting me go.

Martinson placed the coffee cup on a rock and turned to me.

"What now, Myers?"

I exhaled.

"I don't know."

"Bullshit," he said, nudging me with his good shoulder. "You always know. Even when you pretend you don't."

I couldn't help but smile.

"'Knowing' is generous."

He shrugged.

"Fine. You always *feel* your way into trouble."

"That I'll admit."

He took a long breath.

"You're not done, you know."

He was echoing Garrett's words from the night before — a whisper still lodged somewhere behind my ribs.

"I know," I said quietly.

Martinson turned toward the sunrise.

"For what it's worth... you saved people last night."

"Did I?"

"Yes," he said firmly. "Your brother. Sheila. Regina. Half the damn city, probably."

I didn't answer.

Not because I disagreed.

But because the weight of it was too much to hold all at once.

She found me half an hour later, wrapped in a heavy coat, hair still damp from the hospital shower.

She stopped beside us, breath visible in the cold.

"How long have you been out here?" she asked softly.

"Not long."

Martinson gave her a nod.

"Morning, Professor Evert."

"Detective."

He wandered off a few paces to give us privacy.

Regina tucked her hands into her pockets and stared at the lake.

"It's so quiet," she whispered.

"It's resting."

She didn't question it.

That's the thing about Regina — she never requires proof when the truth is heavy enough to weigh itself.

Her voice softened.

"He talked to you again last night, didn't he?"

I nodded.

She stared at me, eyes full of fear and awe.

"What... what did he say?"

I swallowed.

"That I'm not done."

She took a shaky breath.

"Does that mean he's still..." — she gestured toward the water — "...alive?"

"Yes.

In a new way.

A different way."

Her chin trembled.

"Does he know we made it out?"

"Yes."

"Does he... does he hurt?"

"No."

I paused.

"Not anymore."

Regina nodded, tears spilling down her cheeks.

"I miss him," she whispered.

"I know."

She leaned into me, forehead pressed against my chest, and for a moment I let myself hold her — quietly, gently, like we were back in graduate school and the world hadn't learned how to break us yet.

When she finally stepped back, her face looked older.

Sadder.

Wiser.

"Whatever you need next," she said, "I'm with you."

I shook my head.

"That's not safe."

She took my hand.

"I didn't say 'safe.'"

She squeezed it.

"I said 'with you.'"

Sheila found us around noon.

She shouldn't have been out of bed, but she was Sheila — which meant she would've stolen a wheelchair and busted through an emergency exit if they tried to keep her.

She hobble-marched across the muddy shore, wrapped in blankets like a frostbitten burrito, glaring at me.

"You," she said, pointing a trembling finger, "are fired."

Regina laughed.

Martinson muttered, "Here we go."

I smiled softly.

"No I'm not."

Sheila wobbled closer.

"Fine. You're not fired. You're grounded. From everything. Forever."

Martinson folded his arms.

"Pretty sure none of that is legally binding."

Sheila ignored him and stepped right up to me.

"You almost died, Garth. Again. And you dragged me with you. Again. And if you ever—and I mean *ever*—go underground alone again—"

I held up a hand.

"I won't."

She studied my face.

Suspicious.

Searching.

"Promise?"

"I promise."

She narrowed her eyes.

"Good. Because next time? I'm handcuffing you to your desk."

Martinson smirked.

"Can I watch?"

Sheila glared at him.

Regina laughed quietly.

I breathed in the bitter November air and felt something settle inside me — not peace, exactly.

But acceptance.

Sheila nudged me gently.

"Hey," she whispered. "You didn't lose him."

My voice cracked.

"I know."

"Doesn't make it easier," she added softly.

"No."

"But it means he's not gone."

I looked at the lake.

"No," I whispered.

"He's not."

As evening crept in, Regina and Sheila headed back to the hospital. Martinson drove off to file paperwork that would haunt him for years.

I stayed.

One last time.

The wind shifted.

The water lapped softly against the rocks.

And then the link opened — faint, thin, but unmistakable.

"Garry..."

I closed my eyes.

"I'm here."

"Not goodbye."

My breath hitched.

"I know."

"Be ready."

"For what?"

Silence.

Then—

"The others."

A cold ripple shot through me.

"Others?"

But the link faded.

The lake stilled.

And night fell.

I stood there for a long time, staring into the black water, feeling both heavier and lighter than I ever had.

Garrett wasn't gone.

He wasn't human anymore.

But he wasn't gone.

The lake had awakened.

The intelligence had chosen.

And above the water — forces we didn't understand were already mobilizing.

Bob was right.

I wasn't done.

None of us were.

The world had shifted beneath our feet, and we were standing on the edge of something vast, ancient, intelligent... and unfinished.

I finally turned away from the shoreline and walked toward the city lights.

Toward the next mystery.

Toward the next threat.

Toward the next truth hiding in the dark.

Regina would walk beside me.

Sheila would anchor me.

Martinson would guard my back.

Bob would keep me sober.

And beneath the water, a voice I loved — in the only form it could now take — would whisper warnings and guidance when the world grew too loud.

I wasn't alone.

Not anymore.

EPILOGUE

Afterlight

Every darkness leaves a trace—afterlight is simply the proof we survived it.

Winter break hits Madison like a held breath.

Students vanish.

Faculty scatter.

Labs go dark except for a few die-hards running overnight assays.

The campus becomes a skeleton of concrete and wind.

I've always liked it this way.

Quiet.

Stripped down.

Honest.

Tonight, I walk the frozen path along Lake Monona with my coat zipped tight and my breath fogging in the air. The wind is sharp, but the lake is still—slick and black like a mirror turned face-down.

Nothing unusual.

Nothing glowing.

Nothing rising.

If you didn't know better, you'd think the world had never cracked open beneath your feet.

But I know better.

And so does the lake.

I check my phone for the tenth time.

No missed calls.

No texts.

Sheila is back home and recovering.

Regina is safely in her apartment, though she insisted on calling me every two hours "because I'm not letting you brood yourself into another underground death wish."

Martinson is stitched up, casted up, bandaged up, and back to snapping at rookies who bring him the wrong brand of coffee.

Bob left me a voicemail:

"Remember: truth is heavy. Don't carry it alone. See you at the next meeting."

—B.

Normal.

Almost.

But there's something missing.

The whisper.

The pulse.

The gentle tug behind my ribs.

Garrett's presence.

Since the confrontation on the shoreline, he's been quiet.

Not silent.

Just... resting.

I think part of me expected him to speak again immediately.

To explain.

To reassure.

To warn.

But the intelligence—and whatever my brother has become—doesn't follow my schedule.

I sit on a cold bench facing the lake and rub my hands together for warmth.

"I'm here," I whisper.

"Whenever you're ready."

The water stays still.

The first snowflake lands on my wrist just as I notice an envelope tucked beneath the bench plank.

Blue.

Not the color of campus mail.

Not white like interdepartmental memos.

But deep, lake-colored blue.

My heart skips.

I pull it out.

There is no name on the front.

Inside, a single sheet of paper:

A map.

Roughly sketched.

Hand-drawn.

A section of the campus tunnels.

But not the ones we collapsed.

Older ones.

Lower.

Running beneath the humanities wing toward the botanical gardens.

A red X marks a point near the lake's edge.

And below the map, one line:

"Not all of them were asleep."

My fingers go cold.

The handwriting is unfamiliar.

Not Regina's.

Not Sheila's.

Not Martinson's.

And not Bob's.

The message feels... aware.

Like someone who knows the intelligence.

Knows the chambers.

Knows what we found.

A second line is written faintly in the margin, almost an afterthought:

"He's not the only one who woke up."

A chill digs into my spine.

I fold the map carefully, tuck it into my coat, and force myself to breathe.

This is the kind of thing that changes everything.

Again.

The lake doesn't move.

Doesn't glow.

Doesn't ripple.

But something inside me shifts.

A small, warm thrum.

Not pain.

Not fear.

Recognition.

I close my eyes.

Garrett's voice reaches me—not as words, but as presence.

Here.

It's faint.

Weak.

But alive.

I kneel at the lake's edge, letting my fingers hover over the icy surface.

"I got your message," I whisper.

The water is silent.

Then—

Not me.

My heart stutters.

If it wasn't him...

then who?

The link shivers, like fingers brushing over piano strings in the dark.

Others.

The word echoes through my mind.

"Others," I repeat out loud.

A deep, low vibration rolls beneath the ice—subtle, careful, like something enormous turning over in sleep.

The map in my pocket feels heavier.

Garrett's voice fades as the lake quiets again.

But one last whisper slips through, delicate as breath:

"Be ready."

I stand slowly, every hair on my body rising.

Crunching snow behind me.

Martinson's voice grumbles:

"Are you planning to freeze out here or just making the lake nervous?"

I turn.

He stands bundled in a heavy coat, sling tucked neatly under the fabric, coffee thermos in his good hand.

"How did you find me?" I ask.

He huffs.

"You always end up here after a crisis. I can track you in my sleep."

I smile weakly.

He studies my face for a long moment.

"You heard him again."

I don't answer.

He nods.

"I figured."

He hands me the thermos.

"You're freezing. Drink."

I take it.

The warmth spreads through my palms.

We stand there for a while, side by side, looking out at the dark lake.

Martinson finally breaks the silence.

"This isn't over, is it?"

"No," I whisper.

"It's only the beginning."

He nods slowly.

"Good. Means I won't get bored."

I slip the blue envelope from my pocket and hand it to him.

He scans the map.

Frowns.

"Shit," he mutters.

"And this wasn't you?"

"No."

"You think it's friendly?"

"No."

Martinson folds it up and hands it back.

"Then we start tomorrow."

I blink.

"We?"

He smirks.

"You think I'm letting you walk into hell alone? Not a chance. I'm too old to break in a new idiot professor."

I laugh despite myself.

He pats my shoulder.

"Let's get you warmed up. You look like a haunted raccoon."

We turn toward the path leading back into the sleeping city.

Behind us, the lake stays silent.

But underneath, deep below the ice, something shifts.

Something new.

Something awake.

Something waiting.

As we walk, I feel the map pressing against my chest.

A pulse.

A promise.

A burden.

Garrett's whisper repeats in my head:

"Be ready."

I don't know what waits beneath the lake.

I don't know who left the map.

I don't know who the "others" are.

But I know this:

I'm not running.

Not anymore.

Not from the lake.

Not from memory.

Not from the truth.

And for the first time in a long, long time—

I don't feel alone.

TEASER

BOOK II Cold Catalyst

In the quiet before failure, the catalyst is already choosing its path.

Winter settles hard over Madison, the kind of deep freeze that makes the lake look asleep even when it isn't.

Just after 3 a.m., a lone grad student from the Biochem building notices something strange: the emergency stairwell door at the Humanities Sub-Basement 3 is propped open.

No lights.

No sounds.

Just cold air rising from a place that shouldn't have air at all.

He leans in, squinting into the darkness.

A single sheet of paper lies on the bottom step.

Blue.

Folded once.

Edges damp as if carried through mist.

He picks it up.

Unfolds it.

It's a map.

Campus tunnels—old ones, the kind no one has used since the late 1970s.

A red X marks a point beneath the botanical gardens.

A black circle marks a point labeled *SB-3*.

He frowns. He's never seen this kind of mapping before. The scale is wrong.

The angles—unnatural.

As if the tunnels were drawn from memory rather than architecture.

Behind him, the stairwell door groans.

The student turns.

Nobody there.

But the paper in his hand...

changes.

Lines shift.

The X moves.

One tunnel extends, thin as a nerve fiber.

Something is rewriting it.

The student drops the map and bolts up the stairs, slipping on frost, scrambling into the night.

The blue page drifts down the steps.

Settles.

And for a moment—just a breath—

the concrete floor beneath it pulses.

Once.

Twice.

Like a heartbeat trying to remember its rhythm.

Then the light fades.

The map lies still.

But the message it carries does not:

Not all of them were sleeping.

And one of them is awake now.

Author

Frank Doyle is a scientist-entrepreneur whose career has carried him from research labs to global advisory boardrooms to the quiet backrooms where communities confront crises. Along the way, he learned that every mystery begins long before the moment we recognize it — in the small human fractures, buried motives, and unseen pressures that shape what people eventually do.

His fiction reflects that belief. Blending psychological acuity with investigative clarity, Doyle writes at the intersection of systems and souls, tracing how ordinary lives bend toward extraordinary consequences. Before turning to crime fiction, he founded and guided ventures across healthcare, food systems, and emerging technologies — work that honed his instinct for patterns, contradictions, and the hidden logic inside chaos.

Named in homage to Frank Herbert's visionary reach and Arthur Conan Doyle's enduring legacy of deduction, Doyle brings a dual tradition to the page: atmospheric inquiry paired with disciplined reasoning.

Shadows in the Night marks the beginning of his five-book Garth Myers Mystery Series — stories about truth, consequence, and the price of finding what lies beneath the surface.

COMING NEXT IN THE GARTH MYERS MYSTERIES

Book II — Cold Catalyst (2026)

A winter storm locks down Madison just as a breakthrough chemical experiment goes catastrophically wrong. When a researcher vanishes inside a sealed lab, Garth Myers and Detective Martinson uncover a trail of sabotage, buried academic rivalries, and a discovery someone is willing to kill to protect. What begins as a containment failure spirals into a race against a force that refuses to stay contained.

Book III — The Drowned Equation (2026)

A body is found on the frozen shoreline of Lake Mendota—no footprints, no struggle, no logical way it could be there. When strange patterns appear in the victim's notebooks, Garth is drawn into a mystery linking fluid dynamics, encoded messages, and an intelligence hiding in the spaces where physics breaks down. Some equations are meant to be solved. Others are warnings.

Book IV — The Janitor's Ledger (2027)

When a retired UW maintenance worker dies under suspicious circumstances, he leaves behind a ledger filled with cryptic entries about tunnels, missing students, and a decades-old campus secret. As Garth follows the clues, he uncovers a hidden network of people who have been watching him—and waiting. Not all custodians clean buildings. Some guard truths.

Book V — The Last Variable (2027)

A classified government project surfaces with one target: Garth Myers. As old enemies return and new alliances form, Garth faces the final equation—one that ties together every disappearance, every anomaly, and the intelligence beneath the lake. To solve it, he must risk everything, including the one thing he swore never to lose again: his own humanity.

www.ingramcontent.com/pod-product-compliance
Lightning Source LLC
Chambersburg PA
CBHW051054030726
47504CB00006B/1624

*9 7 9 8 9 9 3 6 9 1 1 4 5 *